T0354735

FASHION GIRL 3.0

FASHION GIRL 3.0

ROBY GRAHAM

ARCHWAY
PUBLISHING

Archway Publishing books may be ordered through booksellers or by contacting:

Archway Publishing
1663 Liberty Drive
Bloomington, IN 47403
www.archwaypublishing.com
844-669-3957

ISBN: 978-1-6657-6035-5 (sc)
ISBN: 978-1-6657-6036-2 (hc)
ISBN: 978-1-6657-6037-9 (e)

Library of Congress Control Number: 2024910542

Print information available on the last page.

Archway Publishing rev. date: 05/22/2024

DISCLAIMER

The Style Chicks are named after department and specialty stores. They do not represent, promote or sell any merchandise for the stores they are named after. All names in this story are fictitious. Any similarity to actual persons living or dead is purely coincidental. Because of the nature of this story, it is not intended for readers under the age of 18. Therefore parental discretion is strongly advised.

INTRODUCTION

In the superhero genre, there are times when a hero or heroine needs to evolve or become something more than they are. Or in the case of the She-Ra controversy, it's also best to leave well enough alone. Fashion Girl is a heroine that will always change and become more than before. In the year 2029 this will become reality.

Fashion Girl's eldest daughter Daphne Bates will turn eighteen and will take her mother's place as The Stylish Crime Fighter. How will Daphne Bates be as Fashion Girl? Will she be the same as her mother and grandmother by being vain about her looks like her grandmother was? Or will she be like her mother by traveling the world as a model? Or will she be her own heroine?

What's more, Daphne Bates, who just graduated from high school, was the leader of her own clique. You know what was known as Plastics in "Mean Girls." But this clique is different by setting a good example to others. In 2019, her mother Daphne Jones Simpson decided to give up modeling by becoming a darker and more free wheeling wild child called Madame D.

As Madame D, the woman formerly known as Fashion Girl retired from modeling and became a dominatrix still able to perform as Fashion Girl. She bought property in a neighboring county and built on it a motor court known as Aurora Gardens. Aurora Gardens was designed to attract both families on road trips and be a haven for savory individuals.

As Fashion Girl, Madame D befriended a motorcycle gang called The Skulls as she saved them from let's say a fate worse than death. Their leader known as The Skull King made her their queen as she is also known as The Skull Queen. Madame D or The Skull Queen enjoys the company of good-looking men. So much so that she used her charm and sex appeal to lure criminals in her clutches to the point that they become resistant to being arrested or surrender to the police.

The question remains will Daphne Bates follow in her mother's footsteps, or will she take a different path? Or could she become evil? Find out in this new story as the third woman to become Fashion Girl will take the mantle.

CHAPTER 1

It's the morning of July 22, 2029. The morning when Daphne Sandra Bates and Harold Fredrick Bates Jr. turns eighteen years old. It's also the day when Daphne takes over the mantle of being Fashion Girl. That night, she will take the oath of allegiance to become Fashion Girl. What's more and unknown to her knowledge, her group of friends will also become the next generation of Style Chicks.

As it has become a custom in the Fashion Girl Universe, if and when Daphne has a daughter herself, that daughter will take her place when she turns eighteen too. At the Mystique Boutique, preparations were being made for the birthday party of a lifetime. But that morning, Victoria was preparing a special breakfast for the twins, their mother and stepfather.

Madame D stayed at the mansion to help celebrate this occasion. She knocked on Daphne's bedroom door and asked to come in, Daphne let her in as Madame D said, "Happy Birthday baby girl. Only you're not a baby anymore. Just let me look at you for a moment or two. How lovely you are. When I held you in my arms for the first time, I knew you would be an incredibly special girl. After tonight you will be the new Fashion Girl."

Madame D shed a tear as a mother beaming with pride and delight. Daphne replied, "Mom I am glad that you are proud of me. I will not fail you or Grandma Daphne I will make Fashion Girl a force to be reckoned with again." Madame D said, "Honey now that we are alone I want you to know a couple of things. First about your father Greg. He was a good man but one night in 2015, I stopped a sexual predator by dressing in formal wear and got him arrested when he tried to seduce me."

"Your father got mad, something in him snapped and he divorced me, and he seduced the wife of the predator. Your Aunt Cindy, Grandma Sandy and I went to Philadelphia to confront him, and he died in a cave in when the building we found him in collapsed. He blamed me for the deception I put on for the predator, but his last words to me was to tell you and Harry that he loved you both very much."

"To spare you and Harry, I told you both that Dad was in a place where everything is good, and no one is sad." Daphne replied, "Mom it is okay. Grandma Sandy told us about that years ago. We understood that you had to stop that terrible man from praying on young women. The Victor Miller Case is well known here. People still talk about it. But I have one question to ask, why did you give up being Fashion Girl and became if you will pardon me for saying it this way, a man crazy slut?"

Madame D said, "It's okay sweetie, it's a fair question to ask. When I was in high school and going through puberty, I blossomed into a beautiful young woman who made young boys drool. Boys wanted me. They wanted to have sex with me. I did comply but only if they used a condom. No condom, no sex that was my rule."

"I always told the others to be a woman first and a Style Chick second. I wanted the others to live as normal a life as possible and at the same time, to put bad guys in their place. As for giving up being Fashion Girl, I got tired of modeling. I've been all over the world modeling fashions the average woman couldn't afford or use. You know I was allowed to keep everything I ever modeled in. You've seen my closets; I can't keep the doors closed."

"After we helped She-Ra overcome the controversy she was facing in 2018, we made her a Style Chick. I took a road trip with her from Maryland to here on an adventure of a lifetime. It was then I told her about my feelings about being Fashion Girl. During that trip, I changed my look, clothing, appearance, everything and permanently became Madame D. I admit, I am addicted to handsome men. These men also were vile criminals. I bought the land Aurora Gardens sits on now and made it a haven for both families and criminals."

"I also was pregnant with Charlotte and Dean Jr. during that time. By becoming Madame D, I felt relieved. I felt better about myself, and your Aunt Cindy followed my lead. We became blood sisters and while I also became The Skull Queen, Aunt Cindy became Queen Serpentina of the Vipers. I rescued the Vipers, and they followed me here and now work for me and Aunt Cindy."

"Daphne, I am going to tell you something that no one else knows right now that I have just found out recently, I'm pregnant again. This time I will be having triplets." Daphne replied, "Mom, you need to stop doing this. I mean you're forty-two years old now. You should get your tubes tied after you give birth. How far along are you?" Madame D said, "About two months. Am I getting fat yet?" Daphne replied, "Not yet but I'm sure you'll be soon. But I'm happy for you. Grandpa Fred, Grandpa Harry, Uncle Freddy and Harry Jr and the other twins will be too."

Madame D said, "You're right honey. I will get my tubes tied after I give birth. I am getting a little old to raise children." Daphne said, "Charlotte and I will help you if you need it." Madame D said, "Thank you Daphne." Just then, Harry knocked on the door and said, "Mom, Daphne, Vicki said breakfast is ready now and wait until you see it."

As Madame D and Daphne headed downstairs to see the master-piece of a breakfast Victoria laid out, the other Style Chicks were also there to wish their new leader a happy birthday. They placed birthday presents on a table that was out in the backyard where the party would take place.

Tiffany who replaced Madame D as leader of the Style Chicks said, "Happy Birthday Daphne! And congratulations on your eighteenth birthday! After tonight, you will enter your new phase of your life as the new Fashion Girl. How do you feel?" Daphne replied, "Right now, hungry. Let's eat first and then I'll tell you how I feel."

After breakfast, Daphne said, "Now as for I feel Tiffany, I feel great. I can't wait to take my rightful place as Fashion Girl." Tiffany replied, "That's great honey, now I have a surprise for you right now. In addition to the present, I got you, I want you to know that tonight, Lisa, Teresa, and Daphne will become the new Junior Style Chicks." Madame D added, "And Charlotte will join them too." Daphne said, "That's wonderful news but aren't they a little young to be Junior Style Chicks?"

Tiffany said, "It's true they are a little young, but remember the first group of Junior Chicks were only a couple of years older." Madame D said, "For now and like before, they will continue their education and will be trained after classes. They won't see action. What's more, Saks, Bloomie and Nine West will continue to be Style Chicks."

Penney said, "Ladies let's wait until tonight to go over all the details. So, Madame D, what are you and Daphne going to do before sunset?" Madame D replied, "Spend quality time with my daughter. The quality time I missed during my modeling days." Daphne said, "Mom, Harry and I always understood what you and the others did. You, all of you made the world a better place. And believe me, any time you did spend with us was quality time."

Just then, the sound of roaring motors filled the front of the mansion. Madame D knew what it meant. She and Daphne went out the front door to see the Skulls the biker gang Madame D rescued many years ago. They got off their bikes, bowed and said together, "All hail the Skull Queen and all hail the new Skull Princess!"

Daphne said in amazement, "Skull Princess? Me?" The Skull King came up to her and replied, "Yes my dear, as of now, you are one of us. Happy Birthday!" Madame D added, "Let me explain honey. You knew I was now a part of this gang, but what you don't know is that as of today, you are now the new Skull Princess." Daphne asked, "I thought Belle K was the Skull Princess? Didn't she join up after she broke up with her husband Bobby?"

The Skull King said, "That's right Daphne. You see Bobby was seriously wounded in an attack on the President of the United States in Washington. He survived, but after he married Belle K for which she was his childhood friend, high school sweetheart and girlfriend. Something in him snapped and he became abusive to her and her first child after he was born. She filed for divorce and decided to join up with us."

"She wanted to be a biker girl and joined your mother. But sadly, about three years ago, she was savagely killed in a gang war with our rival gang known as The Crocs. That gang was a bunch of evil hate mongers. When they learned that Belle K was of Hispanic descent, they killed her in an attack. Your mother and I vowed to get even with them. We not only defeated them, but we also killed their leader. A new leader has since taken her place. The others were in prison but escaped. No charges were filed against us. Belle K had three more children after her divorce, and she had them by us."

No offense to her memory, but she loved sex and didn't mind having it with us and had three children. Femur Fracture is one of the dads along with Brainbasher and Kneebreaker. And now you are one of us. Tomorrow night, you will have an initiation ceremony to officially welcome you. But for now, we have a present for you."

Daphne opened the box to reveal a pink leather jacket. Daphne thanked the Skull King and he said, "This is a brand-new jacket, but it also resembles the same jacket Belle K wore." Daphne asked, "Thank you again your highness but what will this initiation consists of?" Madame D answered, "The same kind of initiation Belle and I had, a gangbang." Daphne said, "What!" Madame D laughed and replied, "Just kidding sweetie, but one member of the gang will be your welcoming committee and you will have sex with him."

Daphne said, "Look mom, no offense everyone, I have a boyfriend. We've been together for nearly four years. We're exclusive and serious about our relationship." Madame D asked, "Just how serious are you?" Daphne answered, "Not serious to the point that I'm engaged to him or that I'm pregnant. But we love each other, and we've been loyal to each other."

The Skull King said, "I respect that Daphne. Tell you what I will do, and I will only do it for you. Bring your boyfriend with you tomorrow night to our hideout. Your mother will make it as romantic as possible. If you and he give up your own virginities, both of you are in. What do you say?"

Madame D interrupted and added, "Daphne before you answer that I have some questions for you. Tell me honestly. Either way you answer is all right with me." Daphne said, "Mom, what are you doing? You are ruining my birthday!" Madame D said, "Honey, I'm not trying to ruin anything. But these questions are important. First are you sexually active?"

Daphne looked embarrassed and answered, "Yes mom. Yes, I am sexually active. I've been having sex behind my boyfriend's back. He doesn't know." Madame D said, "Honey it's okay. I was that way too when I was your age as I said. Did you have your partners wear a condom?" Daphne's face became beet red and answered, "No. I wanted it as much as they did."

Madame D asked, "Are you right now as of this moment pregnant?" Daphne's embarrassment continued and answered, "No not at the moment. But two years ago, I was. The boy's father is an abortion doctor. I had an abortion in secret. I'm sorry mom, I knew you wanted me to be as religious as possible. But my hormones went berserk. As soon as I grew boobs and a nice ass, I became the girl every boy wanted. I obliged one of them and got pregnant."

Madame D looked disappointed but not angry. Then she asked, "I drink, I smoke, do you do any of those things?" Daphne answered continued to look embarrassed, "I'm sorry mom. I drink, I smoke, I party, but I don't do drugs if that's what you're wondering. Was that your next question mom? Am I a drug addict too? Was it mom? WAS IT!?"

Madame D said in anger, "I didn't raise you to be a sex crazed party girl, I raised you to be pure of heart! And this is how you repay me!? I've given you everything!" Daphne replied in equal anger, "Here's breaking news mom, you didn't raise me at all! While you were in some exotic place showing off your sorry ass, Grandpa Fred, Grandma Sandy and Dean raised me! Face it mom, you blew it as a parent! Dad dying because he lost his mind because you were gussied up to stop a sexual predator!" Look at you now! You're old! You're fat! You're pregnant again! Yes mom, you gave me everything! I'm just as much as a man crazy slut as you!"

Just then, Madame D got so angry, she slapped Daphne's face. Then she began to choke her. She said, "YOU UNGRATEFUL BITCH! I BROUGHT YOU INTO THIS WORLD AND I WILL TAKE YOU OUT OF IT! HOW DARE YOU! **HOW DARE YOU!!!**"

The Skull King tried to pull Madame D off of Daphne. He finally did and said, "Easy my queen, you need to calm down." Daphne didn't calm down and continued her tirade, "Face the truth mother, I am another you. I don't care about high fashion; I don't care about strutting my stuff on a catwalk. And right now, I could care less if I am going to be the new Fashion Girl. If this wasn't my birthday today, you can wait until Charlotte turns eighteen to take your place! As of now, we are enemies! I WILL BE YOUR WORST NIGHTMARE!!!"

Madame D still upset said, "Wait Daphne, I'm sorry. I gave up modeling to watch you and Harry grow up." Daphne said, "Sorry doesn't cut it mother! I'm out of here!" Daphne had her own car, got into it and drove away." The Style Chicks heard the commotion and waited until it ended to approach Madame D." Sephora asked, "Daphne, are you alright? What the hell happened?"

Madame D answered, "How nice of you to join me, did you hear how your niece talked to me? Did you know anything about what she said? Were you aware of any of it?" Sephora said, "No I didn't. I'm just as upset. The others and I stayed out of it because you had to work it out. But as her family too, I didn't like it when you were choking her." Sandy came out and added, "I didn't like it either Daphne, how could you do that?"

Madame D said, "Sandy, Cindy, please listen to me. I tried to be understanding. I guess I wasn't pleased with what she said. She blamed me for not being there for her. I retired from modeling to be there for her as she was growing up. Just as I've been there for Charlotte and Dean Jr. Sandy, you weren't too happy when Cindy joined the Vipers as their queen. You also didn't seem pleased when I became Madame D permanently. Cindy, Sandy, I'm sorry. I lost my head. I wouldn't have killed my own daughter and you both know it. She's gone somewhere to cool off and now I will do the same."

The Skull King said, "Let us go with you, my queen." Madame D replied, "Not right now my king. I need to be alone too. I'm sorry everyone." Madame D got in her car and peeled out of the driveway at a high rate of speed. The Skull King said, "Ladies, don't be mad at either of them. The conversation started out pleasantly then became very heated. I feel it's my fault when I gave Daphne one of Belle K's jackets. We wanted to make her one of us by having an initiation. And Queen Serpentina, you know the kind of initiations we have."

Sephora got mad and replied, "Are you trying to tell me that all of you wanted to do it with my niece?" Sandy added, "And with my granddaughter?" The Skull King said, "Then we offered to have Daphne's boyfriend and she to have a romantic night together and do it. That would've satisfied our initiation requirements." Sephora said, "No wonder they went off like they did! Mom, this wasn't the faults of either Daphne." The Skull King was going to say something else when Sephora stopped him and continued, "That's enough Skull King, my mom and I have heard enough."

The Skull King did say something, "Ladies, Daphne turned eighteen today. She's officially an adult now. Like it or not, she's the new Skull Princess now. And if she wants to be whoever she wants to be, let her." Sephora replied, "Skull King, you have the colossal nerve to make my niece the new princess after my best friend was killed the way she was? And you also have the gall to have given her one of Belle's jackets? Why? You are not turning her into a trailer trash slut!"

The Skull King said, "She confessed everything honey! She's more than just a good time. I saw the look in her eyes, her mouth said one thing, her eyes said another. Her eyes said I want to fuck all of you tomorrow night. She smokes, drinks, parties to all hours of the night and she had an abortion…" Sephora and Sandy looked catatonic for a moment as the Skull King continued, "She's not a good girl. She's a bad girl with bad intentions. Remember Serpentina, we are a biker gang, the

Vipers are a biker gang too and we do those kinds of things no matter how good or bad people think we are."

"The Skull Queen is pregnant with my babies. You gave birth to Rattler's. We are on the same side, remember that! Let's go boys, I think we've worn out our welcome." As the Skulls rode away, Sephora said, "Mom, I don't know what to think right now. Daphne's always been a good girl. She's always done the right thing. Is what the Skull King said true? Is Daphne really a bad girl with bad intentions?"

Sandy replied, "I don't know Cindy. When I was the Prom Queen many years ago, I was trying to avenge my sister's death as did Fashion Girl was trying to avenge her mother's death. I'm not too thrilled with what the Skull King told us that Daphne's a party girl. If it's true, if Daphne becomes Fashion Girl tonight? With the powers she'll inherit. Even becoming the Phoenix. Cindy, I don't know. All I can suggest is to find Daphne and try to reason with her."

"I'll go to Aurora Gardens and talk with Madame D. You go find where Daphne went to. Maybe we can fix things before it's too late." Sephora said, "I'm on it mom." Tiffany came out of the mansion and asked, "We all heard everything. Should we continue with the preparations, or should we wait?" Sephora answered, "For now continue with the preparations. Mom or I will inform you of any changes. Mom, let's do it to it!"

Sandy hopped into her car. Sephora got on her motorcycle and headed to where both Madame D and Daphne were. But could they defuse a situation that's out of their hands or was it for nothing? Had the granddaughter of Daphne Blake gone bad or evil?

CHAPTER 2

Since Sandy knew where Madame D was, we'll start with their conversation. Sandy arrived at Aurora Gardens ten minutes after Madame D arrived. Sandy has the special card that opens the elevator that leads expressly to the Den of Sin. Once there, Sandy found Madame D on her bed crying.

Sandy sat at the foot of the bed to try to comfort her friend. She said, "Daphne don't cry. She'll come around." Madame D replied, "She's right Sandy, I ruined her birthday. She told me off. She said so much. How can I look at her in the eye ever again?"

Sandy said, "After you left, the Skull King admitted to me and Cindy that it was his idea to have Daphne replace Belle K as the new Skull Princess. And for her to become property of the Skulls. Level with me Daphne, are you the Skull King's property?" Madame D replied, "No. The Skull King is my boyfriend. Diamondhead of the Vipers is also my boyfriend. We do threesomes together. I'm pregnant with the Skull King's babies."

Sandy asked, "You didn't answer my question. Are you or are you not the property of The Skulls? And why would the Skull King suggest having a gangbang with your daughter?" Madame D answered, "I told you no. I ride with the Skulls yes. I fuck the Skull King yes. Do you see him here right now glued to my hip? No! He knows that I can't belong to anyone like that now or ever. As Madame D, I must use the skills I had as Fashion Girl and the new skills I learned as Madame D to seduce criminals to surrender to the police without putting up a fight."

Sandy said, "Alright Daphne I know you're telling me the truth. Before I left Cindy, I had the impression that if you make Daphne the new Fashion Girl, she'll use it for bad purposes. The Skull King said that she's a bad girl with bad intentions. I know my granddaughter's life hasn't always been easy. She and Harry knew what you had to do. They also knew why you did it. But it wasn't easy on them."

"After I came back here to live permanently, I helped Dean and your dad look after the twins. Daphne especially was always asking for you and asked why you weren't around. I explained why you couldn't be around. Cindy told her the same thing when she was in Atlanta. Belle's death took a toll on them both. Bobby became such a jerk after they were married."

Madame D replied, "I know. As boyfriend and girlfriend, they were joined at the hip. They loved each other very much. I helped Belle that night in DC when Bobby was shot. I prayed with her. I... I... I was with her when she was killed. Those filthy bastards shot her down like she was a dog and all because she was Hispanic. Sandy, Ali Lopez was every bit as much as an American as you and I are. The only thing Hispanic about her was where her parents came from."

Sandy said, "I know. And The Crocs didn't kill you? Why?" Madame D replied, "It was thought that my mother was either Irish or Scottish. But no matter her ancestry, she was an American too. The Crocs were skinheads, belonged to the KKK, and hated everyone, even among themselves." Sandy said, "I think I now understand why the Skull King wants Daphne to take Belle's place. Didn't you and him both say that you killed their leader? And the others are in jail?"

Madame D replied, "I didn't kill him, the others did. I still have no use for firearms. I did want Daphne to carry one when she becomes the new Fashion Girl. Only for her protection." Sandy said, "You don't even use the Sword of Style." Madame D replied, "The Sword of Style was more of an elegant weapon than a practical one. I only used it when necessary. Like Tiffany, I preferred hand to hand combat. I have some martial arts skills too you know."

Sandy said, "Look Daphne, we were at that age. Being a teenager has never been easy. It wasn't easy for you, me, Cindy, Daphne, nobody. We must live by trial and error. Let's go back to Colognia and to the mansion. We have a party to help prepare for." Madame D replied, "That is if Daphne wants it." Sandy said, "Cindy will straighten her out. Let's go."

Sephora found Daphne at the beach sitting on the sand alone and thinking. Sephora sat down next to Daphne, took a deep breath and asked, "Daphne are you alright honey?" Daphne still seething with anger answered, "What do you think Aunt Cindy? I'm boiling mad!" Sephora said, "I understand why you're mad, but your mother is equally upset." Daphne replied, "Didn't you and the others see it? My mother tried to kill me! I almost lost consciousness! If the Skull King didn't pull her off me, I'd be dead now! So, no dear Aunt Cindy, I'm not all right!"

Sephora said, "Grandma Sandy went to set the record straight with your mother. I'm here to do the same. Daphne, were you ever aware that your mother and Grandma Sandy were once bitter enemies?" Daphne replied, "No, I don't think she ever told me." Sephora said, "It's something neither her nor your mother likes to talk about. Twenty years ago, Grandma Sandy was once known as The Prom Queen. She became her after her sister, your great aunt Cynthia for which I was named after was killed in prison after your grandma Daphne put her there."

"As you know, your grandma Daphne was the original Fashion Girl. After your great aunt was killed, her minions went after your grandma and killed her. I was there when it was revealed that grandma Daphne's best friend for your mom called Aunt Velma was responsible for bringing the minions together and killed her."

Daphne replied, "I don't understand why you're telling me this now Aunt Cindy? Haven't I been through enough today and it's not even lunchtime yet." Sephora said, "Look Daphne, both sides of your family have gone through some very turbulent times. Your mom and Grandma Sandy patched up their differences and are now the best of friends. Grandpa Fred lost his soulmate, Grandpa Harry reconciled with Grandma Sandy. Your mom helped Grandma Sandy to get visitation rights so she could see me. I grew up without her and didn't know why. Your mom and dad met at that time and hit it off. Before all went bad, your dad told your mom that he was her biggest fan."

"At six o'clock tonight, you will become the third woman to be called Fashion Girl. You will have the sickest birthday party anyone could possibly have. Your mom loves you and Harry very much. Please come back with me to the mansion. We've all gone through a lot of problems over the years."

Daphne asked, "Aunt Cindy, if I go back to the mansion with you, will mom be there? Will she still be angry with me?" Sephora answered, "Of course not honey. You are her pride and joy. You were the first child she had. Harry came along a few hours later. You have a destiny to fulfill, and you will fulfill it. Without making you more upset, tell me the truth woman to woman. Have you done any of the things you said to your mom that made you both so upset?"

Daphne answered, "No Aunt Cindy. I've always tried to keep out of trouble. But one thing was true though. When I finished puberty and grew tits and a nice ass, boys did want to score with me. But I never did it. I never drank, smoked or party. Dean would've killed me himself if I did. Although I wouldn't mind the gangbang the Skulls want me to do. But I won't do it. If I must have sex with a bunch of greasy bikers, I'll pass. If I am going to have sex, it will be with my boyfriend."

Sephora said, "Hey, those greasy bikers are my friends and I'm the queen of the Vipers. They are all nice guys. Just because they look and act the way they do is why people think they are evil. Some gangs are but not the Skulls or the Vipers. Your mom and I wouldn't have affiliated with them if they were. By the way, you do look nice in one of Belle's jackets. She would've wanted you to have it."

Daphne replied, "Belle K really was that special to you?" Sephora said, "Yes, she was. She was nice, sweet and I loved her. She was like a sister to me and a sister to all of us. C'mon honey, let's have lunch to-gether and we'll meet up with your mom. I know she wanted to do some shopping with you." Daphne replied, "I think I'd like that. Let's Do It to It!" Sephora said, "Spoken like a true Style Chick. Let's go."

Not only did Daphne and Sephora had lunch together, but Madame D also joined them. Before they sat down, Daphne and Madame D looked at each other and hugged while offering the other their heartfelt apologies. Sephora informed the others that the party was to go on as scheduled.

The three spent that afternoon at an exclusive mall with all the stores being of a luxury origin. Madame D and Sephora might not look like Style Chicks but once they flashed enough money to choke a horse and high-end credit cards, the employees of each store they dealt with fell all over them granting their every desire. Back at the mansion, Victoria was preparing a celebratory dinner for more than three dozen people. She closed her restaurant that day so her kitchen staff could help her. Her pastry chef baked a birthday cake unlike anyone had ever seen.

At an exotic car dealership, Tiffany and Penney picked up the new Glam Mobile to take back to the mansion. They put the vehicle in the garage to hide it until later that night. With Godiva's help, Macy prepared a special potion that will make everyone feel good and not drunk.

The former Junior Style Chicks also got in the act by putting up the decorations along with the special surprise Daphne's friends will receive. But when six o'clock rolled around, the birthday party of a lifetime was about to begin.

CHAPTER 3

Before I continue with the story, let's meet Daphne's friends who will become the next generation of Style Chicks. However, I won't determine which girl will become which Style Chick. I'll let the current Style Chicks do that.

First is Daphne's best friend Paula Ormand. She's seventeen years old and will be a senior in high school. They've known each other since childhood. Paula was on the junior varsity softball team. Her family hailed from Canada and her parents moved to California when Paula was a newborn. Paula is also prolific in technology and handles all of Daphne's tech needs.

Next is Isabella Rossi. She's of Italian descent. Her grandfather came to the United States after World War II. She has a fiery temper. She loves the magic arts. She's always admired magicians and how they perform. The DC Comics heroine Zatanna is her idol. She's a cheerleader and will stick up for her friends. Isabella is also a whiz at math and before she graduated, was a member of the Mathletes. She's nineteen and will start her sophomore year in college that fall.

Next is Indira Abdul-Zika. She's sweet sixteen and is of Arabian descent. She wears a hajib, but her parents left Syria at the height of the Civil War going on there and made it to America before the travel ban in 2017. Indira's family wanted to start their new life in America by living like Americans. Although Indira covers up her beautiful black hair, she's allowed to do anything American teenage girls do including date.

Indira dates and boys find her alluring. Indira's intentions after graduating high school and college to study marine biology. For now, she's one girl who knows what she wants. Her father taught her how to use a sword to defend herself.

Next is Sarah Newsome. A California girl born and bred, Sarah loves fast cars and even faster boys. Sarah is one friend of Daphne's who likes to live on the edge. She turned eighteen before Daphne did and when she got her driver's license, she took to the streets after her mother bought her an old car. She fixed it up and turned it into a super-hot rod capable of blasting the doors off any car. In high school, she was a flirty girl who would do almost anything to get the boy she wanted.

Sarah has sarcastic wit and likes to hang out with her fellow racers at various hangouts. She's from a broken family when her father left her and her mother when she was a baby. Her mother worked several jobs to earn enough money to support her and her daughter. Of the friends Daphne has, Sarah is by far the least advantaged as far as money and prestige is concerned. Sarah is also homeless but that never bothered her friends when her mother was no longer able to work due to a major disability.

Next is Amora Takata. She's an exchange student from Japan but became a US citizen after coming to the United States. Amora is a mistress of chemistry and wants to pursue a career in science. She's also eighteen and will be a freshman in college that fall. Amora learned how to speak American slang while speaking with a beautiful Japanese accent.

Next is Lori Denton. She's the youngest of Daphne's friends. She's only fourteen. Daphne and her other friends befriended Lori after she was the victim of bullying and hazing. Lori is the youngest of eight children. She's always seemed to bring up the rear when it comes to just about everything. But one thing Lori excels at is tennis and her aspiration is to become a professional tennis player. She has trouble with her studies and has always spent time in special education. While there's nothing wrong with her per se, she just can't seem to figure out basic studies much less at a high school level.

Lori has also excelled at home economics and probably could match Victoria when it comes to culinary skills.

Next is Denise Menendez. Her family hails from Mexico but she was born in America. Her family is deep rooted in Mexican heritage. Denise is bilingual but wishes to speak more English than Spanish which doesn't please her parents much. She's seventeen and holds down a job as a cashier in a fast-food restaurant. She desires to become a doctor and specialize in veterinarian medicine. She loves animals and has had pets all her life.

In the meantime, Denise's role to Daphne's group of friends is to be the diplomat. She has a knack to solve problems and help people resolve their differences.

And finally, there's Aldea Cicero. She's also eighteen and is of African descent. Her family hails from Kenya and fled the country before she was born. Aldea is one girl you don't want to mess with. She's part of a gang who will kill you if you mess with them. However, Aldea's relationship with Daphne's friends is valuable. She stands at six foot four and weighs two hundred twenty pounds. And because of her African heritage, she's deadly with a bow and arrow.

Aldea is the only one of Daphne's friends who does all the things Daphne told her mother. Aldea smokes, drinks, parties and is sexually active and has been pregnant. She's a mother of two and lives in a trailer park on welfare and unable to get a job because she has a criminal record. Her father became a prominent businessman and spared his daughter from prison. But after he did this, he disowned her because of her actions.

Do these backgrounds sound familiar? They are because in most cases they are the backgrounds of the current Style Chicks. And when the party for Daphne goes into full swing, the current Style Chicks will take a liking to these girls once they know these facts.

CHAPTER 4

As previously mentioned, the party was to begin at six, but before that, Daphne's friends one by one came to the mansion. They brought presents for the guest of honor. Then the Skulls and the Vipers also showed up for the party. Madame D let the Vipers in but before she let the Skulls come in, she had a few choice words for the Skull King. She said, "My king I'm glad you and the others came back for the party. Daphne and I apologized to each other, and we're cool. As for you however, we're not."

The Skull King replied, "Wait my queen, before you continue, I wish to apologize to both you and Daphne. We still want Daphne to join us. But if you don't want us to have our way with her, we're okay with that." Madame D asked, "You really mean that?" The Skull King answered, "Of course my dear. If Daphne wants to do this or not, it's fine by us."

Madame D said, "I'm still angry with you. But I accept your apology. Daphne is my daughter and as her mother, I wouldn't let her do anything she doesn't want to. But if she wants to have an initiation like I did, I won't stand in her way. I admit she's very pretty. She takes after me and her grandmother after all. I can assure you that she likes boys, and I met her boyfriend and he's very nice. Like all of you treat me like a queen, he treats her the same way."

The Skull King said, "We are sorry, we love Daphne, just not the way you are thinking right now." Sephora came out to join Madame D and added, "I speak on behalf of my niece gentlemen. She will have the initiation, she told me so. She wore the jacket you gave her, and she likes it. She loved Belle K as much as I did. She didn't deserve to die like she did."

The Skull King said, "I agree with you. Then we are here as are the Vipers to honor your niece on her special night." Sephora replied, "I'm glad to hear that. Now everyone, it's almost time for the party to begin. Please come inside." As the Skulls went inside, the Skull King whispered to Madame D, "My queen, may I have a moment with you in private?" Madame D replied, "Sure, let's go upstairs so we can talk in privacy."

Madame D turned to the others and said, "If you'll excuse me for a few minutes, the Skull King and I need to talk in privacy for a few minutes." As the others excused them, Tiffany whispered to Penney, "I bet they will talk." Penney whispered back, "Do you think so?" Tiffany whispered, "They will do the nasty, I'm almost sure of it." Penney whispered back, "They did have that major fight this morning and will probably talk things out. Tiffany, you were flirty yourself once, remember that."

Madame D took the Skull King into her bedroom. The Skull King said, "So this is your bedroom here? I've never been in here before, it's very nice." Madame D replied, "Alright my king, spare me the pleasantries, what do you want to speak with me about?" The Skull King said, "My queen, you are pregnant with my children. I will be enormously proud to call them my children. I know how mad you were earlier and still right now, but I want to make it up to you." Madame D asked, "Here? Now? With dozens of people here?" The Skull King said, "Yes, my queen. I want to make it up to you by doing it with you right now. When you start to show, who knows how much longer we can do it to it as you Style Chicks say."

Madame D replied, "Since I gave up being Fashion Girl, I have become a man crazy slut. I live underground and I make men succumb to me. If we are to do it right now, you must try not to scream." The Skull King said, "I don't mind being gagged so I won't." Madame D replied, "Very well then. I will do the same. But first let me do this."

Madame D stuck her tongue down the Skull King's throat in a passionate kiss. Next, she gagged the Skull King. Before she put the gag in her mouth she said quietly, "I also hope you don't mind doing it dominatrix style. You must be punished for earlier today."

She put the gag in her mouth, she tied up the Skull King by hand-cuffing his feet and hands to the bedposts. She kept a whip in her bedroom for such a purpose. She cracked it to signal she meant business. Since she was gagged, she couldn't give him a blowjob instead she unzipped his pants and gave him a hand job.

Once the Skull King was ready, Madame D took off her jacket and skirt, inserted his penis into her and they went at it. The Skull King or Madame D didn't let out any noises but they both knew they had smiles on their faces. Madame D could feel the Skull King's penis penetrate her clit as she reveled in delight. When he climaxed, she could feel more of his sperm go inside her. Madame D thought back at that moment of the time when she dreamt of being evil and got more pregnant everytime she had sex.

When they finished, Madame D took the cuffs off the Skull King and got redressed. They kissed once more before they hugged. Madame D whispered, "I love you, my king. You are mine forever." The Skull King whispered back, "And you will always be my queen, I love you too. I will lay down my life for you." Madame D said, "As I will lay down my life for you. Now let's rejoin the others."

The Skull King and Madame D came back downstairs with smiles on their faces arm in arm. Tiffany whispered to Penney, "Told you so, they had sex." Penney whispered back, "When you're right Tiffany, you're right." Madame D was introduced by Daphne to her friends. Amora said, "It's a pleasure to see you again Mrs. Bates." Madame D replied, "Call me Madame D please. I hope you and the others are having a good time?" Amora said, "I sure am like the others. I'm honored to meet the Style Chicks. I've heard so much about them."

Madame D asked, "I use to model in Tokyo quite frequently. What part of Japan are you from?" Amora answered, "My family hails from Sapporo in Hokkaido Prefecture." Madame D said, "I'm quite familiar with that part of the world too, It's a beautiful place. Please mingle, dinner will be ready soon and I assure you it's a meal you will never forget."

About an hour later, Victoria asked everyone to take a seat out in the backyard as dinner was about to be served. Although the dining room could seat twelve people, more than sixty showed up for this event. As everyone sat down, Victoria's servers began the meal with an appetizer. Oysters on the half shell cooked to perfection. Soon after, the servers gave the guest the next course, a special secret recipe soup of Victoria's design. No one knew what was in it, but everyone enjoyed it.

Next the servers brought out another of Victoria's specialties, a garden salad unlike no one ever saw before with a dressing of Victoria's design. Then the main course was served, a huge prime rib with au jus gravy, seasoned potatoes and a garden medley of vegetables.

Victoria said after all of this was consumed, "Now for my pastry chef's masterpiece." Four servers wheeled out a massive birthday cake as everyone sang happy birthday to both Daphne and Harry. The cake was yellow and devil's food with strawberry, raspberry and blueberry filling and a special combination frosting of vanilla and chocolate.

Everyone was stuffed. One final thing the servers did was pour champagne to the guests. Madame D got up, raised her glass and said, "This will be one night no one will ever forget. Daphne, Harry, you both made it to adulthood. Congratulations! Here's to the beginning of the rest of your lives. May it be happy, healthy and prosperous, Cheers!"

As everyone clinked their glasses and drank down the champagne. The party continued with music and dancing. Madame D wanted everyone to have fun first before the big ceremony. Two hours went by when Madame D stopped the music and asked for everyone's attention. She said, "Ladies and gentlemen, this is not just Daphne's and Harry's birthday party, it's also a special event. For some of you here who might not be aware of this, but tonight on her eighteenth birthday, my daughter Daphne Sandra Bates will become the third woman to bear the name Fashion Girl."

And what's more, ladies, you've been good friends to my daughter for years. Not only will Daphne become the next Fashion Girl, but all of you will become the next generation of Style Chicks. Beginning tonight, I will help all of you to determine on what kind of heroines you will all be. Gentlemen, bring out the armoire."

Madame D locked up her old costume and accessories in an armoire under lock and key after she gave up the role. She continued, "Nine years ago, I locked up my Fashion Girl costume in this armoire waiting for the day it will be opened as my daughter will take my place. Daphne honey, I only wish you the best of luck and all the happiness in the world."

"Being a Style Chick won't be easy. You will see and do things most people can only dream of. You will experience joy, sorrow and traumatic events. But you will also experience all the world has to offer." Madame D opened the armoire and continued, "Daphne these are your power bracelets. With them you will possess superhuman strength. The ability to change your costume to accommodate certain situations. You will also be able to communicate with the others. Speak multiple languages fluently and as of now, you will also become the powerful Phoenix of the Archangels."

Madame D took out her costume and continued, "As you know, your grandma Daphne first wore the Fashion Girl costume in her traditional colors of purple, green and pink. When I took her place, I made it to how it looks now, but now that it is yours, it will be anyway you want." Then Madame D took out her primary weapon. She unsheathed it and continued, "And finally my daughter, this is the Sword of Style. It's an elegant weapon which I had on me in special situations. But if you need to use it, you can. And now if you will all come with me, there is one more thing that needs to be unveiled."

Madame D led the others to the garage and opened one of the doors and said, "And Daphne, this is your version of The Glam Mobile. As you know it's more than just a car. You'll be able to fly it, hover above water and it has all the tools you'll need to combat crime. My daughter all this as this mansion and my fortune is also yours. For all of you, you too will get your own costumes, vehicles and you will be compensated financially for your efforts. Now Daphne as you also know, you must take the oath of allegiance as will your friends. Everyone, raise your right hand and repeat after me."

"I." The others replied, "I." Madame D said, "Your name." Everyone replied with their respected names. Madame D continued, "Hereby swear to the following. My heart will always be pure." The others replied, "My heart will always be pure." Madame D continued, "Use force only when necessary." The others replied, "Use force only when necessary." Madame D continued, "To spread love and peace throughout the world." The others replied, "To spread love and peace throughout the world." Madame D continued, "To protect the innocent at all costs." The others replied, "To protect the innocent at all costs." Madame D continued, "And bring those responsible to justice." The others replied, "And bring those responsible to justice." Madame D continued, "So help me god." The others replied, "So help me god."

Madame D said, "Congratulations everyone! You are now officially the next generation of Style Chicks. Your training will begin in one week from tonight. Daphne for now, show everyone how you will look like as the new Fashion Girl." Daphne replied, "Don't I need to change my clothes first?" Madame D said, "No it's okay, your power bracelets will create a new costume just as it did with me." Daphne replied, "Okay mom, stand back everyone."

At that moment, Daphne raised her arms, crossed her wrists and said, "STYLE ME AS FASHION GIRL!" What happened next no one expected. A cloud of thick black smoke appeared. It enveloped Daphne and when the smoke cleared, Daphne's appearance had completely changed. Daphne was now dressed in a black corset with purple and green accents. A short black skirt with purple and green accents, fishnet stockings, a black cape and knee-high black boots with purple and green stripes.

Madame D looked puzzled and said, "I don't understand this. You should have had a purple costume with a green cape. What happened Daphne?" Daphne's appearance not only changed but her voice and hairstyle as well. She replied in her new voice, "I don't know for sure.

Even the power bracelets are black. And look everyone the car is now black as well. What does it mean?"

Tiffany had an idea about it and said, "I think I know Daphne. Since your mom changed her appearance many years ago and she once said to me that she wasn't crazy about purple, but she wore it to honor your grandmother. You are now Fashion Girl in your mother's image. Maybe a darker, more brooding Fashion Girl who will take care of criminals differently."

Now as Fashion Girl, Daphne asked, "What about the others? Will this happen to them too?" Tiffany answered, "Once training begins and Penney transfers our powers to the others, how they will look could also change. We'll have to wait to find out." Madame D said, "Harry, I didn't leave you out, didn't I Glamour Boy?" Glamour Boy and the Phat Kats were also at the party and replied, "That's right Harry, you will take my place as the new Glamour Boy and the new leader of the Phat Kats. Daphne your boyfriend will also become a Phat Kat too."

Daphne's boyfriend named Felix Higgins asked, "Really? I will become a Phat Kat too?" Glamour Boy answered, "That's right Felix, as Daphne's boyfriend, you will become a Phat Kat as the new Jared. We will find a replacement for Kohl Nordstrom too." Daphne asked, "What about the Cosmo Chicks?" Cover Girl and her group were also there and answered, "We Galaxians don't age as quickly as you humans. We are still at the service of The Style Chicks, and we can't wait to work with you once your training is complete."

Madame D said, "As you know when we had breakfast, Saks, Bloomie and Nine West will continue to be Style Chicks." Saks replied, "That's right Daphne, we also can't wait to work with you. Madame D said, "Charlotte, Lisa, Little Daphne and Teresa, step forward please." Charlotte asked, "What is it mommy?" Madame D replied, "We didn't leave you out as well for as of tonight, all of you will become the next generation of Junior Style Chicks. You will all continue your educations and will be trained at a later time."

"Everyone this concludes the ceremony and tonight's party. But before you go, I know all of you brought presents for Daphne, why don't we all open them to see what she got. I'm sure she'll put everything to good use." The presents were nice but modest. But Madame D was right, Daphne could put them to good use. Before everyone left, Sarah who was homeless until she was made a Style Chick. She asked, "Madame D, is it possible that I could stay the night? I'm homeless."

Madame D replied, "You heard me say that Daphne now owns this mansion, you should be asking her." Daphne added, "No problem, Sarah, this place has thirty rooms. And remember that you will start earning a salary. But mom, I can't take your fortune. You worked hard to get what you made."

Madame D replied, "The money I made as a model is mine. The money I'm giving you is the money Style Incorporated makes. Between Vampira Fragrances, Victoria's two restaurants and the Mystique Marauder cruise ship, you will be set for life." Daphne thanked Madame D, shook Sarah's hand and said, "Welcome to the team my friend."

Sarah replied, "Thank you Daphne. See you tomorrow." Madame D turned to Daphne and said, "Happy Birthday honey. I know we had a rocky start to the day but tonight was a major success." Daphne replied, "It sure was and thank you for allowing my friends to become the next Style Chicks." Madame D said, "It took me a few years to find the current Style Chicks, it only seemed fitting to have your friends, people you already know to be the next Style Chicks."

Daphne replied, "Sarah will impress Tiffany. She's practically another her. She likes drag racing, she's flirty, sarcastic and all she's missing is Tiffany's costume. As for the others, I'm not sure." Madame D said, "We'll figure out everything next week. In the meantime, celebrate with your friends. I'll have Grandma Sandy open an account for you to start getting compensated as for your friends." Madame D pulled out a large sum of money, gave it to Daphne and continued, "Give this to Sarah in the morning. I think she'll need it."

Daphne counted it and replied, "Mom there's five thousand dollars here." Madame D said, "It's okay honey. It's not a loan or an advance. Consider it as your first act as the new Fashion Girl." Daphne replied, "Mom, I don't know what to say except thank you."

Madame D hugged Daphne and said, "You're welcome sweetie, I'm heading back to Aurora Gardens. If you need me, you know how to get in touch with me. Goodnight, Fashion Girl." Daphne replied, "That will take some getting used to. Goodnight, Madame D." Madame D laughed and said, "Now that will take some getting used to you not calling me mom."

Madame D rejoined the Skulls with Dean along with them. Dean said, "Daphne that was some party." Madame D replied, "It doesn't have to end as far as we are concerned. Care to head back with us Dean?" Dean said, "I need to work tomorrow." Madame D replied, "You are the owner, call out sick." Dean said, "I guess I could fake a cough or a sneeze or two. That is if the Skull King doesn't mind, you're being pregnant with his babies."

The Skull King replied, "It's cool bro. You're practically one of us. We did have a threesome when Madame D was pregnant with your babies." Dean said, "Why not, once again Daphne I realize why you call your place the Den of Sin." Madame D replied, "You might go to hell for being there, but you'll roast hot dogs and marshmallows with a smile on your face. Let's live in sin for awhile while we're still young to enjoy it."

Victoria's staff stayed behind to clean up with the current Style Chicks helping them. Moments later, there was a scream coming from upstairs. Sephora recognized the scream as it was coming from Daphne's room. She ran upstairs and began to scream herself. She asked, "Daphne what's going on in here? The walls of your room are black. The doors, window shades, even the clothes we bought today are black. What could this mean?"

Daphne replied, "I don't know. I think Tiffany's right, as the new Fashion Girl, I'll be darker, meaner, and maybe evil? Aunt Cindy, am I going to become evil?" Sephora said, "Tiffany could be right. By wearing all black, driving a black car, even having a black bedroom, maybe you will be darker, but I don't think you'll become evil."

With Daphne's mother becoming the dark Madame D. It was possible that her daughter would end up being a dark heroine too. As for being evil, only time will tell if that will one day happen.

CHAPTER 5

After the mansion was cleaned up and everyone went home, Sephora stayed behind to monitor Daphne and what they both witnessed. During the overnight hours, massive heat began to pour into Daphne's bedroom. Then an evil sounding voice calls to her. Before Daphne could respond, she was magically teleported from the mansion to an undisclosed place.

Daphne asked, "Who are you? What are you? Where am I?" Just then a plume of thick red smoke appeared in front of her. Maniacal laughter filled the air. When the smoke cleared, appeared before her was none other than Satan himself. He answered, "My dear child, I am Satan. God of evil. I've been watching you for years. You have all the makings to be a fine minion to evil."

Daphne said, "I will never serve the forces of evil. Were you the one who turned my new costume, car and bedroom into all black?" Satan replied, "Yes, my dear. Many years ago, if only in a dream, I made your mother evil. She was pure evil. More evil than I could've ever imagined. I promised her that I would never do that to anyone again. I kept that promise. But I never promised her that I wouldn't target someone for real. Think my dear, why did your mother give up being Fashion Girl? She wasn't just tired of being a model, she was tired of being ridiculed."

Daphne asked, "What do you mean she was ridiculed?" Satan

answered, "Do you think dear child she got respect with a name like Fashion Girl? She had to constantly prove to others and the world that she was a serious superheroine. Then she gave up modeling, she gave up being Fashion Girl. Why do you think she's now living in a poor excuse of a tourist trap? Why do you think she's living underground? Why do you think she's been riding with a motorcycle gang? Having sex? Is pregnant at her age? Getting tattoos and piercings? She's truly an evil woman."

"Let those goody-goody Style Sluts find new replacements, but you will be something more than being a source of endless ridicule." Daphne said, "One of those goody-goody Style Sluts as you put it is my aunt." Satan laughed maniacally and replied, "Your aunt was only more grateful to your mother and followed her. Does she live cleanly? No, she doesn't. She too gave up being Sephora. When I made your mother evil, she called herself Aldornia. She caused destruction, had sex at will, got pregnant with multiple children. And all because she was asked to stop a gang of evil goths. Their leader gave your mother a potion he called wolf's blood."

"With this potion my dear, you will be evil, powerful, strong, fertile, you and your friends will not become Style Chicks, but Satanic Sluts. You didn't lie to your mother; you live in sin every bit as much as she does. Drink this potion and fulfill your true destiny. You and your friends will give birth to my army of evil. The army your mother was supposed to give me."

Daphne said, "I'll never become evil because you want me or anyone else. I will take my rightful place as the next Fashion Girl. It might not be the best name for a heroine, but my mother and her mother before her helped to make the world a better place to live in. That's a destiny I'm proud to fulfill. I admit I like the new look if you did this and if so, I thank you. Fashion Girl is back in black, so little man, make like Michael Jackson and beat it."

Satan was furious and replied, "Very well my dear, you will pay for your defiance!" Daphne said, "I will defy you for the rest of my life. Leave me, my friends and my family alone. My mother didn't give up being Fashion Girl because she's evil. She gave up being Fashion Girl to be there for me and my twin brother. She also didn't give up being a heroine either. She fought crime with a different kind of style."

Just then, Daphne had returned to her bedroom and the temperature of the room returned to normal. By dawn, she didn't remember a thing at that moment. And she didn't say anything about it to anyone. She found Sarah was already up. She said, "Hey, Sarah, how did you sleep last night?" Sarah replied, "Like a baby. I haven't slept so good in years." Daphne said, "Before my mom left last night, she asked me to give you this." Daphne handed Sarah the envelope with the money inside. Sarah was thrilled and asked, "What's this for?" Daphne answered, "My mom wanted you to have it. She said to call this not a loan, not an advance, not even charity, but to help you on your new path."

Sarah said, "I sure thank you and your mom for this. When my mother lost her job and our apartment, I've been living in my car. My mother was admitted to a living facility due to her disability."

Daphne asked, "If you don't mind my asking, what happened to her?" Sarah answered, "I wouldn't answer that question to anyone else but you. The kind of work my mother did was very dangerous. She worked in a factory. One day there was an explosion. It happened near where she worked, she lost both of her legs. The company refused to give her any financial help. The bills piled up, we got evicted, I wasn't quite old enough to work myself and even if I did, it wouldn't have been enough for us to live on. She qualified for government assistance; it wasn't enough for both of us. So, she used it to go into this facility and I had to live on the streets."

Daphne asked, "Your mom bought you the car you get around in, right?" Sarah answered, "That's right. She only had two thousand dollars left. And I needed something. I drive it, live in it and race it." Daphne said, "Now all of that will change. My mom thinks this, and I agree with her, that you'll be the next Tiffany." Sarah replied, "I'll become the next Tiffany? Why?"

Daphne said, "Before she took my mom's place, Tiffany was a lot like you. Sarcastic, fast living, fast driving and flirty. Little by little, she became more serious and was ready to assume my mom's role. When she gave up being Fashion Girl, Tiffany took over. Now that I will be the new Fashion Girl, you'll be second in command. If I should fail in that role, you'll take my place. Like my mom said, a whole new world has opened to you. Take advantage of it."

Sarah asked, "What do you want to do today new leader of the Style Chicks?" Daphne answered, "Like my mom said, let's celebrate our new roles. Let's take the new Glam Mobile out for a spin. Let's see what it's capable of." Sarah said, "Sounds good to me. Um, will I too get a new car as well?" Daphne replied, "Yes and much more than that."

Victoria called the girls down to breakfast where Sephora was already seated. When Daphne and Sarah sat down at the dining room table. Sephora said, "Good morning girls. Daphne, before you do anything else today, your mom asked me to take you to city hall." Daphne asked, "City Hall? Why do I need to go to City Hall?" Sephora answered, "I'm sure the mayor would like to know that this city's greatest citizen is back."

Sarah said, "To meet the mayor? What an honor! Go ahead Daphne, we'll cruise the streets later." Sephora added, "We'll go there on my motorcycle. Then what will you do next?" Daphne said, "Well it's not to go to Disney World. Sarah and I were going to tryout the new Glam Mobile." Sephora said, "Excellent. Want to go to Aurora Gardens to show your mom how the new car does?" Daphne replied, "Sure. Aunt Cindy, when mom said she wanted to give me her fortune last night. I told her she shouldn't do that."

Sephora said, "You're right Daphne. I think she mentioned that you will become very rich, and your friends will also benefit financially but she's not giving it all away." Daphne replied, "I'm glad to hear that. Okay Aunt Cindy, let's go to city hall." Later that morning, Sephora and Daphne arrived at city hall. The receptionist was shocked to learn why they wanted to see the mayor.

Peter Marcus the former police chief and mayor of the city had retired in 2024. The current mayor named Olivia Upton allowed the two women to come in. Sephora entered first. Mayor Upton said, "Sephora, how have you been? What can I do for you?" Sephora replied, "Actually mayor, I think there's something I can do for you. Just in case you didn't know about Fashion Girl."

Mayor Upton said, "What about Fashion Girl? She died nine years ago." Sephora replied, "Actually madame mayor, Fashion Girl didn't die nine years ago. She's still alive but now lives in Aurora in the neighboring county. She did this to spend more time with her eldest children. Yesterday, her eldest daughter turned eighteen and as the tradition of the Style Chicks, the daughter of Fashion Girl will take her place on that special day. Madame mayor, allow me to present this city's champion of justice, my niece Daphne Bates, the third woman to be called Fashion Girl."

Daphne walked into the mayor's office as the mayor had a surprised look on her face. Mayor Upton asked, "What's the meaning of this Sephora? This is your niece? This is the new Fashion Girl?" Sephora answered, "Hear me out mayor. When Daphne's mother assumed a new role, she changed everything about her including her appearance. When my niece became the new Fashion Girl, her appearance changed as well. Madame mayor, I assure you, Fashion Girl is back, she's just back in black."

Mayor Upton replied, "No AC/DC reference will convince me. Young lady, if you are the new Fashion Girl, prove it to me." Daphne turned to Sephora and whispered, "Aunt Cindy what am I going to do? How can I convince her?" Sephora added, "Mayor can you give us a moment please?" Mayor Upton replied, "Make it quick Sephora, I'm a very busy woman."

Sephora asked, "Mayor Upton, I know it's been nine years and I also know you haven't lived here that long but what do you remember about Fashion Girl?" Mayor Upton answered, "Well, Fashion Girl had super strength, she was a mistress of disguise, and she also changed her outfit to accommodate certain situations." Sephora said, "That's right ma'am. Okay Fashion Girl, you heard the mayor, prove it to her." At that moment, Daphne took the heaviest object in the mayor's office she could find and lifted it over her head.

Sephora asked, "Well mayor, convinced?" Mayor Upton replied, "No

I'm not Sephora. You've wasted more of my time than I have allowed, if you and your niece aren't out of city hall in the next five seconds, I'll have you arrested." Sephora asked, "On what charge?" Mayor Upton answered, "I'll think of something." Just then, Peter Marcus happened to have been at city hall at that moment, heard the commotion and walked into the office.

He said, "Sephora, Daphne, what are you both doing here?" Sephora replied, "Mayor Marcus am I glad to see you." Mayor Marcus asked, "What's going on here Mayor Upton?" Mayor Upton answered, "I was about to throw these women in prison for wasting my time." Mayor Marcus said, "Your honor, don't be upset. I've known these women for years. This is Daphne Bates, the daughter of Fashion Girl. But Daphne why are you dressed in black?"

Daphne replied, "Yesterday was my eighteenth birthday. I finally took my mother's place as the new Fashion Girl. The mayor here doesn't seem impressed. My new costume is black on account of what my mom did nine years ago." Mayor Marcus said, "That's right Mayor Upton. I knew that Fashion Girl didn't die, she faked her death to live in privacy and to be there for Daphne and her twin brother. Madame mayor, this young woman is the new Fashion Girl."

Mayor Upton replied, "I'm sorry ladies. Fashion Girl was my child-hood heroine. When I learned she died, I was devastated. The idea that I lived in the same city she protected. I know Tiffany took her place, but it wasn't the same. Young lady, your mother was beautiful, smart, powerful and she gave it all up. I think I understand. I have children too. I'd be honored to have you back in our city again, Fashion Girl."

Daphne said, "Yes mayor Fashion Girl is back. But promise me one thing only for now. Next week, I will begin my training. Until then, the current Style Chicks will still handle any criminal activity like they've always done. When I complete my training and my friends complete theirs, the Style Chicks will be newer, younger and better than ever before."

Mayor Upton replied, "That's a simple request. Okay Fashion Girl, I won't say anything to anyone else about this for now." Daphne said,

"Thank you mayor. Thank you as well Mayor Marcus." Mayor Marcus replied, "I always thought highly of your mother. I know Mayor Upton will think highly of you too. Good day ladies."

As Daphne and Sephora left the mayor's office, Daphne said, "Well, that went well. For a moment there, I thought we were going to spend the night in jail. And for what? That I'm not dressed like my mother or even my grandmother?"

Sephora replied, "I think Tiffany had something when she said that you are going to do things differently than your mother or grandmother. And dressing the part might have something to do with it. Think what Tiffany said last night. Your grandmother wore a purple minidress with a green scarf. As Fashion Girl, her costume also reflected this. Your mother did inherit the mantle of Fashion Girl, but it wasn't passed down from her mother. So, her costume still reflected what her mother wore."

"With that said, when your mother gave up the Fashion Girl mantle and became Madame D, how you look now as Fashion Girl reflects how she's dressed now. I wouldn't worry too much about that. Once we make it known that Fashion Girl is back, we'll explain everything to the public. That is if that big mouth mayor can keep a secret."

Daphne said, "For now we'll have to trust her. I just hope that wearing an all-black outfit won't mean that I will become bad, or God forbid evil." Sephora replied, "Wearing any color shouldn't represent that a person is good or evil. It's how you are. Your mom wears black, is she evil? No. I now wear black too, am I evil? Of course not. It's personality not your colors that makes you what you are."

Daphne said, "You're right. If it's okay, let's rejoin Sarah and head to Aurora Gardens. I want to set the record straight with the Skull King. I can't believe my mother would even suggest my doing a gangbang." Sephora replied, "Your mother developed a weird sense of humor since she became Madame D. Now that she's pregnant again, her humor really has gotten weird."

Daphne asked, "Aunt Cindy, I've heard of an illness if it's called that nymphomania. Is that what my mother might have?" Sephora answered, "It's a real illness. Maybe she does suffer from it. You know she's been sexually active since she was a teenager herself. You've heard her say, no condom, no sex. She kept those urges in check until she gave up Fashion Girl's mantle. Since then, she's been one big bag of hormones. Daphne there's nothing wrong with liking boys or men but it's not okay when it takes over your life."

"Daphne, I worry about her all the time. I gave birth to five babies at one time when I became sexually active. After they were born, I had my tubes tied. Giving birth like that was the most painful experience I ever had. So, I tied my tubes. Now she's pregnant again. With triplets this time. Alright Daphne let's go there right now. Your mother isn't turning my niece into a sexual predator."

The three got into their vehicles and headed towards Aurora Gardens to settle a score with Madame D. When they arrived at the motor court. Sephora used her special card and they headed into the elevator that leads directly into the Den of Sin. When they got down, no one was there. Then Sephora forgot that Madame D doesn't use the den in the daytime. Instead, they went inside the bar and went down to the strip club.

Sephora stopped the elevator and told the others to wait for her. She stepped out of the elevator, and she found Madame D in her office with her business manager. Sephora couldn't believe her eyes. Madame D and her business manager were going over figures of a different kind. She got mad and asked, "Hey Madame, how much profit did you make last quarter?"

Madame D covered herself up as quickly as she could and answered, "Sephora you couldn't knock?" Sephora said, "I don't think it would've done any good." The business manager asked, "Hey Sephora, what are the chances of you doing a threesome with us?" Sephora answered, "None but the chances of my physically throwing you out of here is almost certain. Get out."

Sephora banged her fist into her palm and continued, "Don't hear good, I said get out!" Madame D said, "I hope you're happy Cindy. We were going over my figures." Sephora replied, "Yeah, I saw that 36, 24, 36 soon to be bigger than that. Daphne what the hell is the matter with you?"

Madame D asked, "What do you mean what the hell is the matter with me? What the hell is the matter with you? My business manager and I were really going over my business capital here." Sephora answered, "No business meeting I know about involves you lying naked on your desk with your business manager literally going over your assets. I ask you again, what's the matter with you? Yesterday, you practically gift wrapped your daughter to be a buffet table to the Skulls. Then you tried to choke her. Now her costume makes her look like a female version of Dracula. Then overnight, she dreamt that Satan wanted her in the same way he tried to do with you, only for real."

"Daphne, I love you; we're blood sisters now. We've been through a lot together. You're my kids' godmother as well as their aunt as am I with your kids. Now you're pregnant again, why? Didn't you learn anything from that horrible experience? Is Satan trying something with you again? Or who did you sleep with to permanently become Madame D? I am beginning to doubt the notion that you gave up being Fashion Girl so you could become a man crazy slut."

"Madame D got up, approached Sephora and replied, "Give me one good reason why I shouldn't kick your ass? You've got a lot of gall coming here like you did." Sephora said, "I've got every reason to be here right now. I've got Daphne and her friend Sarah in the elevator waiting to talk with you and The Skull King. She doesn't want to do what you've been doing the last nine years. You used to stand for something special. Something meaningful. Something heroic. I heard what Daphne said to you. You've gotten old, fat, and dare I say it, ugly."

Madame D replied, "Keep on talking bitch, you're doing just fine." Sephora said, "I will! We just came from Colognia City Hall. The new mayor didn't believe that Daphne had become the new Fashion Girl because of how she's dressed. She was about to throw your daughter in jail. What Tiffany said last night is accurate. Because of whom you've became is what your daughter will become as Fashion Girl now, the mayor thinks anyone dressed in black is evil."

Madame D replied, "Wearing black means nothing." Sephora said, "Take a good look at yourself in the mirror. I know you aren't vain, but you used to take better care of yourself. Look at you now. Whether you're pregnant or not, you've put on a lot of weight. You drink like a fish, you smoke like a chimney, your skin used to be so smooth and silky, now it's about as leathery as your outfit. And your hair is wild and unkempt. Now you will get even bigger with three babies growing inside you. Does the name Aldornia ring a bell?"

"Did you make a deal with Satan nine years ago? If you did or didn't, why would he approach Daphne in a dream? He offered her and the others to become a group called The Satanic Sluts. He would provide them with enough wolf's blood to create a new body of water. She turned him down. I ask you again, did you make a deal with him to spare you in exchange for her? Did you promise her to him? Is that why you offered the Skulls a gangbang with her? You better answer me before I get really mad!"

Madame D replied, "No Cindy, I didn't make a deal with anyone especially the devil himself. Can't you understand that I got sick and tired of being a living mannequin? I had to have perfect hair, perfect makeup, perfect clothes, the perfect lifestyle. Did you know my modeling agencies wanted me to stop fighting crime? Even though I didn't have the battle scars of fighting villains, but they went ballistic when I broke a fingernail."

Can't get drunk, can't eat decently, can't smoke, swear, party or do what I wanted. I often got made fun of because all of you were named for department stores. I am a sex crazed, wild child. I like sex, I like to drink, smoke, party. If I get pregnant, oh well. I call it an occupational hazard. The Skulls worship me, why do you think why they bow to me and say "all hail the Skull Queen" every time they're in my presence? Yes Cindy, I enjoy being a biker slut. I enjoy the fun and adventure. You followed my lead, and you have your own biker gang that worships you too. And you seem to enjoy it every bit as much as I do."

Sephora replied, "Daphne, yes, I do enjoy it but not as much as you. Yes, I had sex, yes, I gave mom grandchildren from me. Rattler loves me and I love him. But we are parents now and we settled down. Plus, that street drug Drain-O did a number on me remember. And as for Belle K,

I miss her. I loved her like a sister. Those bastards shot her down like a wounded animal. And for what? Because she was Hispanic? She enjoyed sex, she had three kids from Skullbasher. She's dead Daphne, and unless you change your ways, you'll be dead too."

Madame D asked, "You said Daphne and Sarah is in the elevator? Bring Daphne to me and have Sarah enjoy one of the many facilities here. I'll talk with her as well but later." Sephora answered, "I'll send her over. Let me know when you're ready to talk with Sarah."

Sephora motioned Daphne to join her mother while Sephora showed Sarah around the motor court. Daphne went up to her mother and said, "Aunt Cindy told me that you wanted to speak with me mom." Madame D replied, "Yes sweetie I do. Again, I wanted to apologize for yesterday. I'm also sorry for trying to choke you. You're right about me honey. I've become an old, dirty, slut. I wanted you to understand that if you think you're disappointed in me now, you would've been more so then."

"In my modeling days, I had to watch my weight, what I ate, how I looked. My agencies didn't want me to solve cases during modeling season. I couldn't have a single strand of hair out of place. I made a fortune, but I wasn't happy. Daphne it was more than traveling the world, modeling in fancy clothes, but I simply wasn't happy." You know when I was pregnant with you and Harry, I had your aunt pose as me to not throw suspicion. If anyone else saw me pregnant, my face would've been plastered all over the tabloids and social media."

"Neither you, Harry, your dad or I would've had any peace. When I got pregnant with Charlotte and Dean Jr., I decided to put Fashion Girl's identity away. Faking her death. I wanted to spend more time with my family. After I gave birth again, I didn't want to miss out on anything. So, becoming Madame D felt right with me. I wake up every morning now knowing that no matter what I did, what I ate, what I looked like or anything else, I wouldn't be in magazines or on the evening news."

"I hope you can understand to some degree why I'm not Fashion Girl anymore. I only suggested a gangbang with the Skulls was my way to say welcome to adulthood baby. But I see now that it was very tacky. Your grandma Sandy told me too. And I can't apologize enough for trying to choke you to death." Daphne said, "I know why Aunt Cindy wanted to talk with you first. She told you about Satan approaching me about becoming evil. He mentioned the name Aldornia. Tell me about her mom, that is if you want to."

Madame D replied, "If you were to have asked me that ten years ago, I wouldn't have said a thing. Now I can talk about it more freely. In 2015, I had the nightmare to end all nightmares when I dreamt of becoming a very evil woman named Aldornia. In the dream, I was asked by Mayor Marcus who was the chief of police in those days to stop a gang of evil people terrorizing major cities across the country."

"They were called "The Crypt Keepers". They dressed like goths with ghostly white skin, black eye shadow around their eyes, black nail polish, black lipstick, and rode around in hearses, they had left a trail of destruction in San Francisco and were headed to Los Angeles when they detoured to Colognia. To try to stop them, I tried to pretend to join them to stop them from the inside out. But my plan backfired. I looked like a goth myself and called myself Aldornia. Macy gave me a different set of powers to separate myself from my true identity."

"I stopped them on I-5 that was eerily quiet for a major highway. Their leader was named Lucifer. I admit he was tall and incredibly handsome. But I had a job to do and pretended to join up with him and his gang. He had others with him, fourteen other handsome men along with fifteen gorgeous women all of whom were pregnant by him. Lucifer was a very sick man. He thought he was the disciple of the devil himself. For me to join his gang, he gave me an initiation."

"He first asked me to burn down an oak tree off the side of the road. I did somehow, I chalked it up to the new powers Macy gave me. Then he made me drink a potion he called wolf's blood. Thinking it was real blood, I drank it down without tasting it. That was my big mistake. It completely changed my personality to the point where I really thought I was Aldornia. Then he lured me into the back of his hearse where we had non-stop sex for hours. He impregnated me almost instantly."

"During the course of this dream, I cause destruction, I got more pregnant every time I had sex. And I was to marry him and become his queen for all eternity. He called me his queen." Daphne interrupted her and asked, "Isn't that what the Skull King calls you, his queen?" Madame D answered, "In that dream, I called Lucifer my king. The same way I call the Skull King... oh my god, I've become Aldornia! Wait a minute though. I'm not evil, I'm just a biker babe."

Daphne said, "Okay mom continue with the story." Madame D replied, "Macy realized I wasn't wearing my power bracelets and with the other's help, she presented them to me and told me to say, "Style me normal!" When I did, I knew who I was. When I was told of what I did, I kicked Lucifer's ass, but Mayor Marcus arrested me. I was acquitted and my career and reputation ruined." Daphne said, "And I heard you woke up from the dream to use the bathroom and the dream changed."

Madame D replied, "That's right. When I went back to sleep, I destroyed my bracelets, and it made me more powerful than ever. I married Lucifer. He read a text from an ancient scroll in an ancient language. It destroyed him and I became the female version of the devil. Macy tried once more for me to change my mind. I told her no and I destroyed Colognia with a powerful earthquake and hurricane. There was nothing left, and I woke up screaming. Dean was right there next to me as he slept with me that night. Satan confronted me for real and I told him off. However, he asked me to dinner and explained everything. The Archangels was created shortly after that."

Confused Daphne asked, "It is an amazing story, but it still doesn't explain why you're like this now. Why are you like this now?" Madame D answered, "Again I wanted to change everything about myself except for being a heroine. I just became a different kind of heroine more than I was before. Now you are the new Fashion Girl, and you'll do fine. But if you don't want to be called Fashion Girl I understand."

"Daphne said, "No mom it's okay. When you told me when I was six that I would take your place as Fashion Girl when I turned eighteen, I couldn't wait for that day. But I want to be a different Fashion Girl than you or Grandma Daphne was. I will compromise, I will have sex with only one member of the Skulls and one member of the Vipers only.

It will be done back in Colognia at the mansion. I will make it a party. Provide the booze and cigarettes and I will do it to them."

Madame D replied, "Are you sure about this? Really honey, I was only kidding with you about that." Daphne said, "Aunt Cindy told me how the Skull King figured that I became an adult and should start making my own decisions. Have Bonecrusher and Cottonmouth come to the mansion at six. Furnish them with everything, after all I'm Fashion Girl now. A darker, more daring Fashion Girl. Who's a bitch and proud of it. I want to please you mom."

Madame D replied, "Okay Daphne if you want to do this, I'll tell them to come. But I'm coming along with the Skull King and Diamondback for a threesome of our own. We'll stay in my bedroom." Daphne said, "One more thing, bring me one of your whips, a mask, one of your outfits and two pairs of cuffs. I will do them like you do them, dominatrix style."

This pleased Madame D. She smiled and replied, "A girl after my own heart." Daphne said, "No a Fashion Girl after your own wardrobe." The two shared a laugh then Daphne left the strip club. While this was going on, Sarah was looking around the complex her friend's mother had built. She met members of both gangs. Unknowingly to Sephora, Madame D and Daphne, she was the teenage version of the man crazy slut Madame D was and not her daughter. On the other hand, Sarah didn't know what Daphne was cooking up either.

Daphne approached Sarah and asked, "My mom wanted to talk with you. She asked me to get you. What have you been up to?" Sarah answered, "Just hanging out with both biker gangs. They are so cool. They asked me to come to their hideout tonight. Babe we are going to get laid." Daphne said, "Sarah, I agreed to a gangbang tonight at the mansion with one member of each gang. Bonecrusher of the Skulls and Cottonmouth of the Vipers. I agreed to do this, but I really don't want to."

Sarah replied, "Bonecrusher and Cottonmouth you said? That's who I was talking with just now. Daphne, I don't mind taking your place if you want." Daphne said, "I have no problem except for one thing, they now know who you are and you're a blonde while I'm a redhead. Let me see. You could wear a wig, but I think I have a better idea. When I was younger, I would play hide and seek with mom and the other Style Chicks. There's a room that's the darkest in the whole place. I asked my mother to bring one of her outfits from here along with a mask, whip, booze and cigarettes. I'll get her clothes before we head back. You put it on, go to the room I told you about and wait there. I'll have Victoria let my mom know that I'm waiting there. But I'll be up in my room with the door locked. They'll never know the difference."

Sarah liked the idea and said, "Daphne I'm more of the kind of girl who your mom would approve of. However, if I switch with you, I don't think she'll like it." Daphne replied, "Sarah yesterday, she called me some unsavory names and tried to choke me. I forgave her but I only pretended to do that. I love her but she needs a taste of her own medicine. By posing as me, I'll put her in her place."

Sarah asked, "I'm not sure about this now? I love boys and I love sex. I've done the slut thing when my mom and I was evicted out of our apartment. I had to live on the streets. Where do you think I got money from? From not only being a drag racer but a cheap prostitute. Now you want me to do it again?" Daphne said, "Just make like you are, and when they are about to begin, there's a light switch on a chain. Pull on it and surprise them to the point where they'll hightail it out of there."

Sarah said, "Or they'll like it. Now that I'm about to become a Style Chick, I want to make a new start, a fresh start." Daphne replied, "You will. But before my mom gives me one of her outfits, I'm going to get another one for you. You're the same size as us. Come with me."

Daphne and Sarah snuck into the bar known as The Speed Bump, went to a broom closet where the elevators are. Daphne used her card to open the secret elevator that only goes to one place The Den of Sin. Sarah had to take a quick look around and said, "Daphne, your mother is so fucking cool. This place is amazing. The whips, chains, handcuffs, the eerie sounding music in the background. The way this place is decorated. And her wardrobe, she is so fucking cool. If you don't want to be the next Fashion Girl, can I take her place?"

Daphne replied, "Sorry Sarah, you can take the place of any Style

Chick but as for being Fashion Girl is concerned, only the daughter of the current Fashion Girl can take her place. When I have a daughter, she'll take my place when she turns eighteen just like I did yesterday." Sarah said, "May I remind you my friend that your mom gave up being Fashion Girl nine years ago. So, Fashion Girl is up for grabs."

Daphne grabbed Sarah by the shirt and replied, "Is that a challenge? The fact remains that my mother is the daughter of the original Fashion Girl who died thirteen years before my mother took her place. My grandma Daphne was ambushed and killed by a bunch of assholes who were led by her so-called best friend." It's an honor to be chosen to be any of the Style Chicks. You can do more than Fashion Girl can. So don't forget that!"

Sarah said, "Daphne I didn't mean anything by that. For more than twenty-four hours and suddenly, your life has been literally turned upside down. This should be the happiest time of your life. Since you woke up yesterday, you and your mother have been at each other's throats literally. Now we are about to do something that's way out of our league. What are we really trying to accomplish here?"

Daphne replied, "I want to give my mother a taste of her own medicine, remember? Now get what we need and let's bail." Both Daphne and Sarah each grabbed an outfit, mask, whips, chains, and handcuffs. Daphne tried something as she used her power bracelets to turn herself into a clone of Madame D. Sarah asked, "Nice look but why are you dressed like her now?" Daphne answered, "To go to the gas station before we leave here and get the ultimate party favors. Alcohol and tobacco."

As Madame D, Daphne went inside the gas station on the Aurora Gardens property to get beer and cigarettes. The clerk behind the counter didn't seem to care who he was selling any merchandise to. For all he knew, he was selling Madame D groceries. He rang up the merchandise, took Daphne's payment, bagged everything up and wished her a good day all not looking at her once.

When Daphne rejoined Sarah in the new Glam Mobile, Sarah said, "Girl do you know how many laws you just broke right now?" Daphne replied, "The police in this shithole of a town doesn't care even if the clerk realized that he didn't ring up an order for Madame D. That's why she's here, to do their work. Do you think my mother is going to put me into submission? Let's get out of here."

Sarah said, "Oh, I noticed that I didn't have to pay for the gas first." Daphne replied, "No, don't tell me." Sarah said, "Yep, I did the gasoline equivalent to the ol' dine and dash." They both began to laugh as they went back to Colognia. Back at the mansion, both girls put their outfits on and armed themselves with the whips, chains and handcuffs.

Sarah asked, "Daphne, are you sure no one else is around right now?" Daphne answered, "I'm sure. Vicki is at her restaurant. Aunt Cindy is enjoying the day with the other twins along with Grandma Sandy. I heard the others were called away on business so until six o'clock, it's just you and me. Shall we celebrate properly my friend? Beer? Smoke?" Sarah said, "Don't mind if I do."

Daphne handed Sarah a beer and a pack of cigarettes as she got one of each for herself. They drank the beer and smoked a cigarette, and both felt good. Daphne said, "I don't see what the fuss is all about, this isn't bad." Sarah replied, "I've been drinking and smoking for years. It's never bothered me." Daphne said, "Tonight, we are going to make patsies out of those dumb bikers." They both began to laugh as they finished getting ready for their act.

CHAPTER 6

When six o'clock rolled around, Madame D and the others arrived at the mansion to have the party she and Daphne agreed to. Madame D called out Daphne and Sarah's names, but no one answered right away. Cottonmouth found a note in the living room. It was folded and the front part of the fold said to go to the secret room and its location. Cottonmouth showed Bonecrusher the note and quietly left the main room.

They opened the door and entered the dark room. Cottonmouth asked, "Bonecrusher, what's going on here? This room is dark, I can't see anything." Bonecrusher answered, "I don't know dude. All we know is this is where we are going to score with the daughter of Madame D." Cottonmouth said, "Yeah dude, tell me about it. She's an uber babe and sexy as hell. Her friend Sarah isn't bad either." Bonecrusher replied, "Yeah dude, that chick is majorly hot too. She looks like she wanted to score with you dude."

Cottonmouth said, "You may be right. As for Daphne, I know you must initiate her into the Skulls, but she really didn't seem to want to." Just then, they heard two beer cans opening and the sound to two lighters lighting up cigarettes. A voice neither of them recognized said, "Turn on the light stud. There's a chain right in front of you."

Cottonmouth turned on the light and they both saw Daphne and

Sarah dressed like Madame D. Bonecrusher asked, "Babes, did you raid the Den of Sin?" Daphne answered, "Hmm, we sure did." Cottonmouth asked, "Where did you both get beer and cigarettes from?" Daphne answered, "Hmm, your clerk at the gas station in Aurora Gardens sold it to me. He seemed too interested in his cell phone to notice who he was selling stuff to." Bonecrusher asked, "And which one of you stole gas there?" Sarah answered, "Hmm, that would be me boys. Daphne told me what the Skull King said to her aunt and grandma, that Daphne is a bad girl with bad intentions."

Cottonmouth asked, "The way you two have been acting right now, if I didn't know better, I'd say you're both drunk. Am I right ladies?" Sarah walked up to Cottonmouth, she opened his shirt and felt his hairy chest and answered, "What's your definition of being drunk stud? Daphne and I are both a little buzzed but if we do it to you both tonight, we'll be anything you want us to be."

Cottonmouth said, "I think I should let Madame D know where we are first. She might get worried about us." Daphne replied, "If I know my mother Snakehead, she's in her room doing it with Diamondhead and the Skull King." Daphne was more drunk than she let on. She was never that belligerent by calling anyone names. Cottonmouth didn't like the remark and said, "Snakehead am I huh?" I don't like being called names. You may be Madame D's daughter and Queen Serpentina's niece, but I don't have to put up with that."

Daphne replied, "Yes you do. If you and Bonecrusher want to put eggs and bones into us, you must put up with us." Daphne began to laugh and continued, "The Skull King is right about me. I'm a bad girl with bad intentions. Your princess wants you to impregnate her and her friend. And that's an order!" Cottonmouth said, "Ladies please excuse us for a moment."

Cottonmouth and Bonecrusher left the room where they ran into the Skull King. The Skull King asked, "Cottonmouth, what's wrong with you? You look like you've seen a ghost." Cottonmouth answered, "In a manner of speaking yes. Daphne and her friend are in that room behind us. Daphne's drunk, they've both been smoking she's been acting erratic. You're right man, she's a bad girl with bad intentions. She wants us to impregnate her and her friend."

The Skull King asked, "We brought beer and cigarettes for this party, how and where did they get their supply?" Cottonmouth answered, "From that excuse for a clerk at the gas station in Aurora Gardens. He didn't see who was buying it and Daphne's friend Sarah didn't pay for gas for the new Glam Mobile. I don't know what they are trying to prove man?"

The Skull King said, "I do. Listen, go back in there. Make like nothing's wrong. I'll tell Madame D and I'll have Diamondback get a hold of Sephora. When she comes, we'll deal with the situation. Just be cool, okay." Cottonmouth replied, "I'm glad they're not armed but they're both crazy man." The Skull King said, "Just be calm, leave everything to me, okay?"

The Skull King was kicking himself for telling Sephora and Sandy that Daphne could be a bad seed. Now he has proof of it. The Skull King cautiously approached Madame D with the news. He said, "My queen, I think you should know this. Don't worry about the initiation, Daphne is having one of her own." Madame D replied, "What! When I get my hands on that crazy bitch I raised, so help me I'll…!"

The Skull King said, "No! You will do no such thing! Daphne and her friend Sarah are both dressed in one of your outfits. Pretending to be you, she bought beer and cigarettes at the gas station. Sarah pumped gas without paying for it. Cottonmouth found a note here into the living room telling him and Bonecrusher to go to a secret room somewhere here."

Madame D replied, "I know of that room, Daphne used to hide in there whenever we played hide and seek. My king, where did I go wrong as a parent? Why is she doing this?" The Skull King said, "My queen, my fellow bikers and I are in your debt. We will follow you to the ends of the earth. I remember how you were before. You were beautiful, alluring, and damn sexy with your flowing red hair, skimpy outfit and tall boots. You were the answer to a prayer. You saved our lives, and we made you one of us to show our appreciation."

"Madame D replied, "Skull King, I was going to give up being Fashion Girl whether I met you and the others or not. You came along at the right time in my life. Have you ever modeled any kind of clothing? Have you ever eaten watercress and cucumber sandwiches? Have you ever been pursued by the paparazzi?" If you to have answered yes to any or all those questions, you can now understand why I gave up modeling."

"Posing for fashion magazines? I once posed for Playboy in 2011. My heart was racing when I did that. But I had full control of how I wanted the shoot to be done. Skull King, I don't mind doing what I do now. I don't have to worry about whether my hair is quaffed properly. That my outfit isn't wrinkled. That I don't consume no more than five hundred calories a day. I once enjoyed modeling, but the more I did it, the more I became disenchanted by it."

"By becoming Madame D, I felt like the weight of my world had been lifted off my shoulders. Maybe I have taken it a bit too far. But I don't care. After we've helped She-Ra overcome that horrible controversy ten years ago, she wasn't too pleased with my decision to become Madame D. Want to know why? For the exact same reason how I'm feeling about Daphne now. She was mad at me because she helped my mother become Fashion Girl. Fashion Girl was her idea. Fashion Girl was the evolution of who Daphne Blake was. And where did it get her? Dead!"

"Now my daughter will become the next Fashion Girl, where did I go wrong? Now she wants to be a sex-crazed, drunken, party slut. Skull King, I want to find her and kick her sorry ass." The Skull King couldn't stall Madame D any longer. She went to the secret room Daphne used to play hide and seek in. Before she opened the door, she heard laughter. She opened the door but before she said anything, she saw Daphne, Sarah, Cottonmouth and Bonecrusher having a good time, with their clothes on."

Madame D asked, "Daphne Sandra Bates! What is the meaning of all this?" Daphne answered, "Chillax babe, we're just having a nice conversation with two gorgeous hunks. Having a couple of beers, feeling mellow, care to join us?" Madame D asked, "A few moments ago,

Cottonmouth came to us looking pale." Daphne began to laugh and replied, "Sarah and I wanted to give you a taste of your own medicine mom. I am honored to be the next Fashion Girl as is Sarah becoming one of the new Style Chicks. I'm not ready for sex yet, but Sarah on the other hand has had it before."

Cottonmouth added, "Madame D, we couldn't go through with it either. Besides I wouldn't have felt comfortable knowing that Bonecrusher or I did it with your daughter." The Skull King said, "See my queen, she was just playing around with you. But girls, I hope you realize that you are in trouble nonetheless." Daphne replied, "What do you mean?" Madame D said, "I'll tell you what he means. For starters, it's illegal to buy alcohol and tobacco at your age. Pumping gas and driving off without paying for it. And you stole from my private lair. I called your aunt and grandma. When they get here, they won't be too happy with you either. There's a huge punishment coming to the both of you."

Twenty minutes later, both Sephora and Sandy arrived to get an update on what's going on. Then a huge shouting match took place with everyone talking over one another. Daphne got tired of it and screamed, **"EVERYONE STOP RIGHT NOW!"** She took a deep breath and continued, "First you mom. I'm sorry for what happened not just today but yesterday. When you told me when I was six that I was going to take your place as Fashion Girl, you also said to not let it run your life. Well, mom, it did."

I only told my friends about it including Sarah. Once I did, an enormous amount of pressure was put on me. I had to be perfect, I couldn't make mistakes, and I had to be a lady about it." Sarah added, "That's right Madame D, it wasn't us that spread the word about it, everyone knew in school since the second grade that we knew the daughter of Fashion Girl. Teachers, other classmates, everyone expected this of her."

Daphne continued, "Aunt Cindy, Grandma, I think the world of you as well as mom. You were there last night as mom told us all to celebrate becoming the next generation of Style Chicks before training begins. I guess you could say that I was letting off more than a decade of steam." Then she continued, "Skull King, I'm honored to be the next

Skull Princess. I will do everything I can to live up to Belle K's expectations. She was a valued friend to all of us. I would never trample on her memory or legacy."

Then she said, "Cottonmouth, Bonecrusher, Sarah and I were just playing around with you both. I think Sarah likes you Bonecrusher, you seemed to hit it off well. Cottonmouth, as far as you are concerned, I like you. But I have a boyfriend, and I haven't done it with him or anyone else. I would be honored to ride with you, but I need to make that decision. And one more thing mom, you were the one who suggested that I have a gangbang in the first place. I guess Skull King, you went along with it thinking that it was a charade. But I realize now that you and mom were serious."

"Mom, why would you even suggest such a thing? I don't understand why." Madame D replied, "Daphne you're right about everything. I did put a lot of pressure on you when you were six. I only explained it because if you remember how that phony DCF agent was trying to take you and Harry away from me all because I travelled the world modeling and being wealthy. But you will become Fashion Girl like it or not."

"As for what you did today, I guess it was a bit foolish, but I see why you and Sarah did it. I suppose that I'm as much at fault about this as anyone else. Daphne from now on, I want you and the others to enjoy being a Style Chick and at the same time, be serious about criminals. And I think you gave me an idea about something."

"I've always noticed that your sense of style is entirely different from mine. I admit you look good in black. The purple and green accents do pay tribute to me and your Grandma Daphne. I think the femme fatale approach might work out for you. But the others will follow the same ideals as the current Style Chicks. Again honey, I'm sorry. Can you forgive me?"

Daphne replied, "Of course mom. Apology accepted and given." Then Daphne felt a sensation in her stomach and continued, "If you will all excuse me, I need to drive the porcelain bus." Daphne ran to the nearest bathroom and threw up. Sarah said, "Madame D, Daphne only drank one beer I swear. I can handle it more than she can. She's telling you the truth, she's not a party girl. She's not a drinker, smoker or a sex fiend. As one of her friends and as a new Style Chick, I will help her out as will the others."

That statement not only satisfied Madame D but the others. Sarah gave Madame D the money for the gas she didn't pay for and apologized herself. And once Daphne stopped tossing her cookies, she and the others would celebrate their new status as Style Chicks with a more lady like nature.

CHAPTER 7

The week of preparation and celebration was over. Madame D along with the surviving Style Chicks along with the Phat Kats and Cosmo Chicks had everyone assemble at the mansion. Madame D said, "Good morning, everyone. Starting today, all of you will begin your training to become the next generation of Style Chicks and Phat Kats."

"I've instructed the others to look at you and find the person who will take their place and within their element. Of course, Daphne will be the next Fashion Girl. I learned last weekend that Sarah would make out best as the new Tiffany, but I'll let the current Tiffany decide. Everyone relax and we will begin the processing."

Madame D was right when Tiffany selected Sarah to train. She asked, "Sarah what do you know if anything about the martial arts?" Sarah answered, "All I know about it is nothing except colored belts, white robes and names I can't pronounce." Tiffany said, "It's okay, once you gain my powers, you'll know. I understand you're a drag racer. I've been a professional racer for years. But now I'm retired. The NHRA misses its star performer."

Sarah replied, "Not to worry Tiffany. I won't let you down or at least try not to." Tiffany said, "That's the spirit. And not only will you become the next Tiffany, but you will also become the next Solara of the Archangels. I will teach you everything." Sarah replied, "I can't wait to begin." Tiffany said, "Excellent. Since I moved here, I have a dojo in town. I'll train you there."

Penney was next and noticed Isabella and asked, "I understand that you like magic, am I right?" Isabella replied, "I sure do Miss Dillard. I've been a fan of yours for years. I find it amazing the magic you can do. And I'm eager to learn." Penney said, "Wonderful. I don't have a studio but not to worry, I can train you right here at the mansion." Isabella asked, "I understand that you always called Fashion Girl Boss. Do I get to call Daphne that too?"

Penney answered, "Yes. And you are the only one who can call her that. It's been that way even with Daphne's grandma and the original Penney. It's a sign of respect." Isabella said, "Like Sarah, I'm eager to learn." Penney replied, "Then come with me out in the backyard and we can start right now. Oh, like with Tiffany, you'll be an Archangel too and will go by the name of Nighthawk."

Penney and Isabella went right to work right away, Victoria was next and asked, "I understand one of you likes to cook, which one of you is it?" Lori stepped up and answered, "That would be me, Victoria. I've excelled in food prep and my goal is to be a famous chef just like you." Victoria asked, "You seem kind of young sweetie, how old are you?" Lori answered, "I'm fourteen."

Daphne added, "Vicki, weren't you the youngest member until Aunt Cindy came along. She doesn't disappoint when it comes to food." Victoria asked, "Lori do you have a specialty dish? Or are your talents broader based?" Lori answered, "I try to be diverse in my culinary skills." Victoria said, "Lori, you're too young yet to work and the child labor laws in this state are strict. But you can still master your craft and perform the most important role in the Style Chicks, to be a lookout for the team. Come with me and I'll explain further."

Victoria pointed out the command center and continued, "Lori, this is our command center. Whenever any kind of criminal activity in the world is detected, an alarm will ring out. Two things will happen afterwards. The screen will put up the activity with a breaking news alert. If the alert is in another language other than English, the command center will print out a transcription of it. Or it will do a printout if there's no TV or internet coverage. As the lookout, you are to inform any Style Chick who happens to be in the immediate area, and they will investigate it."

"Otherwise, you not even Fashion Girl is the lady of the Mystique Boutique. You will prepare food for whoever is here. You will assign chore duties to the others. And take care of the business aspect of this awesome mansion. Can you do this? And in time, I'll hire you initially as a server in my restaurant and then I'll train you personally in my kitchen." Lori replied, "Thanks for the trust you are putting in me Victoria. I won't let you down." Victoria said, "Until your training is complete, and you take my place, call me Vicki. If the others want to call you Vicki or Victoria, it's up to them."

Then it was Zara's turn. She asked, "Which one of you lasses likes the sea? I understand one of you does." Indira answered, "That would be me, Captain Zara. Your legend perceives you. It's amazing how you can take people on a pleasure cruise and at the same time, conduct research missions." Zara said, "Well I don't do both at the same time. But it's how I make my money."

Indira asked, "Something I don't understand about all of this. I always thought superheroes don't get paid for their services. Why do you get paid?" Madame D answered the question, "Indira you're right as a rule, heroes and heroines don't get paid at all. That's why they have careers. But we live in the real world, and we get paid. However, there is a rule, unless compensation is offered, we do not, and I'll repeat do not ask for it. You see Indira, the money I made as a model bankrolled this group for years. That money Daphne will use. Other money is made including the cost for passengers to sail on Zara's ship. She has a crew you know. They're not heroes or heroines but their service is invaluable and get paid well."

Zara asked, "Before I sail on my next excursion, I will show you the ship, meet the crew and you'll see that you will like it aboard The Mystique Marauder. Any questions new captain?" Indira answered, "Just one, I understand about taking your place as my friends will do the same, at the same time though I don't want to fire anyone. Are you sure it's, okay?"

Zara answered, "It's a legacy Daphne will soon fulfill. You're not squeezing anyone out; you're filling a vacancy. What's more, I will still be onboard the ship doing a different service. One more thing, I know that you're of Arab descent and I know you can't show your hair outside of your home. But with your new outfit, you'll be masked and will wear a pirate type hat. You will dress like how I'm dressed now so you don't have to worry about any tradition at all."

"Indira said, "Captain, I'll tell you something, my parents came to this country to live a new life free to do what we want without any kind of persecution. So, once I take your place, the Hajib comes off." At that moment, Indira took off her hajib to reveal the most beautiful black hair anyone had ever seen. Daphne said, "Indira you didn't have to do this." Indira replied, "It's alright Daphne. If I can keep my true identity as secret, I don't give a shit. I'm an American now, An Arab American but an American nonetheless." Daphne said, "For a girl Indira, you got some extra-large huevos."

It was Godiva's turn, and her choice was obvious. Aldea was practically the spitting image of her. She said, "Aldea, I understand that like me, you have deadly aim. I need to ask you this, were you banished from your hometown too? I only ask because it happened to me. For many years, Chicago, where I'm from wouldn't allow me to even visit. Thanks to Madame D, I was finally able to go there. Especially after my father died. My kids live there and once you fully take my place, I'm going back there to live for good."

Aldea replied, "I'm from Nairobi but I didn't cause the trouble I heard you once caused. But after I came to America, I did get into the wrong crowd as well in New York. My kids live there, and I can't go to see them just for like a weekend visit." Godiva said, "Now that you are going to be a Style Chick, you'll be able to get back in New York's good graces again. It will take time, but you'll get there. I also understand you are good with a bow and arrow. There's a setup out in the backyard for archery. Once we begin your training, you'll be ready for action." Aldea replied, "I can't wait. The sooner the better. I miss my kids." Godiva said, "No one here understands that more than me."

It was Macy's turn, and her replacement would be Amora. Both Macy and Amora bowed to each other in respect. Macy said, "Well mate, I will help you to take my place. I will teach you the fine art of alchemy." Amora replied, "I am honored to become a Style Chick. Like the others, I can't wait to begin." Macy said, "I'm glad to see that everyone's eager to begin. However, it will take time to learn this craft. For all of you, it will take time for you to master how the Style Chicks do their jobs. It's good that you know chemistry Amora but it's not so easy."

Amora replied, "I will do you proud Miss Sears." Macy said, "Remember mate, that's what people will call you. Macy Sears." Amora asked, "I understand that your outfit resembles one you might have worn as an aborigine. How will I look like?" Macy answered, "Since you're from Japan, not to worry, you won't look like a Geisha if that's what you're asking. Your costume will be nice I promise." Amora said, "I'm glad to hear that."

Macy said, "The Style Chicks would never stereotype anyone. Indira is an Arab, but she'll wear the same kind of costume Zara's wearing now. Denise is Mexican and she won't be seen in a sombrero. And Aldea is from Kenya and will not look like she does." Amora replied, "Thank you Macy." Macy said, "Remember mate, I will no longer go by that name. Call me Soon-Li from now on." Amora replied, "You got it Soon-Li."

Sephora had the daunting task of training two recruits. Paula was the perfect replacement for her since she's had the same kind of relationship with Daphne as she's had with Madame D. And Denise would become the new Belle K. Sephora said, "Okay ladies, I will be training the both of you since the current Belle K is no longer with us. Denise, as the new Belle K, you will learn other skills besides diplomacy.

Daphne interrupted Sephora and said, "Wait a moment Aunt Cindy. Mom just told me something. Like what she did when Chanel died and retired her name, she just told me that she wants to do the same with Belle's name too. And as you know, not only will Belle's name be retired but her color scheme as well." Sephora replied, "She never told us of this. Belle's been dead for three years. I need to talk with her. Excuse me girls."

Sephora pulled Madame D aside and asked, "Daphne, Belle died three years ago. So why retire her name now?" Madame D answered, "I'm sorry Cindy I forgot to do that for her and Wendy too." Sephora said, "Daphne, do you realize there isn't a lot of feminine sounding department store names. When Denise's training is complete, what do we call her? And what will her color scheme be?"

Madame D said, "I didn't think about that. You know why I did that for Chanel. I didn't think at first not to do it for Wendy and Belle." Sephora replied, "Chanel was a special person. But Wendy and Belle were too. They deserve for their names to be retired. So, what do we do now?"

Madame D said, "You're right Cindy. Alright, I'll let Belle's name and Wendy's name to be retired and I have a good name. Many years ago, there once was a shoe company called Florsheim. It's feminine sounding and it will work. We can call her Flo." Sephora replied, "And her color scheme?" Madame D said, "We'll figure that out." Sephora replied, "You mean I will figure it out since you'll be training Daphne." Madame D said, "Not to worry about that. I will have others to help me out."

Sephora asked, "Like who for instance?" Madame D answered, "Who do you think Cindy? We do have another Style Chick who'd be willing to help." Sephora said, "If you're talking about, She-Ra, I don't know if she wants to help. She hasn't been here for years. I don't know why." Madame D replied, "I do know Cindy. You'll see when we get in touch with her."

Sephora said, "She seemed pretty mad at you the last time she was here." Madame D replied, "Yes, I know but I will make amends. It was ten years ago." Sephora said, "I was there remember? I was about ready to kill Dean." Madame D replied, "When she left here, I thought we were cool with each other. But I guess when she thought about it more often, it angered her."

Sephora asked, "Alright Daphne level with me. Why is she mad at you? What did you do or say?" Madame D answered, "Well, if you remember we had a threesome with King Cobra after we rescued him. She was even doing him before we hit Vegas. But when she got to her home world, she discovered something soon afterwards. The Princess of Power may had gotten laid, but she wasn't ready for it. She became pregnant."

Sephora said, "What!? She got pregnant! And King Cobra? Does he know he's a father?" Madame D replied, "No he doesn't know. He's got an eight-year-old son or daughter he knows nothing about. I guess she's ashamed she got pregnant." Sephora replied, "What should she be ashamed of? And why should she be mad at you?" Madame D said, "I've haven't spoken to her in eight years. When I try to get in touch with her, she disconnects the call."

Sephora said, "I'll call her. I'll try to reason with her. But I'm warning you Daphne. When the Cobra King finds out that he's a father and no one knows about it, the Skulls and the Vipers will end their alliance and we'll be on opposite sides. I hope you're proud of yourself Madame D."

Sephora now had to train two new girls to become Style Chicks. Coming up with a new name and color scheme for Denise. To inform the Cobra King about what she learned and to clean up a major mess made by Madame D. And it was up to Sephora to make things right, but how was the question.

CHAPTER 8

First thing Sephora did was to suspend Paula and Denise's training until this crisis had passed. Next, she contacted She-Ra first to get more information. Sephora went into the command center to call She-Ra. She did answer but thinking Madame D was calling her, she said, "Look Madame D, I want nothing more to do with... oh, Sephora. I'm sorry what can I do for you?"

Sephora replied, "Maybe there's something I can do for you. My niece turned eighteen more than a week ago. She will become the new Fashion Girl. I'd like for you to come here to help." She-Ra said, "Not on your life cupcake. I have nothing more to do with Madame D." Sephora replied, "May I remind you that you are a Style Chick." She-Ra said, "Oh really? I don't feel much like one. Madame D made me do things I wouldn't had done. I had sex, I got tattooed, and worst I got pregnant."

Sephora replied, "She-Ra what did you have a boy or a girl?" She-Ra said, "A girl. She's beautiful. She takes after her mother after all." Sephora replied, "What about King Cobra? Do you know that he's waited for you to return? He doesn't know he's a father. You stopped a war once, but you'll cause one if you don't come back here." She-Ra said, "Madame D taught me a few things, that included being a bitch. I don't care if I never see her again."

Sephora replied, "What about the rest of us? We went to bat for you!

We helped you out when you were at your lowest! And this is the thanks you give us? Look I wasn't too crazy with Daphne's idea to become Madame D. But I understand why she did it. She wanted to be there for her kids. She missed out on her first set of twins growing up, but she was there for them soon afterwards. You have an obligation to uphold to us and to King Cobra. What's it going to be princess?"

She-Ra said, "Alright I'll be there, just keep that slut away from me." Sephora replied, "Interesting choice of words for someone who was once slut shamed. Sephora out." That's a fine how you do. Sephora was right. The Style Chicks helped She-Ra at a time when she was being bashed for who and what she is. Now she thinks that what Fashion Girl did to become Madame D to her was a slap in the face because of her friendship to her mother.

You see, it was She-Ra's idea for Daphne Blake to become a superheroine in her own right. To fight crime in different ways. In other words, to deal with real bad people who's not hiding behind a mask or in a crazy costume. She had enough experience to deal with the likes of bad people to start dealing with real criminals like Lex Luthor and the Joker.

Fast forward to 2004, with Daphne Blake having been dead since 1991, her daughter also named Daphne took the mantle of being Fashion Girl. She tried to live up to her mother's expectations as told to her by her father. Three of the surviving original Style Chicks approached Daphne with the fact that she would be the next Fashion Girl. She had no idea about this fact. She knew her mother was Fashion Girl, but she had no idea about becoming Fashion Girl. It's one thing to be surprised about something, it's quite another when the surprise is a life changing event.

So, when Madame D had her first daughter, she knew that her baby would one day become the next Fashion Girl. And she would make sure that she would know that one day she would take her place. Madame D told Daphne about this when she was six on account of that phony DCF agent who was trying to take her away from the third book.

No one knows for sure how this information got out, but it did and all of Daphne's friends, teachers, and other such people all expected her to live up to this fact. Madame D also wanted to make sure when

Daphne turned eighteen, she wanted to celebrate her daughter's next phase of her life to not only be an adult, but the next Fashion Girl. Her actions in the previous chapter were just a way to alleviate twelve years of unnecessary pressure.

We all at one time or another in our lives where we must throw caution to the wind. But why would She-Ra be upset? She also threw caution to the wind ten years before. She ended up pregnant and had a beautiful daughter as a result. My guess would be that on her world, if word got out that she became a mother, questions would be asked, she wouldn't have any peace. So, in turn, the less people knew the better.

And now, She-Ra it seems doesn't want to be associated with the Style Chicks because of what Madame D had done. By giving up Fashion Girl's title, Madame D could live in peace and privacy. She could watch her older children grow up and prepare for her second set of twins to be born and to take care of them. Now she's pregnant with triplets by the Skull King, and she doesn't care. But what she does care about is to still fight crime. And that's one thing that she still cares about. She-Ra must see that unless she doesn't come back to Earth to help Daphne Blake's granddaughter to become the next Fashion Girl, she might get the much needed experience she once gave to her grandmother.

CHAPTER 9

Well, She-Ra did come back to Earth. A dimensional portal opened in the backyard of the mansion. She-Ra went through it, and she wasn't alone. Her daughter was also with her. Her daughter was nine and was the spitting image of her mother. Sephora greeted her and said, "Welcome back She-Ra, it is good to see you again." She-Ra replied, "Sephora I'm only here after what you told me. I guess I owe it to be here."

Sephora said, "You certainly do. After all the third generation of the Style Chicks will soon take all our places. And who is this lovely young lady?" She-Ra replied, "Sephora this is my daughter. Her name is Amanda." Amanda had long, blonde hair and wore a similar outfit her mother wore except it wasn't as revealing. She-Ra asked, "I need to see King Cobra, I think he needs to know all of this. Where is he?"

Sephora answered, "He's not here but I can get in touch with him. As I told you, he hasn't seen you in nearly ten years. So much has changed. While we wait for him, let me bring you up to date and Amanda it's very nice to meet you. Let me take you upstairs and you can meet the next group of Junior Style Chicks. Tiffany's, Penney's and my kids would love to meet you." She-Ra added, "It's okay sweetie, I think you will like that." Amanda replied, "Okay mommy."

After Sephora came back downstairs, she escorted She-Ra out to the gazebo to try to explain everything. She said, "Now that we are alone, I can talk more freely. You heard me right. You knew Tiffany and Penney became parents and I became a mother myself seven years ago. I had quintuplets or five babies all at one time. I had three boys and two girls. I got pregnant by one of the Vipers. Remember Rattler? The tall muscular guy? I fell head over heels for him and he was crazy about me. We got married soon after and we've been happy ever since."

"I'm still Sephora of the Style Chicks but I'm also now called Queen Serpentina. I ride with the Vipers now but don't worry, it's only a title. Look She-Ra I know how you might feel about Daphne's decision but she's still every bit as much of a heroine as she was when she was Fashion Girl. We are now blood sisters. We took an oath and mixed our blood together. I had a hard time over her decision too, but I accepted it."

"You should see what she has done lately, it's quite impressive. I don't understand why you're mad at her. She made this decision before you two took that road trip together and after you defeated that sorry excuse for you. She talked with us. She learned she was pregnant with Dean's babies. Remember she was married to him at the time, and she was thrilled. When we were in Maryland for that rematch, remember we tailgated in the parking lot for that game."

"We knew that she didn't want to be Fashion Girl anymore. Not to be Fashion Girl not to stop being a heroine. She's still a Style Chick, just a different kind of Style Chick. And she's not that much of a slut as you told me in the command center. I think you need to see Aurora Gardens. After she retired, she bought this large piece of land in a town in the neighboring county fifty miles from here. She decided to use her charm and appeal to put criminals in her place."

"All she was trying to do on that trip was to see how she could pull it off. She saved those bikers as you know." After hearing all of this, She-Ra replied, "I guess I was being kind of harsh. It hurt my feelings to think that my good friend's daughter would throw away the title of Fashion Girl. Alright Sephora, I'll go and see this place." Sephora said, "Good, just remember that within a few weeks, there will be a new generation of Style Chicks. We aren't sure just yet what the new Fashion Girl will do, but whatever she will do, it will still fall within what the Style Chicks are all about."

They left the mansion and drove the fifty miles to the small town of Aurora and Aurora Gardens. She-Ra might still not be convinced of what Madame D had done. Sephora did her best to point out everything. Sephora said, "You see She-Ra, this is what used to be known as a motor court. It was the type of place where families, businesspeople or just about anyone could come to unwind, eat something, spend the night if they had to or make a pit stop. Madame D did something more with it though."

Sephora then pointed out the seedier side to the complex and continued, "One thing Madame D did was to attract all kinds of people including the criminal element. See that one building over there? It's called "The Speed Bump" it's a dive bar. It only opens after 4 o'clock. I have a key, let me show you inside."

When Sephora was showing She-Ra around, she began to realize where Madame D was going with this. Sephora continued, "It's just the tip of the iceberg because this bar is like the tip of the iceberg. See that door marked private? There are two elevators behind it. Step in and I'll continue further." Sephora took She-Ra to the level below the bar to show her the strip club and continued, "This place is called "The Wild Bitch". Yes, it's a strip club but Madame D doesn't perform here as we don't either. This place does attract a rather uh em, savory crowd."

"But if everyone behaves, they all can have a good time. Now let's go back into the elevator." Sephora showed She-Ra the casino that was below the strip club and continued, "Remember when you were in Las Vegas with Madame D? Madame D made a deal with one of the hotels there and they set up shop here. They control everything and Madame D gets a large cut of the profits for having it here. Now there's one more place you need to see."

"Sephora brought the elevator back to the bar's level and continued, "There's a reason why there's a second elevator. It only works with one of these cards. But brace yourself and you'll see why the woman formally known as Fashion Girl really has been up to." Then She-Ra saw The

Den of Sin, her mouth opened so wide you could've shoved a watermelon in her mouth. Sephora continued, "Welcome to the Den of Sin. Before you say anything, let me explain. Madame D uses this place as her new home. She does live here. And she uses this place to put bad guys in their place. The police department in this town are incompetent."

Before they take away bad guys, Madame D roughs them up a little. Once she's done with them, they're putty in her hands." After all of this, She-Ra replied, "I don't know what to say. It's amazing and disturbing all at the same time. What's with all those chains and whips? Why did she decorate this place with skulls and crossbones? Her wardrobe is so outrageous, and they say I'm scantily clad? And that weird music? Where is it coming from? And she did all of this? I still don't know why?"

Sephora said, "Madame D told me why just last week. As a model, she was practically at the mercy of her agencies. The more photo shoots and fashion shows she did, the more disenchanted she got by it. Not being able to eat decent food, and they even found fault with her crime fighting activities. They were afraid if she broke a fingernail, messed up her hair or ripped her dress they would go ballistic. She's happy now and I hope now you understand why she did what she did. One more thing, her being a slut isn't true. She only does it with men she loves and not with just any bum off the street."

"Oh god, I just remembered something, last week Daphne and one of the new Style Chicks a friend of hers named Sarah pulled a dirty trick on her mother and she went nuts. Like mother, like daughter. She-Ra, I think you need to talk with Madame D right now. But first, let's go back topside."

Once topside, Madame D noticed them coming out of the secret elevator in the garage. She went up to them and said, "Well, well, look who's here. If it isn't the Princess of Party Poopers herself. What are you doing here?" She-Ra replied, "Now you've resorted to name calling huh. I've got a few choice words for you too. Have you taken a good look at yourself in the mirror lately? When you took on this new identity of yours, I was against it from the very beginning and still do."

"Just look at you, your skin used to be flawless, now look at yourself, it looks like a worn-out wallet. You used to be fit and trim, now look at yourself, you've become a fat stupid looking cow. And your clothing, not only do you look like a cow, but you also look as if a cow exploded all over you. Dressed in leather from head to toe. I still don't know why you did all this, but now for my words. I'm ashamed of you. I'm embarrassed to know you. And I'm disgusted with what you've done to yourself. It's not just my sentiment, but your mother's as well. If she could only see you now, I know she wouldn't be pleased."

Madame D said, "If you're done insulting me blondie, I have a few choice words of my own. This isn't Eternia or Etheria, this is Earth. It doesn't matter what a person looks like, it's what's in a person's heart that counts. Let me refresh your memory about a few things."

"First, we were all in support of you ten years ago when you were under attack on social media. We were there to see you in action. After the second game, we made you a Style Chick, I bought you a car, and we took the road trip of a lifetime. I was pregnant with my second set of twins. I decided to stop being Fashion Girl before that game. I talked it over with the others and they understood why I made that decision. I wanted to stay closer to home to be with my family. I was missing my first set of twins growing up."

"With every fashion shoot I did, every time I was on a runway or doing fashion shows, I was getting more disgusted by it. As a model, I couldn't consume more than five hundred calories a day. My agencies found fault with the fact that I was a superheroine. If I messed up my hair, clothes or makeup, I was given the riot act. My mother was like that but I'm not. I made a splash by being Madame D when we dealt with that bogus police chief, police force and judge who was making things a living nightmare."

"If you want to know how I got involved with a biker gang, I'll explain. Many years ago, I saved the Skulls after they were involved with a rival gang. Many gang members were killed or severely injured. The Skull King and I pretending to be his girlfriend and being the Phoenix in disguise, we put an end to the war as I made things hot under the collar."

"Grateful to me, The Skull King made me an honorary member.

Now I'm a full-fledged member as The Skull Queen. As for my being a fat cow, I'm pregnant again this time with triplets. I'm his girlfriend now and I'm proud to carry his children. Sephora became the queen of the Vipers after they agreed to settle down here. One of their members Rattler became her husband and she gave birth to quintuplets. She's proud to be their queen too."

"Now my grown daughter will become the new Fashion Girl soon. I did tell her that she had to have an initiation into the Skulls by having a gangbang. Sephora and I also did this too. We're not ashamed of our decisions. Since then, Daphne has gone out of control. Sephora thinks she's letting off some steam. But the Skull King can somehow sense that she's out of control. If this is true, she'll be dangerous as a Style Chick."

"And now Satan is going after her by trying to do what he tried to do with me fourteen years ago. He doesn't seem to realize that as Fashion Girl, Daphne will resist turning evil. Now she's drinking, smoking and is acting badly. She-Ra, I'm willing to call a truce with you. Would you be willing to talk with her? I think if you tell your story about how you were evil, discovered the fact, that He-Man is your brother and how you turned your life around as a result. Maybe also explain how you helped her grandma become Fashion Girl. If you can't convince her, no one will."

She-Ra said, "Okay I'll talk with her. I admit, I had fun on that trip. People have seen that tattoo I got, and I've been paid compliments. But there is something you don't know, and I also need to tell Ike about it too. He's father." Madame D replied, "What!? When did you have a baby?"

She-Ra said, "After I last saw you, I discovered weeks later that I was pregnant. I went into seclusion during the pregnancy. If anyone saw me pregnant, people would ask me who got me pregnant and when I would be due. After the baby was born, I let my parents raised her until she was old enough to rejoin me."

Sephora added, "Wait 'til you see her Daphne, she's gorgeous. She looks just like her mother. Long blonde hair, beautiful smile, the works." Madame D replied, "You're right She-Ra, you need to tell Ike. But I also think that you're ashamed of your daughter." She-Ra said, "It's not like that." Madame D replied, "Is it princess? You're a major figure, people will ask questions. They won't leave you alone until you give them answers. I went through the same thing when I was pregnant the first time. My mother also went into seclusion when she was pregnant with me too. It's unfair for you to criticize me when you could get the same criticism."

Moments later, The Vipers arrived at Aurora Gardens. But before any of them could hail their queen, King Cobra said, "I don't believe it. She-Ra. It's good to see you again. It's been ten years, where the hell have you been!? I don't see you, heard from you, a call would've been nice! We had a blast, then you disappear! Why!? Why did you do that!?"

Madame D replied, "Well princess, your answer for all that?" She-Ra said, "Ike, can we talk in private, and I'll explain everything." Madame D replied, "Cobra, go to the motel, ask Macy for a key to a spare room. I think you two have a lot to talk about." Ike said, "With pleasure Madame D. I'd drag you by that mop you call hair She-Ra, but I know you'd kick my ass if I did, just follow me please."

Cobra did just that. Macy gave him a key to an unoccupied room so he could discuss with She-Ra and relieve ten years of anger and frustration. But She-Ra in return must reveal the biggest secret since the day she became She-Ra.

CHAPTER 10

King Cobra was given the key to room sixteen, which was on the second floor and the other rooms on either side were also vacant. She-Ra was about to realize that sixteen was going to become her unlucky number. Madame D and Sephora were also in the room too. She-Ra asked them to leave but King Cobra asked them to stay since part of it did involve them.

Madame D and Sephora sat quietly while King Cobra did the talking. Madame D whispered in Sephora's ear, "Get ready for the fireworks. And we have a front row seat. This is going to be good." Still fuming, King Cobra said, "I just want to know one thing for starters, that night outside Las Vegas ten years ago when we had that threesome with Madame D, didn't that mean anything to you? It meant a lot to me. I had a sexual encounter that would make other guys jealous. To do it with not one but two major hotties who are also superheroines. Didn't that mean anything to you? DIDN'T IT!?"

She-Ra most of the time wouldn't stand for such treatment, but on this occasion, she was on the losing end. She couldn't put a sentence together. She simply didn't have an answer for it. Madame D stepped in and said, "Cobra give her a moment to gather her thoughts. You'll see she does have a good answer for you." King Cobra stepped outside of the room and replied, "I'll give you five minutes princess. And I expect

68

an answer then, if not, I'll be even more angry than I am now. Excuse me ladies."

She-Ra turned to Madame D and asked, "When I give him the answer he wants, he'll really be mad. What am I going to do?" Madame D said, "You gave me a hard time when I decided to become Madame D permanently. I understand you called Sephora a cupcake and you think I've become this man crazy slut. I got tired of being a model. I retired as one. I bought this land and built it up. Now it's a tourist spot for anyone who's passing through on their way to either Los Angeles, San Francisco or San Diego."

"People can gas up their cars, get a bite to eat, spend the night here if they're tired, and simply enjoy their time here. As for Sephora, she's no cupcake. She's proven herself time and again that she's a worthy adversary to criminals both as a Style Chick and an Archangel. She liked one of the Vipers and became their queen. We are now blood sisters. She now has five beautiful children and married the Viper known as Rattler. He fell in love with her, and she fell in love with him. So, before King Cobra comes back in, keep all of this in mind when you give him the news that he's a father."

Just as King Cobra was about to return inside, he heard the loud sounds of motorcycles in the distance. He busted inside the room and said, "She-Ra what you have to tell me will have to wait. We got company."

The company wasn't good. The motorcycles Cobra heard belonged to the Crocs the sworn enemy of both the Skulls and Vipers. The group approached their leader, The Gator Queen.

She said, "Well, well what do we have here? The Skull Queen is pregnant again? Who did you screw to get so big or how many men did you screw? Are your kids going to be caramel colored? Have slanted eyes?" The Skull King replied in anger, "If you must know, I knocked her up. We're having triplets." Madame D added, "What do you want? You and your gang aren't welcomed here." The Gator Queen said, "We came to bury the hatchet. What can we do to bring peace to our respected gangs?"

Madame D replied, "You want peace? Okay, bring Belle K back from the dead and all will be forgiven." The Gator Queen said, "Are you drunk or stoned? You know no one can bring back anyone from the dead not even Serpentina." Serpentina added, "I can only bring back the dead temporarily. And I can only revive them at night inside the cemetery."

Madame D said, "You killed a very good woman. Belle K was well liked here by everyone. So maybe she was of Hispanic heritage, but she was born and raised in this country. Her father wanted her to live her life as an American instead of being just a Hispanic American. She was more American in her little finger than all of you have in your hate mongering bodies combined. Get out of my sight Gator Queen or I will pregnant or not kill you with my bare hands."

The Gator Queen saw She-Ra and asked, "Who's the blonde in the Halloween costume? She looks like she a good fuck too. What name do you go by?" King Cobra answered, "That's none of your damn business! She's my property and would never join up with the likes of you!" The Gator Queen said, "Too bad. When your done slumming with these losers blondie, I can picture you as one of us. You'd make a good fuck for my boys." She-Ra replied, "You heard my friends get out of here and I mean now!"

The Gator Queen gulped and ordered her riders to leave the premises. Madame D said, "Imagine the nerve of her and those skinheads wanting to make peace after they brutally killed Belle! I am so mad I could scream!" Sephora replied, "Calm down Daphne, don't get upset. It's not good for you especially now." Madame D said, "You're right Cindy, I'm sorry." Sephora said, "Don't be Daphne, I'd be just as mad too. Now let's go back to the room to continue our conversation."

As Madame D, Sephora, She-Ra and King Cobra returned to the motel room, Cobra said, "Now where were we? Oh yes, She-Ra was about to tell me something. Now then She-Ra tell me this news you have for me, now!" Madame D and Sephora nodded their heads as She-Ra replied, "Ike you're a good man and you should've been told this a long time ago. That night we had ten years ago was the best night of my life. After I returned home to my world, I got some news, and I was afraid of sharing it with anyone. Ike, I got pregnant. I had a girl, she's nine years old now."

Sephora added, "Wait till you see her, she's absolutely gorgeous." Cobra's eyes began to well up with tears and said, "I'm a father? I'm a father! I'M A FATHER!!! But why didn't you tell me sooner? I would've helped you with everything." Madame D interrupted and added, "I think I can answer that question better than she can. When my mother was pregnant with me, she hid it from the rest of the world. She wasn't Fashion Girl all the time, so it was easy for her. She was afraid if the media, press or any other news outlet got wind of it, neither her or my father would have no peace and if they were to discover that she was also Fashion Girl, all bets would've been off."

Sephora added, "I posed as Fashion Girl when Daphne was pregnant with the first set of twins for the exact same reason." She-Ra replied, "I went into hiding once I began to show. Only my brother and parents knew of this." Sephora added, "Your daughter is at the Mystique Boutique waiting for this moment that she can meet her father. Daphne and I will go with you both."

Cobra said, "Thank you ladies. I am also anxious to meet my daughter. But just one thing, is she mad at me for not being in her life?" She-Ra replied, "Of course not, once she was old enough to understand, I told her, and she understood." Cobra said, "What are we waiting for? I have a daughter to meet! Let's go!"

When Cobra, She-Ra, Madame D and Sephora arrived back at the Mystique Boutique, Sephora was asked to get She-Ra's daughter to be formally introduced to her father. As she came downstairs, Cobra whispered in She-Ra's ear, "You're right, she's beautiful she looks just like you." She-Ra whispered back, "She has your spirit too, she will adore you."

The closer She-Ra's daughter came, the more Cobra's heart filled with pride. Cobra got down on one knee and said, "Amanda, my name is Ike Pipestone. I'm also known as King Cobra of a motorcycle gang called "The Vipers". I am your father and I'm honored to finally meet you." Amanda's reaction was speechless until she hugged him and replied, "I am equally honored to finally meet you too. Mom has told me all about you." Cobra said, "I think we are going to get along just fine."

She-Ra said, "Cobra I have an errand I need to do with Madame D and Sephora, I think father and daughter need some quality time together." Cobra replied, "I like that. And I understand, Amanda, prepare for the ride of your life." She-Ra interrupted him and said, "Wait a moment Cobra, use one of the Style Chick vehicles instead." Cobra replied, "I was going to ask if I could borrow one of the cars. I wouldn't dream of putting my daughter in danger on a motorcycle no sooner after I met her."

Sephora added, "Cobra, use my car gladly, I need to go with Madame D in her car anyway." As Madame D, Sephora and She-Ra left in the Widow Maker, they went to the cemetery for the errand She-Ra had mentioned. She especially wanted to tag along because she was going to be reunited with a long-lost friend, the original Fashion Girl.

CHAPTER 11

Madame D, Sephora and She-Ra waited until it got dark so they could do what they needed to do in the cemetery. She-Ra asked, "Just exactly what we are doing in the middle of the cemetery after dark?" Sephora answered, "You might not be aware of this so I will tell you now. I can do one thing no other Style Chick can do, bring the dead back to life."

"What I am about to do is bring the original Fashion Girl back to life so she can help Madame D take care of the situation with her daughter and my niece. Now I need absolute silence. She-Ra, Daphne, join hands with me and prepare to be amazed."

Sephora went into a trance and said, "I, Sephora of the Style Chicks hereby summon the ghost of Daphne Blake Jones, the original Fashion Girl." In seconds, fog surrounded the area. An eerie glow began to form, and a figure arose from it. The figure of the original Fashion Girl. The others separated and Madame D said, "Mom it's good to see you again." The original Fashion Girl said, "Daphne, you've changed why do you look like a biker? And you have put on a lot of weight, are you alright?"

Madame D said, "I'm fine mom. I am called Madame D now. I ride with a motorcycle gang called The Skulls. I am their leader. I am also called The Skull Queen. I did put on some weight and altered my appearance. I am also pregnant." The original Fashion Girl replied, "Why

Daphne? Why did you do this?" Madame D said, "Mom in a way you told me to do this. Remember what you told me the last time I saw you?"

"You told me that you weren't there for me when I was growing up and you asked me to not do the same for your grandchildren. After that ordeal was over with, I grew less and less enchanted with being Fashion Girl. The more I strutted myself on runways and catwalks, the more I began to despise it. I made a fortune sure, but I just got tired of it. Modeling in clothing the average woman can't wear or afford. Living on a diet of five hundred calories a day, the more I modeled, the more disgusted I got."

"I was always away most of the time, I missed Daphne and Harry growing up. So, I made a conscious decision to give up being Fashion Girl and retire from modeling. I used the money I made modeling and bought a plot of vacant land fifty miles away from here. I used that land and built what is or was known as a motor court. I still am a Style Chick but I'm no longer the leader. I live on that property, I run it and I attract both good and bad people alike and I now deal with criminals my own way."

"I am also a dominatrix, and the name Madame D is what I'm now known as. As Madame D, I put criminals in submission. On half of the property, I put in a bar and a strip club. I hired gorgeous young women with incredible bodies to run the many buildings I have there which I will show you. You see if a man tries something with any of these women, my security team will send them to me, and I deal with them my own way."

"As for being pregnant, it wasn't on account of these men. I am pregnant with my boyfriend called the Skull King and I am proud to carry his children. I am going to have triplets this time. I was also pregnant by my second husband with two other children who you will meet. I faked my own death so I can live in peace. Now my eldest daughter has officially become the new Fashion Girl, but she's been acting crazy ever since. I even allowed her friends to become the next group of Style Chicks. Everyone but Daphne have begun their training and they're doing good. But Daphne also wants to take Fashion Girl on a different path too. Mom this is why you've been summoned to help me try to put some sense in her. Can you help us?"

The original Fashion Girl took a few moments to let what Madame D said sink in. Then she replied, "Daphne, I will help you straighten my granddaughter out. When can I see her?" Madame D said, "As soon as we find her. She's not at the mansion, she's been hanging out with one of Sephora's guys named Cottonmouth. She wants to be his girlfriend. She was also named as The Skull Princess."

"I told her that she needed to be initiated by doing a gangbang. I only meant that as a joke. Mom, I love men, I love sex, I'm over forty now and I'm pregnant again. I have to be very careful. Daphne told me that she was pregnant in high school and had an abortion. Even the Skull King thinks that she is bad. She also had a run in with the devil himself. I told you about the ordeal I had about him. Thank you, mom, for understanding. And speaking of princesses, someone else is here to see you too."

She-Ra stepped forward and said, "Hello Daphne, it's good to see you again." The two hugged and the original Fashion Girl asked, "What are you doing here?" She-Ra answered, "I'm here to help out. Now that your eldest granddaughter is the new Fashion Girl. And as Madame D pointed out, she's become kind of wild."

The original Fashion Girl said, "I think I understand what's going on here. My granddaughter might be acting out for whatever reason. Maybe deep down she's scared of the responsibility being a superheroine brings. Maybe she's not ready yet. Or maybe she wants to do something else. I'm here and let's not waste anymore time." Sephora replied, "I couldn't agree more. I'll call her now and find out where she is at the moment. She's been talking with me more than her mother. Let me try."

Sephora got out her cell phone and called her niece, the phone picked up, Daphne said hello. Sephora asked, "Daphne where are you at the moment?" Daphne answered, "I'm at the Skulls hideout with Sarah, Bonecrusher and Cottonmouth. We were just hanging out and nothing is going on except for talking if that's what you want to know Aunt Cindy."

Sephora said, "Listen to me Daphne, for the time being I brought your maternal grandmother back to life so she can talk with you. Will you allow her to do this? It's of the utmost importance." Daphne replied, "It's so cool that you can bring anyone back from the dead like that, okay Aunt Cindy, I will talk with her. I'll wait right here." Sephora said, "That's the niece I used to know, we'll be there in fifteen minutes. See you then."

Sephora hung up the phone and continued, "Well Mrs. Jones you're all set." The original Fashion Girl replied, "Thank you Sephora but you don't have to call me Mrs. Jones. Call me Daphne please." Sephora said, "Thank you, your daughter has always said that you were down to earth." She-Ra looked at the tombstone from which the original Fashion Girl arose from and asked, "Can someone tell me who's grave this is? And why does it look like a do not disturb sign?"

Madame D answered, "As you know She-Ra, my mother is buried in Atlanta where we lived at the time of her death. After all these years she still lies in state at the state capitol building. This marker belongs to another Style Chick named Chanel. She died here. She was a vampire over three hundred years old. I made sure that no one ever disturbs her resting place ever again."

Sephora added, "Before she died, she knew of my ability to raise the dead and gave me her blessing to use her site and marker to perform this ritual. Now let's go and fix this mess once and for all." The four got back into Madame D's car and drove to the Skulls hideout. As Daphne pointed out, nothing was going on outside conversation. When the others arrived, Bonecrusher and Cottonmouth both got up and said together, "All hail the Skull Queen and all hail Queen Serpentina!"

Both the original Fashion Girl and She-Ra were taken back at the respect Madame D and Sephora gets with their respected gangs. Madame D said, "Thank you both. Bonecrusher, Cottonmouth, Sarah, meet my mother the original Fashion Girl Daphne Blake and She-Ra the Princess of Power."

The trio were stunned by meeting the two legendary heroines. Bonecrusher and Cottonmouth were especially taken back by their incredible beauty as well. Their mouths were hanging open as Sephora said, "Alright guys put your eyes back in your heads and close your mouths, an airplane could fly in them."

Cottonmouth replied, "Forgive us Serpentina, Bonecrusher and I have heard about these two ladies, but we never thought we'd meet them. Forgive us ladies, it is an honor to meet you both and we are at your service." The original Fashion Girl said, "It's a pleasure to meet you both and you as well Sarah." Sarah replied, "I'm sorry for being speechless but now I see why Daphne and I both should take our new roles seriously."

Madame D said, "If you three will excuse us, my mother, Serpentina and I need to talk with Daphne." Sarah replied, "Of course it's a family matter, guys let's go outside." The others left the hideout so Madame D, Sephora and the original Fashion Girl could begin their conversation. She-Ra sat down quietly and listened to the conversation."

Madame D began and said, "Daphne I am so sorry for being so cross with you these last few days. I am also sorry for suggesting joining the Skulls by doing a gangbang. I taught the others over the years to be women first and Style Chicks second. I told them to enjoy life as well as being heroines. But honey, you just turned eighteen and I want you to be the best heroine you can be. I hope you can forgive me and understand where I'm coming from."

Daphne hugged Madame D and replied, "Of course I forgive you mom. I guess you took me kind of by surprise. Like you I do enjoy the company of boys. I did make a mistake getting pregnant in high school, but I learned my lesson. But I'm falling in love with Cottonmouth, he is so cool. I want to be his girlfriend as well as being the next Fashion Girl. Can't I do both?"

Sephora said, "Daphne you can be anything you want to be, but you have to be smart about it. That's why your grandma Daphne is here. She wants to tell you something that might help you finally figure things out." The original Fashion Girl took a moment to look at her granddaughter and said, "The last time I saw you, you were only six years old. But look at how lovely you are now. You make me proud even if I can't be a permanent part of your life. Your mother, your aunt and your other grandma I'm sure love you very, very much."

"But here is what I want to tell you. That time when I did meet you, your mom, aunt and the other Style Chicks were at war with a crooked politician and police force. I spoke with your mom alone in private and I told her to be there for you and your brother Harry. I guess afterwards, your mother decided to make sure that she would be there for you as you got older. If you want to blame anyone for why your mom gave up being Fashion Girl when she did, blame it on me. Did she do that? Was she there for you?"

Daphne answered, "Yes Grandma Daphne, she sure did. But I still don't get it though. Again, I ask can't I be both a free thinking independent young woman? A superheroine and have a boyfriend all at once?" Madame D replied, "Yes you can. But you must for now learn what it takes to be the next Fashion Girl. Okay let me also put it this way, you don't have to be a mystery solver like your grandma was and you don't have to be a model like I was. I guess the role of Fashion Girl will change."

"Maybe that's why you're not wearing Fashion Girl's colors. Mom, I wore your colors to honor you. But Daphne, you don't have to be another me or your grandma. The Style Chicks will be different with every new version. I am sure that when you do become a mother and have a daughter, she will also take your place when she turns eighteen and she too will do something different. Daphne look at all of us and tell us exactly what you want to do with the Fashion Girl name? I promise we won't get upset by your answer."

Daphne took a deep breath and said, "Mom you once said that sometimes you weren't taken seriously as Fashion Girl. You also said that Grandma Daphne had a better time with it. I think if Fashion Girl is to be taken seriously, she needs a different look, a different coat of paint and a different attitude. So, if you remember, I said that Fashion Girl should become a femme fatale type of heroine. I don't think mom was off the wall by becoming a dominatrix/biker babe. I love her look of black, gold and red. She wears it well. I think it will work for me too. But just to satisfy all of you, I will throw in a mix of purple and green. Or maybe the new look could be in purple and green. So, what do you think?"

Madame D replied, "Okay Daphne, if you'll give us a few minutes we will consider what you said and I'll say this now, you made your case well. We'll call you back in when we've decided."

When Daphne went outside to join the others, Sarah said, "Based on what we could hear, your conversation went well." Daphne replied, "Yes, I think it did too. I made a case that Fashion Girl needs a major makeover with everything. The way she looks, the way she acts and the way she battles crime. I don't think the other Style Chicks need to change. You will become the next Tiffany and you already seem to possess her traits."

Cottonmouth asked, "Babe did you happen to talk about us?" Daphne answered, "I did but I didn't go into it too much. But I think when they're done talking in there, I think my mom will talk with you as well." Sarah said, "We'll just wait and see what they will say."

Inside the hideout, the four were deliberating about Daphne's words. Madame D said, "As I said, she made a good case. Fashion Girl should be mentioned in the same breath as other heroines that have come before her and be a symbol of inspiration for new heroines who will come after her."

She-Ra replied, "In the last day or so, I've been reminded of how I in a way gave birth to the Style Chicks. It also reminded me of what I went through when I first became She-Ra." The original Fashion Girl added, "Although I had intensive training, I wasn't too worried about people's reaction to me at least not at first. Sephora added, "Being a regular Style Chick hasn't been easy, but I wouldn't trade my life for anything."

Madame D said, "Okay then it's settled, the new Fashion Girl will take on an entirely different path. Cindy, bring Daphne back in with Cottonmouth. I want to talk with him too." As Daphne and Cottonmouth came inside, Madame D said, "Daphne I think what you said to us made perfect sense. Using style to fight crime is all well and good but doing things differently might not be such a bad idea. Then my daughter from this night forward, Fashion Girl's personality will be that of a femme fatale type heroine."

Daphne replied, "Thank you mom, it means a lot to me." Madame D asked, "She-Ra, can you once again teach the new Fashion Girl all she needs to know about being a heroine including using a sword? Daphne, if you're going to learn, learn from the best." She-Ra answered, "Who am I to say no to the new leader of the Style Chicks." Daphne's eyes began to tear up and said, "Thank you everyone, I will do my very best."

Madame D said, "I know you will honey. As for you Cottonmouth, I think you're a very good man. But I want Daphne to thrive in her new role. Can you delay any plans you might have for her until at least her training is finished and she completes her first mission?" Cottonmouth replied, "For everyone involved, I'll do it, but I would like to do one thing right now." Madame D asked, "What is it?" Cottonmouth answered, "I'd like to kiss Daphne good luck." Madame D said, "Go for it."

Cottonmouth turned to Daphne as she smiled softly, as he kissed her firm on the lips as Daphne returned the favor. When they finished, Cottonmouth said, "I'm sorry ladies, I needed one more for the road. Good luck babe, I'll be rooting and waiting for you." Daphne's voice also softened and replied, "I'll be thinking of you too." Madame D said, "You two can talk on the phone during down time but she makes the call, understood?" Cottonmouth replied, "Crystal Skull Queen."

Madame D said, "Excellent everyone, I think we all did good tonight. Daphne, your training begins tomorrow morning bright and early. I'll help you as much as I can but as you know, I can't do too much right now. But I'll be your rock emotionally. Everyone, get some sleep we all have a big day tomorrow. Cindy and I will escort my mom back to the cemetery, goodnight, everyone."

Before Madame D and Sephora brought the original Fashion Girl back to the cemetery, Madame D showed the original Fashion Girl Aurora Gardens. The original Fashion Girl said, "This place is amazing, but why do you want the criminal element hanging around here harassing young women?" Madame D replied, "I have someone who can answer that question better than me?"

Madame D took the others to the apartment complex where she allows the employees to live in. She knocked on the door of one of the employees. As the door opened, the server at Victoria's Café named Mary Lou Abbott answered and said, "Madame D, Sephora, this is a surprise, please come in."

As they did, She-Ra also came in as Mary Lou asked, "Who are your friends Madame?" Madame D answered, "Mary Lou meet my mother Daphne Blake world famous mystery solver and the original Fashion Girl and She-Ra The Princess of Power." Mary Lou shook their hands and said, "It's a great pleasure to meet both of you. I've heard so much about the both of you. So, what do I owe the pleasure of this visit?"

Madame D replied, "Mary Lou on the way over here, I pointed out to my mother and She-Ra the fact that I hired only the most attractive young women to work on the complex. I figure you can point this out better than me." Mary Lou is a young, tall blonde with big tits and an hourglass figure. She replied, "Well ladies, Madame D made a deal with the mayor and sheriff of this county to try to curb the crime that goes on in this area."

The original Fashion Girl asked, "If the county is full of crime, why put such women like yourself in danger?" Mary Lou answered, "I've been working here since the complex first opened and I've never felt safer. With the Skulls and Vipers acting as security guards and Madame D's interventions, crime has gone down." Madame D said, "You see mom, She-Ra, I count on the fact that whoever comes here tries anything with any of my employees, they will have to face me in the Den of Sin."

The original Fashion Girl asked, "The Den of Sin? Where did you ever come up with a name like that?" Madame D answered, "It's where I live and deal with criminals. I dress the way I do to convince criminals that I don't fool around. I have a supply of dominatrix tools such as whips, handcuffs, chains, and three different colors of clothing. Red lighting envelopes the room, evil sounding music plays in the background and unless you have a card, there's only one way in and one way out by an express elevator."

The original Fashion Girl asked, "You're along the San Andreas

Fault, aren't you afraid that an earthquake might trap you down there?" Madame D answered, "About two years ago, there was an earthquake here, and I was down there when it happened. Everything below ground is reinforced with concrete. I also have a private stairwell that I can leave from if the power does go out."

Mary Lou added, "Madame D thought of everything to ensure that in such an event, everyone's safe. She spared no expense to make that happen. Fashion Girl, you should be proud of what your daughter has accomplished. Yes, there's a criminal element, yes things could go wrong but it has yet to happen. Some of these people look bad but they aren't bad." Madame D added, "I look like a badass, but as you all know, I'm not a badass. But criminals take one look at me, and they do seem to change their ways."

Mary Lou said, "I would love to continue this chat, but I have to open the café tomorrow. I've become Miss Vicki's right-hand girl and head server. It was lovely to have met you Fashion Girl, She-Ra, you have one great daughter and friend in your corner. Thank you for coming."

Madame D replied, "Thanks Mary Lou, see you tomorrow." As everyone left, Madame D continued, "Mom, I want you to see the Den of Sin before I take you back to the cemetery so you can see for yourself how I do things." The original Fashion Girl said, "Being a former mystery solver, I admit The Den of Sin has piqued my interest." Madame D replied, "I assure you mom, there are no ghosts, ghouls or goblins down there but it's still a sight to see." She-Ra added, "I've seen it Daphne and it's cool I admit."

Madame D said, "Mom and I will go down there alone. Cindy after I show her, take over for me after I take mom back." Sephora replied, "So that you know, since Daphne got pregnant, I've taken over for her as Mistress C. I love doing it. Maybe I'll get my own lair someday." Madame D said, "Keep up the good work Cindy and you might get your wish. Mom, if you'll come with me, please."

Madame D took the original Fashion Girl to the other elevator entrance in the garage. She inserted the card, the doors opened, and they went inside. As the elevator stopped, Madame D said, "Mom, prepare to be amazed." The doors opened as they entered The Den of Sin. Madame D continued, "Mom, welcome to the Den of Sin." As the original Fashion Girl looked around, she replied, "Daphne, this place is fantastic! It's so cool!" Madame D laughed and said, "Criminals don't like it too much. They think at first that they will score with me but then they're in for a big surprise." The original Fashion Girl asked, "So, you're not pregnant with some strange guy's babies?"

Madame D answered, "Of course not mom. I only have sex with my boyfriend The Skull King, my ex-husband Dean Simpson and Macy Sears. Before you say anything, I am bisexual." The original Fashion Girl said, "I can't believe my daughter is bisexual, how did this happen?" Madame D replied, "I discovered that during my first modeling gig in Japan more than twenty years ago. It was by accident."

The original Fashion Girl said, "I understand." Madame D replied, "When I'm pregnant, I get so horny, I will do it with her and only with her. I do prefer men; I didn't lie about that." The original Fashion Girl said, "I do understand honey, I want my only daughter to be happy." Madame D replied, "I am happy mom, very happy indeed. C'mon, I'll take you back to the cemetery."

When Madame D arrived back at the cemetery, she said, "Mom, thank you for doing this favor for us tonight, helping Daphne see things through and seeing my complex." The original Fashion Girl replied, "You're welcome sweetie and if you should need me again, have Sephora summon me." Madame D hugged the original Fashion Girl and said, "We will mom. See you again soon."

At that moment, the original Fashion Girl walked back to Chanel's marker and slipped back into the earth the same way she emerged. Madame D went back to the Mystique Boutique to finally help her daughter achieve her full potential as the new Fashion Girl.

CHAPTER 12

During the night when everyone in the mansion was asleep, Daphne was restless. The kind of restlessness where a woman is in love. Daphne wasn't lying when she said that she was in love with Cottonmouth. She made a promise to take her new role as Fashion Girl seriously, however, she wanted one more chance to be with the man she's fallen in love with.

It turned out that Cottonmouth was hanging around the mansion in the shadows, he too couldn't hold his feelings any longer. But how to get Daphne's attention was easier said than done. Daphne looked out her window and did spot Cottonmouth hiding in a clump of bushes. She went down to investigate, and, in a way, she was performing her first act as the new Fashion Girl.

She got dressed and went down to the courtyard to see for herself if what she saw was true. She said in a whisper, "Cottonmouth? Are you here?" Cottonmouth came out of the bushes and replied, "I'm here babe, I'm here for you. I made a mistake agreeing with your mother not to bother you during your training. I want to be a part of it not being apart from it."

Daphne said, "I only agreed with it to satisfy my mom and aunt. But I have been thinking about it too, I think you have something there to help me out. And if mom agrees, we can be together. But now that I'm here with you, what do we do now?" Cottonmouth replied, "Daphne, I love you, I can't stand to be away from you not even for a minute. You're so wild and so damn sexy. Want to do it to it?"

Daphne said with a wide smile on her face, "If you mean have sex? Then let's do it to it. But where?" Cottonmouth replied, "Didn't your mom say that she's here?" Daphne said, "Yes, so?" Cottonmouth replied, "If you have one of those elevator cards I've heard about, let's commit sin in the Den of Sin." Daphne said, "I like what you're thinking, and I do have one of those cards, but how do we get there? Your motorcycle makes enough noise to wake my grandma Daphne again." Cottonmouth replied, "The new Glam Mobile isn't exactly silent either."

Daphne had an idea. She said, "I'll call my stepfather and have him meet us down the street. We can wait for him there and he'll take us to Aurora Gardens." Cottonmouth replied, "Better yet, "I'll ask Diamondback to come over. He can use the complex's courtesy van. He can pick us up at the end of the block." Daphne gave Cottonmouth a kiss that symbolizes true love. When she finished, she said, "Cottonmouth, I'm ready to lay down my life as the new Fashion Girl and I'm also ready to commit myself to you. Let's not wait any longer, call him and let's begin walking to the end of the block where we can meet him."

After Cottonmouth gave Diamondback a call, he and Daphne began walking down to the end of the block. They walked arm in arm all the way. As they walked, Cottonmouth asked, "Do you remember the time when your aunt fell for Rattler?" Daphne answered, "I was eight at the time, so I don't know the details. Tell me how that happened."

Cottonmouth said, "Just like I fell for you, he fell hard for your aunt. And she fell for him just as hard. Your mom and your other grandma didn't think that our queen would ever find anyone that didn't like or love her for who she is." Daphne replied, "That she wasn't one of the Style Chicks, right?" Cottonmouth said, "Exactly. He fell for Cindy Bates not Sephora. She appreciated it very much."

Daphne replied, "Cottonmouth, be honest with me right now. Do you love me because I will be the new Fashion Girl? Do you love me because I'm now incredibly wealthy? Or do you love me for being Daphne Sandra Bates?" Cottonmouth said, "That's a fair question to ask but it wasn't necessary. I love you for being you. You are the most interesting young woman I ever met. And I don't care about anything else but you."

Daphne and Cottonmouth spent the next few moments locked in a passionate embrace until Diamondback arrived with the courtesy van. He got out and said, "Hey you two, get a room!" Daphne and Cottonmouth broke off from their kiss and she replied, "That's why we called you over Diamondback, we came from the mansion. Take us to Aurora Gardens so we can as you put it, get a room."

Diamondback ordered them into the van. As they drove away, he asked, "Cottonmouth, you are aware that Daphne needs to begin her training today?" Cottonmouth answered, "We know man, but we can't stay away from each other, dude we are in love." Diamondback said, "Okay let me guess what's going on here. I know that Daphne was to be at the Mystique Boutique so she could begin her training with her mom. She couldn't sleep thinking of you. Then you came over and hid in the shadows. And by chance, she thought that you were somewhere nearby. She went down to look and sure enough she found you. Dude, you are so predictable."

Cottonmouth replied, "Can't fool you can I dude?" Diamondback said, "I know you too well. You've been in love before, I'm sure both of you have, but I feel that this is serious." Daphne replied, "Diamondback, even though I promised my mom that I would focus completely on my training, but we just can't wait. And if I end up pregnant by him, I will have his baby. Look at how my Aunt Cindy is so happy with Rattler and my mom is happy with the Skull King and is pregnant with triplets. I deserve to be happy too, we both do. That's why we're doing this."

Diamondback said holding back tears, "That's so deep. I also see how Bonecrusher looks when he's near your friend Sarah, Daphne. I think they're falling in love too." Daphne replied, "I know, Sarah can't think straight with him around. It's amazing that she could concentrate on becoming the new Tiffany. But then again, the original Tiffany and the current Tiffany were both flirts. I understand the current Tiffany settled down both as a flirt and as a Style Chick. Right now, Diamondback, I could care less about becoming the next Fashion Girl. Not until I have scored with my man."

Diamondback said, "Usually your mom doesn't keep anything down in the Den of Sin until she's called upon. Is there anything I can get for you to make what you're about to do right?" Cottonmouth replied, "What about it babe, booze and smokes?" Daphne said, "You heard him Diamondback, get what we need." Diamondback said, "I'll get it from the bar, go down to the lower floor through the garage and I'll meet you there in a few minutes."

When they arrived at Aurora Gardens, Daphne and Cottonmouth did just that. In the Den of Sin, Daphne grabbed one of her mom's outfits to change into. Diamondback brought with him a bottle of the bar's finest scotch and two packs of cigarettes. Diamondback hugged his friend to wish him luck. Ten minutes later, Daphne came out from behind the changing area wearing a red bustier and skirt with red gloves and boots. She asked, "Well stud, what do you think?"

Cottonmouth's mouth was hanging out and replied, "Oh, Daphne, if I didn't know any better, you can outdo your mom any day the way you look right now." Daphne said, "Get ready Cottonmouth for tonight, I'm gonna rock your world." Cottonmouth began to undress but didn't notice Daphne doing the same and asked, "Babe, you're not going to strip?" Daphne answered, "No, I'm not wearing underwear and this skirt is short enough for you to do it in. Mom doesn't strip either. Besides, I am about to commit sin, so I am dressed for it. Let's do it to it!"

At that moment, Daphne jumped on the bed and began kissing Cottonmouth long and lustfully. Cottonmouth began stroking Daphne's breasts feeling how big and soft they are. Cottonmouth's prick was hard and big, Daphne gave him a blowjob that would put other women to shame. Daphne could also feel her cunt getting wet. Cottonmouth tasted how sweet her cum was. Daphne opened her legs wide and said, "Now stud, insert your prick in my cunt, plant your seed in me. I want you to impregnate me."

Cottonmouth replied, "Are you sure Daphne?" Daphne said, "I'm sure. I never wanted anything more than for you to fuck me. Fuck me hard big boy and don't stop." Cottonmouth inserted his dick in Daphne's pussy and began to thrust wildly. Daphne screamed with pleasure. She said, "YES! YES! FUCK ME! PLANT YOUR SEED IN ME! GET ME PREGNANT!"

Cottonmouth continued to push his dick deeper and deeper in Daphne's pussy. Then he climaxed with sperm and cum. Daphne sucked his gift of love in her as hard as she could. Daphne said breathing heavily, "Oh… Cottonmouth… That… was… so… good! But not good enough though." At that moment, Daphne got out of bed and grabbed one of her mother's whips and continued, "Now big boy, get on your knees for me."

Cottonmouth did what he asked. Daphne said, "Lick my boot." Cottonmouth again did what he was asked. Then Daphne threw him on the bed and cuffed his wrists and ankles. She got on top of him and said, "Don't move wild thing, get your prick hard as I will do you."

Cottonmouth asked, "I hope you have the keys for these cuffs?" Daphne answered, "Yes, I do, they're in the nightstand. Wait one moment." Daphne remembered something. She got up, went to the elevator and pressed the stop button so no one, not even her mother would disturb them. Daphne realized that Cottonmouth couldn't get hard cuffed by the arms and legs. She got back on top of him and said, "I forgot you can't jerk off if you can't reach it so I will do it for you."

Daphne noticed his dick still dripping with cum. She took her finger to put against his bulb to sample what he tasted like. She tasted it and said, "Hmmm, you taste so good big boy, now make more of it." Daphne began to stroke his dick until it got hard again. The more she stroked it, the more she noticed the veins protruding out from it. She also was stroking his chest. He was chiseled. She said, "I could iron a shirt on your chest with those rock-hard abs of yours."

Cottonmouth replied in a pant, "I… do… work… out…" Daphne said, "And I always thought bikers were fat, even the biker babes." Then she took his dick and inserted in her pussy as she began to thrust hard. With every thrust, she could feel his dick going deeper into her ovaries." She said, "I'm about to cum with you." Cottonmouth replied, "I am ready too. I will plant another seed in you. Have my baby, get knocked up." Daphne and Cottonmouth did cum together. She felt more of his sperm penetrating her uterus.

She got off him and said, "I hope you did just that knock me up. I want to have your baby." She grabbed the keys from the nightstand to uncuff him. When he could feel his hands and feet again, he replied, "Oh, babe, you are so wild. You fuck better than any girl I ever did it with."

Daphne said, "Well stud, there won't be any other girl, you're mine now." Cottonmouth replied, "Then let's celebrate our union." Cottonmouth opened the scotch and poured two glasses. He handed one to Daphne and continued, "Here's to us babe, together forever." Daphne said, "Yes together forever." They clinked their glasses and drank the liquor down. Daphne opened the cigarettes and handed two to Cottonmouth. He lit them both. Daphne said, "I don't know about you but now I'm starving." Cottonmouth replied, "Yeah, me too. Too bad the café isn't open."

Daphne said, "Well stud, my mom's motorcycle is upstairs in the garage. We could ride to the nearest burger joint." Cottonmouth replied, "I'm right with you baby." Daphne opened the elevator again so they could go topside. Once in the garage, they got onto Madame D's motorcycle and drove to find the nearest burger joint. They ordered food and took it back to Aurora Gardens. They got back into the Den of Sin. Daphne once again put the elevator in stop mode so they wouldn't be disturbed.

After they ate, they finished the bottle. Both feeling drunk and mellow, Daphne said, "I admit I've never been drunk before; I like that feeling." Cottonmouth replied, "Now you're living like a true biker babe. Getting drunk, stoned, partying all night. It's a great life." Daphne began to slur her speech and said, "Wanna...hic... elope stud? Wanna... hic... go to Vegas?" Cottonmouth replied also beginning to slur his speech, "Yeah aby... let's go... to Gevas right now."

Daphne said, "Who... hic... needs marriage, iving in... hic... nis is so much etter... hic..." Neither one felt they got too drunk to do anything else. Instead, Daphne got into bed with Cottonmouth and fell asleep in their arms. Daphne got her wish, she got to spend one last night with her boyfriend. But at what price will she pay for this wild night of sex and booze?

CHAPTER 13

Sarah was asked to wake Daphne up for breakfast and to prepare for a long day of training. But just as Sue Ellen saw Bobby in that shower scene on Dallas, Daphne woke up to see Sarah and asked, "Sarah, what are you doing in the Den of Sin?" Sarah answered, "The Den of Sin? Honey, we are in your bedroom in the Mystique Boutique. You must've had some dream if you thought you were in the Den of Sin?"

Daphne said, "Oh, Sarah and what a dream I had. I dreamt that Cottonmouth and I went to the Den of Sin and committed sin. It was so real. I honestly thought I was there." Sarah replied, "Oh Daphne there's no mistake about it, you are in love." Daphne said, "Cottonmouth is all I'm thinking about since we left him last night. You're right Sarah, I'm in love."

Sarah replied, "Daphne, it's great that you're in love. But remember your training begins today. You need to stay focused. I also understand that you will learn how to use your sword. Don't focus and you'll be known as "lefty" for the rest of your life." Daphne said, "You're right again. Sarah, what am I going to do?" Sarah replied, "Wait here Daphne. I will be right back."

Sarah returned with Isabella who would become the new Penney Dillard. Isabella said, "Sarah told me of your predicament. It's great that you're in love but you need to concentrate. I think I can help you. The current Penney Dillard taught me how to cast spells on other people. I can try to put you in a frame of mind where all you think about and concentrate on is your goal to learn your new role."

Daphne asked, "That's great Bella but what if it doesn't work?" Isabella answered, "Try to make it work. I know it's hard, but I know you can do it. Now close your eyes and concentrate on my voice." Isabella tried to cast a spell on Daphne, but she wasn't sure if it made any difference. When it was done, Isabella asked, "Did it work Daphne?" Daphne answered, "I… don't know Bella. I guess I'll see." Sarah added, "C'mon new Fashion Girl, breakfast is being served."

When Daphne sat down to breakfast, she couldn't think about anything else other than Cottonmouth. Madame D noticed this and asked, "Earth to the new Fashion Girl, are you in there?" Daphne didn't respond. Madame D said, "Honey, it's your favorite breakfast, are you okay? Sick?" Daphne still didn't respond. Daphne had a glazed look in her eyes. Madame D asked, "Can someone tell me what's going on?"

Daphne still had no response. Sarah answered, "Madame D, I don't like to gossip but your daughter is in love. She dreamt of Cottonmouth last night. Isabella tried to put a spell on her so she could train with full concentration." Madame D asked, "She's like in a trance. Isabella, put her out of it so I can talk with her please?" Isabella answered, "I'll see what I can do."

Isabella was successful in bringing Daphne out of the spell. Daphne asked, "What's happening to me? I feel so strange. Mom, what's up?" Madame D answered, "Apparently you on cloud nine." Daphne said, "Oh, mom, I had the most wonderful dream of Cottonmouth, he's making me crazy with love. I don't know how I am going to concentrate on today if I can't stop thinking about him."

Madame D asked, "What about Felix?" Daphne answered, "Felix who?" Madame D said, "You know Felix who, your boyfriend that you've had since the ninth grade." Daphne replied, "I spoke with him a couple of days ago. I told him how I fell for Cottonmouth. He's disappointed, oh alright, he's devastated. But he'll understand." Sephora interrupted and said with an angry tone in her voice, "Will he understand Daphne?

You've been through a lot together. You went to the prom together, you graduated together, he loves you and this is how you repay him? You betrayed him!"

Daphne replied, "No Aunt Cindy, I didn't betray him, he betrayed me! Before my birthday party, he cheated on me with my biggest rival from school. We're through! I'll work with him as Style Chick and Phat Kat but other than that, we're through." Sephora said, "Daphne, honey I'm sorry I didn't know. If that's what he did, then fine, you're better off without him." Daphne replied, "It's okay Aunt Cindy, it's okay. Everyone, let me eat what I can, and I will begin my training in exactly thirty minutes."

Madame D turned to Sephora and said, "Cindy, that snapped our lovebird out of her spell. Isabella, you gave it a good try but sometimes you need to put a burr under the saddle to get things rolling." Isabella replied, "Thank you Madame. I tried but I guess my new powers aren't fully developed yet." Sephora added, "It's okay Bella, you did fine. Now let's let Daphne eat in peace so we can see what she'll be made of."

In exactly thirty minutes, Daphne was ready to begin her training. And she made the most of it. Everything she was asked to do, she did it with surgical precision. Godiva taught her how to use a bow and arrow, Daphne didn't disappoint. Tiffany showed Daphne some martial art moves, Daphne mastered them fast. And of course, She-Ra taught her how to use a sword, Daphne learned it well. She even exceeded everyone's expectations.

Around lunchtime, Victoria came out with a basket full of fruit and an empty basket. She asked, "How's Daphne doing with her training?" Madame D answered, "She's doing better than I thought she would do." Victoria said, "That's great, Daphne let's see how well you are doing by helping me with lunch. This basket is filled with fruit and this second basket I will place at your feet. Call this a training exercise. I will toss to you fruit of all sizes except for small fruits, let's see how well you'll do slicing it up. If that's okay with you Madame?" Madame D replied, "Good idea Vicki, let's see how she'll do with actual objects."

One by one, Victoria threw to Daphne large fruit to begin with. First

Victoria threw a watermelon. Daphne sliced it up quickly and perfectly. Next a cantaloupe was thrown, and Daphne sliced it to perfection. Next a honeydew melon was thrown, followed by a grapefruit, bananas, oranges, lemons, limes, peaches, apples and nectarines all perfectly sliced and even peeled. Now with the second basket full of fruit, Victoria said, "Fruit salad for dessert ladies." Madame D replied, "That looks good and Daphne, you've done well so quickly."

Victoria grabbed the basket and said, "I'll give this to Lori, and I'll be right back." Victoria returned with a pitcher of lemonade and glasses and placed it in the gazebo. She said, "Lunch will be ready in fifteen minutes." Madame D asked, "Wait, you're not serving lunch?" Victoria answered, "No, Lori is. She made breakfast and she's making lunch. After all, she needs to learn how to prepare food the way I do."

Daphne said, "Remember Vicki, Lori will be the new you and she will do things a little differently. And she will have to go back to school in the fall." Victoria replied, "I forgot she's so young. Of course, school is important. If she agrees to make dinner during the school year when I'm not here, it will work out just fine."

Daphne said, "On weekends, she can do your other duties as a lookout. Either way, she'll get the training she needs and go to school too." Victoria replied, "I can't argue with logic like that, so I agree with those terms." Madame D added, "And as for you my daughter, you will also further your education. You were accepted into UCLA, and I want you to go. I had the same chance when I learned of my destiny. I put my higher education on hold, I don't want you to do the same."

Daphne asked, "Mom, what about my new role? My friends will need me won't they? And what about my love for Cottonmouth? Nothing or nobody will keep us apart. Nothing! I swear it!" Madame D answered, "Honey, most of the new Style Chicks are still in high school right? So, they will remain here. When they need you, they will let you know."

"Remember Daphne, if any crime occurs anywhere in the world, the Style Chicks will be there. And in Los Angeles, you will be needed there. The chief of the LAPD is a friend of mine. I can let him know of your presence when you go. And as for Cottonmouth, I see that you are in love. I don't want to keep you from him. So, the next time I see him, I will have a heart-to-heart talk with him. Maybe he'd like to further his education too."

Daphne asked, "Mom, do you mean it? Do you want this for me?" Madame D answered, "Daphne, time and time again that great love had been separated with great consequence. Think of Romeo and Juliet, if their parents weren't enemies, their love would have flourished beyond belief. And think of any love stories out there. I don't want to do the same. So, yes Daphne, I mean it. I'll even pay for him to go to school with you."

Daphne said, "Mom, I don't know what to say except thank you." Madame D replied, "Anything for my daughter and the new Fashion Girl. I know the look in my eyes when I fell in love with your dad. And the look in my eyes when I fell in love with Dean. And the look I had in my eyes when I fell in love with the Skull King, so honey, I understand." Then Lori and Victoria came out with a feast fit for an army of queens. Daphne asked, "Lori, did you do all of this?" Lori answered, "Most of it. Vicki did show me a few things and of course you helped with dessert. I understand your swordsmanship is getting pretty good. Now if you all will excuse me, Vicki told me to go to the command center to monitor any possible criminal activity in between the lunch and dinner hours so enjoy lunch. Dinner will be served at eight o'clock."

Madame D said, "Sephora, I think in a few days, we can officially make everyone the next generation of Style Chicks with our ritual of presenting them to their family and friends." Sephora replied, "I think so too. I remember when I was presented, it was the best night of my life."

With Madame D, Sephora and She-Ra's help, Daphne began to get the hand of doing what it takes to be the next Fashion Girl. While Daphne's training continued, Madame D went into her study and called Cottonmouth to talk with him what she talked with Daphne about, the possibility of going to UCLA with her.

When Cottonmouth picked up the phone, he asked, "How is Daphne doing Skull Queen?" Madame D answered, "She's doing better than I did when I first became Fashion Girl. Serpentina thinks she'll be ready in a few days." Cottonmouth asked, "So what do I owe the pleasure of this call besides giving me an update?" Madame D answered, "I wanted to talk with you about the possibility of going with Daphne to UCLA. She was accepted to go there and will begin in the fall. Would you be willing to go with her? I'll pay for you to go back to school and get a proper education."

Cottonmouth asked, "Do you mean it? Do you really mean it?" Madame D answered, "Yes I do. I realize that you mean the world to my daughter. Without you there, she might not do well otherwise. With you there on campus, she could do it all. Get a first-class education, and not feel lonely. What kind of education did you get?"

Cottonmouth replied, "My father died when I was in high school. I didn't finish. He was the only breadwinner. My mother's health was failing but after his death it took a turn for the worse. Now she's gone too. That's when I met up with the Vipers. They gave me a place in their gang. Then we met you, you changed our lives. You gave us a purpose, Serpentina is a great woman, Rattler is a lucky man to have her. And now I am just as lucky to have Daphne in my life. I love her and would do anything for her."

"As for my education, I wasn't a bad student, but I wasn't honor roll material either. What do you have in mind?" Madame D said, "If you're willing to get your GED and if you pass, you may go with her. Do we have a deal?" Cottonmouth replied, "Deal." Madame D said, "Excellent, we're having dinner tonight at eight, please join us and I'll tell Daphne in front of everyone."

Cottonmouth replied, "Okay Madame, I will be there. I can't wait to see the look on Daphne's face when she hears the news. But since she's been acting kind of weird lately, I hope she won't get mad at the both of us." Madame D said, "UCLA maybe a coed school, the dorms aren't. So, she can do her thing, you do yours, and can still hang out together." Cottonmouth replied, "I like this a lot, see you tonight."

When the call ended, Madame D's intentions were good, but she and Cottonmouth had a right to worry only because of Daphne's behavior. But now that she's gotten down to business to being the next Fashion Girl, her attitude might have mellowed but only time will tell.

CHAPTER 14

Later that night at dinner, everyone sat down to an equally delicious meal they had at lunch. When everyone finished eating, Madame D took a brief glance at Cottonmouth, then turned back to Daphne and said, "Daphne, you did very well today with your training, we feel that in no time flat, we can make our presentation of the new Style Chicks sooner than we first thought." Daphne replied, "You really think so?"

Madame D said, "Of course, since I didn't know what to expect when I first became Fashion Girl, you know what to expect. You knew how I did everything, and you knew you were going to take my place. But for now, I have a wonderful or I should say Cottonmouth has a wonderful surprise for you."

Cottonmouth replied, "Thank you Skull Queen. She's right Daphne, I have a great surprise for you. Your mom is willing to send me to UCLA with you if I can get my GED and graduate high school. We can be together." Daphne's mouth was wide open and said, "Mom, I don't know what to say except thank you. But why the change of heart?"

Madame D replied, "Honey, I realized that everyone should follow their own hearts and to do what they feel what's right even if everyone thinks is wrong. I spoke with Cottonmouth earlier today and I'm willing to do this. He's got some kind of potential. I want you and me to find out what he's truly capable of. So, if he can get his GED, I'll help him get enrolled in school. Also, I see how happy Aunt Cindy is with Rattler and how happy I am being with the Skull King. If your aunt and I can be happy with a pair of bad boys, I see the look in your eyes when you're with or you think about Cottonmouth."

Daphne looked at Cottonmouth with her eyes growing wide as is her smile and said, "I love him mom, and he'll do fine once he gets his GED." Madame D asked, "What subject did you do well in when you were in school Cottonmouth?" Cottonmouth answered, "I didn't do better in one subject over another, I was relatively equal in my studies." Daphne said, "I'm going to UCLA and I'm majoring in drama. I took drama classes in high school and my teacher and my classmates both thought that I could become the next big thing in Hollywood."

Cottonmouth replied, "Daphne I could learn drama and accompany you in at least one of your classes." Daphne said, "I would love to do a love scene with you, it would be more genuine than just an act." Madame D added, "Daphne, also look into joining the Alpha Beta Omega sorority. The original Tiffany and Penney Dillard started it up. Aunt Cindy also was a member there. You're her niece meaning you're a legacy and anyone who's a legacy in a fraternity or sorority are automatically eligible to join."

Sephora said, "I can call the headmistress of the chapter at UCLA, it will help prove the issue." Daphne confused asked, "What do you mean the original Tiffany and Penney Dillard started up a sorority?" Madame D answered, "When they went to school at Georgia Tech, they joined another sorority but when they were caught in a trap set by the number one member realizing that they were Style Chicks, they started a sorority of their own. Alpha Beta Omega. "The first and last name in sororities." Since then, it's become the number one sorority in the country."

Cottonmouth asked, "Did the original Phat Kats start a fraternity of their own?" Madame D answered, "No I'm afraid they didn't. But I'm sure you will be asked to join one for sure." Daphne was so pleased and happy over the news. Madame D and Cottonmouth both agreed that they did the right thing. It made the next few days all the easier.

In Daphne's next day of training, she learned about the cosmetic weapons Fashion Girl is famous for. Sephora presided over this part of the training. She said, "Today Daphne, I will show you the contents of the utility belt your mom and grandma wore and used as Fashion Girl."

"The belt contains six compartments. One compartment is empty for you to use as a purse/wallet. Keep your driver's license, cash and a credit card in it so you won't have to worry lugging a purse around. Now for what's in the other compartments. Keep in mind that these are weapons to look like everyday cosmetics, don't mistake them for real cosmetics."

"First you have exploding lipsticks. When you take the top off and twist to reveal the lipstick, you have ten seconds to aim it at your target or else it will explode in your hand. Next you have metal eating nail polish. Reminiscent of your grandma's time as Fashion Girl and when she was known as "Danger Prone Daphne", Fashion Girl's only weakness is if you get captured, you will lose your powers. I want to take you to the city jail to demonstrate this in better detail."

Once at the jail, Sephora continued, "Daphne as the new Fashion Girl I want you to understand what I said back at the mansion. You see one of your weapons will help you escape. The jail let us use a cell for what we need. Now step inside and I'll explain further."

Daphne went into the cell and Sephora closed and locked the door. She said, "Now then Daphne, try to get out of this cell. Your newfound strength should be no match for iron bars." Daphne tried to free herself from the locked cell and said, "Hey? What gives? I can't get out! Aunt Cindy, is this some sort of trick?" Sephora knew that Daphne was freaking out and replied, "Calm down Daphne it's okay. You can free yourself trust me."

Daphne asked, "Are these bars made of kryptonite or something? I know I'm not Supergirl so what do I do to get out of this?" Sephora reassured her niece that everything was okay and answered, "In your utility belt is the metal eating acid nail polish I mentioned earlier. With it you can free yourself from any cell or cage regardless of what the metal is, even titanium."

"Now apply the polish to two neighboring bars. Apply it to both to the top and bottom of the bars and watch what happens." After Daphne applied the polish, in seconds the compound reduced the bars to dust allowing Daphne to get out. She said, "That's a powerful tool it really will come in handy." Sephora replied, "Remember Daphne to always be vigilant and not get caught. And one more thing, more than likely no one will realize that your belt is just a belt and part of your costume. Just stay on your toes. Now let's get out of here and I'll show you what the other weapons do."

Next, Sephora took Daphne downtown to the city's tallest building, the McNair Building. Sephora said, "Get to know this building well Daphne because as the new head of Style Incorporated, your offices occupies all of the top floor. As for being here is for you to try out your next weapon. In your belt you will find a tube of mascara, but it's not an ordinary tube. This is a grappling hook with unlimited length. With it you could scale any tall building or structure. You could climb Mount Everest with virtual ease. Now aim and shoot for the roof of the building."

Daphne pointed the tube straight up and fired. The hook materialized and latched onto the roof and secured it. She tugged on the line to make sure it was solid. Sephora said, "Well done Daphne, just for fun, let's see Grandma Sandy, I'm sure she'll be surprised." Daphne replied, "Nice idea Aunt Cindy but let's not give her a heart attack either." Sephora said, "No problem for we'll go to the roof and go downstairs. We can't enter through a window anyway; they can't be opened."

Daphne began climbing the rope with Sephora right behind her. Sephora asked, "Hope you're not afraid of heights?" Daphne answered, "If I'm going to get around in a flying car, if I will fly on my own as an Archangel therefore I am not afraid of heights." Daphne saw how far she was up the building, she gulped and said under her breath, "Much."

When they reached the top, Sephora said, "You're doing great Daphne. I'll tell you something, even though your mom had these weapons at her disposal, she rarely used them. In fact, the only time I know of when she used them was her final battle with Grandma Sandy."

Daphne asked, "Mom and Grandma Sandy were enemies?" Sephora

answered, "Sadly yes but it was over a misguided belief on both of their parts. When they buried the hatchet, they never spoke of that time in their lives ever again. Now let's go." When they got down to the top floor of the building, they walked through the front door. The receptionist said, "Welcome to Style Incorporated ladies, what can I do for you?"

Sephora replied, "We're here to see Sandy Bates." The receptionist asked, "Do you have an appointment?" Daphne answered, "Appointment? I am Daphne Bates. For my aunt and I, were here to see her mother and my grandmother. And for that, we don't need no stinking appointments." The receptionist said, "I was just asking ladies, by all means, family is always welcome here. Her office is down the hall and is straight ahead." Daphne replied, "Thank you ma'am, you've been very helpful."

The receptionist said, "You said your name is Daphne Bates? Wait, you're the new Fashion Girl. Oh, I'm sorry I really and honestly didn't know who you are." Daphne replied, "It's okay. It's going to take a lot of getting used to it for everyone. Just know that I am the new Fashion Girl and your new boss. Thanks for the info."

Sephora said, "Your mom and I were going to teach you about being diplomatic. You handled that well." Daphne replied, "I've seen and heard you; mom and the others deal with others, so I knew about diplomacy the easy way."

When they arrived at Sandy's office, they went inside. Sandy rose from her chair and said, "Cindy, Daphne, this is a surprise, what are you both doing here?" Daphne replied, "Aunt Cindy was showing me the cosmetic weapons in my utility belt. We scaled the building to demonstrate. Besides, now that I'm the big boss here, I thought I'd see what exactly I will do here."

Sandy said, "Your mom came here once a month to oversee everything. Since you'll be going to college soon, the office manager has taken care of everything since your mom faked her death." Daphne replied, "Grandma Sandy, Aunt Cindy told me that you and my mom were once enemies. What exactly was the rift between you two?"

Sandy said, "That's a fair question to ask Daphne. Your mom and I don't mention it because it was all on account of misguided beliefs on both of our accounts. Many years ago, my sister Cynthia, for whom I named my daughter after, was the granddaughter of a famous Hollywood director. On the night of her senior prom, she and her boyfriend who were both named the king and queen of the prom."

"On route to the prom, the car they were driving in was sideswiped by a pair of actresses who were too drunk to drive. Cynthia's boyfriend was killed instantly, and Cynthia suffered cuts all over her hands, face and legs. A plastic surgeon tried to repair the damage but was unsuccessful in restoring my sister's looks. So, what she did next I never approved of, she bought another prom dress, altered it and became a villain as she called herself the Prom Queen."

"As the Prom Queen, something in my sister's mind snapped and she started to get her revenge in the worst way imaginable. She would attack young and coming actresses by throwing acid in their faces disfiguring them beyond belief and repair." Before she could continue, Daphne gasped and replied, "How horrible. Why would she do something like that?" Sandy replied, "My sister also was an up-and-coming actress. She used her portion of her fortune to do this."

"It was around the time your Grandma Daphne was getting recognition as Fashion Girl. Your grandma and She-Ra was in Los Angeles doing the rounds of the talk shows. One of my sister's minions kidnapped her and forced her to be introduced to my sister. In one respect, my sister admired your grandma for the way she combat crime. But my sister wanted to do the same to your grandma and ruin her good looks."

"Your grandma literally put my sister through a brick wall and was later sent to jail. She spent the rest of her life there and was killed in a failed jailbreak. Then as you know, your grandma's best friend and your mom's godmother Velma was jealous of your grandma's success. She hired the remainder of my sister's minions, ambushed your grandma and killed her."

"When I learned of my sister's death and when your mom learned of her mother's death, we sort of picked up where they left off. After a failed plot cooked up by me and the Joker, yes that Joker, I called a truce with your mom. At first the only thing I wanted her to do was kick that sorry son of a bitch's ass. The Joker pushed me off this tall platform we were standing on and I broke my leg in three places. Macy bandaged my leg while your mom and the others knocked out my minions and the Joker's jokers."

"Before I was transported to the hospital, I called your mom over. And I made the truce permanent. We both realized that day that we were at odds through no fault of our own. Your mom couldn't have had anything to do with my sister's death because she wasn't born yet. And I was in Philadelphia at that time working in public relations and raising your dad, Aunt Cindy and Uncle Johnny. We became friends from that day on and it changed our paths and lives forever."

Daphne heard every word with her mouth hanging open and replied, "Wow, that was some story Grandma Sandy. I guess in a way, I wouldn't have been born if it weren't for that truce." Sephora added, "And I wouldn't have been made a Style Chick either. Our lives are intertwined not just by blood or marriage. But by the way of how everything turned out."

Sandy said, "That's why neither your mom nor I talk about this Daphne. But one thing you will never have to worry about is having an archenemy. The criminals you will deal with will be that of real-world issues. And not some insane maniac trying to take over the world or steal top secret documents or stealing priceless jewelry or artwork. They will be drug dealers, pimps, and ordinary criminals doing otherwise normal criminal activities."

Daphne replied, "In other words grandma, I won't have to deal with the likes of the Joker or Lex Luthor?" Sandy said, "On your own and that of the Style Chicks, no. But there will be times that you might have to deal with them if you're asked by Batman, Superman, Wonder Woman or any other hero or heroine when they're dealing with them. The Style Chicks are unique to the point that these villains don't know what hit them. Just ask Batman how your mom kicked the Joker's ass that day many years ago."

Sephora said, "We're also here mom to see if you're interested in having lunch with us? And afterwards, I'll show Daphne how to use the quick freeze hairspray." Sandy replied, "That sounds nice Cindy, sure I'm in. Daphne take it from me sweetie, I was a victim of that hairspray, I never skated on such ice before." Daphne asked, "What do you mean that you never skated on such ice before grandma?"

Sandy answered, "Your mom used it on me once and I just couldn't stand up straight. I'm a good skater but believe me, bad guys won't know what will hit them if they try to stand on that slippery ice. Enough reminiscing, let's have lunch, I'm starving."

After lunch, Sephora showed Daphne how to use the quick freeze hairspray and where. They found a patch of sidewalk in a nearby park. Sephora said, "Now Daphne here is why this spray is quick freezing, let's say that I'm a bad guy and I'm about to attack you. You spray the spray on the ground and as if on contact, the surface becomes a slippery surface as grandma pointed out, no one can stand on it."

Sephora handed the can to Daphne. She stepped back two hundred feet and started to run towards Daphne. Daphne sprayed twenty-five feet of the sidewalk. The moment Sephora stepped on the icy surface, she began to slip, slide and fall onto the surface. Scared that Sephora could've injured herself; Daphne ran out onto the ice and to her surprise, she wasn't slipping or falling. She pushed Sephora back onto a dry patch of sidewalk.

Daphne ran up and asked, "Aunt Cindy, are you okay?" Sephora answered, "I'm okay honey. Good thing I have a padded butt." Daphne asked, "How come I wasn't slipping or sliding on that ice? I too should have a padded butt." Sephora answered, "I was going to tell but you found out for yourself. As Fashion Girl, you and only you can actually stand on it. You will not fall." Daphne said, "It was as if that spray knew it was me." Sephora replied, "The spray is mixed with a special compound that will know who's standing on it. The soles of your boots also has this compound too. Now let's go back to the mansion so I can show the final weapon in your arsenal."

Before they left the scene, Daphne said, "Wait Aunt Cindy, shouldn't we do something about that dangerous patch of ice? I don't want anyone to get hurt." Sephora replied, "Relax Daphne, no one will get hurt because there's nothing for them to get hurt on. Look behind you, after five minutes, the spray you applied will melt and leave the surface bone dry."

For the final cosmetic weapon Daphne will use as the new Fashion Girl, she and Sephora went back to the mansion as Sephora explained, "The reason why we came back to the mansion is because the final weapon you'll have is dangerous. Your mom didn't want to use it, but you need to see it." Sephora reached into the compartment where the final weapon is and continued, "This may look like an ordinary compact but it's dangerous because when you press the button on top, you have only five seconds before razor sharp blades will protrude and they will slice off fingers and entire limbs. If you must use this weapon, please do it with the utmost caution."

Daphne asked, "Okay but what exactly will it be used for?" Sephora answered, "Let's say that someone is trying to attack you with a club, a martial arts weapon or even a gun. With the right throw, it will make their weapon useless. Now I placed a block of wood fifty feet away from us. On that block a stick is sticking out of the side. Now when I say go, press the button and throw the compact within five seconds and see what happens."

Daphne pressed the button on the compact, quickly aimed for the stick and threw the compact. In mid-air, the blades came out and cut the stick in half. But what Sephora didn't say was that the compact will come back to Fashion Girl and the blades will go back into the compact. In other words, this weapon was a boomerang compact.

When Daphne safely caught the compact, she said, "This is awesome. But I do see your point Aunt Cindy. Now that I've seen what it can do, I will use it if I have no other alternatives." Sephora replied, "You did well today Daphne. Now all you need to know at this point is about your powers as one of the Archangels. She-Ra will preside over this, and she'll show all of you your powers as Archangels. They're waiting for you outside town near Makeout Mountain. Go now, and good luck." Daphne replied as she hugged Sephora, "Thanks Aunt Cindy. I too believe we'll be ready to take over for all of you very soon."

Daphne got into her car and drove to where the others were waiting for her to arrive. Then Daphne and five other future Style Chicks will learn how to use the ultimate weapon, to become the Archangels. Upgraded Style Chicks that have been nothing short of unstoppable.

CHAPTER 15

W hen she got out of her car, Daphne joined the others where they would get a crash course in becoming Archangels. As Sephora pointed out, She-Ra would preside over this last portion of training. She said, "Now that Daphne is here, I will help you become the Archangels. The Archangels were created to possess ten times the power each of you will soon have. Ten times the ability and the ability to fly."

Daphne raised her hand and asked, "She-Ra, why aren't Lori, Amora and Denise here with us?" She-Ra answered, "Daphne, watching your mom and the others you of all people should know the answer to that question."

"As the new Victoria, Lori's job as lookout is by far the most important job of the Style Chicks and the Archangels. As the new Macy Sears, Amora's ability to make and create potions and elixirs is also an influential part of the team. And as being the new Belle K, Denise has already mastered her skill as an ambassador to the Style Chicks and can hold her own in a fight. You six will become the new faces of the Archangels. Now I will tell each of you what kind of powers you will have as Archangels."

"First Daphne I'll begin with you. As the new Fashion Girl, you will also be the powerful Phoenix of the Archangels. As the Phoenix, you can accumulate fire and disperse it at anything or anyone. I saw your mom do this and she nearly roasted a man to death. However, he died from the injuries he sustained so please don't do this but rather to use it for intimidation."

"Next Sarah, as the new Tiffany, you will also become Solara the Sun Goddess. As Solara, you can turn night into day by producing sun spheres. You can also shoot them at anything or anyone. The current Tiffany along with your mom, used the sun spheres to defeat the Vipers former leader named Aspina. Again, use this power at your discretion."

"Next Isabella, although as the new Penney Dillard you'll be able to fly, and you'll rule the night. But as an Archangel, you will also become Nighthawk. As Nighthawk, you will be able to summon all creatures of flight at your command. Also, you will be able to disrupt the radar, guidance system or anything on a plane to render them useless."

"Indira, as the new Zara you don't possess any special powers. Your knowledge is your power which is better than super strength, sorcery and more. But as an Archangel, you will become Seagirl. As Seagirl, your will have powers one of which, you can control water at your command. You can get water from any source."

"Aldea, as the new Godiva, as an Archangel you will become Firebolt. As Firebolt, you can harness lightning even on a clear, sunny day. You can use lightning to stop objects cold but as with the Phoenix and Solara, do your best not to strike people with lightning."

"And finally, Paula, as the new Sephora, you will become Whirlwind as an Archangel. As Whirlwind, you will literally be able to control the weather. You can make a hurricane out of a calm breeze. You can enhance Firebolt's powers by using a rainstorm. You can freeze people in their tracks by blowing on them with a very cold blast. But like with the others, use it with discretion."

"Daphne, when your mom made me a Style Chick, she didn't want to change my name or appearance from the controversy I had ten years ago. But she made me an Archangel giving me the name Earthshaker. As Earthshaker, I can create new lands, find new sources of energy, stop climate change and be an ambassador to the world. Now you will use the bracelets you were given to become Archangels. You will practice how to accumulate your new abilities and finally, we will take a trip. We will fly to Hawaii and back. For us it will be a trip around the block. Now with all that said, let's rock."

"When you are Archangels, remember let's rock is your battle cry, Daphne, your mom came up with that on a whim, but it works. Now let's rock." Once each Style Chick became an Archangel, they took to the air. Daphne now as the Phoenix said, "This does rock. I can't believe I'm flying. This is great!" The Archangels noticed that it was getting dark. She-Ra now as Earthshaker said, "Solara, produce a sun sphere to light our way."

Sarah now as Solara replied, "You got it." Solara put her hands together and produced a sun sphere to light up the darkening sky. She added, "This is so cool. And the view of the ocean is beautiful." Earthshaker said, "Now we are going to do something really cool. We are going to create an artificial island. Are you ready ladies?" The Phoenix replied, "Yes we are just tell us what to do."

The Archangels were about halfway between the west coast and Hawaii. Earthshaker said, "Now everyone swoop down and reduce our altitude by half." Once they did that, Earthshaker continued, "Now ladies here's how we are going to make an artificial island. Whirlwind, Seagirl come with me and follow my lead." Earthshaker went into the water and found an underwater mountain and raised it to the surface.

Once secured, Whirlwind and Seagirl used their powers to produce an ice boundary to temporarily keep the mountain and surrounding ground in place. Next Whirlwind and Earthshaker used their powers to create sand to create a beach. Then with seeds that Earthshaker had on her, planted trees and other such greenery. Finally, The Phoenix used her fire powers to create a hot spring.

Nighthawk summoned birds nearby to allow them to make the new island home. And Firebolt made the mountain erupt with just enough lava to help prevent the island from sinking back into the ocean. When everything died down, the island was stable. The Archangels landed on the beach to look at what they had done. Earthshaker said, "Ladies, welcome to Archangel Island. We will come back here to have buildings built so people can come here for rest and relaxation. What do you think of what we done?"

The Phoenix replied, "It's beautiful! We can do just about anything as Archangels." Earthshaker said, "You can do even more when it comes to fighting crime. Now as I promised, we will have a great evening in Hawaii. Solara, light our way please." Solara produced a sun sphere as the Archangels headed west towards Hawaii. They enjoyed a Hawaiian luau and a Hawaiian style show.

Earthshaker called Sephora and said, "Sephora, the Archangels are ready as well. We made an island out of nothing and we're enjoying ourselves right now in Hawaii. When we get back, tell Madame D that they are ready to be presented three days from now."

Sephora replied happily, "That's wonderful news Earthshaker. I'll let her know because we need to prepare costumes and send out invitations. Vicki and her staff will need to prepare food for the event as well as alert the media. Thank you for helping us out. Sephora out."

The Archangels decided to spend the night in Hawaii when they realized that no one had money to stay in a hotel. But the Phoenix remembered that she had the credit card her grandmother got for her. She said, "When my mother was Fashion Girl, she carried a credit card with unlimited credit, and it was also her expense account. Grandma Sandy has a card issued to me and told me the same thing, ladies we will spend tonight in style. Then it's back home for our presentation."

Yes indeed, the Archangels enjoyed their evening and night in Hawaii. When they left the next morning it was 8 o'clock in Hawaii and 11 o'clock in California. But when they did come back and resumed their normal identities, Daphne said, "Mom, Aunt Cindy, our training both as Style Chicks and Archangels are complete. We are ready to be presented to the world as the new Style Chicks."

Sephora replied, "That's great news. We will have this presentation three days from now. We will invite your parents, the media, and other honored guests to witness this historic event." Confused Daphne asked, "What do you mean by it being historic? You've done these presentations before right?" Sephora answered, "Of course we've done this type of event. I meant by it being historic, it will be the largest presentation ever with all of you being presented."

"You see Daphne, Penney found a way for the Cosmo Chicks to be on Earth without having to wear those helmets. They will be finally able to breathe our air for the first time ever. Charlotte and Tiffany's kids as you know will become the next generation of Junior Style Chicks and they will have a presentation of their own. All the local stations that reports on the news will be here to see and document this event along with reporters from the Colognia Times and Colognia Gazette. However, they can only tape and report on certain parts of the presentation that will not reveal such things like your true identities and that of the Archangels."

Daphne said, "It sounds so thrilling, but can you do such a presentation in three days from now? If it as big as you say it will be, it might not be enough time." Sephora replied with confidence, "We will all pitch in. New costumes can be made quickly. Vicki and her staff are ready to prepare a banquet unlike anyone has ever seen and when you are presented, for most of you, your fathers will escort you to the stage and Daphne, your boyfriend, uncle, Grandfather Fred and Grandfather Harry will take turns to provide your escort since you will become the next Fashion Girl. Now everyone, relax, take it easy and in three days, your lives will have changed forever. Congratulations to all of you."

As everyone left the scene, King Cobra and Amanda came to the mansion to greet She-Ra back from the training session. King Cobra said, "Welcome back She-Ra, I'm sorry that I didn't keep in touch with you sooner, I figured that you were helping out the new Style Chicks." She-Ra replied, "It's okay Cobra, I told you that you and Amanda needed to get acquainted with each other. So, tell me what did you two do together?"

Amanda said, "Mommy, Daddy and I did so many things together. He took me to see the animals at the zoo. I was impressed with the fact that the animals aren't in cages." King Cobra added, "In just about every zoo across the country, the animals are situated in a natural habitat type setting. Go ahead sweetie, tell mommy more."

Amanda continued, "Daddy took me to see several movies. I saw Disney movies, lots of them. One night, he took me bowling which I understand uncle He-Man learned from grandma. Next we went to the museum and saw a baseball game in San Francisco." At that moment She-Ra noticed that Amanda was wearing a leather jacket and asked, "Honey, why are you wearing a leather jacket? Cobra what happened?" Amanda answered, "Nothing happened mommy. The Skulls and Vipers had a party, and I was the guest of honor. I was made an honorary member of both gangs."

King Cobra added, "Relax She-Ra, we were just celebrating the fact that I'm now a father nothing more. Tiffany also made Amanda an honorary Junior Style Chick too." She-Ra replied, "It sounds like you both had a lot of fun. What else did you do?" King Cobra said, "Nothing else happened but we both learned something, Amanda inherited your powers."

She-Ra replied in disbelief, "Really?" King Cobra said, "Really. First at the zoo, a patron fell somehow into the lions exhibit. A lion was about to kill this person, but Amanda stopped it. She must've communicated with the lion with some form of telepathy. You do the same right?" She-Ra replied, "Yes I can communicate with animals with telepathy."

King Cobra continued, "One day, the car we were riding in had a flat tire. I discovered there was no jack in the car. Remember we were using a Style Chick vehicle. Amanda lifted the car high enough for me to change the tire. She has your super strength. And finally, Bonecrusher of the Skulls suffered a serious injury to his arm. Madame D was going to call 911 but Amanda instinctively touched his arm, and the injury was fixed. Yes She-Ra, Amanda is another you. She'll break hearts someday and she will someday do for you what Daphne will do for the Style Chicks. Our daughter is amazing. And I'm sorry that you had that ordeal of keeping your pregnancy a secret."

Amanda asked, "Mommy, is that true that when you were pregnant with me, you kept it a secret?" She-Ra answered, "Cobra you shouldn't have said that in front of her, but I understand. Honey, I wasn't ashamed of my pregnancy. I had to keep it a secret because of who I am. If I were an ordinary woman, it wouldn't have been no big deal. Women give birth every day. Think about this, I am a famous heroine on three different worlds. If it became known that I was pregnant, questions would be asked, people would talk, accusations would be made, and we would never have any peace. Amanda, please don't think for one second that I am ashamed of you or that I was pregnant with you. I love you and now that you know your father too, I can see that he's proud of you."

Amanda said, "I understand mommy. Daddy you're not ashamed of me are you?" King Cobra replied, "Of course not sweetheart. I wasn't aware that I had a daughter until about a month ago. My heart was bursting with pride the moment I laid eyes on you. And no matter what happens from now on, nothing will ever change that."

She-Ra said, "Now that's been settled, I will help the others with the preparations. I've been asked to host this event and I have to also prepare a speech and program." Sephora replied, "Nine West is now a writer when she isn't a Style Chick so she will help you with that. See you all in three days."

Yes this was going to be a significant event as a whole new group of young women along with the largest gathering of dignitaries, politicians, media and special guests will converge on the Mystique Boutique for the biggest event in the history of the Style Chicks.

CHAPTER 16

The big day finally arrived. The day that would change nine young women, four girls and three young men forever. The morning began with a breakfast banquet for all sixteen participants. After breakfast, Madame D and Sephora came out with sixteen boxes each with the name of the new group. Madame D said, "In these boxes are your new costumes. Tonight, you will be introduced in these new outfits. Then after tonight, you will get a second set of costumes for everyday use. Once again congratulations everyone. Prepare to be ready three hours before the ceremony begins. It will begin at six and be ready."

Daphne replied with a hug, "Thanks mom. I promise to do you and Grandma Daphne proud." Madame D said, "Honey, there's no doubt in my mind that you will do well. Remember that no one is perfect, even if I have made a mistake or two along the way. The Style Chicks are always ready for anything that comes your way, so always be alert and on your guard. The everyday individual will count on you."

Daphne replied, "And I have heard you mom say many times over the years to be women first and Style Chicks second." Sephora said, "Your mom did tell me that many times. I have done both with equal time. I'm now a wife, a mother and always and forever a Style Chick. I've done justice for all of that."

Madame D said, "Enjoy your day everyone, you've earned it."

Daphne replied, "Thanks mom and I know what I want to do today." Sarah added, "And I'll go with her Madame D. We both have something in mind together." Zara said, "And I have plans for Indira aboard ship today. She's excited about her new role. Even though I showed her the ship and all it has to offer, but I saved the bridge for last." Indira replied, "I can't wait to see it, let's go Zara, I might as well see the bridge now."

Madame D took Daphne aside to her study and said in private, "Daphne I know what you want to do today and that's to be with Cottonmouth right?" Daphne replied, "You got me mom, yes I want to spend the day with him. Sarah wants to be with Bonecrusher as well. Do you really have a problem with that?"

Madame D said, "No Daphne as a matter of fact, it's okay. I was going to save this for after the ceremony, but I have got good news for you. Cottonmouth passed his GED exam. Now he can go with you to UCLA. I spoke with the registrar and made all the arrangements. He will study for and will try to get a degree in Mechanical Engineering."

Daphne replied, "Mom, Cottonmouth could rebuild an engine from scratch. He's worked from time to time in Dean's garage." Madame D said, "I know sweetie, Dean likes his work, but I want him to get a degree. After all, if he's going to be my future son-in-law, I want him to support you well. Now go on, enjoy your day with him." Madame D gave Daphne an elevator card and continued, "Go ahead and make some sin in The Den of Sin."

Daphne couldn't be happier. She left the mansion to find Cottonmouth, and when she did, he was at the Vipers hideout. She came inside and said, "Cottonmouth, I heard you passed your GED exam, congratulations! You'll be able to join me at UCLA." Cottonmouth replied, "I guess your mom told you. It was supposed to be a surprise." Daphne said, "Well stud, I have a bigger surprise for you, mom gave me one of her elevator cards. She's giving us the okay to use The Den of Sin."

Cottonmouth replied, "Really? Then that means that we…" Daphne interrupted and said, "Yes that means we can fuck our brains out. Let's not waste this opportunity. I have to be back by three at the mansion because I have to get ready for the presentation, it begins at six."

Cottonmouth replied, "What are we waiting for. We're burning daylight and as the Style Chicks would say, "Let's Do It To It!"

Daphne and Cottonmouth got on his bike, and they headed to Aurora Gardens and to the Den of Sin for a session as they've never had one before. While this was going on, Zara took Indira to the Mystique Marauder to show her the bridge of the ship. As they walked in, one of the ship's navigators said, "Captain on the bridge." Indira asked, "Zara, do they always say that when I would walk in?"

Zara answered, "Yes, it's a sign of respect and so everyone here is doing what they're supposed to do. Now Indira, this is the captain's chair. Sit down and take your rightful place as the new captain." Indira sat down and said, "This is nice, really nice." Zara replied, "After tonight, call me Ursula. Tomorrow we will take passengers on the "Love Boat" route."

Indira asked, "The Love Boat route? What's that?" Zara answered, "Many years ago, there was a TV show called "The Love Boat". It was set on an actual cruise ship, and they sailed from Los Angeles to Acapulco and back. I want you to be in charge, to get the feel of the ship and be in command. Remember, people who've sailed on this ship before knows that I take time to meet and greet and get to know who's onboard. For now, get a feel for the bridge, and get to know your crew. And my boyfriend Jim and I will be here to sail the ship. Don't be afraid to ask any questions. Okay?"

Indira said, "Okay, Zara, I can't wait to set sail." Zara replied, "I know you're anxious but it's always best to be calm and relaxed." Indira said, "I understand Zara." During this time, the new Style Chicks are getting final preparations for their new roles. Even though they are getting their costumes for their presentation. Sephora approached Denise and asked, "Denise, can I speak to you for a few moments?" Denise answered, "Sure Sephora, what can I do for you?"

Sephora said, "Actually there is something I can do for you. After tonight, this is your regular costume. It's different than what you'll get. This outfit belonged to the previous Belle K. The one who got killed a few years ago. I'm sure that if she was still with us, she would've wanted you to have it." Denise opened the box to see what Belle K's costume was like. She said, "This is beautiful. I love pink. She wore all kinds of pink. I will always treasure this outfit, thank you very much Sephora."

Sephora replied, "You're welcome Denise. After tonight, call me Cindy or Serpentina. I am still the queen of the Vipers." Denise said, "I understand. I can't wait for tonight." But the real action involved Daphne and Cottonmouth in the Den of Sin. Daphne told Cottonmouth to wait for her because she wanted to use one of her mother's outfits. Before she changed outfits, there was a note taped to the closet door. The note was for Daphne, and it read as follows…

Daphne,

Tonight, your life will change forever. You will take my place as the new Fashion Girl. But for now, enjoy your day, wear any outfit and use any tools you like. You are going to make me and your grandma Daphne proud. I love you…

Mom

Daphne opened the closet to find an outfit and the other closet for either a whip or crop to subdue her "prey". After she changed outfits and found a tool she liked, she sent for Cottonmouth to come downstairs. Cottonmouth saw Daphne in an all-black outfit with a cat-o-nine tails and said, "Welcome to the Den of Sin Mr. Cottonmouth."

Cottonmouth replied, "Daphne, you look amazing. I can only imagine how you'll look tonight at the presentation." Daphne said, "I know it will be black mostly, but I don't know what it will look like for real. A few days ago, I dreamt of us being here. We even talked about eloping to Las Vegas to get married. This is how much I love you."

Cottonmouth replied, "Daphne, do you really want to marry me?" Daphne said, "We'll see how we do as a couple. So, for now stud, let's get fucked." Daphne cracked the whip at Cottonmouth but did not hit him. She said, "You will do as I say. I want you to please me. If I'm not satisfied, you will have to pay the penalty." Cottonmouth replied, "I'll do my best to please you Daphne." Daphne said, "For now stud, call me Mistress D. I am going to enjoy this."

Daphne told Cottonmouth to kiss her thigh. Her silky-smooth skin felt good on his lips. Next she told him to feel her perky breasts. His hand felt good to her. She said, "Make my nipples hard stud." As he rubbed her breasts, her nipples became rock hard. She cracked the whip and said, "Now stud, throw me on the bed." Cottonmouth replied, "Are you sure mistress?" Daphne said, "Do it!" Cottonmouth outweighed Daphne by one hundred pounds. But it didn't affect her. He threw her but softly on the bed.

Daphne said, "Look stud, champagne, fresh strawberries and chocolate. Mom thought of everything." Cottonmouth grabbed the bottle and looked at the label. He said, "This is fine, it's non-alcoholic. I'm sure the real stuff will be given out tonight." Daphne said, "Yes I agree, I certainly don't want to be drunk before tonight. Go ahead, open it."

Cottonmouth opened the bottle, poured two glasses and replied, "To us mistress. Our new lives begins right now." They clinked the glasses and drank the champagne down. Daphne said, "As you saw, I'm wearing the skimpiest outfit I could find. I'm not wearing underwear. Do it stud, let's have some raunchy sex."

Daphne suggested that Cottonmouth to get her pussy wet and at the same time, she got his dick hard with a hand job. Daphne said, "Let's begin by doing it "69" style. You can eat my pussy as I will give you a blowjob." Cottonmouth replied with delight, "Yes ma'am."

Daphne saw how rock-hard Cottonmouth was and started the blowjob. Cottonmouth fingered Daphne's pristine pussy and began to eat it. Daphne said, "Hmm, Cottonmouth, your dick is sooooo good in my mouth." Cottonmouth replied, "Mistress your cunt is the sweetest tasting I ever had."

They changed positions. Daphne lifted her skirt and said, "Put your dick in me. I want to feel it inside me. I don't care at this point if you get me pregnant today. I want to have your baby." Cottonmouth replied, "Anything to please you Mistress."

Cottonmouth positioned his dick and put it in Daphne's cunt. As he did the motions, Daphne moaned with delight. She never felt such elation. Cottonmouth also let out groans as he never felt a pussy so wet and so pristine. Then he climaxed, Daphne felt his cum go right inside her. She continued to moan with joy and elation. She said, "Oh, Cottonmouth, that was the best sex I ever had." Cottonmouth replied, "I also feel that way too. You are so hot and sexy as hell."

Daphne grabbed some strawberries, dipped them in chocolate and began to feed Cottonmouth. As he ate them he said, "Food always taste better after sex." Cottonmouth also fed Daphne and she replied, "I agree, these are the best strawberries I ever had." Cottonmouth poured out more champagne and as they drank, Daphne said, "Cottonmouth, do it to me again. I want this moment to last forever. Get me pregnant, I don't give a fuck."

Cottonmouth continued to please Daphne by granting her this wish. She continued, "I want to be a biker babe. I want to dress sexy, have orgies, and be a true Style Slut." Daphne got Cottonmouth's dick hard again. Cottonmouth got Daphne's pussy wet again. She got on top of him as she did the thrusting. She screamed with pleasure, she said, "YES! YES! YES! IMPREGNANTE ME STUD!"

The thrusting and screaming continued until she climaxed all over him. Cottonmouth took a taste of her cum and replied, "This is sooooo good! You taste so sweet." Daphne also tasted Cottonmouth's cum and said, "You are so bad that it's good. Your cum is sooooo good. Got a cigarette?" Cottonmouth took out a pack from his jacket and replied, "Yes I do." Cottonmouth took out two cigarettes, lit them, handed one to Daphne and continued, "Anything to please you mistress."

Cottonmouth poured more champagne and asked, "Hungry for lunch my mistress?" Daphne answered, "I'm hungry for you. Your cum is my food." Cottonmouth said, "Let's eat real food first before we do it again." Daphne asked, "You want to do it a third time stud?" Cottonmouth answered, "I wouldn't be a badass biker if my supply of cum ever ran out. We can keep this up until we have to go back." Daphne said while catching her breath, "For your handsome face and your badass ways, I will follow you anywhere. Okay let's have lunch."

Cottonmouth got on the phone to Victoria's Café and ordered two double cheeseburgers with the works, two orders of large fries and two large chocolate shakes. Fifteen minutes later, an alert was sounded that the food was ready. Daphne got up and took the order from the delivery person. She paid him along with a tip. She opened up the bags, placed the food on the bed and they began to eat.

Daphne asked, "Have you ever dipped a fry in a shake? It's really good." Cottonmouth was doing just that and answered, "All the time baby, all the time." When they were done eating, it was still early. Daphne said, "That was a good lunch, but I'm still not pleased." She cracked the whip and continued, "I'm satisfied with food, champagne, and cigarettes but I'm still not satisfied sexually. I'm ready to do it again."

Cottonmouth replied, "One quick question, when we are in LA and attending school, will we keep this up? I mean what if we can't share a dorm?" Daphne said, "If we can't, we'll find a way. The Skull King was right about me stud, I will be the best Fashion Girl I can be. But at the same time, I want to be a slutty, nasty whore of a bitch. After all I am dating a bad boy." Let's do it again."

This scenario proves that Daphne Bates may become the next Fashion Girl, but she won't be as prim and proper as her mother or grandmother was. But it's a different time and place. So, Cottonmouth had to obey to his girlfriend's demand by having sex for the third straight time. Ten minutes later, Daphne said in a low tone of voice, "Now I'm satisfied stud. Let's head back to the mansion. I'd like to know how Sarah and Bonecrusher did. I hope she banged him good."

Out of breath, Cottonmouth replied with concern in his voice, "D-D-Daphne, are you going to be like this? I'm glad we had this time together but you're a wild little bitch." Daphne turned to her prey and said, "Stud, in a few hours, my friends and I will become the next generation of Style Chicks. As I said earlier, Fashion Girl stands for something, but I'm young and I want to be wild. Remember I'm going for the femme fatale route. But I admit something, in this inner sanctum my mother calls The Den of Sin, this place can really give you an attitude adjustment. Let's clean up and go."

When they got back into the elevator, Daphne stopped it and French kissed Cottonmouth. When she finished she said, "Thank you

Cottonmouth for spending the afternoon with me. Tonight's going to be a blast." Cottonmouth was still out of breath and replied, "You're welcome Skull Princess. Remember what I said about us bikers having unlimited sperm? I was wrong I'm all tapped out. Honey, you give the best sex I ever had."

Daphne restarted the elevator and when they got out she said, "You're the best lover I ever had too. If we did conceive down there, I don't regret it. I love you." When they headed back to Colognia, Daphne held Cottonmouth in her arms extra tight. She also whispered in his ear about how they were going to spend time after the presentation. They got back before the three o'clock deadline.

When they walked in, Sarah and Bonecrusher approached them. Sarah asked, "Hey Daphne, you look happy. How did it go?" Daphne answered, "It went great. Cottonmouth satisfied me in every way. Bonecrusher looked at Cottonmouth and asked, "Dude you look like I feel. Daphne must be wild in the sack. Am I right?" Cottonmouth answered, "If you feel like I look, Sarah must be equally wild too."

Cottonmouth and Bonecrusher left the scene both walking kind of funny. I'll let you leave this to your imagination. Daphne and Sarah both laughed at this. Daphne said, "They may look badass, they might act badass, but look at them now, a pair of cupcakes." Sarah replied, "Yeah we are more of a badass then they are."

Sephora came up to them and said, "Okay ladies, the time has come for you to prepare for the biggest night of your lives. As you see, the preparations for tonight is being done in secret which is why the blinds are over the backyard windows. Except for me, the others won't disturb you. I instructed the others to be in their rooms and to get dressed. I'll be here if any of you need us. So as for both of you, you need to shower. I know the scent of sex better than any of us."

Daphne replied, "Aunt Cindy, mom gave me the okay to spend the day with Cottonmouth in the Den of Sin. He's everything I imagined him to be." Sephora said, "I am happy for you Daphne but remember, you are going to be the next Fashion Girl not the next flavor of the month. All I can say is I hope you didn't get pregnant today. That will happen in due time honey. You have your whole life ahead of you. Now go get ready. You and Sarah are already behind."

As they went upstairs, Daphne mumbled to herself, *"I hope you didn't get pregnant today. You have your whole life ahead of you. Really Aunt Cindy? You didn't need permission to have five babies all at once. Mom didn't need my permission to get knocked up by the Skull King. Yes I will get ready. I hope you'll be ready to rock tonight Aunt Cindy."*

Everyone was instructed once dressed to wait in the gymnasium where they would come out to the backyard by the back entrance. Once everyone was dressed and waiting for their big moment, Daphne was the last to be seen. She said, "Ladies, you look fantastic. I like these new costumes. I like mine as well." Sarah replied, "Honey, you'll rock as the new Fashion Girl. But there's something I want to say that we all are thinking."

"No matter how long we've known you, we've known that for two thirds of your life, you knew tonight would happen. We are proud to call you our leader Daphne and we are all willing to lay down our lives for you. We were known as The Style Chicks in school, now we will be Style Chicks for real. Style Chicks for one, Style Chicks for all, Style Chicks forever!"

At that moment, everyone put their hands in together and raised them over their heads. Sephora saw this and said, "That was a great speech Sarah. And I'm glad all of you feel that way about your leader. Can I take a picture of all of you having your hands together like you just did?" Daphne replied, "Sure Aunt Cindy, this is a night we will all remember. Go ahead."

After Sephora took the picture, she continued, "For now ladies, relax. Your big moment will happen sooner than you think." As Sephora went to the backyard, three rows of folding chairs lined the scene. A stage was constructed where everyone would be presented. A podium also was put onstage. The media one by one arrived to set up their equipment. Dignitaries began to file in and took their seats. The kitchen was filled with a variety of smells as Victoria's restaurant staff was preparing a feast fit for royalty. Madame D and She-Ra were going over their notes for the event. Everything was running smoothly on all cylinders.

The four English language stations and two Spanish stations pre-empted their newscasts to show the event live on television. Then right at six o'clock, the festivities began. Since She-Ra was presiding over this event, she stepped up to the podium and said...

"Good evening ladies and gentlemen. Forty-six years ago, I saw the true potential of Daphne Blake the famous mystery solver that she could do more than chase criminals all over the world dressed like ghosts and monsters. She could fight crime in a different way. And after she saved my life, I gave her that chance to become a true superheroine. Her husband said to her that in her new outfit, she looked more of a fashion girl than ever before. She loved the name and she decided to use it. And her widower Fred Jones is here tonight as he will take part in tonight's event. Fred, please stand up."

As Fred stood up, everyone gave him a round of applause. She-Ra continued, "Before we continue, I would like for everyone to observe a moment of silence to honor the members of the Style Chicks who couldn't be here tonight including the original Fashion Girl." As this happened, the soon to be former Style Chicks and the three surviving first generation of Junior Style Chicks shed tears for their fallen counterparts. When the moment of silence was over, She-Ra continued speaking.

She said, "Tonight's event is unlike any presentation ceremony we've ever done as for you will all witness history in the making as we will present the third generation of Style Chicks as Daphne's granddaughter will become the next Fashion Girl along with friends of hers who've she's known since elementary school."

"Before we continue, I would like to acknowledge special guests with us tonight. First the surviving original Style Chicks, the original Tiffany Brenda Adams Green. The original Penney Dillard Sister Chrissie James. The original Zara who tonight will mark her retirement from the sea Maria Sanchez and the original Sephora, prima donna of the Metropolitan Opera in New York, Michelle Norton."

The audience applauded for them as She-Ra continued, "We also have with us tonight three of the greatest superheroes of all-time from the Justice League, Superman, Batman and Wonder Woman." After the audience applauded for them, She-Ra continued, "We also welcome members of the press and media covering tonight's event along with the mayor of Colognia the honorable Olivia Upton and current police chief Reggie Stanton." After the audience applauded, it was Madame D's turn to say a few words.

When Madame D stepped up to the podium to speak, she gave everyone in the audience the ultimate bombshell. She said, "Ladies and gentlemen before I introduce my daughter as the next Fashion Girl, I have a confession to make. You heard ten years ago that the previous Fashion Girl died at the hospital after she gave birth. The truth is that it was all a rouse. You see ladies and gentlemen; my daughter and her twin brother was growing up at the time and I was missing it by posing for magazines and doing fashion shows."

"When a rogue DCF agent tried to take them away from me because I wasn't there for them, it made me think. And the more fashion shows and modeling shoots I did, the more I became disenchanted. So, when I became pregnant with my second set of twins, I made a conscious decision to put Fashion Girl to rest until my eldest daughter took my place. I hope you'll understand why I did this. But I didn't give up crime fighting, this is who I really am. And I'm not ashamed of it. Now I will soon give birth again and I will be there for them too. Tiffany took over for me and she did the best job she could under the circumstances. I am sorry to have deceived you."

No one in the audience booed Madame D, but they were more stunned than anything. After a few moments of silence, the crowd began to applaud her for coming up with this information and confession. They realized that only the persona of Fashion Girl was dead but not the woman who portrayed her.

Next Penney Dillard stepped up to the podium and said, "Before we present the next generation of Style Chicks, we would like to present to you the next generation of Junior Style Chicks and Phat Kats. Everyone please come out to be presented."

At that moment, four young girls and three teenage boys in their new costumes approached the stage and podium. Penney continued, "Here are the second generation of Junior Style Chicks and Phat Kats. The girls will continue their education until they're old enough to begin their training in their new roles. As for the Phat Kats, after tonight, they will take over for their older counterparts in their new roles. Please give a round of applause for them."

After the crowd applauded, Penney continued, "For twenty years, the Cosmo Chicks have been powerful and faithful allies of ours. However, they live in a space station orbiting the earth because they couldn't breathe in our atmosphere. So, I finally figured out how to change this and as my next to last act as a Style Chick, I will make them be able to breathe our air and be able to live on earth as well as protect it. Ladies, please come up here."

One by one Cover Girl, Revlon, Maybelline and L'Oréal came up on stage. Penney continued, "Now then ladies, you will soon be able to breathe our air and never have to wear those helmets ever again." Penney concentrated with all her might as a ray of light extended from her hands onto the Cosmo Chicks. When the light stopped, Penney said, "Now ladies, remove your helmets." When they did, something else happened. Their grayish tint to their skin was gone. Their pink hair turned brunette, and their pink eyes became blue.

Cover Girl said, "We can breathe your air finally! We can live here on earth! Thank you so much Penney! We will never forget this!" The crowd rose to their feet to give the Cosmo Chicks a standing ovation as they left the stage. She-Ra took over the podium and said, "Now ladies and gentlemen. Distinguished guests, members of the press and media, and other dignitaries the moment you've been waiting for. Escorted by the men in their lives and one by one, we will now introduce to all of you the third generation of Style Chicks. First escorted by her father, the new Belle K."

The new Belle K was wearing the outfit Sephora gave her. She held her head up high and proudly walked to the stage with her arm in her father's. She-Ra continued, "Next escorted by her father, the new Sephora." The new Sephora's outfit was also in the same design as the soon to be previous Sephora's outfit but a little shorter and the boots a little taller. She too had her head held high and walked proudly with her father's arm in hers.

She-Ra continued, "Next escorted by her father, the new Macy Sears." Since the new Macy is Japanese, she came out of the gym, bowed to her father, took his arm and proceeded to the stage. Her outfit was that of a modern-day Geisha girl but without the traditional makeup with a short skirt and knee-high boots. She looked a little nervous, but she too came to the stage with her head held high.

She-Ra continued, "Next escorted by her brother, the new Godiva." Godiva's new outfit was totally different than her soon to be predecessor's as it paid tribute to her African roots with a quiver of arrows behind her and her bow in her other hand. Walking proudly to the stage to join the others.

She-Ra continued, "Next escorted by her father the new Masked Mistress of the Seven Seas Zara." Indira's version of Zara's outfit continued the tradition of looking like a modern-day pirate and wearing a mask over her eyes. Her father was beaming with pride. He kissed his daughter's hand, and she joined the others onstage.

She-Ra next said, "And now escorted by her uncle, the new Victoria." The new Victoria's costume was still red, white and blue but without the stars and stripes. The crowd seemed pleased with the new design. Victoria joined the others onstage hugging the others.

She-Ra continued, "And now please welcome escorted by her father the new Streetwalker for Justice, the new Penney Dillard." The new Penney's outfit continued the tradition of looking like a hooker's outfit but instead of a green tiger striped dress, the dress was a black tiger striped dress with silver stripes and a green cape and shorter green boots and black gloves. Her father wasn't crazy about her daughter dressed like a hooker, but he understood that it's how Penney Dillard is expected to look. The new Penney also hugged her friends onstage.

She-Ra continued, "Now escorted by her boyfriend, the new Queen of Bling, the new Tiffany." Sarah's new costume continued the tradition of Tiffany being the only Style Chick not to wear a dress. The colors of red and gold were still there but it also followed the tradition first brought on by the original Tiffany as her costume was gold with red racing stripes, red boots and a red diamond on her chest. Unlike the other escorts, Bonecrusher gave Sarah a kiss on the lips as he let her come up onstage.

Before She-Ra could continue, a group of men began blowing a fanfare on trumpets to signal the big moment had finally arrived. She-Ra said, "Now for the moment you've been waiting for, first escorted by her paternal grandfather Harold Bates Sr., her maternal grandfather Fred Jones Sr., her uncle Fred Jones Jr., her stepfather Dean Simpson and her boyfriend may I present to all of you the third woman to be called Fashion Girl!"

As described, each man in Daphne's life took turns escorting her to the stage. As Daphne figured, her new outfit was black with purple and green stripes all along the borders of the dress with purple and green stripes going down the center of her boots. She also wore a sinister looking black cape with purple and green stripes going down the borders but what did change was the logo. The logo now features the hex shaped FG in black surrounded by a red and gold border.

Harold said, "I am honored to be here with you tonight Daphne, your dad would be so proud of you." As he gave Daphne to Fred Sr., he said, "I also am honored Daphne. Your grandma Daphne is looking down from heaven right now smiling from ear to ear." Next Fred Jr. took her arm and said, "You've always been my favorite niece. Look at your mother, her heart is about to come out of her chest, she's so proud and happy for you."

As Dean took over he said, "Daphne even though I'm not your biological father, you're the best thing to have happened to me in my life. I love you as if I was your biological father." Daphne held herself close to him and replied, "I love you too Dean. Biological or not." Dean kissed Daphne's hand before handing her to Cottonmouth. Dean said, "Son, watch out for her and be there for her no matter what." Cottonmouth replied, "She'll be in good hands sir I promise."

As they approached the stage, Cottonmouth said, "If I hadn't seen this with my own eyes I wouldn't believe it. All this for you. It's incredible." Daphne replied, "Now I understand why mom was so adamant about this. She wasn't prepared to be Fashion Girl when she was eighteen, so I now see why she did all this for me. I am now prepared for almost anything." Cottonmouth also kissed Daphne on the lips before he let her come onstage. The others hugged her in gratitude and pride and the crowd gave Daphne a standing ovation. She-Ra said, "And there they are, the next generation of Style Chicks!" Daphne was to give a statement for the media and press. She asked the audience to retake their seats.

She said, "Thank you ladies and gentlemen. When I was told that this would be the best night of not just my life but the lives of my friends, we now see why. This is definitely a night none of us will soon forget. I give you my promise that from this moment forward, we will continue the traditions my grandmother Daphne Blake and the original Style Chicks as well as my mother's group of Style Chicks have done for over forty years."

"When I've heard stories about my grandmother's adventures as Fashion Girl from my grandpa Fred, I always had a thought that maybe he was simply telling me a story to entertain me growing up. Plus, the stories my mom told me when I was younger about her adventures as Fashion Girl, I knew they were true because I witnessed them either first hand or what I saw on television."

"Even though I will be going to attend college at UCLA in a few days, rest assured that my friends will assist the police and other agencies here in town and I understand that if I'm needed, I will answer the call and will come back. When my mom turned eighteen, she too was about to go to college at UCLA until she was approached by Brenda Adams Green, Chrissie James and Maria Sanchez and was given one of my grandma's costumes and The Sword of Style. She had no idea of the legacy that was waiting for her."

"However, my mom little by little began to take on her role with help from journals my grandma kept before her untimely death. Now that I'm the new Fashion Girl and my friends are the new Style Chicks, my mother was diligent that we prepared, trained, and practiced for our new roles without any surprises. My mother did so much for the Style Chicks by having more and different Style Chicks onboard, the Phat Kats and Cosmo Chicks joining them and the Archangels whoever they happen to be. And making peace with the sister of my grandma's arch enemy."

"And as soon as the soon to be former Penney Dillard and Style Chicks transfers their powers to us, our duty will begin at that point. I wish to thank you all for being here with us tonight. Please stay after the power transfer for the biggest, sickest party you've ever seen. Okay Penney, we are ready now for the power transfer."

Penney replied, "Thank you... Boss. I had to say that once more. Now then ladies, join hands while I begin to concentrate. A few moments later, Penney continued, "I Penney Dillard of the Style Chicks and as my last act as a Style Chick hereby grant the powers and abilities to the new generation of Style Chicks."

Penney raised her conversion staff high over her head various colors of bright light shined on the new Style Chicks for several moments. When the lights were gone. Penney said, "The transfer is complete. You all now have what we had. Our powers and abilities. To prove this, I will ask the new Penney Dillard to fly. If she can do this, all of you will now have your own set of powers."

The new Penney jumped up and began to hover above the stage. Then she began to fly around the mansion's perimeter. She landed back onstage with a smile on her face shouting, "I did it! I can fly! The new Style Chicks are here!" After a round of thunderous applause, She-Ra retook the podium and said, "Ladies and gentlemen, the ceremony portion of this evening's events are over. We invite you as the new Fashion Girl said to join them for the biggest, sickest party you've ever seen. And now, "LET'S PARTY!""

As music began to play and the audience began to mingle around the area along with trays of food to be served and champagne corks popping and overflowing, the new Fashion Girl said, "Mom, She-Ra, thank you for this evening. We will never forget it." She-Ra replied, "You're welcome Daphne er um I mean Fashion Girl. And we wish you all the best." Fashion Girl said, "Now for my first act as Fashion Girl, I want to take a picture of the now previous Style Chicks to always remember this night after tonight." Madame D replied, "Anything for you Fashion Girl." Fashion Girl said, "Thank you for everything mom er um I mean Madame D."

After the picture was taken, Fashion Girl asked Cindy, "Aunt Cindy, now that Paula is the new Sephora, can she do what you used to? Bring back the dead?" Cindy answered, "Of course. Now that your friends are the new Style Chicks, they can do what we used to, why do you ask?"

Fashion Girl said, "I want to talk with dad. You've never brought him back not once since he died." Cindy replied, "Your mom, my mom and me weren't too happy with him before he died. He deserted your mom, he had an affair, abandoned you and Harry and went crazy. I was afraid that if I brought him back from the dead, he could wreak havoc once again."

Fashion Girl said, "Now that I'm grown up and the new Fashion Girl, I don't think he'll do that." Cindy replied, "Alright honey, if you're heart is set on speaking with him, I'll go with you, and we'll ask Harry if he wants to join us." Fashion Girl kissed Cindy on the cheek and said, "Thank you Aunt Cindy, you're the best." Cindy replied, "Anything for my favorite niece. Now let's join the party. We'll conjure up your father tomorrow night."

As the evening progressed, both the new Fashion Girl and the new Glamour Boy were mingling with the guests especially the dignitaries in attendance. But it was Jackie Newman who had to speak with Madame D since she was part of the deception Madame D made when she gave birth to her second set of twins. She asked, "Madame D, why did you tell everyone about what happened when your second set of twins were born? This could mean my job."

Madame D answered, "Jackie, before tonight's presentation, I spoke with your boss at channel 8. I explained everything to him, and he understood. You are in no danger of losing your job." Jackie said, "I was afraid it would ruin my credibility as a reporter and Fashion Girl as a superheroine."

Madame D replied, "Jackie, the only credibility it might have ruined is my own. Can't people understand that sometimes we have to sacrifice for our families? My kids were growing up. I wasn't there for them after my first husband was killed. Remember that bogus DCF agent tried to take them away from me. I was even convinced at one point that maybe I only cared about was my career both as a model and a superheroine. Look Jackie, everything is okay as far as your job is concerned. With your boss' approval, you will do a tour of Aurora Gardens with me to let the viewers here see what I've been doing for the last ten years."

Jackie said, "Okay Madame D I understand. I do have an interview with your daughter for the 11 o'clock news not to mention give her my friend's contact in Los Angeles. I'll see you later."

When 11 o'clock came, all four news stations showed the presentation of the new Style Chicks and her allies and here is how each station opened their newscast that night. First from KTVJ the CBS affiliate...

"Tonight, on CBS5 news, it's official, the new Fashion Girl is presented before top local dignitaries, other superheroes and the governor at the Mystique Boutique for a live report."

From KCCA the NBC affiliate that Jackie Newman works for...

"Live from KCCA NBC8 in Colognia. Tonight, we were at the Mystique Boutique as the changing of the guard happened as the new Fashion Girl is revealed. Our own Jackie Newman will interview the new Fashion Girl live and exclusively in a few moments."

From KLVN the ABC affiliate...

"Right now, on ABC11 news at 11. The Mystique Boutique was the place to be tonight as the new Fashion Girl and the new Style Chicks were presented before a packed backyard of other heroes and dignitaries. We're there live with a report."

And from KFXT the FOX affiliate...

"Coming to you from KFXT Fox in Colognia. It's a party at the Mystique Boutique as the third generation of Style Chicks and their leader the new Fashion Girl, we will go live to the Mystique Boutique to tell you about all of the festivities."

As promised, the new Fashion Girl was to give a live interview with Jackie Newman. But she insisted that all the reporters be on hand to hear what she had to say. She said, "As you heard me say in the mansion, my friends and I will do our very best to keep this city safe and at the same time to do what we need to do to ensure that. Now then everyone, there's still a party going on, enjoy yourselves."

After Fashion Girl finished her statement, Cindy was there and said, "Aunt Cindy, I changed my mind about seeing dad. I can't wait any longer, I want to see him right now." Cindy replied, "Are you sure of this?" Fashion Girl said, "Yes. Get Paula and we'll go to the cemetery to conjure him up."

After Cindy got Paula the new Sephora, they headed to the cemetery for the new Fashion Girl to see her departed father. But was he willing to see her was the question.

CHAPTER 17

When they arrived at the cemetery, the eerily quiet and a moonless night was all the new Sephora needed to conjure up the dead. She asked, "Cindy, this is one thing you didn't teach me. How do I raise the dead and how long will they last?" Cindy answered, "It's okay Paula now you will learn. All you have to do is ask who's here with you and say that you wish to bring back to life the name of the person who you're trying to conjure up."

But before this happened, Madame D got word of what the new Fashion Girl wanted to do. She approached her and asked, "Just what the hell are you doing?" The new Fashion Girl answered, "I wanted to talk with dad. I've never spoken to him since he died." Madame D said, "He abandoned us, he went with a two-timing floozy and got killed in a building collapse. Do you really think he wants to have anything to do with us?"

Cindy replied angrily, "Daphne you should be ashamed of yourself. I was there when he died too. He brushed me off as well. But I think I understand why the new Fashion Girl wants to do this. She misses him and I think she's entitled to talk with him." The new Fashion Girl said, "That's all I wanted to do mom. To talk with him and tell him how I feel about him. I'm sorry if this is a sore spot for you, but it needs to be done."

Madame D replied, "Okay I'll allow it, but I warn you Fashion Girl, if he says something or does something wrong, I'll kill him again." The new Sephora asked everyone to hold hands and said, "I Sephora of the Style Chicks hereby ask for..." She stopped and asked, "Cindy what's his first name?" Cindy answered, "His first name was Greg."

Then Sephora continued, "Greg Bates to materialize before me." Just then a foggy mist formed and then the figure of Greg Bates stood before them. He looked solid and not ectoplasmic and said, "Where am I? What am I doing here?" Fashion Girl came up to him and said, "Daddy, it's me Daphne." He looked at her and replied, "Oh, really, did you bring me back from the dead to kick my ass. And why did you call me daddy?"

Fashion Girl said, "No daddy it's me your daughter Daphne all grown up." Greg looked more closely and realized that it was his daughter talking to him and not his ex-wife. He replied, "Sweetie! I don't believe it! You are all grown up! This is a surprise, but again why am I back from the dead?"

Fashion Girl said, "I asked Sephora to bring you back from the dead so I can talk with you. I haven't done so since you died." Greg replied, "Sephora you said? Is Cindy here too?" Cindy said, "I'm here Greg only I'm not Sephora anymore. The reason why Daphne wanted to talk with you was because she's now the new Fashion Girl. This is Paula Ormand the new Sephora. You see Greg, Daphne turned eighteen recently and as you know she was destined to take her mother's place as the new Fashion Girl."

Greg replied, "I remember now. When your mother held you in her arms after you were born, I remember her saying that you would take her place someday. Speaking of her, how is she? What's she's doing now?"

Madame D interrupted him and replied, "I'm right here Greg. I'm sorry to say that you're a sorry sight for sore eyes." Greg said, "I figured your still mad at me at what happened. I know it might not make a difference now, but I'm so sorry for that." Madame D replied, "Your mom told Cindy and me both why you did what you did. How you lost your first sister and why. But it doesn't excuse what you did. I can't accept your apology."

Greg said, "I understand Daphne. I know I put you, mom, Cindy, Johnny and my dad through a lot at that time. Just tell me one thing, why do you look like a biker chick?" Madame D replied, "I'm not Daphne anymore, call me Madame D and yes I am part of a biker gang and their leader."

Greg said, "You look so different. You got old and fat and dressed in black leather." Madame D replied, "I'm old because I'm forty-two and will be forty-three in a couple of weeks. As for my being fat, I'm pregnant with triplets by the Skull King. I'm also known as the Skull Queen. I also became a dominatrix. I did this because unlike you I wanted to be there for Daphne and Harry. I did get married a second time and had another set of twins and gave up being Fashion Girl as a result."

Greg asked, "Where's Harry? Why isn't he here?" Fashion Girl answered, "He's back at the mansion still enjoying the party we are having to celebrate the new Style Chicks. I didn't tell him that I would be here. I assure you that he misses you as much as I have. I wanted to have this discussion first."

Greg said, "Daphne you are my daughter and even though I did your mom dirty like I did, nothing ever changed the way I feel about you. I love you very much." Fashion Girl gave Greg a big hug and replied, "I love you too daddy. I just wished you could take back all that happened, but I see mom is still very bitter about what happened between you two. You might still be with us instead of being in a box six feet under."

Greg said with a sad voice, "I know princess, being in the ground for the last fifteen years I've had time to think about it and I've regretted it ever since I was buried in a ton of bricks." Madame D replied, "Your mom, Cindy and I consoled each other after that warehouse collapsed but the tears I shed that day were tears of hate. I hate you with every fiber in my body. You deserve what happened to you, you sorry son of a bitch."

Fashion Girl said in an angry tone of voice, "Mom that's enough! I'm sure Grandma Sandy and Aunt Cindy weren't too pleased either! But he's still their family and you need to show some respect for the dead! You once loved this man, he was crazy about you, you married him, and you had me and Harry as a result! Doesn't any of that mean anything to you?!"

Madame D replied in an equally angry tone of voice, "Yes Daphne he did meant something to me! When I first met him, he said that he was my biggest fan! Your Grandpa Harry told me that he had posters of me hanging on his bedroom walls! We had lunch together that day and we did hit it off I admit! That New Year's Eve, I admitted to Sandy that I was falling in love with him!"

"A year later, we got married! I got pregnant on our wedding night! Then I had you and Harry, that I don't regret. Because I dressed up to stop a sexual predator, your dad lost his fucking mind! I kicked him out of the mansion and then he shacked up with the wife of that sorry excuse of a man! He committed adultery!!! I'm sorry Daphne I can't forgive him! As I said earlier, that if he wasn't already dead, I would've killed him myself! If you will excuse me, I need air!"

Fashion Girl turned to Greg and said, "I'm sorry daddy that you heard that." Greg replied, "Daphne your mom's right, everything she said was true. I met her, I fell in love with her, I married her, and we had you. She has every right to be angry." Fashion Girl said, "I think I better go as well. But no matter what mom said, I'm glad I had this talk with you." Greg replied, "In spite of it all princess I'm glad too. You'll do great things now that you are the new Fashion Girl and I wish you the very best of luck."

At that moment, Greg disappeared in a cloud of fog and returned to the earth. Cindy asked, "Daphne are you okay?" Fashion Girl answered, "Yes and no. I am glad to see daddy again, I just wished mom would lighten up on the issue." Cindy said, "It is a sore spot for her. I wasn't too happy with him either but like you said he's family and he's my brother. Grandma Sandy, Grandpa Harry, Uncle Johnny and I forgave him in our own ways. C'mon honey, let's return home and finish up the party."

Fashion Girl said, "I'm ready to go but I kind of lost the mood to party." Cindy replied, "I understand but you had to do what you felt was right." The new Sephora who had been quiet said, "Daphne, I agree with both your mom and aunt. I couldn't imagine what that could have been like for your family. Look anytime you want to speak with him again and as long as I now have the power to conjure the dead, I'll do it. Just let me know."

Fashion Girl hugged Sephora and replied with tears going down her face, "Thank you Paula, it's no wonder why you're my best friend. Sephora hugged Fashion Girl back and said, "That's what friends are for. Let's go back to the mansion."

By the time they returned back to the mansion, Madame D ran up the stairs and slammed her bedroom door as hard as she could as she was still fuming over the conversation she had with her ex-husband. Fashion Girl also went to her bedroom, but she didn't slam the door shut. When Cindy and Sephora went back to the backyard, the party was over, and Victoria's Bistro's staff began to clean up.

The new Tiffany asked, "Paula, Queen Serpentina, what happened? Where's Fashion Girl and Madame D?" Cindy answered, "Fashion Girl went to see her father at the cemetery as did Madame D, Paula and I. It didn't go over well for Madame D, but Fashion Girl lost the mood to continue the party. It was a bittersweet reunion." Tiffany said, "Some of the dignitaries wanted to speak with her. I didn't have an answer to give. But I was told that they will speak with her in the next day or two." As you can imagine, neither Madame D nor Fashion Girl slept that night.

Fashion Girl was tossing and turning in bed and said to herself, *"Did I do the right thing by going to the cemetery to talk with daddy? I had no idea what happened between him and mom. I also had no idea that mom could be that bitter or was capable of being bitter towards anyone. Will what I did have some kind of repercussion? Or will mom forget about it? I don't know. I just don't know."*

Put yourself in both Madame D and Fashion Girl's place, what would you have done in a similar situation?

CHAPTER 18

At the same time, Madame D also couldn't sleep for she was furious at her daughter for summoning her father to speak with him. She said to herself, *"The nerve of that little bitch! He was never there for her or Harry, he didn't deserve to know how she's doing! Okay, maybe Cindy and Sandy forgave him, but I haven't! I kept it bottled up inside me all these years! Now I'm going to make my daughter who I gave life to, who've I've supported both in comfort, health and finance, will pay for this act of treason! So, Satan wanted her to become evil did he? Well, my dear daughter, I gave you what you need to become Fashion Girl, but I will make the deal with the devil, and I won't be alone about it!"*

When dawn arrived, Fashion Girl and her brother now the new Glamour Boy were sitting in the gazebo talking. Glamour Boy said, "That was some party last night wasn't it sis? I mean the festivities, the ceremony, the food and the people who showed up. Where did you go after eleven?! Everyone was looking for you!"

Fashion Girl replied, "Cool it bro, I got an earful from mom last night! I went to the cemetery to speak with dad, that's where I went. Aunt Cindy, Mom and the new Sephora went with me. As you know that anyone with Sephora's abilities she can literally raise the dead."

"Let me ask you something, do you remember what mom told us why dad isn't around anymore?" Glamour Boy said, "Sure I remember.

She told us that he's in a place where it's always sunny and happy and no one is sad." Fashion Girl replied, "Harry, we were only four when mom told us that. It was a nice way of saying that he was dead in a way a young mind could understand. Don't you remember that Grandma Sandy told us what really happened to him?"

Glamour Boy said, "Yes I remember her telling us how he lost his mind when mom got gussied up to lure and stop that sexual predator. How he lost his sister in a car accident caused by an actress dressed formally." Fashion Girl replied, "Yes and do you remember how he lost his mind, stormed out of here and shacked up with that scumbag's wife?"

Glamour Boy said, "I remember that too, but I didn't want to put it so cruelly. Yes sis, I do vaguely remember that. So, you left the party that was pretty much in your honor to go and conjure him up and speak with him. Daphne your my older sister and I love you very much, but I agree with mom on this one. It was one thing that he ran out on mom like he did, but he also forgot about us, why? What did we do to him that would have made him do that?"

Fashion Girl replied in anger, "Bro, the last thing he told mom before he died was to tell us that he loved us you ungrateful jerk! Look when Grandma Sandy told us what really happened to him, yes, I also was upset! But I also realized that no matter who he was or what he did, he was our father, and he did love us very much. He made a terrible mistake and paid the ultimate price for it, but now that I'm Fashion Girl and you're Glamour Boy, we need to put any animosity aside and focus on our new roles! I didn't realize how upset it would make mom. I honestly don't know why she tagged along. But she did say how she felt at him and now she's mad at me."

"Harry, becoming the new Fashion Girl was supposed to be a time for not only a changing of the guard but to celebrate a new chapter in my life. And so far, chapter one isn't going well."

Glamour Boy asked, "Sis, can I talk to mom on your behalf? What you said makes perfect sense." Fashion Girl answered, Sure Harry. If you think it would calm her down a bit, do it to it." Glamour Boy asked, "Daphne, do you think mom also could be overreacting because she's pregnant?" Fashion Girl answered, "I suppose. Most women when pregnant can become irritable, moody and yes downright mad at times. But I think even if she weren't pregnant, I believe she'd be just as mad as she is now."

Glamour Boy got up to go back inside the mansion but before he did he said, "Sis, I've seen how you are when you have PMS, you can be a bit bitchy yourself. See you later."

Fashion Girl remained where she was to continue to think and keep her distance. While this was going on outside the mansion, inside everyone gathered in the dining room for breakfast. Madame D came downstairs with a basket of material. She said, "Good morning everyone. If you're wondering why your leader left the party last night after she gave an on-camera interview was because she went to the cemetery and had the new Sephora conjure up the spirit of her late father. A man I despise very, very much."

The new Sephora got up and replied, "Now just a minute Madame D, Queen Serpentina was okay with Daphne doing this. If you want to be mad at her go ahead! I've known some of my classmates who grew up without a father for whatever the reason was. They would've given anything to have the chance Daphne had to speak with him! I commend her for what she did!"

Madame D said with an angry tone of voice, "You are out of line young lady! Who the hell do you think you are talking to me like that?" The new Sephora replied with an equally angry tone, "I'm the new Sephora, her best friend and now she's our leader! That's who I think I am! And we'll back her up no matter what!"

Madame D got up out of her chair and asked, "Is that a challenge? You forget I used to be Fashion Girl. I can still kick your sorry ass!" The new Sephora answered, "No, it's not a challenge, it's a promise! A promise we all made to your daughter that we are all in her corner and are willing to lay down our lives for her!" Madame D approached the new Sephora to try to slap her face. But she stopped the attack by grabbing her wrist.

Sephora was actually hurting Madame D's wrist and continued, "Daphne is right about you. You've become soft. You're old, no longer beautiful, and pregnant past forty. You thought you were doing right about giving up being Fashion Girl. But look at you now, go ahead and take a good, long look in the mirror. See what you've become! A sorry sack of shit! A man crazy whore! You like dick too much! It's commendable that you wanted to be there for your eldest kids when they were growing up, but you didn't have to do this, all of this!"

The silence in the dining room was deafening as no one added to Sephora's words. Madame D said nothing, as she stormed out of the mansion, got in her car and drove away. Serpentina noticed the basket of materials Madame D left behind. She looked inside and saw what it was. She said, "Sephora those were some very strong words. Madame D and I have been through a lot together. We became blood sisters, but I am not mad by what you said. I actually commend you for standing up to her."

Sephora replied, "Being the former Sephora yourself, I'm sure you would've done the same. You saw she was trying to attack me." Serpentina said, "I know and I'm sorry. As for this basket of materials she brought down, I saw what's inside and she was to give you all these." The basket contained blank journal books as Serpentina continued, "Both Fashion Girls kept a journal of their adventures so they could recall some of the cases they worked on while working on new ones. Use them, be descriptive because you never know how handy they can become. By the way, where is your leader?"

The new Tiffany said, "She and Glamour Boy were outside in the gazebo. He came back inside and she's still out there." Serpentina noticed that her niece had her head down on the table with her arms around it. She approached the gazebo and heard Fashion Girl crying. Serpentina sat down next to her and said, "Daphne? Honey don't cry. Please don't cry. Everything will blow over you'll see."

Fashion Girl replied, "Really Aunt Cindy? What has happened to mom? If she still wants to be mad at daddy that's fine it's her right. But this isn't right. I'm the new Fashion Girl, I should feel happy, proud and excited. All I feel is nothing but loathe and despise. Truth Aunt Cindy, has mom become a drug addict or an alcoholic? I know she's become a nymphomaniac for sure!"

Serpentina said, "Your mom does drink, she smokes cigarettes, and she loves sex but she's not a drug addict or an alcoholic. Look honey, I forgave my brother. Grandma Sandy forgave her son, but your mom was hurt the most by his betrayal. I remember that you got mad at Felix for shacking up with your high school rival right? He was your boyfriend, you dumped him and now you found Cottonmouth and you do make a lovely couple. He loves you very much."

Fashion Girl asked, "Why did mom allow us to have sex yesterday in the Den of Sin if she's so upset at me? She's ran hot and cold since my birthday." Serpentina answered, "I don't know either honey. I'm not too thrilled with her right now." Fashion Girl asked, "I heard commotion inside what happened?" Your mom and Sephora got into a fight a few minutes ago. Your mom was going to attack Sephora and she stopped it. She had some choice words for her too. Your mom left the mansion, probably going back to Aurora Gardens."

Fashion Girl asked, "What's in the basket Aunt Cindy?" Serpentina answered, "Your mom wanted to give you and the others blank journal books to record your new adventures as sort of a diary. I kept one during my time as Sephora too. But there's an envelope here with your name on it. I don't know what's inside. We'll open it together."

Fashion Girl opened the envelope and discovered an amazing surprise. She said, "Mom bought me a house? In Beverly Hills no less? Now I'm really confused." Serpentina looked at the document further and replied, "Honey, your mom didn't buy you a house in Beverly Hills, your adopted sisters did." Fashion Girl said, "What?" Serpentina replied, "Remember Daphne, they're richer than all of us former Style Chicks combined. I guess they figured since you're going to UCLA soon, they didn't want you living on campus."

Serpentina also noticed a small box at the bottom of the basket and handed it to Fashion Girl. She opened it to find two key fobs for two cars. She asked, "I got the new Glam Mobile, Cottonmouth has his motorcycle, why would we need two other vehicles?"

Serpentina answered, "I do know why. Your mom didn't care if other people knew that she and Fashion Girl were one and the same. But she wants you to keep her a secret. That's why we didn't mention your actual names at last night's ceremony." Keep the Glam Mobile in the garage along with Cottonmouth's motorcycle and keep the new vehicles out in the driveway and for your new neighbors or anyone else there will know that a new young couple is moving in the neighborhood."

Fashion Girl asked, "Are my adoptive sisters going to live there too?" Serpentina answered, "No. They bought another house two blocks away. But they've been housesitting waiting for you to arrive." Fashion Girl hugged Serpentina and said, "Thank you Aunt Cindy. Those girls are the best. I feel so much better now. I am still concerned about mom though."

Serpentina replied, "Don't worry about her, I'll have a woman to woman talk with her. Oh, Saks said that you should come to Los Angeles tomorrow. Again, they'll be waiting for you." Fashion Girl said, "I can't wait to tell Cottonmouth the great news about this." Serpentina replied, "The house is also his too. They furnished it themselves with both of you in mind." Fashion Girl said happily, "I'll call them up and thank them for their generosity!"

While Fashion Girl went to tell Cottonmouth the good news, Serpentina went back inside the mansion to address the others only to find She-Ra, Cobra and Amanda there too. Serpentina asked, "She-Ra I'm glad you haven't left yet, I need a favor from you. I hope you can help me?" She-Ra answered, "Okay Serpentina, what is it." Serpentina said, "I would like to borrow Amanda for a little while. Madame D and Fashion Girl are at odds with each other. I just comforted Fashion Girl with some great news. But I think Amanda can help me to get through to Madame D."

She-Ra agreed and let Amanda go with Serpentina to talk to Madame D. Serpentina knew where to go and drove to Aurora Gardens. Before she went to see Madame D, she said, "Amanda, there's a diner on this property. Go ahead and get something to eat or drink. Where Madame D is isn't appropriate for kids. Tell the blonde waitress that you're with me." Amanda replied, "Okay Serpentina, I'll wait for you there."

Serpentina went down to the Den of Sin and found Madame D on her bed crying. Serpentina said, "Not you too. I just came from The

Mystique Boutique where your daughter also was crying." Madame D replied, "Oh really Cindy? She should cry. She had no right to go to the cemetery to talk with her father. Seeing him made me sick and not because I'm pregnant."

Serpentina said, "Daphne, you should be ashamed of yourself! Fashion Girl had every right to see him! He is her father after all! If it makes you feel any better, Harry agrees with you that she shouldn't have seen him!" Madame D replied, "He agreed with me?" Serpentina said, "Yes he agreed with you. I gave Fashion Girl the deed to the house Saks, Bloomie and Nine West bought for her along with the fobs for two cars. She's happy now and that's how I left her."

"She-Ra and her daughter stopped by. Amanda is waiting to speak with you. She's in the diner." Madame D replied, "Is she alone? Or is her mother with her?" Serpentina said, "She's alone. Based on what Cobra told us, she can take care of herself." Madame D asked, "And she wants to speak with me? Why?"

Serpentina answered, "I think that Amanda not She-Ra can possibly reason with you." Madame D said, "Cindy I knew that She-Ra also grew up without her family too, but they aren't dead. Greg is. I am sorry if I seemed rough last night, but you and Sandy of all people knew what he did." Serpentina replied, "Daphne I know, mom knows too. But we did forgave him even though we didn't tell him so."

Madame D said, "Okay Cindy, I'll go see Amanda and I'll talk with her." Serpentina replied, "That's the spirit Daphne. I promise that you won't be disappointed but please try to keep an open mind." Madame D said, "I will, let's go see her."

When they entered Victoria's Café, Serpentina asked, "Mary Lou, where is a young girl sitting, Madame D is here to talk with her?" Mary Lou answered, "Sure hon, that cute little blonde girl? She's in the last booth on the left." When Madame D and Serpentina approached the booth, they saw Amanda finishing a chocolate milkshake.

Madame D broke the ice and said, "The shakes here are absolutely delicious. But I know you're not here to talk about milkshakes. You wanted to speak with me, what's on your mind?" Amanda replied,

"Madame D, I heard that you're upset with your daughter about her seeing her father at the cemetery. Madame D, mommy once told me that she and your mother were very good friends. That in a way she gave birth to the Style Chicks. She's not really mad at you she's just disappointed."

"When I heard mommy say that she had to hide her pregnancy from her friends and even her family at first. After I was born, Uncle Adam and my grandparents all fell in love with me, and I love them. I also saw the look on daddy's face when he first saw me. It was like his heart was going to jump out of his chest because he was so proud."

I understand now why mommy did hide her pregnancy from others. Questions would be asked; she wouldn't have known how to answer them. But now I know who my daddy is, I'm proud of him. So, what if he's the leader of a motorcycle gang? So, what if mommy was trying to protect me? None of that matters now."

"Whatever your ex-husband did or why he did it, the fact of the matter is that he's still her father. She had a right to be with him, to talk with him even if it were only for a few minutes. Be honest with me Madame D, are you proud of your eldest daughter? For what she has accomplished? And now she's the new Fashion Girl, don't you think she'll do fine in her new role?"

It took Madame D a few moments to let what Amanda said sink in and then replied, "My daughter accomplished quite a lot especially in high school. Like when I was her age, she was class president, head cheerleader, and class valedictorian. I guess I was being hard on her."

Amanda replied, "Madame D, mommy thought the best of you too. In time she'll cool off herself. Please do me a favor, go back to the Mystique Boutique and have a heart-to-heart talk with your daughter. She's young but she's not dumb or stupid. I think you should see her for what she is now, the third woman to become Fashion Girl. If you want mommy to be there, I think she'll assist you. Like the Style Chicks say, do it to it."

Madame D said, "Actually the phrase is let's do it to it. But I understand. Thank you Amanda. Your mommy gave birth to a wise young girl who is mature beyond your years. Who knows, you might take her place someday." Amanda replied, "Let's all go back and get this straightened out together."

The three left the diner, got into Serpentina's car and headed back to the mansion. When they got back to the mansion where everyone was glad to see them. Madame D asked, "Where's my daughter at the moment?" The new Tiffany answered, "She came back in after Serpentina talked with her. She went to give Cottonmouth some news. Do you want me to get her?"

Madame D said, "No that's okay Tiffany, I have an idea where she is." Madame D went upstairs and saw Fashion Girl with a huge smile on her face. The smile quickly disappeared and turned to a frown as she said, "Mom, if you're going to pour more salt in the wound, go ahead. I'm not sorry for speaking with daddy last night."

Madame D said, "No honey, I'm calm now. I'm sorry for last night. I shouldn't have taken it out on you. Of course, you had every right to see and talk with your father. But I can't help after all this time that I'm still bitter with him for what he did to us. In a way I am glad that he got to see his baby girl all grown up. Honey I have a confession to make, when I got home last night, that I was going to make that deal with the devil after he tried to get you. But I'm not going to do that."

Fashion Girl replied, "Since were pouring our souls I too have a confession to make. I was never pregnant in school, and I didn't get an abortion. I only said that because you got on my case about it. Mom you've given me so much, I would never make you feel ashamed or upset. I promise that for whatever the time I have to be the next Fashion Girl, I promise to do right by her. I also promise to make her name be feared by criminals once again. The femme fatale route is still how I want to take her. But she will do fine and her very best. You have my word."

Madame D hugged Fashion Girl with tears streaming down her face and said, "Oh Daphne, honey you've never disappointed me in any way. You were my first-born child and remember what I told you when I held you in my arms for the first time that you would one day take my place and you would do many great things."

Fashion Girl asked, "Mom, I know why you became a dominatrix and why you joined the Skulls. But I'm worried about you, can't you stop being a dominatrix, being a biker chick and once again do something good? You have Aurora Gardens and it's done great. You're a good businesswoman why can't you be that exclusively?"

Madame D replied, "Daphne, I love being a dominatrix. Being a dominatrix has more to do with submission rather than sex. When a criminal is sent to me, I make them worship me. I put them into submission, and they become putty in my hands. You should see some of the men I'm given. I wouldn't have sex with them if they were the last men on earth."

"I told you why I became a biker chick. As Fashion Girl, I saved the Skulls from getting killed by a rival gang. The Skull King was so grateful that he made me an honorary Skull at first because it wouldn't have looked good for a heroine like Fashion Girl being a biker chick. After Charlotte and Dean Jr. was born that I became a full-fledged member. Yes I'm pregnant but I got pregnant by the Skull King. I'm proud to be pregnant by him."

"And yes I still have sex with Dean. I still love him, and we got divorced in secret when I faked my death after the other twins were born. Fashion Girl died in childbirth. Sometimes we do threesomes, but I'm not a slut, a whore or a skank. I just make like I am one. And yes I like to drink alcohol, yes I smoke cigarettes and yes I like to have sex. But I keep it under control."

Fashion Girl took a moment to think about what Madame D said. Then she replied, "I understand mom. Cottonmouth and I had sex yesterday in the Den of Sin. We did it three times. He was nothing short of amazing. I hope he didn't get me pregnant. But if he did, I would care for that child. Hope I do have a daughter someday. For now, I will check my urine stream with pregnancy tests. But I am in love with him, and I do hope we will get married someday."

"I see how Aunt Cindy is happy with Uncle Rattler. I also see how happy you are with the Skull King. I'm not crazy when he said that I'm a bad seed. I'm not a bad seed. As Fashion Girl I will be a badass, I already look like a badass but I'm good and will do my new job with both service and justice in mind. You can tell him that for me."

Madame D said, "I will tell him that. I thought he was out of line too. I'll take care of that, I promise. Oh, I forgot to mention, I live in the Den of Sin to again prove that I'm a sex crazed bitch even though I'm not. I'm worried about being more than two hundred feet below ground especially after the earthquake we had two years ago. But I made sure when it was built that it would be secure, and it was made with concrete and cement. I also made sure that the underground casino and strip club was secure too."

Madame D and Fashion Girl hugged each other again and Madame D said, "The former Style Chicks will be here soon for a farewell lunch. They should be here any minute now. Let's go downstairs to join them when they arrive." Fashion Girl replied, "Okay mom, I want to say goodbye to them too."

When Madame D and Fashion Girl came downstairs to meet with the former Style Chicks for lunch, neither of them realized at that moment that a different chapter that wasn't intended to happen would happen to them both and soon.

CHAPTER 19

Moments after Madame D and Fashion Girl went back downstairs, the former Style Chicks arrived for their farewell lunch. Everyone was glad to see each other for the last time at the Mystique Boutique. Between the former and new Victoria, they prepared a lunch unlike any other either of them had ever made.

While eating Madame D began asking the others now that they were the former Style Chicks what they would do from now on. First she asked Lisa Mobley the previous Tiffany and she replied, "Now that my girls are the new Junior Style Chicks and they'll be going to Atlanta and live at Belphora Manor, I'm going to be with them that is if it's okay with you Madame D. That is since it was your mother's original headquarters."

Madame D said, "Of course it's okay Lisa. I remember you're from Atlanta so it will be a homecoming for you too." Teresa Andrews the former Penney Dillard added, "And of course I'm going to live there too. It's big enough for everyone including my son and our husbands." Madame D said, "I wish you both the very best and I wish the new Junior Chicks the best of luck in their new roles. Don't forget Charlotte is going to be there too so I will come whenever I can especially during the holidays."

Candace "Candy" Munson the former Victoria her plans has already been mentioned that she'll still be there to help the new Victoria since she's only fourteen. And she'll still be the Victoria in Victoria's Bistro and Victoria's Café. Ursula Swensen the former Zara also has had her plans mentioned that she'll be aboard The Mystique Marauder and be the new Zara's first mate. She said, "This reunion is great, but I need to go back to the ship to help my captain on her maiden voyage."

Madame D replied, "But before you go my daughter will take a picture of all of us and we'll send it to you and everyone else too." Then Lakesha Johnson the former Godiva said, "Now that I've earned the right to go back to Chicago, I can finally be with my kids at long last. Sure, they're all in their twenties now, I can still be there for them." Fashion Girl replied, "Lakesha, no matter how old a child gets, no matter what they might endure, they will always be your babies. Mom told me the same thing; I'll always be her baby girl no matter what might happen to me."

Lakesha said, "You're right Fashion Girl. I never thought of it that way." Fashion Girl replied, "Most parents don't think that not at first but when they realize it, then they'll know. Next was Soon Li Chang the former Macy Sears and she said, "I'll still be here mates. Only now you have to call me Dr. Chang now that I'm a doctor. Madame D you always believed in my talents of my days as a tribal medicine woman. Now I can practice my profession legally and I owe it all to you."

Madame D replied, "You're welcome Soon Li, you deserve it and about you're helping me at Aurora Gardens, you don't have to be at the motel anymore." Soon Li said, "Are you kidding? I love helping people settle in only now I'll continue to do it on the weekends but if I should have an emergency, I'll have to go." Madame D replied, "Of course Soon Li I understand. By the way you didn't say what kind of medicine you'll be practicing?" Soon Li said, "I'm a general practitioner. I figured since I can patch up injuries, help with other ailments I felt there was no need to specialize."

Of course, the former Sephora is Fashion Girl's aunt and Madame D's blood sister, she will also remain where she's at. The Cosmo Chicks were also in attendance and were enjoying their first full day as earth residents. Cover Girl said, "And we will also be here too. It feels so good to be with you all the time now. Teresa thanks again for doing this for us." Teresa replied, "It was my greatest pleasure to do that for you Cover Girl. The Cosmo Chicks have been so instrumental to our cause it was the very least we could do for you. And don't worry, the spell is permanent you can live without those toxic helmets for as long as you live."

The celebration soon turned to sadness for a few moments as they remembered the memory of their fallen comrades Chanel, Wendy and Belle K. Madame D said, "Ladies I'm sure that all of you will agree that our friends couldn't be here to celebrate with us. I mean how Chanel died in my arms so long ago. I still feel guilty how Wendy died. If I had known that she was under the influence of Drain-O I would've been more sympathetic to her. And Belle K, such a waste of life, how she died, being killed for being nothing more than a Hispanic American. Those Crocs will one day pay for what they did. And when they face justice, I'll be there in the courtroom enjoying every minute of it."

No one in the room disagreed with Madame D's words. And if the Crocs do go to court, the others will be there too. Fashion Girl replied, "I loved her too and rest assured mom, the new Style Chicks will also be there too." Everyone pause for a moment of silence to honor their memories.

Afterwards, Fashion Girl pulled out her cell phone camera and said, "Okay everyone, I know we just had a sad moment but please gather around and give me all a big smile." Fashion Girl took the picture and thanked everyone for coming one last time. As everyone left the mansion one by one, She-Ra remained, and she wasn't asked about her endeavors, but Fashion Girl did.

She-Ra replied, "It's okay if I wasn't asked before but I will continue to do what I've always have done to right the wrongs of innocent people." Cobra added, "And I will join her for a while, meet her friends and family and see where she lives both on earth and her home worlds. It's the vacation and adventure of a lifetime."

Serpentina said, "That does sound like a great trip indeed. Good luck to you all. She-Ra you have to admit, you three make a great looking family and be proud of it." She-Ra replied, "You're right Serpentina and Cobra I am again sorry for not telling you about Amanda sooner." Cobra said, "It's okay and I accept your apology. Being famous is all well and good but I also understand that some people can be cruel and think the worst."

They were the last to leave except for Madame D, Serpentina, Fashion Girl, Candace and the new Victoria. Madame D said, "It was a great celebration. The food was great and now we know where everyone will be." Fashion Girl replied, "It sure was. Now I need to start packing and go to Los Angeles. Now that I have a home in Beverly Hills, I was told to come tomorrow. One thing, Saks, Wendy, Bloomie and Nine West were the Junior Style Chicks, what do I call them now?" Madame D said, "They are regular Style Chicks now. And I let them continue to be Style Chicks. They're all in their twenties and they are now your Style Chicks. That's why they're in LA."

Fashion Girl replied, "Thank you for allowing me to join you all for lunch. If you'll excuse me please." Madame D said, "You're welcome honey. I need to leave myself. I do have a motor court to look after." While Fashion Girl went upstairs to pack her bags, Madame D left the mansion, got in her car and drove back to Aurora Gardens.

On the way back she said to herself, *"Hmm, I got that bitch thinking everything is okay between us now. But little does she knows what I truly have in store for her. Yes I miss both Wendy and Belle K. And if I play my cards right, I can have them help me. But first, I have a date to keep."*

When she got back to Aurora Gardens, the date she had to keep was an appointment between the leaders of two gangs. More like a Menage a Trois. Madame D has this threesome with the leader of the Crypt Keepers the gang she stopped many years ago and the leader of Hell's Hotties the female members of the Crypt Keepers now a separate gang in itself.

Madame D was a couple of minutes late but they began their session with Lucifer the Third and La Diablo. Madame D was a little more sexual than normal. Lucifer said, "Madame D, you are one freaky woman. You don't mind having sex being another man's girlfriend?" Madame

D replied, "The Skull King is my boyfriend, but he doesn't own or control me."

Lucifer asked, "You fuck like a man crazy slut, La Diablo and I have asked you each time to join us. You have no loyalty to the Skulls, so c'mon join us please?" Madame D answered, "Today my dear Lucifer and my dear La Diablo, you're in luck. In a dream I had many years ago, I dreamt that I was evil, very evil. I became a baby making machine by your father."

"I became a willing participant in the ways of evil. I enjoyed being evil. Day by day, I have given it serious thought. Recently, Satan came after my daughter. I won't allow her to become evil. But I do. Yes Lucifer, La Diablo, I will become a member of Hell's Hotties. But there are some conditions."

Lucifer with a big smile on his face asked, "Name them my dear, what are your conditions?" Madame D replied, "When I speak to Satan, I want to first become young again. If I'm to be a baby making machine for evil, I need to be in my late teens. Next, I don't want to be called Aldornia again. I want a new name. Next I have two others who will join me as well, two former Style Chicks named Wendy and Belle K. And finally, I want us to not only become evil, but I want us to get revenge for how they were killed. Wendy died from a drug overdose, although one faced justice and was put to death himself. I've heard his widow continues to exploit young girls."

"As for Belle K, her real name was Alicia Lopez. She was born and raised in Miami, Florida to Colombian parents. She had good fighting skills along with being compassionate. I made her a Style Chick with the name Belle K. Her father once told her that even though she had Colombian heritage, he wanted her to be as American as possible."

"That meant that she should speak English only. But she did everything Latinos do like having a quince for instance. She was killed last year by a rival gang called the Crocs. They belong to the KKK, and she was killed for being Latino and nothing else. She deserves to get her revenge."

La Diablo said also with a smile on her face, "I can grant you one of those conditions now, your new name will be Satanra." Madame D replied, "Satanra? I like the name." Lucifer said, "Good. We will now conjure up Satan to appear before us." Lucifer and La Diabla recited an ancient and evil spell and soon before them appeared Satan himself.

He asked, "What can I do for you my children?" Madame D replied, "It is I who wishes to speak with you." Satan asked, "Madame D I presume? What can I do for you my child?" Madame D answered, "Mighty Satan Prince of Darkness, I wish to join the ranks of your evil gang." Satan said, "I wanted your daughter, I don't want you." Madame D replied, "My daughter won't join the forces of evil. But I do. Many years ago, I dreamt that I was evil, and I loved it. Let me join you and I assure you that you won't be disappointed."

Satan said, "You seem willing my dear, but what do you want to do to serve me well?" Madame D replied, "For starters, I will serve you by being a baby making machine." Satan said, "I have no further desire to have an army of evil by having my women be constantly pregnant." Madame D replied, "Okay, so even though I'm pregnant, I've been feeling like I can do more by being evil. Look around you this is my home it's called The Den of Sin. It's also where I put evil doers into submission until the police arrive."

Satan said, "Sounds interesting. What else do you want?" Madame D replied, "I'm over forty and I'm pregnant. I want to be young again and be immortal." Satan gave it some thought and said, "My dear, I think I can grant you what your asking for. You sound sincere." Madame D replied, "I am. I rule the night by doing this which I will continue to do only I will do it a different way."

Satan said, "Everything you asked for will be granted. As of this moment, you will become a sex vampire called Satanra." With a wave of his hand, Madame D changed to become the evil Satanra." Lucifer and La Diablo were also pleased. Satan asked, "How do you feel now my dear?" Now as Satanra she answered, "I feel much better, I feel becoming evil. And I'm horny as hell! I will enjoy this."

Satan said, "Excellent my dear child. You once dreamt of this, and I do remember that. You were eviler than I thought someone who once was called Fashion Girl could be. So now Satanra, as of now you are younger, stronger and have evil tendencies." Satanra replied, "I will still give birth to my babies and then I will devote full time to the forces of evil."

Satanra laughed maniacally and continued, "Tonight I will have the new Sephora to conjure the spirits of Wendy and Belle K so you can make them evil too." Satan said with a smile on his face, "If you think they'll turn evil, I will bring them back to life so they can get their revenge and they too will live again permanently. Are they also baby making machines?"

Satanra replied, "Wendy got pregnant at eleven years old and was pregnant again when she died. Belle K married her childhood friend and sweetheart. After their divorce she became such a whore and had three children by both the Skulls and Vipers. They will serve you well master."

Satan said, "I couldn't have asked for better minions, very well Satanra, all you've asked will be granted." Satanra again laughing maniacally replied, "They want their revenge but what should we call them?" Satan said, "I do have the perfect names. For Wendy, she will be called Slutan. As for Belle K and being Latin, she'll be called Miss Muertos or Miss Death."

Satanra replied, "Perfect names indeed for a pair of dick loving sluts. See you tonight master of all evil." Satan disappeared in a cloud of red smoke as La Diablo said, "Now that you're evil, do you want to know what the Hell's Hotties do?" Satanra replied, "Yes but you know by being here I too like both dick and cunt. So please tell me."

La Diablo said, "You will ride with my gang from now on. You will do anything that's considered evil like terrorize drivers, looting stores and here on your property, you'll fuck the men that will be sent to you along dominating them. From what I've heard, you're rather tame as a dominatrix, they will change after we conjure up your friends. Let the babies you're carrying until they're born. Give them to whoever the father is and you'll become the baby machine our master demands."

Satanra asked, "How many babies have your gang had?" La Diablo answered, "Between the members of my gang, we've had seventy-five children, and we'll have lots more once your friends join us." Satanra asked, "I'm sure not only is Lucifer handsome, the others in his gang too. Do I fuck them? Or can I fuck anyone I see fit?"

La Diablo answered, "I know in your dream you could only fuck Lucifer, now you can fuck anyone you want. You are now a sex vampire. Just like a regular vampire can't live without blood, you can't live without sex. And you will also need to do this, you must drink wolf's blood in order to be strong, have an appetite like a plague of locusts and be fertile." Satanra said, "Okay La Diablo, I'll do it. Just one thing, I hope wolf's blood tastes better than in my dream." La Diablo replied, "Yes it does taste better and it's also very addictive too. You already like alcohol and tobacco so you will like this."

Later that night, La Diablo and Satanra kidnapped the new Sephora to conjure up the spirits of Wendy and Belle K. Satanra said, "We will let you go after you do a favor for us, conjure up the spirits of Wendy Blake and Alicia Lopez aka Belle K." The new Sephora replied, "Who are you and why are you doing this?" Satanra said, "Don't you know who I am? I helped to make you a Style Chick, I am Madame D, but you can now call me Satanra."

Sephora replied, "Madame D? I don't believe it. What happened to you?" Satanra said laughing maniacally, "I now serve the forces of evil. I'm now a member of Hell's Hotties and this is their leader La Diablo, she convinced me that I can do more by being a member of Hell's Hotties. Conjure up their spirits or I will show you just how evil I am now."

Sephora replied, "You will release me if I do this?" Satanra said, "I'm evil now but I still keep my word. Just do your thing and you can leave unharmed." Sephora said nothing more and conjured up the spirits and once they arose, she left the cemetery. Satanra stopped La Diablo and said, "Let her go, I gave her my word. No one will believe her anyways." La Diablo replied, "Alright if you say so, I won't go after her."

Both Wendy and Belle K looked confused and appeared solid. Belle K asked, "Who are you and why were we conjured up? Haven't we been through enough?" Satanra answered, "Relax ladies, I'm Satanra and this is La Diablo and we're members of an evil gang called Hell's Hotties. We had you conjured up because we want you to join our gang."

Belle K asked, "We aren't evil, we served the forces of good. We will never become evil. Again, I asked, why are you doing this? Why do you want us?" Satanra answered, "You both knew me as Fashion Girl and later Madame D. I know how and why you both died. I'm giving you the chance to get your revenge. Belle, don't you want to get revenge against the Crocs? And Wendy the widow of that corrupt sheriff is still exploiting young girls for profit. You made friends with those girls; don't you want to help them?"

Wendy and Belle K talked it over between them and Belle K said, "Yes we both want revenge. We will become evil to do this." Satanra replied, "Excellent. Now we will call for Satan. You will be given new names, eternal life, and with wolf's blood, you'll both be strong, hungry and fertile."

Wendy said, "I got pregnant at eleven by a sexual predator. To have all the sex I want, and get revenge, I'm in." Belle K added, "I too love sex and I became a biker slut. We both love us some good dick. Call your master, we will do whatever you ask." As Satan appeared in a cloud of red smoke he said, "You must be Wendy and Belle K, welcome ladies. I will grant you both eternal life and become baby making machines and the ability to get your revenge."

Wendy and Belle K both drank the wolf's blood and the evil started to flow through them. Satan continued, "Wendy from now on you will be known as Slutan and Belle K you will be known as Miss Muertos or Miss Death. And together, you will serve me well."

Now as Slutan she replied, "We thank you all. We'll do our very best to show how evil we are now." Satan said, "Excellent, now you can leave so you can do what we will." Satan left in a cloud of red smoke as Satanra said, "Now then ladies, starting tomorrow, we will put our plans together."

They left the cemetery never to return again. But what about Fashion Girl? Would she have to deal with her mother, adopted sister and friend? Or will they leave her alone? Only time will tell.

CHAPTER 20

While this was going on with the former Madame D, Wendy and Belle K, the new Fashion Girl and her boyfriend Cottonmouth were finishing packing bags to go to their new home in Beverly Hills while they'll attend classes at UCLA. As they brought their last bags downstairs, Cottonmouth said, "I can't believe this Daphne, we're going to live in Beverly Hills! I hope we'll rub elbows with famous celebrities!"

Fashion Girl replied in equal excitement, "I can't wait to see it too! But remember Cottonmouth, we're going to college and not have wild Hollywood parties." Cottonmouth said, "I know I'm just curious and anxious at the same time." Fashion Girl replied, "Of course baby, it's okay to be excited, curious and anxious. My heart is also racing."

The new Tiffany came up to them and said, "I'm absolutely green with envy that you're going to live in Beverly Hills while you're going to college. I'm so jealous." Fashion Girl replied, "There's no need to be jealous Tiffany. I didn't buy the place; it was given to me by my adopted sisters. And of course, you and the others are welcome to come down anytime you want or when nothing is going on."

Just then the doorbell rang, the new Victoria was near the door and answered it. As she opened the door, a young woman with green hair and a grayish tint to her skin stood there and said, "My name is Saks. I'm

Daphne's adopted sister." Victoria didn't know what to say at first then replied, "I'm the new Victoria by all means please come in."

Fashion Girl's expression was both exciting and confusing. She said, "Saks! It's good to see you but what are you doing here? I thought you were waiting for us in LA?" Saks replied, "That was supposed to be the case. But you don't know which house is yours so I will escort you there. I take it that you did get the deed and fobs for your new cars?" Fashion Girl replied, "Aunt Cindy gave it to me yesterday."

In confusion Saks asked, "Aunt Cindy? Wasn't mom supposed to give it to you?" Fashion Girl answered, "Oh Saks, something's terribly wrong with her. Since she's been pregnant again, she's been acting strange, and I don't mean the kind you are when you're pregnant. I mean she tried to strangle me on my birthday. She and the new Sephora got into an altercation. Then she acts sweet, kind and understanding."

"I asked Aunt Cindy if she's become an alcoholic or a drug addict, she assured me that wasn't the case. Something's wrong with her no doubt but I don't know what." Saks said, "You're right Fashion Girl, that doesn't sound like her at all." Fashion Girl replied, "Maybe we can find out together now that you, Bloomie and Nine West are my personal Style Chicks. But relax, I won't pull rank on you since you're older than me."

Saks replied, "Yes but you're Fashion Girl and you are the leader of the Style Chicks and as long as you are the leader, no one can pull rank on you regardless." Fashion Girl said, "Where are my manners? Saks, this is my new boyfriend Cottonmouth of the Vipers the gang Aunt Cindy leads. Cottonmouth this is Rosie Blake AKA Saks of the Style Chicks."

They shook hands as Cottonmouth said, "It's nice to meet you Saks. I've heard a lot about you and the others." Saks replied, "It's nice to meet you too. Although we haven't heard too much about you, but I think once you're down in LA, we'll all get acquainted. If you're ready Fashion Girl, let's get going. LA, Beverly Hills and Hollywood awaits you."

Saks loaded up the Chicken Coup motorhome and headed towards I-5 going south towards LA. Cottonmouth sat up front with Saks while Fashion Girl sat in the back still worried about how her mother has been acting. Cottonmouth couldn't help staring at Saks. Saks got self-conscious and asked, "Cottonmouth, why are you staring at me?" Cottonmouth answered, "Forgive me I didn't mean to stare. I thought I knew the occupations of the current and former Style Chicks, but I didn't know one of the Style Chicks is a punk rocker. I thought it explained the green hair."

Saks said, "I don't have green hair because I'm a punk rocker. I have green hair because of something that happened to me when I was younger. When I was younger, none of us knew how to read, write or count. Wendy and I swam in a lake that turned out to be a toxic waste dump. It turned my hair green, I lost both of my eyes, and it turned my skin to this grayish tint. For Wendy, it made her go through puberty at a very early age. She got pregnant at eleven from that sexual predator Victor Miller."

"Even though he had no idea that she was so young, she was the only one to get pregnant by him. When she reached the final stage of puberty, she became a young woman on the outside but was a child on the inside. She wasn't stupid, she was twelve years old."

Cottonmouth asked, "Wendy? Wasn't she the one that died several years ago?" Saks answered, "Yes and she died such a horrible death. Before we met Fashion Girl and the Style Chicks, Wendy sold herself for money. I made her do it. We had no parents, no supervision and no money. She even worked in strip clubs too. But it all changed thanks to the former Fashion Girl."

"Both Wendy and I got huge cash settlements from the company that turned Lake Colognia into a cesspool. Daphne's mom made us the first group of Junior Style Chicks. I had my eyes restored. We were homeschooled until we got caught up. Wendy continued to be homeschooled because we felt she would be teased on account of her mature appearance."

"After we all graduated high school, we moved to LA and got our home in Beverly Hills. We were only happy to do the same for you and Daphne. Believe me you will love this place."

Cottonmouth said, "Daphne and I are excited to see this place. But right now, she don't look too happy." Saks replied, "With good reason if what you told me about mom is true." Nothing more was said for at that moment, the RV arrived Fashion Girl and Cottonmouth were staring at their home away from home. Fashion Girl had her mouth wide open and said, "Saks? You bought this for us? It's bigger than the Mystique Boutique!" Saks replied, "If you like what you're seeing on the outside, wait until you see the inside."

As they opened the door, Bloomie and Nine West said together, "Welcome home Fashion Girl!" Fashion Girl replied, "Thank you ladies. This is my boyfriend Cottonmouth. Cottonmouth, this is Brittney and Lisa Blake AKA Bloomie and Nine West." They shook hands as Cottonmouth said, "Nice to meet you both." Saks added, "Both Bloomie and Nine West didn't sustain the same damages Wendy and I suffered. They're two normal young women."

Jokingly, Bloomie said, "Nine West and I are women but we're not too sure about being normal." Fashion Girl replied, "Okay enough with the banter girls, how come you didn't come up with Saks?" Bloomie said, "We first wanted to make sure that the house is perfect before you came. And second, we also were minding a special new member of the Style Chicks."

Just then, sounds of yapping was coming from another room and out came a four-legged friend. Fashion Girl said, "Who's this little guy? He's so adorable!" If anything could've brighten her day, it was this. The girls gave Fashion Girl a puppy. Fashion Girl continued, "What kind of dog is he?" Bloomie replied, "He's a cockapoo." Fashion Girl asked, "A what a poo?" Bloomie answered, "A cockapoo. Half Cocker Spaniel and half Poodle."

The puppy began to lick Fashion Girl's face. Fashion Girl was laughing hysterically and said, "He's so lovable." Bloomie replied, "We had a picture of you, so he knew who his owner is but I'm sorry Cottonmouth we didn't have a picture of you." The puppy went to Cottonmouth and began licking his face too. Cottonmouth replied, "He is cute, and I think we'll get along just fine."

Fashion Girl asked, "I'm sure his name isn't puppy so what do we call him?" Bloomie answered, "Well, um, I'm afraid Nine West named him." Nine West got her name because her love of shoes. Fashion Girl

said, "Don't tell me, let me guess, his name is Foot Locker right?" Nine
West replied, "Very funny Fashion Girl. It just so happens that I did
give him a shoe name. A name I think you'll like. His name is Nike."

Fashion Girl said, "Nike? Nike. I like it. I think it suits him." Sure
enough when Nike heard his name, he came over to Fashion Girl and
continued to lick her face. Fashion Girl kept laughing and continued,
"Okay, okay Nike it is." Saks said, "He's three months old, he's had all
his shots, his papers are in order, and he'll get the Bob Barker treatment
in three months."

Cottonmouth replied, "The Bob Barker treatment? What's that?"
Saks said, "It's Hollywood for he'll be fixed." Cottonmouth replied,
"Being a guy, I think the Bob Barker treatment sounds better."

Saks, Bloomie and Nine West showed Fashion Girl and Cottonmouth
the rest of the house. They furnished everything very tastefully.
Cottonmouth saw his mancave and said, "This is so amazing. Big screen
TV, pool table, video games and even pinball, girls this is great thank
you so much."

Saks replied, "I'm glad you like it. Fashion Girl how about you?
You've been quiet since you met Nike." Fashion Girl said, "Saks remem-
ber what I said earlier, I'm very worried about mom and her behavior."
Saks asked, "Tell me what you think about your new home?" Fashion
Girl answered, "It's nothing short of magnificent. I really love it too."

Bloomie showed one more thing to Cottonmouth and Fashion Girl
and said, "And no Beverly Hills home would be complete as Jed Clampett
once called a "cement pond."" Both Fashion Girl and Cottonmouth
loved it. Bloomie continued, "Not only do you have the swimming pool,
but there's enough space if you wish to have a pool party. That's it for
the tour of your new house."

Fashion Girl replied, "Girls again, I can't thank you enough for your
generosity. It sure beats living with someone in a dorm. But mom paid
for me to live on campus, what can I do to refund the money?" Nine
West had an idea and said, "Find out which dorm you were to supposed
to go to and give it to someone who might be struggling financially.
They'll worship the ground you walk on."

Fashion Girl replied, "Not a bad idea Nine West. I'll do that." Saks said, "The two cars you saw in the driveway are yours. Put the new Glam Mobile in the garage along with Cottonmouth's motorcycle and use them instead." The two cars were a black Ferrari and a red Corvette. Cottonmouth replied, "I'll take the Vette. As they say, "The Vette gets them wet."

Fashion Girl said, "If anyone is going to get you wet, it's me! Got it!" Cottonmouth replied, "Just kidding babe. I know when I have a good girlfriend." Saks said, "We left our phone number by the phone, we're just two blocks away if you need us. Good luck with everything we'll talk again soon." Nine West added as she whispered, "Cottonmouth, if you want an even better girlfriend, call me." Getting mad, Saks said, "That's enough Nine West. Forgive her Cottonmouth, she's been boy crazy since she finished puberty. Besides she already has a boyfriend and he's a good young man."

Fashion Girl asked, "What was that all about?" Cottonmouth answered, "I think Nine West wanted me to dump you for her." Fashion Girl said exhaling hard, "Saks is right, since she finished puberty, Nine West is a walking bag of hormones. And I met her boyfriend once, he really is a good guy. So, let's make ourselves at home, shall we?"

Fashion Girl and Cottonmouth went to the kitchen to see what they could eat for dinner. However, Saks failed to mention that there was no food in the refrigerator for fear that anything inside could spoil. They decided to go out to dinner instead. Cottonmouth asked, "Where's a good restaurant around here that we could eat at?" Fashion Girl answered, "Let's see online where there is a good place to eat here."

Fashion Girl saw some very trendy looking restaurants in the area. She said, "Cottonmouth, based on what I see here, there's no McDonald's in Beverly Hills. But there are some interesting choices. Steakhouses, Italian, Asian, and Brazilian. See what you like, and I'll call for a reservation."

Cottonmouth saw the choices and replied, "Let's go for this place. Il Fornaio." Fashion Girl said, "I'll call them. We may have to dress fancy to go to this place." Cottonmouth replied, "Based on the description, it doesn't seem like a kind of restaurant you have to dress fancy. Besides, you're the new Fashion Girl. Go as you are now. That way you can get some exposure. Think about it, if Fashion Girl loves to eat here, we will too. It's good for your image and it's good for the restaurant." Fashion Girl said, "You made perfect sense. We'll go there as we are but let's go there in the Glam Mobile. Fashion Girl is going to make her Hollywood debut." Cottonmouth was right for when they drove through Beverly Hills, people on the street both as drivers and pedestrians noticed them driving by. When they got to the restaurant, diners also noticed her as they sat down to order.

After their order was made, somebody approached Fashion Girl and asked, "Please pardon me ma'am, but are you Fashion Girl?" Fashion Girl answered, "I'm Fashion Girl, is there something I can do for you?" The diner said, "I saw your introduction online a couple of days ago. I just wanted to meet you and wish you the very best of luck in your abilities to fight crime." Fashion Girl replied, "Thank you very much for your kind words. Please keep in mind that although I'm a superheroine now, I'm just a normal girl who lives just like everyone else. Thank you again and take care."

Cottonmouth said, "What did I tell you? You will be a big hit here even if you do nothing at all." Fashion Girl replied, "You're right. Just sitting here drew attention. But also think about this. If I am seen in a restaurant, a nightclub or any other public place, will I be able to enjoy myself? Or will it turn into an autograph session? It does remain to be seen."

Cottonmouth said, "At least when you're in school, you don't have to go as Fashion Girl. Everyone wants you to succeed in school not to mention your desire to become an actress." Fashion Girl replied, "My mom made a fortune strutting her stuff on catwalks and doing photo shoots, I want to make my fortune doing what I love too." Cottonmouth said, "We begin classes Monday morning, so let's make the best of anything or everything that comes our way okay?"

Fashion Girl replied, "Anything and everything that comes our way we'll deal with it." After dinner, they returned home, and both agreed to go grocery shopping in the morning. Fashion Girl said, "Listen stud, let's do it. Let's fuck our brains out."

Cottonmouth said, "What about what your mom said about us sleeping in separate bedrooms?" Fashion Girl replied, "Right now Cottonmouth, I don't care what she said. I'm an adult now. I can make my own decisions and I can do what I want. And if I want to have sex with my boyfriend, that's what I'm going to do."

The next morning, Cottonmouth found that Fashion Girl was up before him. When he came downstairs, he saw Saks in the kitchen. He asked, "Saks what are you doing here?" Saks answered, "I brought some food over. I forgot to tell the others to do some shopping before I brought you here." Cottonmouth asked, "Where's Fashion Girl?" Saks answered, "She's out by the pool. I made coffee and she took a carafe out with her."

Cottonmouth said, "Thank you Saks. I'm really worry about her. It's our first day of college tomorrow and I have a bad feeling that she won't be able to concentrate." Saks replied, "Cottonmouth don't worry. Mostly the first day of college for freshmen consists of finding where their classes are, where they're dorms are located and to see if they want to do some elective classes, join a club, joining a fraternity or sorority, that sort of thing."

"I know you're both going to UCLA, we went to USC, and this is what we went through. Nine West is in her junior year while Bloomie is in her senior year, and I graduated two years ago."

Cottonmouth said, "Thank you Saks. I see at least you bought us dishes, glasses and silverware. We were planning to go shopping today. Would you like to join us?" Saks replied, "It's okay Cottonmouth, you two should be together today and prepare for college life." Cottonmouth grabbed a coffee mug and went out to the pool area to see how Fashion Girl was doing.

Cottonmouth found Fashion Girl sitting on a deck chair holding Nike as she was scratching his ears which he loved. Cottonmouth sat next to her and asked, "Good morning. I was wondering where you were since you weren't next to me in bed." As he was pouring a cup of coffee she replied, "I'm sorry Cottonmouth. I just can't shake this feeling that mom has done something terrible. Think about this, she lives underground in a place called The Den of Sin."

"Her car is called The Widow Maker. Her motorcycle is called The Assassin. She's tattooed from head to toe. She told me she only has sex with those she loves and not with the men she's ordered to subdue. I agree with Sephora. She loves dick too much. She claims she got pregnant by the Skull King, but I'm beginning to doubt that."

"Who knows who got her pregnant again. She's over forty now, it's dangerous for any woman to be pregnant especially with triplets. I love her of course but at the same time, I don't like what she's doing. If she wants to be a slut, whore and a skank, that's her problem. But it will look bad on me now that I'm Fashion Girl. Look I love you and when we do it, it's amazing. But I don't want my time as Fashion Girl cut short because I got pregnant too soon."

After hearing all this, Cottonmouth said, "Um, Daphne I have a confession to make to you. Ten years ago, I met your mother for the first time along a riverbank near Dodge City, Kansas. All of us were under the influence of an evil woman called Aspina. As you know of all of the snakes in the world, the asp is more dangerous than a cobra. We met your mother who was looking for some action. She was pregnant at the time also with your kid sister and brother."

"Needless to say, Aspina wasn't pleased with your mother's intrusion. So Aspina challenged your mother to what she called a fuck off. Your mother won and took Cobra as her prize. We briefly went our separate ways until Aspina brought us back together to confront your mother again. That was when Cobra met She-Ra who was travelling with your mother in a car your mother bought her."

"They travelled until they got to Las Vegas where Aspina and the rest of us confronted your mother again. Aspina eventually was not only defeated but was killed by your mother and the former Tiffany as The Phoenix and Solara. We didn't know who they were as Archangels at the time. So, your mother once again fucked us, and it broke the spell Aspina had over us for good."

"Rattler, Diamondback and Cobra went with her and as you know she gave them jobs at Aurora Gardens. Another Viper Python and I came along later, and we also were given jobs. Daphne, you were only eight years old when this happened. I'm grateful to your mother for giving me this opportunity to get a college degree. I'm also grateful to your aunt for becoming our leader. And I'm grateful to you. I love you and I'll be as loyal as Nike is."

After hearing this incredible story, Fashion Girl asked, "How old were you at the time this happened?" Cottonmouth answered, I was young then, I was younger than you. I was sixteen." Fashion Girl asked, "You mean you had sex with my mother when you were only sixteen?" Cottonmouth answered, "Compared to how things were back then, how I live now is an improvement. Aspina liked her men young. No kidding I wasn't the youngest, Rattler he was only fourteen. And no kidding on this either, this woman was so into snakes she laid eggs instead of being pregnant."

Fashion Girl said with slight confusion, "So now you're twenty-six? I can live with that." Cottonmouth replied with assurance, "Aspina may have like her men young, but I don't do jailbait. Granted you're eighteen now but you're an adult and I wouldn't be with you now as your boyfriend if you were still a minor. I hope you understand that I fell in love with you."

Fashion Girl said, "I do. After breakfast, let's go grocery shopping and prepare for tomorrow." Cottonmouth replied, "Saks dropped off some food for us but didn't make anything other than coffee." Fashion Girl said, "I told her not to go to any trouble. Besides I've eaten her cooking, it's an interesting experience to say the least."

Cottonmouth replied, "It's that bad?" Fashion Girl said, "It's not that it's bad but more like she's trying to cook without recipes. Otherwise, as I said, it's an interesting experience." They said nothing else as they prepared to go out and shop for food. Nike already had dog food and treats at his disposal. Cottonmouth again suggested that she should shop as Fashion Girl. She agreed. But neither car didn't have much cargo space so Fashion Girl called Saks to ask if she could borrow a bigger car to shop. She agreed and Fashion Girl and Cottonmouth found their house and got their cargo van to do what they needed to do.

And like in the restaurant, people noticed in the grocery store that Fashion Girl is there. After they shopped and returned the van, they spent the rest of the day preparing for their first day of college.

But as this was going on, something more diabolical was taking place. In the Den of Sin, Satanra, Slutan and Miss Muertos met up with La Diablo and something very evil was about to happen. La Diablo said, "Ladies, as your first full day as Hell's Hotties your first job is to again pledge your allegiance to the all mighty. Once you drink the wolf's blood, you will become evil, strong and fertile. Satanra, in order to accomplish this, you must purge the babies you're carrying. Are you willing to do this?"

Satanra replied, "Yes I'm willing to do this. I will purge the good I'm carrying. Now that I'm younger again, I will get pregnant by the evilest men on this forsaken planet." La Diablo said, "Excellent. Together with Slutan and Miss Muertos, you three will help to create the Army of Evil. Now then Satanra, purge the good and get pregnant by evil."

They drank the elixir, and they could feel the evil take over them. Satanra deliberately broke her water and in a matter of moments, three premature babies were born but were lifeless. Satanra laughed maniacally and said, "It is done, the good is dead. From now on, I will fuck enough men to get pregnant and the babies will be very, very evil."

Satanra continued to laugh maniacally as Slutan and Miss Muertos looked in horror and shock as Satanra continued, "When I meet with my daughter again, she will know the evil her mother really is. I can't wait to take her down." La Diablo replied, "Excellent! The new Fashion Girl declined to join us. When we get done with her, she'll be willing to do whatever we want." The four evil women all laughed maniacally as phase one of the plan was complete.

CHAPTER 21

The big day had arrived, the new Fashion Girl and Cottonmouth were in their first day of college. As Saks said, the first day was to get acquainted with everything they needed to go to classes and their location. Both dressed like college freshmen, Cottonmouth tried to join a fraternity, but no one wanted him. Fashion Girl wanted to join a campus acting troop to further her wish to become an actress.

After a busy morning, they met up near the main entrance of the college. Cottonmouth said, "I think we have everything in order don't we?" Fashion Girl replied, "I think so too. Let's have lunch and look around this place." Cottonmouth agreed to do so too. But as they were going to the parking lot, a young woman stopped them and asked, "Pardon me please but are you Daphne Bates?"

Fashion Girl answered, "Yes I'm Daphne Bates. What can I do for you?" The woman handed two envelopes to Fashion Girl and said, "I was asked to give you these envelopes. I know that you are the new Fashion Girl. Don't worry I won't say anything. My name is Amber Watley and I'm at your service. I want to help you adjust to this new life as a college student."

Fashion Girl replied, "Thank you Amber it's nice to meet you. This is my boyfriend. He's called Cottonmouth and I don't know his real name. Cottonmouth added, "I never told her my real name it's Darren

Bowes and it's nice to meet you too. One thing, why do you want to help Fashion Girl out?"

Amber said, "I was a fan of her mother and the former Style Chicks. What they dealt with and how they lived. So, when I heard that the new Fashion Girl was to attend college here, I want to do this with no other intention." The envelopes Fashion Girl was given were in fancy stationary. She opened them up and gasped and said, "Cottonmouth listen to this, I've been invited to lunch by the Dean. He points out other dignitaries in LA to join us."

Cottonmouth replied, "What does the other letter say?" Fashion Girl said, "I've also been invited to the Alpha Beta Omega sorority to have dinner with their members. Remember Aunt Cindy was in this sorority. In a way, I'm a legacy and this sorority was started by the original Tiffany and Penney Dillard."

Amber replied, "That's right and no matter which college has this sorority, it's the best one on any campus. Joining up with them will be a big feather in your cap." Fashion Girl said, "Aunt Cindy enjoyed her time there too. It's a sorority where women become women. Responsible, caring, and they don't throw wild parties like some sororities do."

Amber replied, "I happen to be a member myself and it's great." Fashion Girl said, "According to this invitation, lunch is at two. We need to get going, thanks again Amber. Amber replied, "Let's exchange phone numbers so if you both need me, call me. Who knows, I could become an honorary Style Chick." Fashion Girl said, "Consider it done Amber. As of now because of your kindness, you are an honorary Style Chick."

Amber thanked Fashion Girl for her kindness and parted company. The lunch with the Dean was in the fanciest restaurant in LA. When they arrived, they were directed to a banquet room where the Dean was waiting for them. The Dean got up out of his chair and walked over to them and said, "You must be the new Fashion Girl. I'm Dean Gerald Montgomery and it's a pleasure to meet you."

He even went as far as to kiss her hand. Fashion Girl replied, "It's nice to meet you too Dean. But there's something I don't quite understand. I'm also to meet some of LA's dignitaries?" Dean Montgomery said, "That's right Fashion Girl. I don't greet new students like this. But because you're here both new here in LA and UCLA, I want you to get acquainted with them."

"You'll meet the mayor, police chief, fire marshal, a reporter friend of the reporter that dealt with Fashion Girl in Colognia, and a director at First and Ten Pictures." Fashion Girl replied, "I understand that the reporter is with KCBS." Dean Montgomery said, "That's right. By the way who is this man with you." Fashion Girl replied, "This is my boyfriend Darren Bowes." They shook hands as Dean Montgomery said, "It's nice to meet you Mr. Bowes."

Cottonmouth replied, "I know I wasn't invited here; I was escorting Fashion Girl over here. I can go somewhere else while this luncheon is going on." Dean Montgomery said, "I'm sorry Mr. Bowes, I didn't realize that Fashion Girl has a boyfriend. Tell you what I'll do, have lunch in the main part of the restaurant on me. Just tell the server to give me the bill." Cottonmouth replied, "That's very nice of you sir. Fashion Girl can tell me all about it later. Please keep in mind that as long as I'm her boyfriend, I'll look after her even though she can take care of herself."

As Cottonmouth left the banquet room, Dean Montgomery pulled out a chair as Fashion Girl sat down. He said, "Before the others arrive, I want to talk shop for a moment. What is your major?" Fashion Girl replied, "Unlike my mother who modeled for a living, I aspire to be an actress. My mother gave me a lot of tools to become the new Fashion Girl including half of her fortune, her bulging closets full of clothes she once modeled in, the Mystique Boutique mansion back home and many other things."

Dean Montgomery said, "UCLA has a great program for aspiring actors. If I may say my dear, you have the look Hollywood is always looking for. That's why a movie director was invited to join us. I think he'll agree with my sentiment." Fashion Girl replied, "Like my mother and grandmother, Fashion Girl is just a name and not an attitude or lifestyle. They both proved that they could kick ass and doesn't take no crap from anybody. I'm waiting to do my first official mission as Fashion Girl."

Dean Montgomery said, "That's a reason why you'll meet the chief of police. Like your mother was friends with the chief in Colognia, I want you to have a good rapport with our chief." Just then, the other dignitaries came in and to get acquainted with everyone.

Dean Montgomery continued, "Fashion Girl, may I present his honor the mayor of Los Angeles, Seth O'Malley. The mayor kissed Fashion Girl's hand and said, "A pleasure to meet you my dear and welcome to Los Angeles." Dean Montgomery continued, "This is the chief of police in Los Angeles, Curt Gilmore." He also kissed her hand and replied, "I equally welcome you to Los Angeles Fashion Girl. It's not everyday that you get to meet a superheroine in person."

Dean Montgomery continued, "Fashion Girl this is the friend of the reporter that reported on your mother in Colognia, Jane Lansing of KCBS-TV. She shook Fashion Girl's hand and replied, "A great pleasure to meet you Fashion Girl. If you're anything like your mother was when it comes to fighting crime, you will help us get great news and ratings." Fashion Girl said, "Don't worry about ratings Ms. Lansing, you'll get as many exclusives as I can give you."

Dean Montgomery continued, "I made a mistake, this man isn't a director at First and Ten Pictures but he's now the head of the studio. May I present Mr. John Smith." He also kissed her hand and replied, "It's an honor to meet you my dear. I am looking forward to doing business with you." Fashion Girl asked, "John Smith? Why does that name sound familiar to me? I know it's not just the character in Pocahontas, oh yes, you directed the movie Chanel's Revenge that my mother starred in, right?"

Mr. Smith answered, "Then you've seen the movie I take it?" Fashion Girl said, "Every year at Halloween when I was growing up, my mother made my friends and I see it. No offense, it was awful." Mr. Smith replied, "None taken. Your mother was kind of apprehensive in making the film because she and Chanel were good friends thinking that my staff and I were trying to mock Chanel's memory. But the film I understand is now a cult classic."

Just then Dean Montgomery said, "Pardon the interruption Fashion

Girl but I just learned that the fire marshal won't be attending today on account that he had a prior engagement. Let's all sit down and get started."

The first order of business was to place orders for lunch. During lunch, the conversations were pleasant. After lunch, Chief Gilmore said, "Fashion Girl I know that you will be needed elsewhere you might be and help out with a case. But in Los Angeles, you will help to represent the LAPD and therefore while you're here, you will be an honorary member of the force complete with badge."

Everyone in the room pleasantly applauded. Then Mr. Smith got up and said, "Fashion Girl it is my understanding that you're here to pursue a career in acting. When you're not in school, I hope that you will consider being for the moment a consultant to bring Fashion Girl and the Style Chicks to life on television and the movies. After graduation, I also hope that you will star in this series."

Fashion Girl replied, "It will be my pleasure Mr. Smith. I'm sure my fellow Style Chicks would also help me in this endeavor." Again the group applauded as Dean Montgomery said, "Fashion Girl, I want you to know that once I found out which classes you'll be taking and who your professors will be, I will instruct them to not be too hard on you if you do miss a class or lecture. That's why Amber Watley will assist you in keeping up with your classes."

Fashion Girl asked, "That's very nice of you Dean but I wouldn't want her to suffer in her studies on my account. Will she be alright with this?" Dean Montgomery answered, "She's a senior who's studying to become a nurse. Her class schedule doesn't collide with yours, so she'll be able to help you." Fashion Girl said, "I met her and that's how I knew about this meeting, and she told me that she would be at my service. My mother was supposed to go to UCLA after graduating from high school. But when she became Fashion Girl, she put college on hold and attended Colognia University instead."

Dean Montgomery replied, "I wasn't dean here back in 2004 and I learned this when I became dean here. To make sure that this wouldn't happen again, all of this was done for your benefit. As Chief Gilmore said, it's not everyday that you meet a superheroine and if you graduate, just about any good student would want to follow suit."

Fashion Girl said, "Gentlemen and Miss Lansing, just because I'm a superheroine doesn't mean that people should worship the ground I walk on. As my mother once said that the Style Chicks should be women first and Style Chicks second. That meant that if they wanted a career, a family or anything else they might wanted to do, that they should do it."

Dean Montgomery replied, "Well spoken Fashion Girl. It's good to know that not everyone with privilege acts like it. And with that everyone, this concludes our meeting and I thank you all for coming." The group wished Fashion Girl the best of luck. As Dean Montgomery promised, the server that waited on Cottonmouth gave him the bill for his lunch and gratuity.

Fashion Girl met up with Cottonmouth and he asked, "By the smile on your face, I take the meeting went well?" Fashion Girl answered, "It sure did. I was made an honorary member of the LAPD. I was made a consultant by the head of a motion picture studio to bring me and the others to life on television and the movies. And Dean Montgomery will help to make things easy as far as my education is concerned just in case I miss a class or lecture. Amber was assigned to me in order to accomplish this."

Cottonmouth said, "That is wonderful news and congratulations on everything." Fashion Girl replied, "I also said however, that I'm just an ordinary woman too. Just because of how much money I have or the legacy I inherited doesn't mean that I'm better than others." Cottonmouth said, "And you have a dinner engagement tonight. Are you nervous about it?"

Fashion Girl replied, "I'm not nervous, after all I'm a legacy with a sorority that was started by two of the original Style Chicks. It should go over well."

While this was going on in LA, at Aurora Gardens, The Skulls were getting worried about their leaders. No one had heard from Madame D or the Skull King in three days. The new Tiffany was there with Bonecrusher and went to find Serpentina. Tiffany found her and asked,

"Queen Serpentina, the Skulls haven't heard anything from either Madame D or the Skull King in days. Where could they be and what happened to them?"

Serpentina answered, "Unless they're both down in the Den of Sin, I have no idea where they could be. Tiffany, Bonecrusher, come with me. I have one of those cards that will take us down there." As they got in the elevator and went to Madame D's quarters, that was when the shocking and gruesome discovery had happened.

Tiffany gasped and asked, "What happened here, what is that on the floor?" Serpentina examined the goo on the floor and answered, "This is placenta otherwise known as afterbirth. Madame D is pregnant with triplets. Something bad has happened here." They also noticed what were the remains of three premature babies. Tiffany asked, "Who could have done this? And why to three innocent lives?" Serpentina answered, "Tiffany whether you like it or not, you are about to take part in your first official case as a Style Chick."

So, where were Madame D now called Satanra and the Skull King you might ask? They were in another hideout that the Crypt Keepers and Hell's Hotties had. The Skull King not knowing that his girlfriend turned to evil asked, "Who are you people? And what do you want with me?"

Laughing maniacally Satanra answered, "Don't you recognize me my king? I'm the Skull Queen Madame D. But now you can call me Satanra." Satanra continued to laugh maniacally. The Skull King asked, "If you are the Skull Queen, what happened to our babies? You're not pregnant with them anymore?"

Satanra answered, "That's right. I purged our babies. The good inside me was making me sick. After a threesome with the leaders of the Crypt Keepers and the Hell's Hotties, I decided to join them. I made the deal. I'm young again, immortal and very evil. Join me and we can get pregnant again but this time, our babies will serve evil and the almighty Satan."

The Skull King said, "I will never become evil! If you were once Fashion Girl, you saved our lives, and we served you and the Style

Chicks." Satanra replied, "Those goody two shoe Style Sluts are too sweet for my taste. It's amazing I didn't end up with diabetes." The Skull King asked, "If I were to join you, what do I have to do?" Satanra answered, "Simple, all you have to do is pledge your allegiance to the almighty and drink the magic elixir Wolf's Blood. It will make you strong, horny and very evil. Do it or I will make your life and the Skulls a living hell."

The Skull King asked, "Just tell me one thing. Does this have anything to do with when I said that your daughter was a bad girl? Or does have anything to do with her contacting her father? Why are you doing this?"

Satanra answered, "Satan approached my daughter and offered her the same offer I accepted. As for her contacting her father, it made me furious. So again, when I had a threesome with Lucifer of the Crypt Keepers and La Diablo of Hell's Hotties, that was when I decided to join them. I will deal with the new Fashion Girl in my own way. Join me my king, we will make horrible babies together and I will also spare the other Skulls. I had Wendy Blake and Alicia Lopez brought back to life to get revenge on those who killed them and will now serve our cause."

Satanra poured two glasses of Wolf's Blood, handed one to the Skull King. The Skull King said, "Alright you win, I will do what you ask." Satanra replied, "Here's to evil, immortality and endless love." Satanra clinked the Skull King's glass and as he drank it, the properties of the elixir took hold. Satanra asked, "How do you feel now my king?" The Skull King answered, "I feel the elixir go through me. I am feeling stronger, my dick is getting rock hard, and I am feeling like striking fear in our enemies. I feel so evil."

The Skull King laughed maniacally as Satanra said, "Your first order of business is to impregnate me with the seeds of evil. You now have golden sperm as I have golden eggs. Only golden sperm can impregnate golden eggs. You can have gangbangs with my fellow Hotties. Let's go back to the Den of Sin and commit real sin."

The Skull King and Satanra got on his motorcycle as they headed to the Den of Sin where their new lives as evildoers had begun.

CHAPTER 22

As Satanra and The Skull King headed back to Aurora Gardens to head down to the Den of Sin, they ducked behind the garage where Madame D kept her vehicles and noticed police everywhere. The Skull King asked, "What's going on here? Why all the pigs?" Satanra answered, "I killed our babies down in the Den of Sin. I'm afraid it's become a crime scene."

The Skull King asked, "Why did you kill our babies and how?" Satanra answered, "Our former babies were conceived good, so I killed them. I deliberately purged them by inducing labor by striking my stomach. Now when we conceive again, it will be for evil." They disappeared in a cloud of thick black smoke and headed elsewhere to do their bad deeds.

At the same time in Los Angeles, Fashion Girl wasn't made aware of what happened as of yet. After she and Cottonmouth left the restaurant and back at their house, she was preparing for her dinner date with the Alpha Beta Omega sorority. She asked, "Hey Cottonmouth, what outfit should I wear to this dinner? Any suggestions?" Cottonmouth answered, "We ate together with you dressed as Fashion Girl. We went grocery shopping with you dressed as Fashion Girl why not go to this dinner dressed as Fashion Girl."

Fashion Girl said, "Except for at school, going as Fashion Girl seems to have worked out so far, what's one more appearance. I'll go there in the Glam Mobile too." Cottonmouth replied, "Why not, it might give those girls a thrill unless they have nice cars too."

Fashion Girl said, "Judging by the fact that Amber Watley told me she's a member and looks like she's hanging on by a thread, I'll take a wild guess that these girls also might be in the same boat. But I can't tell by a book's cover. Cottonmouth, dinner is at eight so just relax here, keep an eye on Nike and check out your new mancave." Cottonmouth replied, "Okay I will."

It was after seven when Fashion Girl left. Cottonmouth turned on the huge TV as one of the local stations was doing a seven o'clock newscast. The anchor talked about, and images were shown of what happened in Aurora Gardens. Then the phone rang. Cottonmouth picked up the phone as Saks was on the other end. She asked, "Cottonmouth, where's Fashion Girl? And did she see the news?"

Cottonmouth answered, "No she left a few minutes ago to attend a dinner at the sorority house that two of the original Style Chicks founded." Saks said, "Alpha Beta Omega. I am familiar with it, but we didn't belong to any sorority when we were in college." Cottonmouth replied, "She was invited to come because her aunt belonged." Saks said, "The news said that the dead babies were found in the Den of Sin. Plus, Madame D and the Skull King are both missing. Cottonmouth I fear the worst."

Cottonmouth replied, "Let's not assume the worst for now. The other Style Chicks I'm sure are on the case. If it makes you feel any better, I'll call Serpentina. She could give us more information. Come on over with the others, we'll get to the bottom of this." Saks asked, "What about Fashion Girl? She needs to be notified." Cottonmouth answered, "Not to worry Saks, when she gets home, we'll all tell her."

Cottonmouth called Serpentina and said, "Queen Serpentina, I saw on the news about something happening at Aurora Gardens. What do you know about it?" Serpentina replied, "Three babies were found dead in the Den of Sin. It turns out that they were Madame D's babies. She and the Skull King are missing. This is going to be the first mission the new Style Chicks will face."

Cottonmouth asked, "Should Fashion Girl come back home to look into this?" Serpentina answered, "Not at the moment, after all you both are now in college. If we need her, I'll ask her." Cottonmouth said, "She went to a sorority house for dinner. Before that, she met with the Dean of UCLA along with other high-ranking people including the mayor and police chief."

Serpentina replied, "I had a feeling that she would meet them at some point. I know about the dinner she's having. Remember I belonged to that sorority many years ago. She's a legacy and they will want her to join." Cottonmouth said, "Are you aware that Saks, Bloomie and Nine West bought us a house in Beverly Hills? If not that's what happened along with a new member of the Style Chicks, a puppy Nine West named him Nike. My question is if Fashion Girl is accepted in a sorority and I know that both fraternities and sororities have houses, would she move into it?"

Serpentina replied, "I knew the girls would do something nice for Daphne. They love her especially when she visited us, and they got along with her very well. But I had no idea that they bought her a house in Beverly Hills. And a puppy too? What kind of dog is he?" Cottonmouth said, "A breed I never heard of before, he's a cockapoo. He's cute and lovable."

Serpentina replied, "I've heard of cockapoos. It's like a designer breed. Lots of wealthy people would have such a dog." Cottonmouth said, "He practically gave Daphne a bath with his tongue. He also gave me a good licking. But we are getting off the subject. As for Madame D's babies, I'll tell Daphne the news. I hate to think that she just lost three future siblings before they were even born."

Serpentina replied, "I know Cottonmouth, I also lost three future nieces and or nephews. When I find out who did this, he or she will answer for it." Thank you for getting in touch with me Cottonmouth, bye-bye." When Cottonmouth hung up the phone, he had a strange look on his face. He asked, "Ladies, you're Style Chicks, tell me what Daphne can do when she finds out about this?"

Saks answered, "We've been Style Chicks for fifteen years now. We grew up knowing and learning about crime and how to fight it. The former Style Chicks dealt with a lot of cases, but this is one case they couldn't handle directly but indirectly. Madame D allowed us to continue to be Style Chicks after Daphne turned eighteen. All I can promise is that we are here for her."

"But how she'll take the news that her future siblings are dead? All I can say is that she will get mad, and we can't blame her for that. It makes me mad how we found out about this, seeing it on the news! Cottonmouth, you're new to this sort of thing so be strong for her. Comfort her anyway you can, and we'll help her and kick the ass of whoever did this."

Back in Aurora Gardens, Satanra and the Skull King returned to the motor court and to The Den of Sin. Satanra said, "My king, not only have I turned evil, but I now have powers. They suspect its my babies they've found, with my new magical powers, I can make the DNA of those dead babies into the DNA of other babies. They suspected that I was pregnant with other men's babies, so let them think that. I will disguise myself as Madame D again pregnant with those ugh goody good babies."

The Skull King replied, "After you do that my queen, we'll make new babies. Hideously evil and unstoppable. He laughed maniacally as Satanra said, "Miss Muertos when she kills the leader of the Crocs, she'll make that gang hers and she's just as fertile as I am. And Slutan once she kills Mrs. Z, she'll make her girls ours. Mrs. Z has already found young girls who are fertile and eager to be impregnated. Satanra also laughed maniacally as they proceeded with their plans.

Back in Los Angeles, Fashion Girl pulled into the sorority house where the entire membership body greeted her. Amber said, "Welcome to Alpha Beta Omega the first and last name in sororities." Fashion Girl replied, "Thank you Amber, thank you all for allowing me to come tonight."

Then a young woman approached Fashion Girl and said, "Fashion Girl, my name is Linda Green, my grandmother was the original Tiffany who along with the original Penney Dillard helped to find. I personally welcome you. We hope that finally that a Fashion Girl will join our sorority." Fashion Girl replied, "Thank you Linda. I am here tonight on your invitation. I haven't decided yet whether or not I will join."

Linda asked, "Do you have any reservations as to why you might not be able to join?" Fashion Girl answered, "First and foremost, I'm a superheroine. If it's mandatory for me to attend certain events, I might be working on a case. I might not even be here in LA and already my plate is full, and I haven't had a class yet."

Linda asked, "Exactly what do you have on your plate already?" Fashion Girl answered, "I met Dean Montgomery in person today as he invited me to have lunch with him along with the police chief, a reporter for KCBS and the head of First And Ten Pictures. The chief made me an honorary police officer. The head of First And Ten Pictures wanted me to be an advisor as he is making a TV series based on me. He wants realism in this series and I'm to provide advice."

"Three of the former Junior Style Chicks bought me and my boy-friend a house in Beverly Hills, so I don't know if I have to live here or there." Linda said, "This is the reason why we invited you to dinner. And I think we can work something out if you decide to join."

Fashion Girl replied, "What about wild parties? I've heard so many stories about how some fraternities and sororities have gotten in trouble with excessive drinking and parties that have cause chapters to be expelled from campus." Linda said, "That is reasonable as to why most students would join. But throughout the history of this sorority, we've been praised for being a model place for young ladies to be young ladies. Now Fashion Girl, please join us in the dining room, we have a fabulous dinner waiting for you,"

Linda wasn't joking on using fabulous for how the dining room table was set. The dinner consisted of prime rib cooked to perfection, roasted red potatoes, homemade buttermilk biscuits and the most dec-adent chocolate cake Fashion Girl had ever seen with imported French champagne. Fashion Girl replied, "The former Victoria couldn't have made a better meal. I am deeply honored."

Conversation was lively as Fashion Girl was impressed with this group of young women who were dedicated to setting a good example not just to her but all people in general. Linda asked, "Well Fashion Girl, what do you think? Are we a perfect fit for you?" Fashion Girl answered, "Earlier today, I made Amber an honorary Style Chick because of how she is. So, it's only fair if I do the same. I'm in ladies and I thank you."

The group applauded as Amber said, "Congratulations Fashion Girl! Welcome to Alpha Beta Omega!" Fashion Girl replied, "Being a super-heroine will also give you some clout. Think about it, being a member, you'll be the envy of all groups like this all over the country. I will not let you down." Amber said, "Just like you took a pledge to become a Style Chick, stand up, raise your hand and repeat after me."

The pledge was similar to the Style Chick pledge stating being pure of heart, spreading love and peace, etc. The dinner was over and before Fashion Girl left, Linda added, "We understand that you might be able to be here at all so don't worry. I also offer my congratulations as well. Thank you for coming tonight, enjoy the rest of your evening and we'll have Amber tell you of any events we have and if you're able to come."

As Fashion Girl left, the group waved goodbye. Little did Fashion Girl know what was waiting for her when she got home and the terrible news she would receive.

CHAPTER 23

When Fashion Girl arrived at home and walked in, she noticed Cottonmouth, Saks, Bloomie and Nine West sitting in the living room with strange looks on their faces. She asked, "Cottonmouth, girls, what's going on? Why do you all look so strange?"

Cottonmouth got up and answered, "Honey, I don't know how we can tell you this without crying. Something bad happened at Aurora Gardens. We all saw this on the news and your aunt called. She and Tiffany found three dead babies inside the Den of Sin. Autopsy concluded that they died after someone had a miscarriage. But the police suspects murder. Honey they were your mom's babies."

The color in Fashion Girl's face completely drained and asked, "Where's mom? Is she alright? Is she in the hospital? What? WHAT!" Cottonmouth answered, "Calm down honey please. Your mom and the Skull King are missing. No telling about your mom's condition. All the Style Chicks and your aunt can do now is to investigate, and all we can do is wait for any news."

Fashion Girl began to cry and said, "I lost three future siblings tonight on a day that was otherwise great. Excuse me please, I'm going to be sick." Fashion Girl ran upstairs to the nearest bathroom. The others could hear the retching she was doing. Cottonmouth said, "Ladies, I don't know about you but when Fashion Girl feels better, we're going back home to do some investigating of our own."

Nine West replied, "Cottonmouth we know how you feel, but we can't go there without a lead. First, let's recap what has happened according to the news and Cindy. We know that three babies and afterbirth were found in the Den of Sin. We don't know why Cindy and Tiffany went down there to begin with. And we know that Madame D and the Skull King are missing. If we go back now literally blind, we could make things worse. Tell you what, I'll call Cindy and I'll try to get an update of any kind."

Nine West picked up the phone and called Cindy to get any updates. Cindy picked up the phone and said hello as Nine West asked, "Cindy this is Nine West. We just told the news to Fashion Girl, and it shook her to her core. She's in the bathroom throwing up. Is there any updates we need to know about?"

Serpentina replied, "There was a mistake at the coroner's office. Yes three babies were found, the coroner thought the same thing we thought that the babies belonged to Madame D. As it turned out, the babies belonged to another girl. Apparently somehow an unauthorized user of the Den of Sin got down there pregnant with triplets too. These babies were Asian meaning either a Chinese, Japanese or Korean girl was down there."

Nine West said, "The previous Macy is Chinese, but we now know it couldn't been her since she's come out as a lesbian. The new Macy we know is Japanese and she's never been sexually active, so who could had gone down there and had a miscarriage?"

Serpentina replied in puzzlement, "We're still investigating the matter. But there is some good news, Madame D and the Skull King came back earlier tonight. And there's something else, she announced that as of tomorrow morning, no families or weary travelers are no longer welcome here and she fired everyone including me."

Nine West said, "You're kidding. Madame D made that place into an oasis for everyone, why won't she allow just anyone anymore? And why did she fire your fellow Vipers and the Skulls?" Serpentina replied, "It's her property and she can do with Aurora Gardens anyway she wants. She also severed ties with Style Incorporated, she figures she can make money without mom."

Nine West asked, "If you and the others need money, let us know okay. Is there anything we can do to help now?" Serpentina answered, "Give Daphne this update. Tell her that her mom did return pregnant as ever and what she's going to do now. As far as all of us are concerned, we are still on the payroll. We'll just have to find other work that's all."

Nine West said, "Thanks for this update Cindy. I'll let Daphne know what you told me." The call ended and Nine West's expression on her face was puzzling. Fashion Girl returned downstairs and asked, "I overheard you talking with Aunt Cindy Nine West, what did she tell you?" Nine West answered, "Well um, your aunt told me that the babies that were found in the Den of Sin weren't your mom's after all. The babies were of Asian origin and that some Asian girl somehow went down there and had a miscarriage. Also, your mom and the Skull King returned but she fired everyone from Aurora Gardens."

Fashion Girl couldn't believe her ears and said, "At least my mom returned but something isn't right. Not right at all." Just then, the doorbell rang. Saks was near the door and answered it. A man and a woman were at the door and asked for Fashion Girl. Saks let them in, and the man said, "Fashion Girl, I'm Lt. Bailey Pollack of the Las Vegas Police Department. The woman added, "My name is Vivian Ramirez of LA Escorts. We're both here to offer you a job."

Fashion Girl asked, "What kind of job do you want me to do? Am I in trouble somehow with the Las Vegas Police? And I'm not a call girl or an escort." Lt. Pollack answered, "No you're not in trouble with the police in Vegas and we both know you're not an escort. We want you to help us stop a major criminal. His real name is George Steinberg and he's known as "The Frog". He's called that because he bounces around from city to city and has no roots anywhere."

Saks said, "My friends and I have heard of him, but we've never encountered him. So, what do you want with Fashion Girl?" Vivian replied, "We want Fashion Girl to become an escort for him tomorrow night so we can finally stop him. He's considered armed and extremely dangerous." Fashion Girl said, "Well I decided to be a femme fatale, so I'm figured to be the right person for the job right?"

Lt. Pollack replied, "Correct. We'll be around as well as helping you. He's planning to go to Vegas tomorrow night and that's why I'm here in LA to recruit you." Fashion Girl said, "Lt. Pollack, Ms. Ramirez, I appreciate the offer, but I got some disturbing news from back home and I may have to return there."

Saks said, "Tell you what Fashion Girl, I'll stay here to mind the phone. Bloomie and Nine West will go with Lt. Pollack to assist you if necessary." Cottonmouth added, "I am going too. No criminal mastermind is going to try anything with my girlfriend. I'll stay with Bloomie and Nine West to keep away from any action that we can't handle."

Vivian said, "Fashion Girl, be ready by five o'clock tomorrow. He's going to pick you up at my office. He'll fly you and his gang to Vegas. He will wine and dine you for he is charming but the minute something happens, the police will intervene." Fashion Girl replied, "And so will I Ms. Ramirez. I happen to be a mistress of disguise."

Lt. Pollack said, "Fashion Girl, I know you're a superheroine but you're not indestructible. Just keep in mind that you're going to help us lure a dangerous criminal into our custody. I know you have powers, but you aren't known to be armed with a gun. I'm not telling you not to help, I'm telling you to be careful."

Fashion Girl replied, "It's true I've only been a Style Chick for about two months now. But I have more than forty years of experience and know how behind me. My mother let the original Junior Style Chicks continue to be regular Style Chicks. They've had fifteen years of training and experience along with assisting in more than twenty cases. Their here to help me become the Fashion Girl that my mother and grandmother were before me."

Vivian said, "Five o'clock tomorrow Fashion Girl. Be sure to look your best, remember you're going to be a high-class escort." Fashion Girl replied, "Ms. Ramirez, even though I'm not a model like my mother was or an investigator like my grandmother was, my mother however, let me have her entire wardrobe. I can be any kind of woman needed on the case. I'll be ready and dressed to kill."

This satisfied both Lt. Pollack and Vivian Ramirez. They thanked

Fashion Girl and left. Fashion Girl looked at the others and said, "I feel like I've been drafted into service." Cottonmouth replied, "I guess this is your first official case. Do you remember your mom telling you what her first case was when she first became Fashion Girl?"

Fashion Girl said, "All I remember hearing about that was she was presented to the Colognia Police Department. She took on a case for them and that's all I remember about it." Cottonmouth replied, "Don't worry about a thing honey. Bloomie, Nine West and I will be nearby wherever you're at without you seeing us."

Bloomie added, "Daphne if it was one thing we were taught was surveillance. We'll place a small transmitter in your purse tomorrow morning it's silent and it will blink quickly when we pinpoint your location." Fashion Girl said, "I'll be prepared for tomorrow night. This does make me feel better. Thanks Bloomie."

Back in Aurora Gardens, Satanra, Slutan and Miss Muertos put their plans in action. Satanra asked, "Ladies, do you know what you need to do?" Slutan answered, "Yes I do. I can't wait to see that witch Mrs. Z again. When I kill her, I'll take those little tramps of hers and make them ours. I hope they'll like the kind of sex the Crypt Keepers and Hell's Hotties likes. Nonstop, hot, and creating evil life."

Miss Muertos added, "And I can't wait to choke the life out of Queen Croc. I'll make those skinhead racists of hers into real evil minions of the Crypt Keepers. I'll make her gang worship the ground I walk on. I can't wait for the evil, steamy gangbangs I'm going to have with them. With the right amount of wolf's blood, I'll create Satan's Army all by myself."

Satanra said, "Excellent. Now that the Den of Sin has been clear of the cops and the paramedics, my king and I have our own sin to make. Make sure you all have enough wolf's blood to make these people yours to command. Enjoy your evening ladies." The three laughed maniacally, grabbed enough bottles of their magic elixir, loaded up their vehicles and went to find those who did them wrong.

CHAPTER 24

True to her word, Satanra and The Skull King went down to the Den of Sin to have a sexual encounter she only experienced in her dream of becoming evil fifteen years earlier. Once they drank more wolf's blood, The Skull King began his conquest of his queen as they had nonstop sex for hours.

While this was going on, Slutan went back to the hideout of Mrs. X and her sex slave operation. Slutan approached Mrs. X and told her to come outside. Mrs. X asked, "And who the hell are you and what are you doing here?" Slutan answered, "Don't you recognize me Mrs. X? I'm Wendy Blake or I used to be her." Mrs. X said, "That's impossible, I heard you died about ten years ago."

Slutan replied, "I live again but you won't for much longer. Thanks to your husband and Drain-O, I died from that dangerous drug. I was pregnant again and my unborn baby died with me too. Now I live again as Slutan, and I serve Satan's will. And once I dispose of you, I will take those girls and turn them into minions of evil. Prepare for your demise for I will see you in hell!"

Mrs. X tried to defend herself, but Slutan was too powerful. She grabbed Mrs. X by the throat and choked the life out of her until she was dead. Slutan began to laugh maniacally as she stood over Mrs. X's lifeless body. She said, "I hope you're judged the way I was judged. I hope you rot where you lay." She continued to laugh maniacally as she went down to the lair, she said, "Girls I am Slutan your new leader. I know you were raised to be sex slaves to make Mrs. X rich. But now you have a choice."

"If some of you wish to leave this place and never return, you may go in peace. But if you wish to stay, you will serve the almighty Satan and produce his Army of Evil. With this potion called wolf's blood, you'll become strong, evil and incredibly fertile. With me and wolf's blood, scour this county and attract men and make them do your bidding. And get impregnated for the glory of Satan. Now who's with me?"

There were twenty girls, but they were older than Slutan remembered. None of them left the scene and all stayed on. One girl replied, "We were all taken away from our homes at an early age to do Mrs. X's bidding. Thanks to Drain-O, we had no minds of our own. You have a deal Slutan, we will do your bidding and will drink this wolf's blood. We all want to get pregnant if it means to be rewarded."

Slutan laughed maniacally and said, "Excellent ladies! Take these bottles with you. Pour the elixir into flasks and trick your prey into drinking it. They also will become extremely fertile, and you'll enjoy nonstop sex for hours. Your eggs will become pure gold and they'll have golden sperm. You can also get pregnant with multiple babies and each of them will become willing participants to Satan's Army of Evil."

The girls took the bottles. They all had flasks and poured out whatever they were drinking and filled the bottles with the elixir. Slutan said, "This place is no more, check back with me to get more elixir. Any money you get is now yours. I have a new hideout so go there and you'll be treated to a feast every meal. Enjoy yourselves ladies!" Slutan laughed maniacally as she was pleased with what she did.

At the same time, Miss Muertos found the Crocs hideout. She said to herself, *"There they are. The bastards who cost me my life. Once I kill their queen, I will have them worship me. Their girlfriends will also do my bidding. For now, it's their queen I want. I want my revenge and I'm going to get it."*

Miss Muertos found The Croc Queen all alone outside her hideout. Miss Muertos said, "I've come for you Croc Queen. I have a score to settle with you." The Croc Queen asked, "Who are you and what do you want with me?" Miss Muertos answered, "Remember me skinhead, I'm Alicia Lopez. You had me killed because of my Latin heritage."

The Croc Queen said nervously, "Y-Y-You can't be her, we k-killed her nearly ten years ago. And we did kill her because she was Latin. She didn't deserve to live in this country." Miss Muertos replied, "Wrong answer you bigoted bitch. I am now Miss Muertos, Latin for death. It's your worthless life I want." The Croc Queen said, "If you want me dead, you will have to fight me. I will strike you dead where you stand!"

Laughing maniacally Miss Muertos replied, "You can't kill what's already dead. I have eternal life now!" The Croc Queen took out her switchblade knife, exposed the blade and swung at Miss Muertos and it did pierce her skin, but the slashes healed. Miss Muertos continued to laugh and continued, "See bitch, you can't kill me. And when I want someone dead, they die."

At that moment, Miss Muertos grabbed The Croc Queen by the throat with one hand and began choking her. She continued, "Like Mrs. Z who killed my friend, I kill you now!" With her other hand, she broke The Croc Queen's neck killing her instantly and continued, "Rot in hell you worthless piece of racist scum."

When The Croc Queen didn't return to her hideout, her gang of bigots came out looking for her. They saw Miss Muertos standing over The Croc Queen's lifeless body. The Croc King asked, "Who are you? Answer me bitch! What did you do to my girlfriend?" Miss Muertos answered, "I'm Miss Muertos. I killed your queen and now you will do my bidding as your new leader."

The Croc King said, "We don't answer to a piece of shit like you! We'll strike you dead!" Miss Muertos replied, "Go ahead and try skinheads, your queen tried, and it cost her, her life. I can take all of you on. I have a proposition for you. I now answer to Satan. I am now one of his Hell's Hotties. Join me and him, and you can be more than what you were before."

"Become Crypt Keepers and Satan will give you all eternal life. With me and an elixir known as wolf's blood, you'll become strong, and extremely fertile. Your girlfriends can also become Hell's Hotties. They too will become fertile and have eternal life. They will help bore many babies for Satan's Army. If you think you were evil before, join me and it can all be yours. Deny me, you will meet the same fate as your queen. So, what's it going to be gentlemen?"

"The Crocs stood in a huddle talking it over. Before the Croc King gave his answer, he asked, "How do we supply Satan with an Army? Do we have to bang you only? Or can we fuck any woman we want?" Miss Muertos answered, "Yes you must have sex with me, but you can bang any woman you see fit too. Give them the elixir, you will have golden sperm while the women will have golden eggs. And it guarantees instant pregnancy. And I have a new hideout for us where you will be treated to feasts unlike anything you've ever experienced."

The Croc King and his thugs were convinced and said, "Okay Miss Muertos, we have come to terms. So, when do we begin this new venture?" Miss Muertos replied, "Does now seem too soon? All the wolf's blood you can drink is with me. Once you start drinking it, your personality will change forever. So, boys, who would like to be the first to put several buns in my oven?"

Once they began drinking the elixir, those who didn't have girlfriends lined up to take part. Miss Muertos laughed maniacally and continued, "We'll have gangbangs every night. Be sure to get other women to join us. We'll give our master what he wants. To conquer this shithole of a planet. FOR THE GLORY OF SATAN!" The others replied, "FOR THE GLORY OF SATAN!"

More than six hours later in the Den of Sin, both Satanra and the Skull King paused to catch their breath. Satanra asked, "How do you feel my king?" The Skull King answered, "I feel incredible. Being evil has made you a sex machine." Satanra said, "Hmm, I feel like you impregnated me with a dozen babies. I will also be a baby making machine so here's a secret my king, the more sex I get, the more pregnant I get. Also, we can fuck whoever we want. We don't have to be exclusive."

The Skull King smiled and replied, "I like that. Before long, we'll infect breeders by the dozens to give Satan his army." Satanra said, "What's more my king, we will feast every meal and we'll eat like a plague of locusts. Victoria's Café is where we will feast as Satan will send lots of food to us." The Skull King replied, "I love you my queen, let's fuck some more." Satanra said, "Fuck me my king, make me more pregnant." She began to laugh maniacally as The Skull King continued his conquest. He asked, "What about your daughter and the new Style Chicks? They will try to stop us."

Satanra answered, "When my daughter dares to show up here or in Colognia, I'll teach that little bitch a lesson she'll never forget. I will thrash her within an inch of her life as will Miss Muertos' new posse and Slutan's group of bitches." The Skull King asked, "What will you do to her? Can Miss Muertos' boys gets to have her way with her? Will she be beaten up or raped?" Satanra answered, "She's still my daughter, but I like how you think. So, yes she'll get a beating and a banging too. She'll wish she was never born and wish she was dead." The two laughed maniacally as they continued to have more nonstop sex.

How can any mother subject her eldest daughter to such a beatdown? In Satanra's mind, she gave up her career as a model and being the previous Fashion Girl. So, she feels like she was somehow betrayed when she knew full well that she had to pass the baton to her eldest daughter as it is dictated by the rite of passage.

But for the new Fashion Girl, she had to fight a menace of a different sort as she was to embark on her first official mission as the new Stylish Crime Fighter.

CHAPTER 25

The next morning in Los Angeles, Fashion Girl was preparing for her first official duty as a Style Chick. She first went to a beauty salon to get her hair done. Next she came home to find the perfect outfit to wear. Bloomie and Nine West helped her with the preparation process. While this was going on, Serpentina contacted her, but it was Cottonmouth who answered, He said hello and asked, "Serpentina, is something wrong? You sound kind of excited."

Serpentina answered, "I am Cottonmouth but not the kind of good excitement. I told you last night that we saw Madame D and the Skull King back to Aurora Gardens. No sooner did I tell you this that she fired the other Skulls and all of us Vipers and had us trespassed from the property. We were all paid off and I am at the Mystique Boutique with the others and the Style Chicks trying to figure out what to do next."

"How's my niece doing this morning? Is she okay after I told her what happened?" Cottonmouth answered, "That's awful news, I'm sorry all of you lost your jobs. As for Daphne, she's preparing for tonight. She's going to Las Vegas as an escort to a major crime figure. His name is George Steinberg, they call him "The Frog" because he's never in the same place for long."

Serpentina said, "We've heard of him, but he is hard to locate and capture. If we as the former Style Chicks couldn't stop him, I don't know if Daphne can. How is she going about acting the part?" Cottonmouth replied, "For starters, she got her hair done and right now Bloomie and Nine West are helping her pick out the right outfit for the job. I'm sure she's going to look good for this mission. What about you and the others? How are you going to get by without a steady income?"

Serpentina said, "I spoke with my mother before I called you. She'll make sure we are still getting paid for our services and she's going to cut off financial support to Aurora Gardens later today. Without any security over there, it's going to become a haven for dangerous people. At least we kept them in check." Cottonmouth asked, "Do you want me to pass along any message you might have for Daphne?" Serpentina answered, "Just tell her that I called to see how she is and that we love her."

Cottonmouth said, "I sure will my queen. I'll talk to you later, I'll let you know how Daphne did in Vegas." Serpentina replied, "I wish her the best of luck, goodbye." Cottonmouth hung up the phone and said to himself, *"I hope she does good too Serpentina."*

In an upstairs bedroom, Bloomie and Nine West were helping Fashion Girl pick out the right outfit. Fashion Girl asked, "Girls, how do you think I should dress for tonight? Should I dress slutty? Or should I dress casually? Or more formally?" Bloomie answered, "I know some people go to Vegas not dressed fancy at all. But for this trip, you should dress to the nines. Pull out all the stops and make a great impression."

Fashion Girl said, "My mother literally gave me a department store full of clothing. It's almost like a kid in a candy store. I think you're right Bloomie, I should dress like I own Las Vegas. My mother modeled in evening gowns so I will wear one of them." Bloomie replied, "I know it's taboo, but I think you should also take one of your mother's furs too." Nine West added, "Your mother also had all kinds of accessories too. I think those long opera gloves would go with the gown along with some jewelry too. We'll help you look like a million dollars."

Bloomie and Nine West helped Fashion Girl get ready. They fixed her makeup; they found the right outfit. They selected a diamond necklace, two diamond rings and diamond earrings. They found a purse that Fashion Girl could sling across her shoulder instead of by her side. And instead of boots, they found a pair of pumps to complete the look and a pair of diamond ankle bracelets.

Along with Fashion Girl's power bracelets, one last thing Bloomie did was to put in the purse a wallet containing money, a cigarette lighter and holder along with a pack of expensive looking cigarettes. This was to show The Frog that he would be with a lady with class, sophistication and style. Fashion Girl isn't a Style Chick for nothing.

By four o'clock Fashion Girl was ready for what would happen that night. Bloomie and Nine West came down first as Bloomie said, "Cottonmouth, Saks, Nine West and I proudly present the Stylish Crime Fighter Fashion Girl in her best disguise ever." Fashion Girl sashayed down the stairs as Cottonmouth's eyes looked like a pair of black marbles.

He said, "Daphne, you look incredible. Honey in that outfit, you could put any Hollywood actress to shame." Fashion Girl laughed and replied, "And you Cottonmouth oh so handsome could put any actor to shame too. But aren't you going to dress up too?"

Bloomie replied, "No we won't but we'll be nearby if you should need us." Saks added, "That Lt. Pollack called. He found out that The Frog will take you to the Bellagio. You know the hotel with the dancing waterfalls. Candy and the new Victoria will wait for us in the Freedom Flyer at the municipal airport after your plane leaves the same airport." Fashion Girl said, "Well, I guess we're ready for what might happen. Now I will wait for the escort service comes for me and go to their office to wait to be picked up by The Frog."

Fifteen minutes later, a car from the escort service pulled up as Vivian Ramirez came out and said, "Fashion Girl, now I see why you're called The Stylish Crime Fighter. You look like a high-priced call girl. And perfect for this mission." Fashion Girl smiled and replied, "Thank you Ms. Ramirez and remember from here on out, call me Daphne."

Vivian said, "I will remember. Now let's go to the office and wait for your date for tonight." Fashion Girl replied, "Before we go, may I talk with my boyfriend for a moment or two please?" Vivian said, "Of course, go ahead." Fashion Girl turned to Cottonmouth and said, "Cottonmouth, I hope you understand why I'm doing this. My father lost his life because he thought my mother was having an affair with a man named Victor Miller."

Cottonmouth replied, "Not to worry Daphne. I've heard about that case, and I fully understand." Fashion Girl said, "It's you I want and the only one I want. If he tries anything funny, I can handle him." Fashion Girl kissed Cottonmouth and continued, "I love you." Cottonmouth replied, "I love you too Daphne. Good luck." Fashion Girl turned to Vivian and said, "Okay Ms. Ramírez I'm ready to go. See you guys later."

Cottonmouth went back inside the house and said to the others, "Ladies, I feel confident that Daphne will do well tonight. But I also feel worried about what's happening at home." Saks replied, "What is happening back home? Fill me in."

Cottonmouth said, "Last night, Madame D fired the Skulls and Vipers except for the Skull King who was with her. Serpentina told me this earlier. Her mother will suspend any money to Aurora Gardens. Remember our money is provided by Style Incorporated." Saks replied, "After Daphne finishes her first mission, let's go back to Colognia just to see exactly what's going on."

Cottonmouth said, "If Madame D fired everyone, my question is just who will keep Aurora Gardens secure? And who will come there without it?" Bloomie replied, "I know I might sound like I'm shooting in the dark, but I think that something bad has happened to Madame D that prompted her to fire everyone."

Cottonmouth asked, "What exactly do you think happened to Madame D Bloomie?" Bloomie answered, "My boyfriend lives near Aurora Gardens, and he tells me everything that goes on over there. He told me that two gang members comes to Madame D and does threesomes with her. One gang member is a man who belongs to a gang called The Crypt Keepers and the other a woman is from a gang called Hell's Hotties. She's been with them for months."

Cottonmouth asked, "Do you think The Skull King knows about it?" Bloomie answered, "Yes. He also told me that The Skull King also has threesomes too. With two more of Hell's Hotties. Cottonmouth, The Crypt Keepers were the gang in the dream Daphne's mother once had where she turned evil. Remember that Daphne visited her father's grave and her mother got so upset? Well, she had a session with those two the next day and they must have talked into her joining up with them."

"And remember how the new Tiffany and Serpentina found those dead babies in the Den of Sin? I don't care what anyone thinks, but those babies were Daphne's future siblings. Madame D and the Skull King have become evil. And if my hunch is right, they have also become willing servants of Satan. Satan wants an Army of Evil to conquer the world. I remember that from that dream Daphne's mother had."

Before Cottonmouth, Nine West or Saks could respond, the phone began to ring. Saks picked up the phone, said hello and the voice on the other end asked for Bloomie. Saks handed the receiver over to Bloomie. She said hello and the voice on the other end replied, "Bloomie, it's Carl. Honey I have some more news for you. I found out more about the situation at Aurora Gardens."

Bloomie asked, "What's going on over there Carl? Talk to me." Carl answered, "I snuck into the facility behind Victoria's Café, and I saw a group of both men and women with enough food to feed every member of the military. Plus, I also saw bottles and bottles of this red liquid on a separate table. I don't think its wine, but it could be something else. But these people were guzzling it down like an SUV that gets two miles per gallon. After they drank it, they began to have sex right there in the café. Bloomie, something needs to be done about this."

Bloomie said, "Carl thanks for the update. Get out of there while they can't see you. Get in your car and go to the Mystique Boutique and inform Tiffany and Serpentina and most importantly stay over there and don't leave." Carl replied, "I will Bloomie and thank you. Talk to you later, Ciao." As Bloomie hung up the phone, she said to the others, "After Daphne's mission in Vegas is done, we need to go back to Colognia immediately. I feel that it's of the utmost importance."

Cottonmouth asked, "What's going on over there Bloomie?" Bloomie answered, "Carl saw lots of people over at Victoria's Café eating enough food for several banquets along with several bottles of a red liquid they drank down as if it were red colored water. Then they had sex all over the café. On the tables, on the floor, everywhere. We are going back to Colognia right after Daphne's done in Vegas. C'mon for now we need to go to the municipal airport and wait for Candy and Victoria."

Carl hurried out of Aurora Gardens before anyone saw him. Victoria's Café got out of control with eating, drinking, partying and sex. Another table had a bunch of pregnancy tests to see if the women got pregnant and how many eggs were fertilized. All the women who needed to pee took a test with them to check. Almost all the women were pleased especially Satanra who grabbed the Skull King and went back to the Den of Sin. Her last instruction to the others were to go wild and go to the motel to continue their sexual escapades.

In the Den of Sin, Satanra was smiling from ear to ear and said, "My king, we did it! I'm pregnant with twelve babies! I'm so happy!" The Skull King replied, "That's wonderful babe! I can't wait to be a father!" Satanra said, "Remember what I told you my king. The more sex we have the more pregnant I will become. I'm sure our master will be pleased. With the other women now in our gang, Satan will have his army by the hundreds or maybe even thousands."

The Skull King replied, "Now my queen, I want us to be together forever since we'll live forever." He got down on one knee and opened a box containing a skull ring encrusted with diamonds and continued, "My queen Satanra, will you marry me?" Satanra said happily, "Yes my king! Yes I will marry you. I am the chosen one. Once we're married, we will read text from an ancient scroll to make us eternal forever. Now then with more wolf's blood, let's celebrate our upcoming nuptials!" They drank the elixir, laughed maniacally and began to again have nonstop sex. Satanra said, "Get me more pregnant! I want to give birth to an entire nation of Satan's Army!"

Her wish was granted and as for Carl, he went to the Mystique Boutique and told the Style Chicks the disturbing news and at the same time, the leader of the Style Chicks was ready for her rendezvous with The Frog in Las Vegas.

CHAPTER 26

En route to the escort office, Fashion Girl and Vivian Ramirez were engaged in conversation. Fashion Girl wanted to smoke a cigarette to get into the act. Although Vivian allowed it, she was confused about it and asked, "Since when does Fashion Girl smoke? I would think that you or any Fashion Girl would be dead set against it."

Fashion Girl answered, "Normally I wouldn't but if I am to be a high-class call girl, I may have to do certain things. Smoking is one of them as is drinking. You want me to catch a dangerous criminal. I need to be good bait to do it." Vivian asked, "What about the other Style Chicks? Do any of them do these kinds of things?" Fashion Girl answered, "The new Tiffany both smokes and drinks too. The new Penney Dillard also smokes but not on a regular basis. Think of it this way, if we deal with some bad people, we have to be that way too. As I said, if I'm going to catch a dangerous criminal, I need to be good bait."

Vivian understood what Fashion Girl said, but she was kind of perplexed about it. When they arrived at the escort office, the "fish" as it were hadn't arrived yet but would be there by six o'clock. So, the only thing Fashion Girl could do is wait. Vivian instructed Fashion Girl to wait into another room and she would introduce her to the frog. This gave Fashion Girl time to freshen her makeup, and to mentally prepare herself for whatever will happen next.

Right at six o'clock, a long black limousine pulled up in front of the office. A chauffer opened the door as George Steinberg AKA The Frog stepped out. Dressed in a tuxedo, he was more than six feet tall, weighed more than two hundred pounds and was ruggedly handsome. As "fish" goes, Fashion Girl was about to attempt to capture Moby Dick.

Steinberg walked in approached Vivian, kissed her hand, and said, "Ah, Vivian, how good to see you again. Vivian replied, "Gracias Senor. How may I be of service to you this evening?" Steinberg said, "I'm flying to Las Vegas tonight and I want one of your girls to escort me while I'm there." Vivian replied, "I have just the girl for you tonight, I recently hired her, but I have a question for you. You are one of the most handsome men I know. I figure you can get any girl you desire so why do you ask for an escort when you are in town?"

Steinberg said, "You're right Vivian, I can land any woman I see fit. But when I go to such places like Las Vegas, I want a woman by my side whose classy and sophisticated and not just some bubbleheaded bimbo." Fashion Girl overheard their conversation and said to herself, *"Bubbleheaded bimbo huh? I'll show you a bubbleheaded bimbo!"*

The conversation continued as Vivian said, "Senor Steinberg, you've been a customer of mine for years. You know full well that my escorts are both pretty and smart. And as I said, I have recently hired a new escort and she's not only gorgeous but intelligent. Wait here and I'll get her for you."

Vivian opened the door to the other room approached Fashion Girl and said, "He's waiting for you Daphne and you aren't going to be disappointed." Fashion Girl replied, "I heard him say that remark about bubbleheaded bimbos and I can assure you that me and the other Style Chicks aren't bimbos." Vivian said, "I asked him why he can't get a girlfriend himself and apparently some of the girls he had were pretty but has a brain the size of a grain of sand. I assured him that you're highly intelligent." Fashion Girl replied, "Well as the old saying goes, "Here goes nothing.""

Vivian came out first with Fashion Girl behind her and said, "George Steinberg, this is Daphne our newest escort." Steinberg was nearly floored by Fashion Girl's looks. Fashion Girl said, "Good evening Mr. Steinberg, it's a pleasure to meet you." Steinberg kissed Fashion Girl's hand and replied, "A pleasure to meet you my dear. You were right Vivian, she's everything you said she was."

Vivian replied, "You know I only hire the most beautiful and charming girls in Los Angeles, so why should Daphne be any different." Steinberg said, "When you're right Vivian, you're right. Well Daphne, if you're ready, we are going to Las Vegas tonight." Fashion Girl replied, "Hmm, I love Las Vegas and I love it even more than with a rich, handsome and powerful man as yourself."

Steinberg said, "My dear, we are about to make beautiful music together. Your chariot awaits for us to fly." Fashion Girl interlocked her arm with his as he escorted her to his limousine. Once inside, Steinberg told the chauffer to take them to his private jet at the municipal airport. Steinberg pulled a cigar out of his coat and as he was about to light it, he asked, "Do you smoke Daphne? Or do you object to my smoking?" Fashion Girl replied, "Yes I smoke just let me pull out a cigarette."

Here was why Fashion Girl took cigarettes with her. She has her power bracelets in her purse as well. So, when she reached for a cigarette and her cigarette holder, she turned on the communicator on her bracelet. This allowed the others to hear everything that goes on. As Fashion Girl's cigarette was lit for her, Steinberg said, "Tonight we will be at the Bellagio in Las Vegas. We will have dinner there and we will gamble. What kind of game do you like?" Fashion Girl replied, "It doesn't matter to me, I play them all." Steinberg said, "Then we'll play them all."

Once the communicator was on, Bloomie said, "Listen now we can hear everything." Nine West asked, "What are they doing at the moment?" Bloomie answered, "From what I can gather, there in a car or limo. The motor sounds powerful. I also heard Bellagio just as Lt. Pollack said." Saks said, "Okay, we are now in the game. Give them a head start of five minutes before heading to the airport. Remember Candy and Victoria are waiting for you there. Wait until Fashion Girl's plane takes off first. Good luck."

The limousine arrived at the airport at six thirty and Steinberg, his entourage and Fashion Girl boarded. The plane took off at six forty-five. Bloomie, Nine West and Cottonmouth arrived at the airport at six fifty-five. They saw the limousine parked where the plane was so they knew Fashion Girl was in the air.

They boarded the plane as Candy was firing up the engines preparing for takeoff. Candy put the plane in the air as Victoria came out of the cockpit and said, "Good evening everyone, we will be flying at an altitude of twelve thousand feet. The weather is clear all the way to Las Vegas with a temperature of ninety-one upon arrival. Coffee, tea or milk? Well how did I do?"

Bloomie replied, "I don't know about your piloting skills yet but as for your skills as a flight attendant, you were spot on. So, Victoria, how are you doing? How's your new role treating you?" Victoria laughed and said, "I'm doing well so far Bloomie. Candy is teaching me well with my cooking and she's teaching me to fly when I'm old enough to take over. For now, she asked me to keep you company while we're in flight."

Nine West asked, "Hey, I hope you have something more onboard than just coffee, tea, or milk? We're hungry." Victoria answered, "You have onboard the new and previous Victoria. Of course we brought food with us. But we also have coffee, tea and milk." Nine West said, "I'm sure you brought onboard nothing short of a banquet so we'll share it. But we prefer to have a soda with our meal." Victoria replied, "Coming up."

As the Freedom Flyer was trailing the plane Fashion Girl was in, there were more people who were listening in. Saks was tuned in too as she expected when there was a knock at the door. She went to answer it and Amber Watley was standing there. Saks asked, "May I help you miss?" Amber answered, "I'm Amber Watley. You must be Saks of the Style Chicks. Daphne has spoken very fondly about you. In case you weren't told, Daphne made me an honorary Style Chick. And when she didn't show up for school today, I got her address from the bursar's office and I came here."

Saks said, "Yes she did mention that she made someone an honorary Style Chick but she didn't go into details. Please come in." As Amber walked in, she said, "Wow look at this place, it's gorgeous." Saks replied,

"I know my friends and I bought and decorated this place." Amber replied, "I heard that you and another Style Chick Wendy were given billion-dollar settlements for what happened to you as kids."

Saks asked, "Yes that's what happened. We knew Daphne was going to live here while in college so we bought this place. Look unless you're looking for a handout, what can I do for you?" Amber answered, "Again I was looking for Daphne since she didn't show up for school. I was curious to see if she is okay."

Saks said, "Daphne's fine. She's on her way to Las Vegas to help capture a dangerous crook who goes by the name The Frog." Amber replied, "The Frog"? What kind of name is that?" Saks said, "He literally hops around from one part of the country to the next." Amber replied, "In case Daphne didn't tell you, I'm studying to be a nurse and I'm in my senior year. After graduating, I have a job lined up at UCLA Medical Center."

Saks said, "Okay Amber, if you wish to help out, I have a feeling someone like you could come in pretty handy." Just then, Nike came downstairs yapping up a storm. Amber had a big smile on her face and asked, "Now who is this little guy?" Saks answered, "This is Nike, he's our gift to Daphne upon moving here. I guess it might explain why I'm here alone. My friends Bloomie and Nine West along with Daphne's boyfriend Cottonmouth are following her to Vegas and report to us and the police."

Amber asked, "Where are they now?" Saks said, "Daphne is in the plane with The Frog while my friends are in a plane we call The Freedom Flyer." Amber asked, "May I properly introduce myself to Nike? I love dogs especially cute and cuddly puppies." Saks answered, "Of course you can, he's so friendly."

Amber called Nike's name and he came over to her with his tongue hanging out ready to kiss her. Amber laughed as she too got the Nike doggy bath. Amber said, "You're right he's so lovable." Saks replied, "He's also the reason why I stayed behind, he's still a puppy and you have to lookout for it like you would a toddler." Amber said, "Listen, if all of you have to go and can't take Nike with you, here's my number. Call me and

I'll look after him." Saks replied, "Thanks for the offer Amber. Actually, Bloomie, Nine West and I live in the neighborhood a couple of blocks away but Daphne I'm sure will accept your offer."

At the Mystique Boutique the command center was turned off since Candy nor Victoria was there to monitor it and the new Style Chicks weren't trained to use it. But in Aurora Gardens they did. A command center was put in both The Den of Sin and in the office of the motel. An alarm was blaring loud throughout the complex and no one knew what was going on except for Satanra and The Skull King.

Satanra calmed the crowd down and said, "That sound you heard is an alarm from a command center in the motel office. It alerted the Style Chicks of any trouble in the world. The Skull King and I will check what's going on. Come with me my king. Oh by the way, The Skull King and I are getting married and you're all invited."

The crowd began to cheer as Satanra and The Skull King went ahead to the motel office to see why the alarm sounded. There was no news report or a printout but they could hear the conversation Fashion Girl and the Frog were having. Satanra smiled from ear-to-ear and said, "Well, well, it looks like my daughter is in league with a known criminal. She is evil too just as I thought."

The Skull King replied, "She might be with a criminal but it doesn't sound like she's planning anything. They're just talking." Satanra said, "Let's just keep listening to them. We'll see what she is up to." Onboard the plane Fashion Girl was on, she was treated very well by The Frog. He offered her champagne and continued to light her cigarettes for her.

Fashion Girl said, "Mr. Steinberg, I'm really enjoying this trip. This plane is so amazing. And you're amazing too." Steinberg replied, "Call me George please, I'm informal." Fashion Girl said, "Okay George. If you will excuse me, I need to use the powder room."

Steinberg rose as Fashion Girl did and said, "By all means my dear, go ahead." As she stepped inside and closed the door, she quietly locked it and tried to call the others. She said, "This is Fashion Girl, can anyone hear me?" Saks replied, "Loud and clear, where are you at the moment?"

Fashion Girl said, "I'm in the ladies room to "powder my nose" if you will. Everything is going smoothly so far. We should touchdown in Vegas within the next fifteen minutes. I don't know how often I can talk so I'm keeping my communicator open." Saks replied, "No worries Daphne, just keep up the charade. Saks out."

Back in Los Angeles, Saks said, "You heard it for yourself Amber, she's doing fine so far." Amber replied, "Just so you know Saks, I'm not like a fan where I'm following Daphne around everywhere she goes. I was asked by the dean to be an escort to her, a liaison if you will." Saks said, "I wasn't thinking that but thank you for telling me. Believe me when I tell you that I saw her grow up to be a strong, confident young woman. She can take care of herself."

Minutes later, the plane Fashion Girl was on landed at the municipal airport in Las Vegas where another limousine was waiting to take them to the Bellagio resort. The Freedom Flyer landed ten minutes later and someone was waiting for them too. The new Penney Dillard and the new Macy Sears. Bloomie asked, "Penney and Macy, what are you two doing here?"

Penney answered, "Once I learned that the previous Penney and Tiffany did a magic act here, we got hired to take their place. We perform at the Bellagio." Bloomie said, "What a coincidence, that's where we're going to. Fashion Girl is also here too performing her first official mission as a Style Chick."

Penney replied, "Climb in folks, Macy and I need to be there in thirty minutes." Nine West asked, "I'm glad to see you both and giving us this lift but how did you know we were coming here?" Macy answered, "Saks told us to wait for you at the municipal airport but she couldn't tell us a time. We did see what looked like Fashion Girl on the arm with an incredibly gorgeous hunk of man."

Cottonmouth said, "That gorgeous hunk of man you put it Macy better mind himself with Daphne or he's going to answer to me." Bloomie replied, "Cottonmouth remember these are dangerous criminals armed to the teeth with guns. Try something and it could be your last. We'd hate to see that happening to you." Cottonmouth said, "Relax everyone, I'm not getting jealous, I just want her to be safe." Penney said, "Fashion

Girl was trained to take on people like these, so let's play it cool. Say while you're waiting, how would you like to see us perform?"

Bloomie said, "Thanks for the offer Penney but we need to stick close by and keep an eye on things. If your act is just as good as the former Penney's was, I'm sure it's a sight to see." Penney understood and pulled into the main entrance to the resort.

They saw Steinberg, his entourage and Fashion Girl go inside to eat dinner first. They went to the most expensive restaurant in the resort. They got a table at one end of the restaurant while the entourage sat at a neighboring table. The entourage featured two beefy looking men and two streetwise women none of which made it on their looks. Bloomie, Nine West and Cottonmouth sat at a table on the other side of the restaurant but could still see everything.

At Fashion Girl's table, Steinberg ordered champagne along with oysters on the half shell. He poured two glasses, handed one to Fashion Girl and said, "To us my dear." He clinked the glasses as Fashion Girl replied, "To us." As they drank, Fashion Girl continued, "If I didn't know any better George, I think you're trying to get me drunk. Champagne always goes to my head."

Steinberg said, "No that wasn't my intention. I'm paying a small fortune to be here, with you, and after we eat and gamble, I reserved a suite in the penthouse where you must fulfill your end of the bargain." Daphne asked, "Bargain? What bargain?" Steinberg answered, "To be intimate with me of course. Didn't Vivian tell you that as one of her girls, when a man wines and dines you, sex is the payoff."

Fashion Girl was going for the femme fatale route and said, "Of course, how silly of me. She should had said something but I should've known. I'm sorry." Steinberg replied, "You were a new hire so I guess she didn't get a chance." After the oysters arrived and the main course was ordered, Steinberg tried to feed Daphne oysters. But to her surprise, he ordered them cooked so they were easy to eat and swallow. Steinberg pointed out that he prefers food like oysters cooked instead of raw.

Fashion Girl also pointed out that food like sushi, raw oysters and other such fare wasn't to her liking either. I guess there's something about eating bait that doesn't appeal to some people. But it sure didn't appeal to Cottonmouth and the girls. They ate more normally than Fashion Girl did.

After they ate and got up, Steinberg, Fashion Girl and his entourage made their way out to the casino floor. Steinberg pulled out a roll of money big enough to choke a horse and peeled out hundred-dollar bills by the dozen and gave it to her. They walked arm in arm and passed where Cottonmouth and the girls were sitting. Fashion Girl spotted them briefly and gave a facial expression as not to arouse suspicion. She fanned out the money and said, "Oh George, you're so good to me."

Cottonmouth asked, "What the hell was that about?" Bloomie answered, "Relax Cottonmouth she's in full mode right now. She's playing her part well." Cottonmouth said, "Maybe a little too well." Nine West replied, "C'mon, we aren't exactly on welfare you know, we have our own wad to flash. Let's spend some of it." Cottonmouth realized at that point that his girlfriend was playing call-girl to Steinberg but he was with two babes as well.

Fashion Girl's first place to gamble was the roulette wheel. She placed down two hundred dollars and placed chips on the red and black boxes that are blank. Steinberg also plunked down money and placed chips on the two green spaces zero and double zero. They both lost. They played their remaining chips on numbers this time. Fashion Girl placed chips down on number twenty-nine. She pointed out to Steinberg that twenty-nine was her birthdate.

Steinberg placed his remaining chips on twenty-three and pointed out that it was his birthdate. As the ball spun, no one could imagine where it would land and to Fashion Girl's surprise, it landed on twenty-nine. She bet one hundred dollars and won thirty-five hundred dollars for it was a thirty-five to one shot.

Cottonmouth, Bloomie and Nine West saw this. Cottonmouth said, "Wow she won all that money! I hope she won't spend it all." Nine West replied, "It's his money she's playing with. C'mon they're going to the cashier to cash the chips in. I learned that there's a different chip used for roulette than the other games. Let's try wherever they're going to try."

As Fashion Girl cashed in the chips, she was allowed to keep it. Steinberg had much more where it came from. She put fifteen hundred dollars in her purse and kept out the other money to try her hand at another game. Next they tried their luck shooting craps.

The entourage acted like bodyguards and kept their distance while staying close. They were acting like spectators looking in on the action. Cottonmouth and the girls tried their hands at another crap table. Steinberg gave Fashion Girl more money and told her to shoot. She placed one thousand dollars worth of chips on various spots on the table. She selected two dice she felt was lucky. She blew on them, rubbed them in her hands and rolled.

The dice wound up on seven and everyone won. She rolled them again and it landed on seven again. This kept up for more than ten minutes and she called it quits walking away with twenty-five thousand dollars. The croupier asked, "Ma'am that was impressive dice playing. Can you do us a favor please?" Fashion Girl answered, "What is it sir?" The croupier said, "Just for fun, roll the dice once more to see if you throw a seven again." Fashion Girl replied, "Okay, I'll roll again."

The croupier told everyone that this was a free roll and not to worry about the outcome. Fashion Girl took the dice and rolled and it came up snake eyes. The croupier said, "You did the right thing ma'am, congratulations!" Fashion Girl asked for bigger chips and replied, "I guess tonight is my lucky night." As Steinberg, Fashion Girl and the entourage left, the table gave her a round of applause as she made them a fortune too.

Cottonmouth, Nine West and Bloomie left their table crapped out. Bloomie asked, "Fashion Girl made a killing at the roulette wheel and the crap table. Do you think she was playing with a crooked wheel or loaded dice? Or is she just plain lucky?" Nine West answered, "Fashion Girl would never cheat in anything. She's simply on a hot streak. That's more than twenty-eight thousand dollars she's won so far. They're going to the cashier's cage again. Let's go to see which game they'll try next."

After Fashion Girl left the cashier's cage, she went to try her luck on a slot machine. Steinberg gave her more money for the slots and she asked, "George baby, you're spoiling me. I've already won a lot of money;

I can use it to play with. Why are you giving me more money?" Steinberg replied, "Daphne honey, you're hot and my money has made you that way. Play with this and good luck."

Steinberg gave her a stack of c notes with a wrapper around it. Fashion Girl said, "This is five thousand dollars. Are you sure you want me to use this?" Steinberg replied, "You're making us rich, keep it up and bet high." One thing to point out is that they have played these games in the high stakes area of the casino, which could explain why Fashion Girl's won so much money.

She sat down at a slot machine that costs ten dollars per credit. She put in one c note in the machine and bet the max and pulled the arm. And in seconds she hit a jackpot worth half a million dollars. The machine made a sound that could wake the dead. A crowd gathered around as it was confirmed that Fashion Girl won a huge jackpot. Cottonmouth said, "This is unbelievable. We're losing our shirts while Fashion Girl's getting wealthy. I'm so green with envy right now." Bloomie replied, "Let's get out of here and see where they'll go next."

Fashion Girl walked by the trio still fanning c notes in their faces again to not arouse suspicion. She said, "George, let's celebrate. Let's go to the lounge for a drink." Steinberg replied, "I'm with you honey." They walked away laughing as if they owned the place and the way it was going, it might just be the case.

The idea of going to the lounge gave Fashion Girl a chance to talk with the others so as to not arouse suspicion. Before she sat down she said, "If you'll excuse me George, I need to use the can." George kissed her hand and replied, "Of course my dear, I'll wait for your return."

Bloomie and Nine West went into the ladies room a moment later and approached Fashion Girl. Fashion Girl asked, "Girls, how's my performance so far?" Bloomie answered, "If this were a movie, you'd be a cinch for an Oscar. But you are spreading it on just a little too thick. The way you're talking with that scuzz bucket as if you were his moll. And all that money you've won. Let me see some of that money he's been handing you and not the money you got from the cashier's cage."

Fashion Girl handed Bloomie and Nine West each a c note so they could examine it and just as they thought, Nine West said, "Daphne, you're playing with Monopoly money. It's not worth the paper its printed on. How can the dealers not spot it?" Fashion Girl said, "I don't know but thanks for telling me. Before I go back, how's Cottonmouth taking this? I mean I hope he's not jealous."

Nine West replied, "Daphne, I think he's more jealous of your winning streak than how you're acting with The Frog." Fashion Girl said, "I'm glad he's okay. I need to go but tell him I love him." Nine West replied, "Don't worry, we will." Fashion Girl left the ladies room to rejoin Steinberg and the entourage. She sat down and ordered a drink and took out a cigarette. Steinberg offered to light it for her but she took out one of his funny money bills and took it to his flame and lit her cigarette.

Steinberg was taken back by that as she said, "What's the matter baby, we've won a fortune with more to come. Tonight we have money to burn." The members of the entourage also were surprised by Fashion Girl's action. George replied, "Um, yes well you're right baby. We have money to burn." Fashion Girl then got up and shouted, "DRINKS FOR THE HOUSE ON ME!"

Steinberg asked, "What do you think you're doing!? Buying the house drinks." Fashion Girl answered, "Nothing but sharing our good fortune. What's a round of drinks compared to winning millions of dollars. Isn't that what you want?" Steinberg had no reaction to it. After Fashion Girl paid for the drinks with the money she won from the casino, she continued, "Let's try one more game, Texas Hold 'Em in the main casino. We can still win big over there."

As they left, Cottonmouth asked, "Girls, does Daphne know how to play Texas Hold 'Em?" Bloomie answered, "No. But the way her luck has been, she'll do well. Let's see what happens." As they sat down, Steinberg took out all the money he had left on him. Fifty thousand dollars and gave half to Fashion Girl to use as he used the other. Fashion Girl acted flustered and said, "All this money is making me so lightheaded but then again, I'm just nothing but a bubbleheaded bimbo."

As they dealt the cards, Fashion Girl once again won big while Steinberg was losing. This kept up for some time. Then Fashion Girl said, "If you will all excuse me, I'm feeling a bit sick and I need to go to the ladies room. Steinberg and everyone else at the table rose to their feet including the dealer as she left the table. A man sitting next to Steinberg said, "Sir, that is by far the classiest lady I've ever seen." Steinberg replied, "At this rate sir, I'll give her to you. She's caused me bad luck since we came here."

Fashion Girl went into a stall and separated the money she won as opposed to the money Steinberg gave her. Nine West was right and Fashion Girl saw what she saw. The picture of Ben Franklin on Steinberg's money had a different look on his face as opposed to a genuine bill. Now Fashion Girl knew how The Frog made his money. He made his own money as a counterfeiter.

While she was still in the ladies room, a scuffle began as Steinberg accused the dealer of cheating for dealing from the bottom of the deck. His entourage flipped the table and drew guns. Fashion Girl peeked out the door and saw what happened. She went back inside and said to herself, *"Well, it looks like Fashion Girl will finally make her crime fighting debut."* She raised her arms, crossed her wrists and said, "STYLE ME AS FASHION GIRL!" A cloud of thick black smoke enveloped her turning her into the Style Crime Fighter Fashion Girl.

Now as Fashion Girl, she snuck behind a row of slot machines and drew her sword and activated her shield. Just then gunfire began to erupt as everyone in the vicinity was ducking for cover. Fashion Girl shouted, "Hey! Don't you know it's illegal to shoot a gun inside a casino?" Steinberg turned around and asked, "Who the hell are you!?" Fashion Girl answered, "My name is Fashion Girl and the game's up Frog, I know what your game is."

Steinberg said, "Fashion Girl huh? I thought she was dead." Fashion Girl replied, "I'm the new Fashion Girl and I'm even better than the previous one." Steinberg ordered one of his bodyguards to get her. Fashion Girl grabbed him by one arm and threw him over several rows of slot machines and crashed into one. Fashion Girl shouted, "Didn't you ever want to break the bank in Vegas?"

Steinberg and the others drew their guns and fired them at Fashion

Girl. Her shield kept her safe but the bullets were bouncing around the place like balls in a pinball machine. Steinberg said, "Stop you fools! Her deflections could kill us. Just rush her and put her in her place!"

Fashion Girl quickly picked up slot machines and threw them at the entourage like they were rag dolls pinning them to the ground. Then she went after the big prize, The Frog. He fired the remaining bullets in his gun until the gun was empty. Fashion Girl grabbed the gun and disintegrated it in her hands. She said, "Give it up Frog! Your hopping days are over!"

Steinberg replied, "It's never over with my dear. I'm the leader of a worldwide crime syndicate. Get rid of me and someone else will take my place." Fashion Girl said, "Not if I and my friends can help it!" Steinberg replied, "We'll just see about that Style Slut!" Fashion Girl took out her sword and said, "Yes we'll just see about that Frog. Give up or I will slice you up like a tube of salami." Steinberg replied, "Not a chance."

Steinberg somehow knocked the sword out of Fashion Girl's hand and resorted to fists. He punched Fashion Girl in the face but she fought back with a barrage of punches to his face, chest and stomach. With the fight out of him, Fashion Girl flung him against a wall knocking him unconscious. She walked up to him and said, "The next time you call any woman a bubbleheaded bimbo, I hope you think of how you were tonight."

Just then, the police along with the hotel manager arrived. The manager said, "Officers, arrest that woman for damaging my casino. I'll throw the book at her." Just then, Cottonmouth, Bloomie, Nine West along with Penney, Macy, and Lt. Pollack arrived. Bloomie said, "Not so fast sir. This woman saved everyone from getting killed. And that man lying over there was all behind it."

Lt. Pollack added, "She's right sir. That's George Steinberg alias The Frog the leader of an international counterfeit ring. Fashion Girl went undercover to stop him and his gang." Fashion Girl gave Lt. Pollack the bogus money The Frog gave her. Nine West said, "And if you come with me, I'll show all the other places they were tonight where the bad bills were given out."

The manager replied, "I'm sorry Fashion Girl. I didn't realize you were stopping these people. I won't press charges." Fashion Girl said, "Thank you and I will pay for the damages." The manager replied, "Money and property can be replaced. People can't. I appreciate the offer but it won't be necessary. You will always be welcome here as are your fellow Style Chicks. Thank you. Officers take these "people" away where they belong."

As everyone dispersed, Cottonmouth and Fashion Girl were all alone. Cottonmouth said, "Honey, you were terrific tonight with everything. Tell me one thing, how did you win all that money without marked cards, crooked wheels or loaded dice?" Fashion Girl replied, "Lady luck was on my side tonight. I won close to seven hundred thousand dollars. I'm surprised no one asked me for it."

Cottonmouth said, "Maybe they figured that you and the Frog was losing big and were a jinks to each other. So all that money is yours?" Fashion Girl replied, "Not mine Cottonmouth, ours. Half of this is yours. I want to cash the chips I got from the poker table and let's get a room. We'll have to stick around for the police." Fashion Girl went back into the ladies room to change back to her normal identity.

After she cashed in her chips, she did wind up with over seven hundred thousand dollars in both cash and cashier's checks. She went back to Cottonmouth and said, "There's one more game I wanted to play and that's blackjack. I've played everything else." Cottonmouth replied, "Sounds good to me. Um, do you think you could lend me a few bucks so I can join you?"

Fashion Girl laughed, handed Cottonmouth two thousand dollars and said, "Be my guest stud." Fashion Girl took out a cigarette, placed it on her holder and asked, "Got a light big boy?" Cottonmouth took out his lighter and lit her cigarette. He answered, "No offense but make sure you have a lighter just in case." Fashion Girl said, "Remember stud, I'm a lady. Now let's see if my luck is still hot."

Fashion Girl and Cottonmouth walked arm in arm and before they reached a blackjack table, Cottonmouth asked, "Daphne, how did you know what The Frog was all about?" Fashion Girl answered, "Actually I can't take credit for that, Nine West and Bloomie told me. They showed me one of the bills in the ladies room in the lounge. They pointed it out to me and sure enough it was counterfeit."

Fashion Girl's winning streak finally ended as she lost five thousand dollars. Cottonmouth fared no better. It was well passed midnight and after Bloomie and Nine West gave their statements to the police, everyone decided to spend the night there. Fashion Girl was able to obtain the penthouse suite The Frog had reserved.

Cottonmouth asked Fashion Girl if she could become her heroic form so they could be intimate since no one had any luggage. Cottonmouth said, "I know we've had sex before Daphne, but this will be the first time we'll do it as Fashion Girl. That is if you want to."

Fashion Girl replied, "I admit I drank a lot tonight. I wasn't joking when I said I felt a little sick when I left the poker table. But I'm okay now. Cottonmouth, you're my boyfriend and I love you very much. I would be proud for you to do it to me. We're in this great room overlooking the strip, we're rich and I'm ready for action." Fashion Girl took off her costume and was completely naked.

Cottonmouth also got naked as Fashion Girl continued, "Remember what I said about getting me pregnant in the Den of Sin. I'm ovulating, I'm drunk, and I want to have your baby tonight. Then afterwards, let's find a jewelry store, buy rings, go to one of those chapels and get married." Cottonmouth asked, "Are you sure Daphne? Are you sure about everything you just said?" Fashion Girl answered, "Stud, we are in one of the most exciting and glamourous places in the world. If I am to get pregnant, it's right here, right now. Go on fuck me up good."

Whether it was the champagne talking or all that happened that night, Fashion Girl wanted it to end with her getting pregnant. And also the possibility of eloping. Fashion Girl's first official mission was a great success and this was her way of celebrating. After more than three hours of sex, Fashion Girl and Cottonmouth fell asleep in each other's arms.

When sunrise occurred, Bloomie and Nine West who also got to stay at the resort and shared the room Penney and Macy had went to look for Fashion Girl and Cottonmouth. Bloomie asked, "Where could they had gone to last night? It's a good thing she didn't have to talk with the police." Nine West answered, "I have an idea that they are here still. I'll call the front desk to check."

Nine West called the front desk and it was confirmed that Fashion Girl and Cottonmouth were in the suite the Frog reserved. They went there to check on them. When Bloomie knocked on the door, Fashion Girl put on a bathrobe and opened it. Bloomie said, "Nine West and I were looking all over Vegas for you. I'm glad you're okay." Fashion Girl replied, "We're better than okay Bloomie, Cottonmouth and I had sex last night."

Bloomie said, "Daphne Sandra Bates you sly dog you. How was it?" Fashion Girl replied, "Bloomie I don't kiss and tell but in this case I will. Come in and I'll tell you." Bloomie and Fashion Girl stepped into the bathroom so Cottonmouth could continue sleeping. Fashion Girl said, "Bloomie, last night was so amazing. I admit I was drunk from all that champagne. When I used the bathroom before The Frog got mad, I did get sick and I really wasn't feeling well."

"When everyone left, I tried my hand at blackjack and lost five grand. Cottonmouth lost two but we are still ahead a lot of money. The resort allowed us to use this suite and I told Cottonmouth that I wanted him to impregnate me. I felt I was ovulating. And we even talked about eloping."

Bloomie asked, "Do you think you are pregnant right now? Do you really want to get married here? Now?" Fashion Girl answered, "Yes. Yes and yes." Bloomie asked, "Daphne, are you sure that you are pregnant right now? And are you sure that you want to get married? Please be honest with me."

Fashion Girl answered, "Since your using my first name I'll use yours Brittney. Brittney I've never been so sure of anything in my life. I love him and I want him as my husband and the father of my baby. Brittney please say you're happy for me, please?" Bloomie said, "Daphne you're an adult now. You're capable of making your own decisions good or bad. But even if you make a bad decision, no one should hold it against you. But yes if any of us deserves to be happy, it should be our leader, you. Congratulations!"

Bloomie let Nine West in on the news and the three were squealing like pigs in a trough. But Fashion Girl wasn't aware of one thing, her communicator was still open and everyone who could hear it, heard it. In Los Angeles, Saks and Amber were also excited by the news. No one in Colognia didn't because the command center was still off. But at Aurora Gardens, Satanra and the Skull King heard everything.

Satanra said, "So, my daughter's first mission was a success. So, she and Cottonmouth wants to be married and start a family. So are we my king. We will be married at sundown tomorrow and I can't wait." The Skull King replied, "You should be happy for Daphne's good fortune." Satanra said, "You fool! I don't want her to be happy, I want her to be miserable! And after tomorrow night, my onslaught of my daughter will take place! And I can't wait!" She began to laugh maniacally. She continued, "We'll join the others for breakfast and while we're there, we have a wedding and a beating and gangbang to plan. Let's go feast and have more sex!"

Again I ask, how can any parent be so cruel to a child even if the child is an adult? The Skull King was right that Fashion Girl should be happy. Satanra did bring Fashion Girl into the world but at the same time, she wished she hadn't but not until years after the fact. But after Fashion Girl and the others remained in Vegas, a confrontation unlike no other will take shape and not for the better.

CHAPTER 27

F ashion Girl, Cottonmouth, Bloomie and Nine West remained in Las Vegas. Bloomie, Nine West and Fashion Girl were shopping for a wedding dress and rings as she was preparing for her wedding. Cottonmouth went his separate way but he needed to make a couple of phone calls.

One call he was kind of dreaded to make but it had to be done, and that was a call to Fashion Girl's mother. Unaware of what her mother had become, he wanted her blessing. So, he called her and as she picked up the phone and said hello, Cottonmouth said, "Madame D, this is Cottonmouth. Um, there's something I need to ask of you."

Satanra replied, "Sure Cottonmouth what is it?" Cottonmouth said, "As Daphne's mother, I want to ask you for something. Your blessing to marry your daughter." Satanra replied, "Are you serious about marrying my daughter?" Cottonmouth said, "Yes I am. You should've seen how she did last night on her first mission. We're still in Las Vegas. Daphne along with Bloomie and Nine West are looking for a dress and rings for our nuptials. Again all I ask is your blessing."

Satanra replied, "Cottonmouth, in the back of my mind, I knew the moment Daphne laid her eyes on you, that she fell in love with you. Yes Cottonmouth, you have my blessing." Cottonmouth replied, "Thank you Skull Queen, I really appreciate it."

Satanra replied, "Congratulations to you both. Are you going to get married there?" Cottonmouth said, "Yes. I know it might sound crazy but we're going to get married in one of those chapels and by a guy dressing probably acting like Elvis." Satanra replied, "That's Las Vegas alright. Thank you for your call and I wish you both the very best of luck. Goodbye."

After the call ended, Cottonmouth needed to make another call he was dreading and was to his leader and Fashion Girl's aunt Queen Serpentina. Serpentina said hello and Cottonmouth said, "Serpentina, this is Cottonmouth. My queen I have news for you and I want to ask you something." Serpentina replied, "Okay what do you want to ask?"

Cottonmouth said, "I already called Madame D and I want the same thing from you…" Before Cottonmouth could continue, Serpentina replied, "WHAT!? You called her why did you do that?" Cottonmouth said, "Please let me explain. I'm with Daphne, Bloomie and Nine West in Las Vegas. Daphne successfully completed her first mission last night. She defeated the Frog."

Serpentina replied, "That's wonderful news. My former Style Chicks and I tried to capture that elusive man but failed each time. That's great. We actually heard about it on the news the command center was turned off." Cottonmouth said, "It was turned off? Why?" Serpentina replied, "Candy was teaching only the new Victoria to use it. But I take it that there's something more."

Cottonmouth said, "Yes ma'am there is. One Daphne made a fortune gambling and it ticked the Frog off. She acted as an escort for him. She even got a little drunk too. He kept giving her champagne. But she was sober enough to beat him. You had to be there. And two, we got to stay here in the penthouse suite the Frog had reserved. Um, Serpentina, she wanted me to get her pregnant. She was ovulating or so she told me and now we are planning to get married. That's why I called Madame D. To get her blessing."

Serpentina replied, "Cottonmouth honey, something bad has happened to Madame D but we aren't too sure what. I think it's noble of you to do the right thing and ask us both for Daphne's hand in marriage.

Even if Madame D did give her blessing, she might have done so under a different pretense. Honestly, I'm not too crazy about the fact that Daphne got drunk last night."

Cottonmouth said in a defensive tone, "My queen, I didn't get her drunk as I said. If you doubt me, ask Bloomie and Nine West. I was with the both of them the entire time following Daphne and the Frog. Once the police learns that the Frog got Daphne drunk and being underage, he could face another serious charge."

Serpentina replied, "Didn't anyone in that casino thought to check Daphne's ID?" Cottonmouth said, "My queen, Daphne might be underage but she looks more mature like a woman in her twenties." Serpentina replied, "We dealt with that before with Wendy. She was a woman on the outside but a child on the inside. And all because of that damn toxic pool she and Saks swam in many years ago."

Cottonmouth said, "Serpentina, I love your niece very, very much. I want her hand in marriage. As for her being pregnant, when Daphne and the others get back, I'll ask Bloomie or Nine West to get a pregnancy test from a pharmacy and make Daphne take it. If I did impregnate her last night and if she was ovulating as she said, then I will take full responsibility for it either way."

Serpentina replied, "Cottonmouth, can you and the others remain there in Las Vegas until I can get a flight over there? I need to get Dean involved." Cottonmouth said, "I can get Candy and Victoria back to you in the Freedom Flyer and come back here again." Serpentina replied, "Thank you Cottonmouth, get them back here and Dean and I will wait for them at the airport. See you later, goodbye."

As Cottonmouth making the arrangements for Serpentina and Dean's arrival, Fashion Girl, Bloomie and Nine West were shopping for a wedding dress and wedding rings for the ceremony. They found a bridal shop right in the resort and went inside to look around. The clerk approached them and said, "Good morning ladies, how may I be of service for you today?"

Bloomie replied, "Our friend is getting married and she needs a dress." The clerk said, "You've come to the right place ladies, who's the lucky bride to be?" Fashion Girl replied, "I am ma'am. My fiancé proposed to me last night. We also need to get rings too. We admit we came unprepared. As you can see I'm still wearing the same dress I wore last night."

The clerk said, "For an evening gown, it's lovely and the fur you're wearing completes the look. Say are you a model by any chance?" Fashion Girl replied, "Well my mother was a model and she was allowed to keep the clothes. What I'm wearing now she once modeled in." The clerk asked in a soft tone of voice, "By any chance Miss, but are you that lady that helped stop that crook last night? Are you Fashion Girl?"

Fashion Girl answered, "Yes I am Fashion Girl. But I'm trying to keep it a secret." The clerk said, "No offense Miss, but there aren't too many redheads these days especially natural ones." Fashion Girl replied, "If I have a daughter, may she have any hair color other than being a red-head." The clerk said, "C'mon my dear, you have a wedding to shop for."

The clerk showed Fashion Girl a variety of dresses from traditional to contemporary. Until she found an ensemble she liked. Fashion Girl found a white leather strapless wedding dress complete with a short skirt and white boots. She said, "Ma'am, this outfit almost matches my costume. I'll take this." The clerk replied, "Your groom to be will love this. Now I take it these ladies will be your bridesmaids?"

Bloomie said, "Yes we are. My friend and I decided to be just brides-maids instead of choosing who will be the maid of honor. We both will be it." The clerk replied, "Then I have the perfect dress for you both." The clerk showed them the same type of outfit but in pastel pink. Bloomie said, "Nine West and I won't mind being pink ladies for an evening. We'll take these too."

The clerk replied, "Excellent choices ladies. How will you pay for these? Cash or credit?" Fashion Girl reached into her purse and pulled out a wad of money and counted out the amount for the dresses and another bill for the clerk and said, "Keep the change ma'am. You've been very helpful." The clerk thanked Fashion Girl and replied, "If you will go right next door, there is a jewelry store like this place that specializes in wedding rings. Good luck to you Fashion Girl."

Before they went to the jewelry store, Nine West got a text from Cottonmouth. She said, "Girls, Cottonmouth is asking us if we can go to a pharmacy to pick up… a pregnancy test." Fashion Girl replied, "Why would he want me to take a test. I'm telling you I feel confident that I'm now pregnant with his baby."

Nine West said, "Look Fashion Girl, last night you were drunk. You said you were ovulating but you might not have had your full capacity to think. I'll buy one and it won't hurt to be sure." Fashion Girl replied, "Nine West, a woman know if she's pregnant when she hasn't had her period. I haven't had mine in two months. I'm pregnant with Cottonmouth's baby I'm sure of it." Nine West said, "Again let's be positive if you're indeed positive. It can't hurt to make sure. C'mon, let's find a good set of rings for you and your groom."

Nine West saw a gift shop that could sell pregnancy tests. She continued, "Daphne, Bloomie, you two go ahead, I'll be with you shortly." Nine West went to the gift shop. They did have health and beauty aids but no pregnancy tests. The gift shop clerk told her that there's a pharmacy not far from the resort on the strip and within walking distance. It was perfect."

Nine West discreetly bought the pregnancy test and headed back to the resort. She rejoined the others to find the perfect rings for the ceremony. While this was going on, in Aurora Gardens, preparations were being made for another wedding. The wedding of Satanra and the Skull King. In the Den of Sin, the couple to be once again engaged in sex. When they were done and after Satanra took another pregnancy test and it revealed she was now pregnant with thirty babies.

She said laughing maniacally, "So, my daughter thinks she's pregnant with one baby, I'm pregnant with thirty and I couldn't be more happy." The Skull King asked, "How can any woman be pregnant with that many babies at one time?" Satanra answered, "Simple my king, the babies won't be born the normal way. After thirty days, I will give our master my fetuses and he'll incubate and cultivate them into his Army of Evil. La Diablo told me she gave her father twenty fetuses at one time. They are now twenty full grown willful mindless servants of the almighty Lord of Darkness."

The Skull King said, "Let's see how the preparations are going for tonight's ceremony. We're finally going to be married." Satanra replied, "Now my king, your queen's posse will help me get ready for tonight. And I can't wait to be your exclusive property." The central part of the complex was adorned with a black carpet, long black roses and a devil's food wedding cake with black frosting.

Satanra's posse were preparing their queen for her marriage and coronation. They got for her a blood-red leather wedding dress with tall blood red boots. They fixed her hair and colored her hair black with red streaks. Dark red nail polish and lipstick. She was going to look as evil as she is. When they were done with her, she was instructed to go to one of the rooms at the motel to wait until sundown.

When lunch was served, The Skull King ate first but for Satanra and her girls, there was a separate feast laid out before them. A cloud of thick red smoke appeared and Satan stood before the bride to be.

He said, "My child, you look beautifully evil, your wedding will make you more powerful and with this scroll, read it to each other after you're married. It will give you both new and special evil powers. It's my gift to the evil bride. Now then ladies, eat your fill, let your babies grow inside you and top it all off with wolf's blood. Satanra, be sure to have a gangbang before you get married. Your man's posse wants to give you gifts of material possessions and their eternal lust."

Satan laughed maniacally and disappeared in a cloud of thick red smoke. Slutan and Miss Muertos were on hand. Miss Muertos were feasting while Slutan wasn't. Satanra asked, "Slutan, why haven't you feasted? You should be pregnant with more babies than me by now. Slutan answered, "My revenge was on a woman not a man. All I have are a gang of teenagers who are getting pregnant at will. In fact here they are now." Miss Muertos added, "The Crocs are mine now and they've become Crypt Keepers too. I've been fucking their brains out. I'm pregnant with fifteen babies so far. Later I intend to get more pregnant."

Satanra said, "Now my whore of a daughter could be pregnant herself." Miss Muertos replied, "Isn't that good news?" Satanra said in an angry tone, "NO IT ISN'T YOU SLUTTY SKANK! I WANT HER

TO BE MISERABLE NOT HAPPY!" Slutan added, "Take it easy, she's your daughter and my friend as is Miss Muertos' remember that. I think it's great that she'll become a mother. And I assuming she's getting married too?"

Satanra said, "Yes she is. She's going to marry that snake Cottonmouth. They've eloped. They're in Las Vegas right now as I'm talking to you." Slutan and Miss Muertos sighed as Miss Muertos replied, "That is so romantic. They fell in love and will get married in Las Vegas. That's how I wish I got married when I was alive."

Satanra said, "To be a part of this gang, there's no love! There's no romance! There's nothing else other than thoughtless, meaningless sex and more sex. We are now sex vampires; we live for unholy lust. Remember where your loyalties are ladies."

Miss Muertos and Slutan got the message loud and clear. Slutan said to herself, *"How can Satanra think so poorly of her daughter? Daphne has always been a good person. She never gave Satanra or Dean grief that I knew of. Somehow being able to have sex at will doesn't sound as good as I thought it would be."*

Back in Colognia, Serpentina got Dean to come to the Mystique Boutique to inform him of the news. Up to now she kept this quiet but now that Dean's there, she can spring what she knows to everyone there.

She said, "May I have everyone's attention please? Thank you. Everyone I have news. Fashion Girl successfully completed her first official mission last night in Las Vegas." Everyone applauded at this news as Serpentina continued, "Wait everyone there's more to this. She's still in Las Vegas with Cottonmouth, Bloomie and Nine West. Penney and Macy are there too performing their first magic act there. But I heard of Cottonmouth that he and Fashion Girl are going to get married either tonight or tomorrow night."

"Candy and Victoria were there too but are at the airport here to take me and Dean there to be there for Fashion Girl. For most of you, board a regular plane bound for Las Vegas. Tiffany, Godiva and Sephora, become the Archangels and fly there yourselves. Get in touch with Zara out at sea and have her come as Seagirl. Saks has also been notified and she has someone else with her. An honorary Style Chick we'll meet when we're there. They're staying at the Bellagio Resort. Get there as fast as you can, good luck everyone."

Back at Aurora Gardens, Satanra said to one of her men, "Listen and listen carefully. My daughter is in Las Vegas and she's marrying her boyfriend Cottonmouth either tonight or tomorrow night. After the Skull King and I get married, go to Las Vegas and wait for when she's alone and in costume. And when she is, knock her unconscious and let me know about it. I'll bring my gang down there and I will teach her a lesson she'll never forget."

The man asked, "How do you want us to attack her?" Satanra answered, "Beat the shit out of her and do whatever else you want to do with her. She's your oyster. By doing this is my gift to you for making me very happy. But first, we celebrate my nuptials with a gangbang of our own. Grab your wolf's blood and get good and horny." The man told his friends of Satanra's plan to have a gangbang with her made them just as horny." Bottles of wolf's blood was passed around and they drank it down completely as did Satanra. She said, "My cunt is wet and my legs are open, so fertilize more of my eggs!"

It seems that Satanra has become sadistic with her actions. Even getting out of control. No one in that group of degenerates realize that wolf's blood is a dangerous even deadly drug. But no one seemed to care as long as they can satisfy Satan with his ultimate goal.

Aboard the Freedom Flyer, Serpentina and Dean were talking over the situation before them. Serpentina said, "Dean, I want to put any ill feelings we've had for each other aside and call a truce. Dean, Cottonmouth is a very nice young man and he would make Daphne very happy. It seems she already is. But I'm afraid that if she gets married now at eighteen, it could be a bad thing. What are your thoughts about this?"

Dean replied, "Okay Cindy I'll call a truce with you and I'm sorry if I ever made you mad at me for anything. I want you to know that when she was away, I treated Daphne very good. I love her as if she were my biological daughter. I want her to be happy too. I told Cottonmouth the night of her presentation that I would get on his case if he ever treated her badly. I believe he truly loves her. And if she wants to be married now, I'd be proud to give her away."

Serpentina asked, "What if I also told you that she might be pregnant right now?" Dean answered, "I'll kill him!" Serpentina said, "Wait a minute Dean, we don't know for sure if she's pregnant or not. Cottonmouth told me the whole story. She got drunk last night but not by him, she told him she was ovulating, and she wanted him to get her pregnant. They had sex last night and he thinks she's indeed pregnant. She asked him to marry her and he asked me and Madame D for her blessing. But asking her could've been a grave mistake based on what has happened since Daphne left for school."

Dean replied, "So, it's her that wanted this? Usually it's the man who has his way with his woman." Serpentina said, "I know Daphne is an adult now and she's capable of making her own decisions, but marriage and possibly motherhood, I just don't know." Dean replied, "I fell in love with her mother almost from the start. I proposed to her the night you introduced the Archangels and told me she was pregnant. It seems like déjà vu to me."

Serpentina said, "Dean look, no matter what Daphne decides, let's agree right now to be supportive of her. Either way, we're family and we need to stick together." Dean replied, "Does her grandma, grandfathers, brother and uncle know about this?" Serpentina said, "They'll know in time but for right now, we're all the family she needs and I have all of the Style Chicks and our friends coming. Those wedding chapels out there aren't big. We can have another ceremony back home for everyone else. Dean I only wish Daphne all the best. Dean replied, "So do I Cindy. So do I."

Later that night at sundown, Satanra and the Skull King were ready for their nuptials to be met. A high priestess was there to perform the ceremony. She said, "Disciples of evil. We have gathered here tonight to witness the evil Satanra and the evil Skull King in the bonds of unholy matrimony. If there's anyone here who wish to not see them become one, let them speak now or forever hold their peace."

"Marriage is a sacred bond that ties two hearts together. For more than ten years, these two people have proved to you and each other that they belong together forever. Now Satanra, place the ring on the Skull King's hand and repeat after me, with this ring, I thee wed." Satanra replied, "With this ring, I thee wed." The priestess continued, "Now Skull King, place the ring on her hand and repeat after me, with this ring I thee wed." The Skull King replied, "With this ring I thee wed."

The priestess continued, "Then by the power invested in me by the evil Satan and this state, I pronounce you husband and wife. Skull King, you may kiss your bride." As they kissed, the priestess continued, "Ladies and gentlemen, before this ceremony concludes. There's an ancient scroll that all of you must read. This happens when a Hell's Hottie and a Crypt Keeper gets married. Open the scroll and everyone read together the text before you."

At that moment everyone read a text in a very ancient language. The text read as follows…

ābētu ḥayalu seyit'ani kifuwini hulu, lehulachinimi yezelalemi ḥiyiwetini sit'eni ina lewedajochachini k'onijo ina k'onijo honeni bet'ela-tochachini fīti yeminidebek'i ādirigeni. yekifu minyoti ina yefitiweti lazarani yech'elemawini t'ik'uri, yekifu imebētini init'et'aleni.

In English, the text read as follows…

Oh mighty Satan all that is evil, grant us all eternal life and make us hideous in the eyes of our enemies while remaining beautiful and hand-some to our allies. We drink the dark, black potion of the evil mistress of evil desire and lust Lazara.

By everyone's seat, there was a bottle of a black liquid. They picked it up and drank it down. At that moment, clouds of thick black smoke enveloped all in attendance. When the smoke cleared, they looked at each other and it looked as if the spell didn't work. But when they looked in a mirror, the spell worked; they all looked hideous in the face.

Satanra said, "My King! My King! It worked! We look as evil as we are! I'm so happy!" The Skull King replied, "I really look like a Skull King now! I am happy too!" The others were also pleased. Satanra said, "Now my king, now that we are married, nothing will stop us from giving Satan an eternity of the Army of Evil. Now we party like we're in hell!"

And party they did. There was food by the truckload and wolf's blood flowing like water. The women were looking forward to their men making more evil babies as was the happy couple." They went down into the Den of Sin with food and wolf's blood to last them all night. Satanra opened two bottles and said, "Thanks to the gangbang I had earlier, I'm now pregnant with sixty babies. Fuck me so I can have one hundred babies." The Skull King replied, "As my queen desires."

Satanra's marriage means she will live forever serving her master as her ability to get pregnant had increased twenty-fold. As for her husband, his ability to get her pregnant had also increased twenty-fold. And it could be a recipe for disaster.

But in Las Vegas, the dress was picked out, the rings were too and by mid-afternoon, all of Fashion Girl's friends and allies converged on the Bellagio. Before any vows were exchanged, a mystery needed to be solved first. Is Fashion Girl pregnant? Bloomie, Nine West and Cottonmouth were in the penthouse suite. Fashion Girl had to wait to use the test. Cottonmouth said, "Daphne babe, I want you to know that if you are pregnant or not, it doesn't change how I feel about you."

Fashion Girl replied, "Cottonmouth, my handsome bad boy, my heart is about to burst with the love I have for you. If I am pregnant, it would be with your baby. I think that you impregnated me when we were in the Den of Sin. I only think this way because I haven't had my period for nearly two months." Nine West added, "Some women do go for months without their period, but it doesn't mean she's pregnant. Cottonmouth, I know now that you and Daphne were meant to be together. I can see it in both of your eyes."

Cottonmouth said, "Bloomie, Nine West, you two are going to make a man very happy one day. Until then, be yourself, don't rush into anything you don't want to do. As for me, I fell in love with Daphne from the moment I laid eyes on her. She even dreamt of us being here eloping and getting married. For her, it's a dream come true. And she's happy."

Fashion Girl kissed Cottonmouth in mouth with her tongue going halfway down his throat and replied, "And I feel the same way about you too. I think it's time for me to check if I'm pregnant or not." Fashion Girl went into the bathroom and locked the door. She opened the box and pulled out the test and followed the instructions. If she is pregnant, chances are she could have a son before a daughter. But if she has a daughter now, it would mean that she would have to give up being Fashion Girl at thirty-six years old.

She waited for the line or lines to appear. When the test was completed, she unlocked the door, opened it and came out. Cottonmouth, Bloomie and Nine West braced themselves for the result. Fashion Girl handed the test to Cottonmouth. She said softly, there are two lines in the window." Then said loudly, "I'M PREGNANT!"

Cottonmouth picked her up and twirled her around in his arms. He was overjoyed. He replied, "Oh Daphne, you've made me the happiest man on earth right now! I can't believe it! I'm going to be a father!" Fashion Girl said, "Yes sir that you will be. And I know you'll make one hell of a father too. So, is it okay for us to get married now?" Cottonmouth replied, "You better believe it we will. Let's go."

Before they could leave, the room phone began to ring. Bloomie picked up the phone and was informed that a large group of people were asking for them. Bloomie told the clerk that they would be right down and hung up. Bloomie said, "Guys, we have company, lots of company. Let's hope their friendly."

They went down to the ground floor and to the lobby. The desk clerk told them that the people looking for them were waiting at one of the restaurants. They went to the restaurant the same one as they were at last night and a crowd shouted, "SURPRISE! CONGRATULATIONS!"

Fashion Girl said, "Aunt Cindy? Dean? Everyone? What are you all doing here?" Serpentina replied, "We're here for you honey. We wanted to congratulate you on the success of your first mission and your upcoming wedding." Fashion Girl asked, "You're not sore at us for doing this?" Dean answered, "Of course not sweetheart. We've always wanted you to be happy." Serpentina added, "Well honey, we heard the rumor about that you could be pregnant. What about that?"

Fashion Girl said, "It's true Aunt Cindy, I'm pregnant. I just found out before we were called down. Now you're mad at me about that." Dean replied, "Mad at you? Sweetie, we're mad about you. We're excited and congratulations to both of you." Tiffany added, "Daphne, you're not the only one who's going to be a mother…" Fashion Girl said, "You mean?" Tiffany replied, "I mean I'm pregnant too."

The two hugged and squealed at each other. Fashion Girl asked, "Are you and Bonecrusher plan on getting married too?" Tiffany answered, "We hadn't thought about it. But Bonecrusher got down on one knee and added, "Well I thought about it. Tiffany, will you marry me?" Tiffany couldn't believe it and replied, "Yes I will marry you." Fashion Girl said, "Ladies and gentlemen, we will have a double wedding. Tiffany get yourself a wedding dress and we'll wait for you. We were going to a chapel later tonight. We have a reason to celebrate!"

And celebrate they did. They had a pre-wedding lunch ordering everything the menu had to offer. Especially for Fashion Girl and Tiffany, now they were eating for two. While Tiffany was shopping for a wedding dress, Saks and Amber arrived late but made it for the wedding.

Fashion Girl asked, "Saks, Amber, I'm glad you made it but where's Nike? Didn't he come with you?" Saks replied, "Of course we brought him. Until he's grown up some, he shouldn't be left alone. He's in his carrier. I'll get him."

Saks let Nike out of his carrier and went straight towards Fashion Girl, leaped up in her lap and began licking her. Fashion Girl laughed and said, "Hey, Nike it's good to see you. I guess you wanted to kiss the bride early." Everyone else began to laugh. Fashion Girl continued, "Everyone this is Nike, my puppy that Saks, Bloomie and Nine West gave me."

Everyone began to pet him, shook his paw and he showed love in return. Fashion Girl continued, "I think we all will need a bath before the ceremony." Penney asked, "Boss, who named him Nike?" Fashion Girl answered, "Nine West did. She likes shoes you know." Penney said, "So I'm told. If the wedding is tonight, what time will it take place? And where will it be held?"

Fashion Girl replied, "Eight o'clock is a good time for it, but where we aren't sure of yet. But there are so many of these chapels, I'm sure there all good." Tiffany returned with a wedding dress and two more for bridesmaids. She chose Sephora and Macy to be her bridesmaids. Everyone seemed ready for the wedding. But someone else was ready too.

Satanra arrived that afternoon along with two of her gang. She said, "I will attend the wedding disguised. You two wait for me in back of whatever chapel they decided upon. I will let my daughter have her wedding and the reception. But when she needs to go to the bathroom, I'll be waiting for her with a hammer. I will knock her out and we'll magically return to Aurora Gardens so you can have your way with her." The three began to laugh maniacally.

To decide to go to which wedding chapel, Tiffany and Fashion Girl looked online and found one. Fashion Girl said, "How does this chapel sound to you, The Lucky Lady wedding chapel?" Tiffany agreed and so did the others. Fashion Girl called the chapel and made the arrangements.

She continued, "Okay everyone we're all set. We'll leave here at seven and arrive there at seven-thirty to register." Tiffany asked, "Is the minister an Elvis impersonator?" Fashion Girl answered, "We're in Vegas, we're going to a wedding chapel here, what do you think the minister is dressed like?" Tiffany asked, "Like Elvis?" Fashion Girl answered sounding like Elvis, "Yes he will. Uh, thank you, thank you very much."

For the rest of the day, Fashion Girl, Cottonmouth, Bloomie and Nine West told their story about the case they worked on last night. How Fashion Girl showed the Frog up and how she defeated him. Everyone was impressed.

Serpentina said, "We tried many times to defeat the Frog and failed. Needless to say we were all frustrated by it. But you got him in one attempt and how you went about it, nothing short of impressive." Fashion Girl replied, "I remember who mom took care of those rogue police officers many years ago and I followed her example. I used style to fight crime and it worked." Serpentina said, "It sure did honey and I'm so proud of you."

The time had come for the wedding to take place. The resort took the wedding parties by limousine to the wedding chapel. They registered and Fashion Girl, Tiffany and their bridesmaids went to get ready. Dean was not only to give Fashion Girl away but Tiffany too and act as best man as well.

Fashion Girl alerted a chapel employee that she and Tiffany were ready. Dean went to where they were and waited for their cue. Organ music began to play, everyone stood up as the brides slowly made their way to the altar. Sure enough, the minister looked like Elvis and talked like him too.

The minister said, "Dearly beloved, we are gathered here tonight to unite the two bodacious babes and the handsome hunks in the bonds of wedded bliss. If anyone here who might feel that these four shouldn't be united, may they speak now or forever hold their peace." No one responded.

The minister continued, "Uh, thank you, thank you very much. Daphne Sandra Bates and Darren Bowes along with William Franklin and Sarah Newsome have decided to give their own vows. We'll begin with Miss Bates and Mr. Bowes."

Fashion Girl said, "Darren, from the moment I met you, I knew you would be the man I want to spend the rest of my life with. I know that we will have our share of triumphs and tragedies but no matter what we'll face, we will face it together. I love you and I promise that no matter what happens, I want you by my side, always."

Cottonmouth replied, "Daphne honey, I too fell in love with you from the moment we met. Babe, you mean the world to me unlike any woman I've ever known. After tonight, we will face the world together. And I wouldn't want any other woman by my side than you. I'd be lost without you. I promise to be faithful and loyal to you like no one else. I love you."

The minister said, "Now we'll hear from Miss Newsome and Mr. Franklin." Tiffany said, "I share Daphne's feelings towards Darren that I have towards you Bill. I was a lost cause until Daphne helped me. Then you came along and everything fell into place. For the first time in my life, I have purpose. And now, I am about to marry the man of my dreams. A caring, kind and loving man who I know will be there for me. I promise that I will make the best wife ever. I love you."

William replied, "Sarah, like you I too was a lost cause. That all there was in life was riding the roads, getting wasted and doing it with anything in a skirt. And then I met you and all of that changed. Since I met you I too now have a purpose. You, Daphne and your friends have changed my life for the better. Now I feel like a human being with a different sense of everything. I promise you that no matter what happens I will make you proud to have me for a husband. We will be together forever."

The minister said, "Now if I may have the rings for Ms. Bates and Mr. Bowes please. Now Ms. Bates place the ring on Mr. Bowes' hand and repeat after me, with this ring I thee wed." Fashion Girl replied, "With this ring I thee wed." The minister continued, "Now Mr. Bowes, place the ring on Miss Bates' hand and repeat after me, with this ring I thee wed." Cottonmouth replied, "With this ring I thee wed."

The minister said, "Now for Ms. Newsome and Mr. Franklin. Ms. Newsome place the ring on Mr. Franklin's hand and repeat after me, with this ring, I thee wed." Tiffany replied, "With this ring, I thee wed." The minister said, "Mr. Franklin place the ring on Miss Newsome's hand and repeat after me, with this ring, I thee wed." Bonecrusher replied, "With this ring, I thee wed."

The minister said, "By the power vested in me by the state of Nevada, I here by pronounce you both husbands and wives. Gentlemen, you may kiss your brides." As Cottonmouth and Bonecrusher kissed Fashion Girl and Tiffany, the minister continued, "Ladies and gentlemen I present for the first time Mr. and Mrs. Darren Bowes and Mr. and Mrs. William Franklin."

Everyone in attendance rose to their feet and applauded as the couples left the altar and headed out to the front of the chapel where a reception was set up. And it was a good spread of food, drink and two wedding cakes. The newlyweds were happy and kissing. The ceremony was a success.

A DJ was also on hand to play music for dancing. The DJ said, "Ladies and gentlemen before you all dance, may we let the honor of the first dance goes to the happy couples." A romantic song began to play as the couples took the floor and slowed dance. Cottonmouth whispered softly, "We did it babe, we're married now." Fashion Girl replied, "Oh Cottonmouth, I'm so happy that I could cry." Fashion Girl rested her head against Cottonmouth's chest as he cradled her in his arms.

The Style Chicks looked teary eyed as they watched this very romantic scene. Bloomie said, "Girls this is what true romance is all about. Not just for married couples but for everyone." No one disagreed. When the song ended, everyone went on to the dance floor and began to dance. Dean and Serpentina danced together. Dean said, "Cindy, now that we are in-laws of sorts, I hope we can let the past die and move on for now and the future. We both have a stake in Daphne's happiness." Serpentina replied, "I agree. We will work together from now on."

Dean asked, "How come Rattler isn't here with you?" Serpentina answered, "Now that he's a regular person with a store to operate and five kids to raise, he couldn't leave them alone." Dean said, "I know. I deal with it too." Just then, Fashion Girl excused herself to use the ladies room. This was the moment Satanra was waiting for. She went in after her. She went into a stall while Fashion Girl was in another. When Fashion Girl came out, Satanra also came out and struck her in the back of the head knocking her unconscious.

Satanra picked her up, alerted her gang and said, "Mission accomplished gentlemen. We head back to Aurora Gardens with our "prize". She and Fashion Girl disappeared in a cloud of thick black smoke. Several minutes passed and Cottonmouth noticed Fashion Girl hadn't come out of the ladies room. He approached Nine West and asked, "Daphne hasn't come out of the bathroom yet, can you check up on her?"

Nine West went inside to find an empty bathroom. She came out frantically and said, "Everyone! Everyone! Listen to me! Daphne is gone!" The crowd began to murmur. Cottonmouth replied, "What do you mean she's gone?" Nine West said, "She's gone as if she disappeared." Cottonmouth replied, "Did she go out a window or something?" Nine

West said, "There's no windows in there and the only way out is through the door. I'm telling you she somehow vanished."

Everyone got up out of their seats as Tiffany tried to calm the crowd down and said, "Look everyone, I don't know how this happened but if she's still here in Las Vegas, we'll find her." Cottonmouth replied, "What if she isn't still here Tiffany? Where could she had gone to?" Tiffany said, "Cottonmouth, don't worry. Daphne's power bracelets not only allow us to communicate with her, but it also allows us to find her or the others. I'm turning on the tracker."

The tracker quickly pinpointed where Fashion Girl had been taken. Tiffany said somberly, "She's been taken to Aurora Gardens back home." Tiffany was right for at that moment, Satanra and her men brought Fashion Girl back to the complex. She placed her in one of the motel rooms and said, "Boys, here she is, the Stylish Crime Fighter Fashion Girl. She's all yours, enjoy it. But be "kind", it's her wedding night after all."

The Skull King said, "Don't worry my queen, Miss Muertos' gang will take good care of her, won't you boys?" They shouted as Satanra added, "Give her the best time, she's also a little slut. She loves dicks too, she's also pregnant." One of the men replied, "Oh she is, is she? She won't be for long." Satanra said, "Don't kill her, I want her alive, but barely."

The men were rough as they began to kick her in the sides, punched her in the face, ripped her dress open and began to sexually assault her. For more than an hour, they worked her good. Satanra returned and said, "Excellent job boys. Leave her there." Satanra magically produced iron bars on the door's entrance that no one can open unless by magic.

When the wedding party returned to California and arrived at the Mystique Boutique, it was quiet as no one knew what to do. But once they find Fashion Girl, it will become a fight for survival and their lives.

CHAPTER 28

Satanra looked in on Fashion Girl the next morning. Fashion Girl was lying on the floor in a pool of blood. Her dress ripped to shreds and her face was beaten up to a pulp. She also had bruises on her arms, legs and body.

Satanra laughed maniacally and said to herself, *"Miss Muertos' boys were especially rough on her. Excellent job they did. Let her friends come to save her. But they won't find her here. I think The Crocs' former hideout would be perfect. I hope she'll remember last night for the rest of her life and not just for her wedding. Her anniversary won't be marked by her marriage. It will be marked by this instead. I hope you had fun little bitch."*

Satanra magically transported Fashion Girl to the Crocs' former hideout. One of her men came to her and she said, "Well minion, our "guest" is over at the Crocs' former hideout. She'll remain there locked in a cage with magical cell bars that can't be opened unless by magic. Let's go to breakfast now, I must feed my many babies." She laughed maniacally as she headed towards the café.

Slutan and Miss Muertos both saw this. Slutan said, "I can't believe that Satanra did this to Daphne. We have to do something about this." Miss Muertos replied, "How? She teleported her to the old Crocs' hideout. How can we notify the Style Chicks if we will look hideous to them?"

Slutan said, "Remember last night Miss Muertos. Thanks to that special potion, we could change our appearance to look more normal." Miss Muertos replied, "It's worth a try. As we used to say as Style Chicks, "Let's Do It To It!"" Slutan said, "Get your bike and we'll go to the Mystique Boutique and alert them."

No one else was standing in the complex as they were all at Victoria's Café feeding on another large quantity of food. Some of the women including Satanra were beginning to show baby bumps for the amount of babies they were carrying. Miss Muertos got her bike, she and Slutan changed their appearance and headed south towards Colognia and the Mystique Boutique.

They both knew time was of the essence. When they arrived at the mansion, Slutan said, "It will be good to see some of our old friends again." Miss Muertos replied, "We won't have time for reminiscing, we must tell them about Daphne. In these disguises, they won't know who we are. Let's go."

Slutan rang the doorbell. Bloomie answered it and asked, "What can I do for you ladies?" Slutan answered, "If you value the life of Fashion Girl, you'll come with us." Bloomie said, "If you will pardon me for just one minute." Bloomie closed the door and continued, "Everyone listen. Two women are standing outside the front door and said that if we value Fashion Girl's life, we need to come with them. I don't know if this is some kind of trick or trap."

Serpentina replied, "I'll handle it from here Bloomie." She opened the door and invited the two women in. She continued, "May we offer you anything?" Slutan replied, "No thank you. Let us introduce ourselves, my name is Slutan and this is my friend Miss Muertos. We belong to a gang called Hell's Hotties along with another gang called the Crypt Keepers, we are tasked to produce babies by the hundreds for Satan's Army. This isn't our normal appearance. We won't show you what we look like now."

"We know that Fashion Girl was severely beaten and attacked last night at Aurora Gardens. She was brought there by our leader Satanra. I'm sorry to say, Satanra was Madame D before and the previous Fashion

Girl and her mother." Serpentina replied, "WHAT!? Why did she do that to her own daughter?"

Miss Muertos said, "I can answer that question better than Slutan can. Somehow, her mother wanted revenge but we don't know why. Satanra followed you to Las Vegas, she witnessed the marriage and reception. When Fashion Girl went into the bathroom, that was when Satanra initially attacked her. She teleported her back to Aurora Gardens where my gang of men had their way with her. Believe me when I say that I didn't make them do that to her."

"Before we came here, Satanra magically put Fashion Girl in a cage again with magical iron bars. That's when we decided to come here. We have no qualms with Fashion Girl and we wish her only the best." Serpentina asked, "If you have both become evil, why are you telling us this?" Miss Muertos answered, "We know you all better than you think. That's all I can say about this. Please Fashion Girl could run out of time. Select a party to come with us."

Serpentina said, "The following people come with me now. Dean, Cottonmouth, Amber I understand you're studying to be a nurse, you're about to become one. Tiffany find the Archangels and tell Solara, Whirlwind, Firebolt and Nighthawk to join us. Slutan, Miss Muertos I swear if this is a trap, you will answer to us." Slutan replied, "We are on the level with you. Please don't waste any more time."

The group ran out of the mansion, got into several cars and high-tailed it onto the street following Slutan and Miss Muertos. Tiffany said, "Ladies the Archangels are about to make their debut, LET'S ROCK!" At that moment, Tiffany, Penney, Godiva and Sephora became the second generation of Archangels and took to the air following the caravan.

Just then, a police car began to tail the caravan for speeding. The officer yelled for the cars to pull over. Serpentina told them that they were going into the next county to save Fashion Girl. When the cop heard this, he stopped the pursuit. The caravan arrived at the hideout where Fashion Girl was kept. Serpentina said, "Dean get an ambulance over here on the double but tell the dispatcher to not sound the sirens." Dean replied, "Right away Cindy."

Cottonmouth couldn't see Fashion Girl too well from behind the bars. He said, "Solara, Archangels thank god you're here. Please help your leader." Solara replied, "Yes she is our leader, she's the Phoenix too. But what can we do here?" Serpentina said, "When I was an Archangel, we never tried combining our powers to solve a case. But I think you can somehow get these bars to disappear. Here's what I think you should do."

"Whirlwind, use your ice breath to freeze the bars. Firebolt, you and Solara combine a sun sphere and lighting bolt and shoot it at the bars and Nighthawk, use your magic to disintegrate the bars. I'm praying it should work." Solara replied, "We're praying right along with you." Whirlwind's ice breath made the bars freezing cold. Solara's sun sphere and Firebolt's lightning made the bars super-hot. And Nighthawk's magic made the bars disappear.

Serpentina said, "It worked! Cottonmouth, Amber get her out of there now!" Amber replied, "Wait, look at all that blood, she can't be moved until I can at least see if she can. Nighthawk, can you produce for me a stethoscope, a blood pressure monitor and a finger pulse monitor and hurry!" Once Amber got what she asked for, she checked Fashion Girl's vital signs. Fashion Girl was conscious enough to speak. She said faintly, "Cottonmouth... is it... really... you?"

Cottonmouth replied, "Yes Daphne I'm here. Amber is checking you out now. Just lie still." Amber finished her check and said, "Blood pressure is 80 over 40. Her pulse is weak. She's alive... but barely." Fashion Girl said faintly, "Cottonmouth..., Amber... help... me. Please... don't let... me die... please." Cottonmouth replied, "Not if we can help it honey, just hang in there."

Two minutes later, the paramedics arrived on the scene. They performed the same check Amber did with the same result. They were about to pick Fashion Girl up but Cottonmouth stopped them and asked, "If I may, I want to carry my wife to the ambulance. Once outside, you can put her on a stretcher. Please, we got married just last night. Please?"

One of the paramedics answered, "I know it's against regulations but I understand. You may proceed." Cottonmouth gently put Fashion Girl in his arms as he carried her down a hallway towards the outside door. Slutan whispered to Miss Muertos, "This is the saddest yet most beautiful scene I ever witnessed. That is real love and not meaningless sex for getting pregnant to serve Satan." Miss Muertos replied, "I agree. He really loves her."

Serpentina said, "Thank you ladies for helping us out, she may owe you her life." Miss Muertos replied, "We wanted to help but keep this in mind. When we leave, we must rejoin the gang of evildoers to do Satan's bidding. We must be enemies after this but we still don't have nothing against Fashion Girl. Good luck to you all."

Serpentina said to herself, *"You may have helped us whoever you are, but if you serve evil, you are enemies of the Style Chicks and Archangels. Fashion Girl will be avenged."*

Cottonmouth put Fashion Girl on the stretcher himself, he along with Amber rode with her to the hospital with the others following the ambulance. They arrived at a nearby hospital and Fashion Girl was rushed into the emergency room as they began to assess what injuries she sustained. Everyone was waiting in the waiting room. Waiting for any word on Fashion Girl's condition.

Serpentina said, "I can't believe that Daphne's mother is behind all this. I'm sorry none of you knew her when she was Fashion Girl. She was so strong, so helpful to everyone. Why did she do this? What did Daphne do that was so wrong, so bad that her mother would attack her like that?" Nine West replied, "We don't know Cindy, we don't know. But I know what you mean. Her mother adopted us, made us Style Chicks. We learned so much since then and continue to learn so much more."

Saks added, "I got my eyesight back because of her. I'd still be blind today if it weren't for her. Serpentina said, "And I'm not the woman I am today if it weren't for her too. But listen everyone. As long as Daphne's mother serves evil, she is now our enemy. While we were there, Miss Muertos told us that the evil they do for the Hell's Hotties is to get pregnant with multiple babies. She's pregnant with fifteen so far." Satanra as she's called now, is pregnant with sixty at last count. She's become a dangerous sex vampire."

Bloomie asked, "What in the hell is a sex vampire?" Serpentina answered, "According to Miss Muertos, just like Dracula sucks on people's necks for blood, a sex vampire does the same thing except with draining men of sperm to get pregnant with multiple babies.

Unless they both drink a concoction called wolf's blood, it makes the women strong and their eggs pure gold. It makes the men strong and fertile too with golden sperm. Only golden sperm can fertilize golden eggs and they fall through the fallopian tubes like cars on a highway. Folks, with all this information, the dream my blood sister had fifteen years ago has come true. Satan wanted Daphne but Satanra agreed to become evil."

Dean asked, "If what you're saying about Daphne's mother turning evil and is having sex at will, what will happen if she runs out of eggs? And how will she react when she learns Fashion Girl is gone?" Amber answered, "Even though I'm studying to be a nurse, I have no idea of how many eggs are inside a woman. Nine West added, "But I do know this, when Satanra finds Fashion Girl is gone, all hell will break loose."

Solara did an internet search and she learned something very interesting. She said, "Dean I have answered your question about how many eggs does a woman carry. Listen to this, according to this article by a doctor from India she pointed out that "At birth, a woman typically has around one to two million eggs in her ovaries. However, this number declines over time. By the time of puberty, the number reduces to about three to four hundred thousand eggs. Throughout a woman's reproductive years, only a few hundred of these eggs will mature and be released during ovulation. The decline in egg quantity and quality is a natural part of aging and is influenced by various factors, including genetics and overall health."

Every woman in the group were stunned by this revelation. Saks said, "One to two million eggs at birth?" Nine West added. "Three to four hundred thousand eggs at puberty?" And Serpentina added, "But only about a few hundred could pass through the tubes if mature enough? This is terrible. I feel kind of sick."

Amber said, "Here's how I look at it. If this Satanra is getting pregnant at an alarming rate, and if she's pregnant with at least sixty babies now, she will stop producing more babies soon." Serpentina replied, "Amber don't forget, with the potion wolf's blood, it won't matter. Satanra could've been given eternal life and made younger so she can constantly produce more babies. And if the others are like this, they could have babies by the truckload."

Nine West added, "That Miss Muertos is pregnant with fifteen babies so far as she told us. But how can any woman bear that many children all at once? And when the babies are ready to be born, then what? I can understand if a woman has twins or triplets, but fifteen? They're not dogs or cats."

Amber said, "Again I'm taking a guess but if Satan himself is over-seeing this project of his, he won't wait for nine months for the babies to come to term. He must stop the process at some point and somehow grow and incubate the fetuses until they become full-fledged babies. Then he might accelerate the growing process until the babies reach adulthood."

Serpentina replied, "And they become mindless soulless drones... The Army of Evil." Amber said, "Exactly." Just then, a doctor came out to the waiting room to talk with the group and said, "Folks my name is Dr. Ethan Hollingsworth. I'm the head emergency room doctor. I've been looking at Fashion Girl and her injuries."

Cottonmouth replied, "Doctor, I'm Fashion Girl's husband. We got married last night. She was kidnapped at the reception and then this, how is she?"

Dr. Hollingsworth said, "It's amazing that Fashion Girl is alive. She suffered a severe concussion. Bruises and contusions on more than sixty percent of her body. And Mr. Bowes I'm sorry, she was raped and if she was pregnant, the blood she was covered with when you all found her was from her vagina. She suffered a miscarriage."

The group gasped all at once and Cottonmouth got mad. He replied in rage, "I WILL KILL WHOEVER DID THIS TO HER! I SWEAR TO THAT!" Serpentina said, "Relax Cottonmouth let me ask the doc-tor something, Dr. Hollingsworth, will my niece be able to have more children in the future?"

Dr. Hollingsworth answered, "The prognosis for her having more children is excellent. It was how she was attacked that caused the miscarriage. As for other injuries, there was no organ damage, which is a very good sign. We want her to recover here until she makes a full recovery."

Cottonmouth asked, "Doctor, my wife was only about two months pregnant, she wasn't even showing, how could she had lost her baby like that?" Dr. Hollingsworth answered, "Mr. Bowes, your wife was not only raped, but she was also the victim of some hideous attack I haven't figured out yet. We need to run tests before we can be definite about it. Mr. Bowes, I know you're upset and you have every right to be. But if you try to go after whoever did this to Fashion Girl, they won't fool around. They could kill you or severely injure you too."

Serpentina asked, "When can we see her doctor?" Dr. Hollingsworth answered, "She's been asking for her husband. You may go inside and you being her aunt and you too Mr. Simpson. Until she gets a private room, it's family only. I'm sorry." Solara said, "No problem Doc, we understand."

When Serpentina, Cottonmouth and Dean looked in on Fashion Girl, she was just as upset and even ashamed of what happened. And like Cottonmouth, she wanted revenge for whoever tried to kill her.

CHAPTER 29

When the doctor showed the others where Fashion Girl was at, she smiled faintly and said in a soft tone, "Cottonmouth, Dean, Aunt Cindy, I'm so glad to see you." Cottonmouth wanted to hug Fashion Girl and continued, "Please Cottonmouth, no hugs for a while. I'm so sore from the beating I took. Cottonmouth, at this time yesterday, we were happy, we were going to get married, we learned we were going to have a baby. Now I was attacked, physically attacked."

She began to cry as she continued, "Our baby Cottonmouth, I lost our baby. I'm so, so sorry. It even hurts to cry." Cottonmouth replied, "The doctor said you will be able to have more babies very soon. You will make a full recovery. Your prognosis is very good if not excellent."

Fashion Girl said, "What does it matter, if I didn't have to pee last night, none of this would've happened." Dean replied, "Daphne sweetie, what happened wasn't your fault." Fashion Girl said, "Maybe not Dean but I was targeted. There was no other reason." Cottonmouth replied, "Honey, I'm afraid you're right. You were targeted and I'm sorry to say that it was your mother who attacked you."

Fashion Girl asked, "Why? Why would she do that to me?" Cottonmouth answered, "We don't know yet. Everyone is working on this case together. Style Chick, Skull, Viper, Phat Kat, Cosmo Chick and Archangel alike. But we did find out some things. For now, try to get some rest. You're young, strong and you'll bounce back like a rubber ball. Amber is here too along with Nike. Amber checked your vitals before anyone else."

Just then, Amber came in and said, "Because I'm a nursing student, I've been asked to assist you exclusively when the actual nurses are too busy. As for Nike, he is with us, but he wasn't allowed in." Fashion Girl replied, "I understand. I don't mean to be rude but I need some rest." Serpentina said, "Anytime you want Dean, Cottonmouth and me, let Amber know, we'll remain here for now. And we'll stay nearby in a hotel as well."

Fashion Girl said, "Thank you everyone, I'm sorry if I'm not too receptive." Cottonmouth replied, "We understand, feel better honey." Everyone but Amber left and before Fashion Girl closed her eyes, she said, "Amber thank you for being here too. No one among us is any kind of medical professional. You've quickly become a member of the Style Chicks even if for now it's honorary." Amber replied, "Anytime Fashion Girl, anytime."

Fashion Girl had trouble trying to rest. She was in so much pain. At least she could breathe and move her arms and legs easily. Otherwise, blinking, sneezing, eating and urinating was painful.

Fashion Girl was finally able to sleep some. About three hours later, she began to get restless and was talking in her sleep. She said, "No! No mother don't hurt me! Don't hurt me! Please!" Amber woke her up and replied, "Daphne, Daphne! Wake up! You were having a nightmare!" Fashion Girl said, "Wow! Amber I dreamt that not only my mother attacked me from behind, but I was conscious enough to see her beat me up herself."

Amber replied, "Alright Daphne, calm down. Everything is okay now. A regular nurse looked in to see what the yelling was about. Amber assured her that Fashion Girl was having a nightmare. A cafeteria worker brought a plate of liquids. Fashion Girl asked, "What's with all the liquids? I can eat." Amber replied, "I heard you say yourself that it was painful for you to eat. I guess the doctor feels for now just to take on liquids."

Serpentina, Dean and Cottonmouth came back for another visit before visiting hours had ended. Cottonmouth put his hand in hers and asked, "How are you feeling honey?" Fashion Girl replied, "I had a terrible nightmare about an hour ago. And I was given this tray of liquids. I can eat maybe not well at the moment. Cottonmouth said, "The doctor told us that you did sustain a fractured jaw. It may have to be wired up."

Fashion Girl replied, "Great that's all I need right now. I really got fucked up didn't I?" Cottonmouth said, "No offense, but do you really want me to distinguish that remark with one of my own. Honey, get well. But it's going to take time." Cottonmouth asked, "Should I ask Tiffany if she should investigate the Aurora Gardens complex? Or should she and the others do nothing?"

Fashion Girl answered, "Unless the others can learn the fine art of being mistresses of disguise, they'll stick out like a sore thumb. But at the same time, we can't just sit around and do nothing. Aunt Cindy, what can we do? What should we do?" Serpentina said, "You're right Daphne. We can't sit around and do nothing. But at the same time, your mother needs to be investigated. Don't worry, I will come up with a plan. Again until then, just get well. See you tomorrow. Oh, is there anything you want me to bring you from the mansion?" Fashion Girl replied, "Maybe bring me my old teddy bear Smokey. I could use him for comfort."

Serpentina said, "I haven't seen him in years. I'll bring him with me. Goodnight honey and get some rest." Dean and Cottonmouth kissed Fashion Girl goodbye and left the hospital for the night."

Amber asked, "How come you named a teddy bear named Smokey?" Fashion Girl answered, "Well the former Style Chicks helped to put out a forest fire at Yellowstone Park. They had stuffed teddy bears that looked like Smokey so my mom bought me one. Now that I am thinking about her, I'm getting madder and madder by the minute."

Amber said, "Why your own mother did this to you is eating me up alive inside. How can any woman do this to their own flesh and blood? I hope the new Style Chicks can solve this case." Fashion Girl replied, "So do I Amber. So do I."

In Aurora Gardens that night, Satanra was celebrating the fact that her daughter was savagely beaten. But she was also mad at Slutan and Miss Muertos. She said, "How dare you help free my daughter from her cell?" What was in it for you? TALK TO ME TRAITORS!" Slutan replied, "Now wait one moment Satanra. Maybe you have a problem with your daughter, but we don't! You had no right to do what you had Miss Muertos' gang did to her. The question is Satanra, how dare you?" Satanra said, "That little bitch has been a thorn in my side from the day she was born."

Miss Muertos asked, "Why? What exactly did she do to deserve what she got?" Satanra answered, "Our master wanted her to serve him, she declined. She went to speak with her father at the cemetery, I forbade it but she still did anyway. Once I turned evil and when she got married, she doesn't deserve to be happy. She was brutally beaten. She had a miscarriage and she's in the hospital probably for weeks. This is only the beginning."

Slutan said, "You know what her husband did for her when she was freed? He carried her out of the hideout then she was put on a stretcher. That's real love as far as I'm concerned." Satanra replied, "We are to have sex, get pregnant and serve Satan. We don't care who we fuck and how we do it. As long as we keep spitting out babies. I see you still have your figure. Miss Muertos is pregnant with fifteen babies. I'm pregnant with one hundred. Soon, Satan will harvest some of my fetuses for incubation. Go fuck lots of men Slutan. After all, slut is in your name."

Slutan left as did Miss Muertos. They did what they were told to do, fuck and get fucked to give Satan his Army of Evil. For Slutan, finding men to have sex with was actually a problem. She needed to do something but what was the question. Then she realized that she was once a prostitute selling herself for money. Her gang has done their fair share, so Slutan must do the same in order to stay alive and not to go back to the cemetery.

At the hospital, it was touch and go for Fashion Girl the next few days. But the doctors still believed that she would make a full recovery. She did have her jaw wired shut. She communicated with everyone either by text or a pad and pen. Her bruises began to heal. Her face began to look better. Physical therapy was also used as treatment. Once she got over the worst, she was moved to a private room where she could have all the visitors she wanted.

And visitors she got. The other Style Chicks were allowed now. Her grandmother came by as did both of her grandfathers. Her uncle Johnny and uncle Freddy also stopped by along with her siblings as well as The Cosmo Chicks and the mayor and police chief paid a visit too. Yes everyone Fashion Girl knows came to see how she was doing.

What's more, fans by the hundreds held candlelight vigils. Churches and synagogues in the area held special prayer services for her. As days continued to go by, Fashion Girl got better and better. Her jaw had healed and the wiring came off. Her bruises were all but gone. She felt better and was almost ready to be discharged.

Serpentina stopped in one day and said, "Daphne, look at you. You've made an amazing recovery. You almost look like your old self again." Fashion Girl replied, "Aunt Cindy, I'd lie if I told you that what happened to me was no big deal. I know better. Aunt Cindy, I want revenge. I want to do to my mother what she did to me." Serpentina said, "Honey, I don't blame you one single bit when you say that. But if you try to get revenge, your mother herself could kick your ass too."

Fashion Girl replied, "I know she herself didn't attack me, I also want revenge for those scumbags who did her bidding." Serpentina said, "Daphne, we have someone in Aurora Gardens posing as a stripper at the Wild Bitch. She's telling us all that's going on and she's learned quite a bit." Fashion Girl asked, "Who do you have working as a stripper there? And wouldn't she be recognized?"

Serpentina answered, "Cover Girl agreed to act as a spy and decoy." Fashion Girl replied, "Mom saw the Cosmo Chicks transformation to become able to live on earth." Serpentina said, "She's in disguise. No one knows any better. She's done a good job so far." Fashion Girl asked, "Okay tell me what information Cover Girl has passed on to the others?"

Serpentina answered, "For starters in spite the fact that Grandma Sandy cut off the payroll to Satanra, money is still coming in. Only the criminal element comes over there. Most of the employees quit including

Mary Lou of Victoria's Café, Randy who manages the gas station and our own Soon Li will no longer help out at the motel. The Speed Bump dive bar, the Wild Bitch and the casino is still up and running with perhaps stolen money."

Fashion Girl replied, "Was Mary Lou, Randy and Soon Li scared of who was going there now?" Serpentina said, "Yes they were. Now some of the Crypt Keepers are running the show and no records are to be kept. If money is missing from the till, Satanra doesn't care. And according to Cover Girl, Satanra is getting as big as a house, she heard she's pregnant now with over two hundred babies."

Fashion Girl replied, "That's impossible. No woman not even an evil woman can't be pregnant with that many babies." Serpentina said, "Cover Girl has seen Satan himself perform C-sections on Satanra and other women and removing fetuses by the hundreds. Remember what I told you before, Satan will incubate these fetuses to term."

Fashion Girl replied, "Aunt Cindy, I hope I can get out of this hospital soon so I can confront my mother and have a knock down, drag out fight. She'll never know what hit her." Serpentina asked, "Daphne, you mean you would fight your own mother?" Amber, who was still in the room, added, "Based on all I've heard Cindy, her mother needs to be stopped somehow, the question is how?"

Fashion Girl answered, "I'm not going to fight my mother as Fashion Girl. I'm going to fight her as The Phoenix." Amber asked, "The Phoenix? You are also the Phoenix? Is that one of the Archangels I've heard about?" Fashion Girl answered, "The Phoenix is not just an Archangel, she is "the" Archangel. She's the most powerful of all the Archangels. I can kick ass as Fashion Girl, but as the Phoenix, I can do it ten times better and we can fly. Amber the Archangels are unstoppable. Ask Serpentina, she was Whirlwind. She'll tell you how powerful the Phoenix can be."

Serpentina said, "She's right Amber. You see each Archangel is ten times more powerful based on their abilities as Style Chicks. But as an Archangel, the Style Chicks who are also Archangels Fashion Girl included have elemental powers too. The Phoenix has the power of fire. Solara has the power of the sun. Nighthawk can control birds and other creatures of flight. Firebolt has the power of lightning. Seagirl has the power of water and Whirlwind has the power of the weather. You see as the Archangels; Fashion Girl can do much more than she is normally."

Amber replied, "Thank you for explaining it to me. Don't worry I won't tell anyone what I learned. It's really interesting how being a superheroine works." Fashion Girl said, "Well not every hero or heroine does what we do. There are so many players involved that it can be complicated but it's also exciting. I'm honored to be the next Fashion Girl."

Amber replied, "And after your mission in Las Vegas was so successful, the world will take notice. You'll see."

Just then, Dr. Hollingsworth came in and asked, "Good morning Fashion Girl, how are you feeling today?" Fashion Girl answered, "Much better today. Doctor, I've been here for nearly a month, when can I go home? Or at least to do what I need to do?" Dr. Hollingsworth said, "Well my dear, I do have good news for you. After our last round of tests and exams, I'm pleased to say that you've been completely healed. In a few minutes, a social worker will come in with your discharge papers."

Fashion Girl asked, "One final question doctor. You said when I first came in that despite my having a miscarriage, that I can have children in the future. I'm not questioning your integrity but please for my sanity, I will be a mother someday?" Dr. Hollingsworth answered, "Fashion Girl, some women can have several miscarriages before they successfully have one. Unfortunately, some women can't not even with treatment. And some women can get pregnant but can't stay pregnant. Trust me when I say, you'll be a mother someday. I know about the Fashion Girl legacy."

Fashion Girl felt relived and said, "Thank you doctor, thank you very much. I hated to think that the legacy could end with me." Dr. Hollingsworth replied, "Not unless you have nothing but sons, I know your first daughter will take your place when she's eighteen. It's been a pleasure to have you, your friends and family here. The best of luck to you."

Twenty minutes later, a social worker brought discharge papers. Fashion Girl read and signed the paperwork and was released. Ten minutes later, an orderly with a wheelchair took Fashion Girl to the main entrance of the hospital. To her surprise, fans by the hundreds were there to wish her well as was her friends, family and fellow Style Chicks. Fashion Girl was completely well.

Back at Aurora Gardens, Satanra got the news of Fashion Girl's recovery. She said, "La Diablo, my daughter is out of the hospital and completely recovered from the savage beating she got. When will Satan have his army of evil?" La Diablo replied, "Very soon Satanra, very soon. You've done well in your efforts to provide babies. I understand Slutan wasn't onboard with this process. Is she now doing what she's suppose to?"

Satanra said, "Yes. She was a prostitute and stripper as Wendy Blake. Because of her huge tits, she was known as "Kid Klevage". She felt she didn't know what to do because of who she got revenge on and who she rescued. Those girls some of them as young as ten, are getting their babies fast. Wolf's blood must work quicker on those who are younger. Their babies will soon be able to be harvested."

La Diablo asked, "How many babies Slutan is pregnant with?" Satanra answered, "I don't know, she hasn't used a pregnancy test yet. She's not very bright. She thinks with her tits and not with her head." La Diablo said, "But you are the star of this project, you're pregnant with more babies than the next fifteen breeders combined. Three hundred fifty babies. Your next harvest should produce seventy-five fetuses."

Satanra replied with a smile on her face, "I am so happy to do this for the glory of Satan and all that is unholy. The Skull King's sperm is the strongest while my eggs are the most potent. We are married now as you know." La Diablo was pleased with Satanra's report but asked, "Now that your daughter is out of the hospital, what are you going to do about it?" Satanra answered, "I don't know yet. I'm waiting to see what she'll do. I will give her one more chance to join us, if she declines, I will kill her. I'm through playing games." Satanra and La Diablo laughed maniacally for their words.

At the Mystique Boutique, Fashion Girl was treated to a welcome home party. Nike was the first to greet her by leaping in her arms and licking her. Fashion Girl laughed as his wet tongue covered her with doggie drool. Amber was very impressed by the mansion and everything it has. Cottonmouth came downstairs and kissed Fashion Girl and was glad his wife was fully recovered.

Although a party was taking place, everyone involved were there for strategy on what to do with Fashion Girl's mother. Fashion Girl said, "Everyone thank you for your prayers, well wishes and support while I was recovering. Now that I'm back, we must do something about my mother and what's happening at Aurora Gardens. The idea my mother had of putting a great rest stop along the highway was a great one."

"But how or why she chose to become evil really is anyone's guess. I feel in some ways that it was my fault for what's happening. Some of you could feel that way too. But we must stop this madness now. I'm open to suggestions."

Mary Lou who worked in the café said, "Fashion Girl first I'm glad to see you up and around. I have more of a comment than a suggestion. Everyday three times a day, food magically appeared in the café. You never saw so much food at one time outside of being in a supermarket. And the food was the most high calorie, high fat and high everything. You'd think Satan was trying to feed the Los Angeles Rams three times a day."

"The women including your mother, chows down on it like it's their last meal. And they're all pregnant. The men eat good too but not like the women. And on another table are bottles of what they call wolf's blood. And there are these pregnancy tests. It seems to say how many babies each woman was carrying. And thanks to my quick thinking, I swiped a bottle and a test and brought it here. It might help you solve this case."

Fashion Girl replied, "Mary Lou, if you weren't a girl, I'd kiss you! This will be very helpful. Okay now that we have something to work with. We need to find out more about these items. Macy, the former Macy was an alchemist before she became a doctor. One of you, give her office a call and have her come here. As for the pregnancy test, I have a feeling that something's screwy about it. Unless there are no volunteers, I volunteer to take the test."

Cottonmouth asked, "What good is it to take a pregnancy test if a woman isn't pregnant?" Fashion Girl answered, "Precisely my point. I'm not pregnant anymore so if I take the test, it might say otherwise. I know it sounds screwy but it might crack this case wide open." Cottonmouth said, "I hope you're right."

Serpentina called Soon-Li's office and told the receptionist about the urgency of her arrival. As for Fashion Girl, she went to the bathroom and took the test. The pregnancy tests that were being used was different than a standard test. It was computerized with a digital readout.

Soon-Li arrived at the mansion after she got Serpentina's message. She said, "It's good to see you mate. You're looking well. I heard about Fashion Girl, I'm so sorry for not visiting her in the hospital. But I know Dr. Hollingsworth, he's an excellent doctor. She was indeed in very good hands. So what do you need me for?"

Serpentina replied, "Now that Fashion Girl is out of the hospital, she's now on a case that she would like to forget about. You know what's been going on at Aurora Gardens. Mary Lou and Randy told us their stories. Cover Girl has been there undercover. What have you learned about what's over there?"

Soon-Li said, "I was the first one to quit. But the last family that stayed there got fed up with the raucous and all the sex that was going on, they fled so fast, they didn't bother to pack their bags. It's Fashion Girl's mother that is behind this. She turned the Skull King evil; she brought Wendy and Belle K back to life. They eat like pigs and live like them too. Cindy, something needs to be done."

Serpentina replied, "Soon-Li that's why we called you here. I know you once wrote down on paper the recipe for wolf's blood. But Mary Lou swiped a bottle of it and brought it here. We think that it's more dangerous than ever. She also took a pregnancy test. Fashion Girl is taking it herself. We need you to help the new Macy to decipher what is now in this formula." Soon-Li replied, "You can count on me Cindy."

Fashion Girl came out of the bathroom with some interesting news, she said, "Everyone hear me out for a moment. This pregnancy test is computerized. There's a digital readout. It tells how many babies a woman is pregnant with. Now I last had sex about a month ago. Cottonmouth and I believe that I conceived about three months ago when we had the presentation. And I had a miscarriage, so you would think the test would be negative right? With these tests, it's wrong. Look at the readout on this test. I also used a regular test too."

She showed the others the regular test and it came up negative. Then she showed the test used by Hell's Hotties, it showed her to be pregnant with ten babies. Cottonmouth said, "This is incredible but how can a test like this do what a regular test can't?" Fashion Girl replied, "Like Grandpa Fred would say, "When we figure that out, we will have solved this mystery.""

Serpentina said, "That settles it! We are going to go there tomorrow night and put Satan out of business. But first, the Skulls and Vipers must join forces." Cottonmouth replied, "But my queen, we already are working together." Serpentina said, "What I mean is to combine our forces to form one team." Fashion Girl replied, "I get it, no more Skulls and no more Vipers. Then what will you call them now?"

Serpentina said, "We will call ourselves by our own names and as a group for now we will remain nameless. Without the Skull King or Queen and without King Cobra, it makes no sense going by a new name. And from now on, we will be called by our given names." Fashion Girl replied, "For now Aunt Cindy, it's a good idea." Then she whispered, "As far as I'm concerned, you're still Cottonmouth to me." Darren said, "I agree honey."

Fashion Girl said, "Now we need a plan but when it comes to my mother, it will be between her and me. Aunt Cindy, Tiffany, come with me. We have work to do." Cottonmouth were putting a plan together with the former gangs and together they might come up with a plan that will work.

Six hours later, Fashion Girl and Cottonmouth with two different plans. Fashion Girl said, "I will take the Style Chicks, Cosmo Chicks and Phat Kats to infiltrate the perimeter of the complex. Cottonmouth and his group would attack from the interior. Fashion Girl said, "Once it's all said and done, it will be between me and my mother with me as the Phoenix. For now everyone, get some rest until tomorrow afternoon. We'll put these evil monsters in their place."

Both Fashion Girl and Cottonmouth had plans to take down The Crypt Keepers and Hell's Hotties. One question remains, can Fashion Girl with good conscience stop her mother from carrying out Satan's final plans?

CHAPTER 30

A t two-thirty the next day, everyone had finished their preparations for Fashion Girl's confrontation with her mother. She said, "If everyone's ready, here's what we'll do. Cottonmouth, take the bikers to their respected hideouts and get your motorcycles. Aunt Cindy, go with the Style Chicks and set up your locations. Phat Kats, Cosmo Chicks, you do the same. Soon-Li you and Macy find out what's in this version of wolf's blood and report it to Aunt Cindy."

"Cover Girl if you're scheduled to work at the strip club, go and make like nothing's wrong. Victoria, stay here at the command center and monitor us. I also need you to look after Nike so he doesn't get into trouble. Tiffany, Penney, Godiva, Zara and Sephora, we're going as the Archangels. Now everyone good luck and let's do it to it."

Penney replied, "Wait a minute Boss, I have something for us and you to use. Since you figure these women have become sex vampires, we need silver to stop them permanently. And I upgraded the Sword of Style with a special silver coating. I know you don't use any weapon as the Phoenix, but we can stop these baby making machines by using silver blades and your sword."

Fashion Girl said, "Why didn't I think of that, nice work Penney. Okay everyone let's go, Archangels, LET'S ROCK!" Fashion Girl raised her arms, crossed her wrist and said, "STYLE ME AS THE PHOENIX!"

Tiffany did the same and said, "STYLE ME AS SOLARA!" Penney did the same and said, "STYLE ME AS NIGHTHAWK!" Zara did the same and said, "STYLE ME AS SEAGIRL!" Godiva did the same and said, "STYLE ME AS FIREBOLT!" And Sephora did the same and said, "STYLE ME AS WHIRLWIND!"

In seconds, each Style Chick underwent an amazing transformation to become the powerful Archangels. They left the mansion from the backyard and took to the skies. At the hideouts, the bikers took to their motorcycles and everyone else in their vehicles began the trek from Colognia to the town of Aurora and Aurora Gardens.

Everyone parked their cars and motorcycles in a lot three blocks away from Aurora Gardens. Only Cover Girl went because of the job she has. The Archangels were flying over the complex in stealth mode thanks to Nighthawk. The rest had no choice was to wait until nightfall. Serpentina said, "Fashion Girl thinks that like real vampires, they will be at full strength at night."

Cottonmouth replied puzzled, "If they're vampires, according to Cover Girl, they've been out in the daytime." Serpentina said, "Yes that's true but no one is there right now. We wait for the Phoenix's signal. Until then, let's do one last check of our weapons." Saks asked, "If we got specially coated daggers, what exactly do we do with them?" Serpentina answered, "We use them on the women. If we cut their bellies, any fetuses they're carrying will spill out. If that doesn't stop them, we kill them."

Saks said, "In all the years I've known about and been a Style Chick, I can't imagine that we would stop people by killing them." Bloomie replied, "You're right Saks. But we might not have any choice." Just then, Soon-Li and Macy reported to Serpentina about what's in the wolf's blood. Soon-Li said, "Cindy, do you remember what I uncovered many years ago? This version of wolf's blood like the original starts with red wine. But the other ingredients are quite lethal. For instance, this stuff has liquid cocaine in it. Also it has various fertility drugs along with male enhancing sexual drugs. And finally, it also has opium. No drug legal or illegal is more dangerous than opium. Remember the opioid epidemic a few years ago."

Serpentina replied, "Thanks for the info Soon-Li. Have Macy come here and if you want to tag along, by all means come too." Soon-Li said, "Thanks Cindy but I need to go to the hospital. I have a couple of patients who's in need of my assistance." Serpentina replied, "Thanks again Dr. Chang. Cindy out."

She continued to the others, "You heard it folks, these so-called sex vampires are hopped on a dangerous combination of drugs. But the women are getting pregnant at alarming rates. They're depleting food supplies, and for what? To take over the world? And Fashion Girl's mother is mostly responsible. I think I'm going to be sick."

Amber gave comfort to Serpentina and said, "Cindy if I may call you that, it's okay. I'm here to offer first aid to anyone who needs it along with any other medical care. For now, stay calm and cool. Things will get tense in the next few hours. Just take deep breaths. I think eating will also help. Can one of you take one of the cars and pick up burgers, sandwiches, whatever you like? Cindy especially will need it."

Bonecrusher offered to do that. He got into one of the cars and went to find a fast-food joint. And it was a good idea. Amber figured everyone could fight better on a full stomach. Once Serpentina ate something, she felt better and was more relaxed.

Just before sundown, the Crypt Keepers and the Hell's Hotties were converging outside in the open. Serpentina and the others could hear everything that was going on. But it was Satanra who made the biggest noise. She said using a megaphone, "Tonight is the night we have the biggest sex party ever. We will feast first, grab all the bottles of wolf's blood you can. We breeders need to get more pregnant. So once we feast, we party. It's time for Satan's Army to be completed. You women will be ready for harvesting and so will I. I'm carrying four hundred babies; therefore, I will make the biggest contribution. LET'S PARTY!"

That was all the Style Chicks and the others needed to hear. Serpentina called the Phoenix and said, "Phoenix, your mother made an announcement to have the biggest sex party ever. The women will get more and more pregnant. The time has come to strike."

The Phoenix replied, "And strike we will. Thanks Aunt Cindy." The Phoenix swooped down in the middle of the complex while her mother was out in the open. She said, "Hold it right there Satanra or should I say mother. You are done as a breeder to Satan or anyone else! If you surrender now, you must leave this complex in peace otherwise I will strike you down!"

Satanra replied, "Well look who dropped in. The Phoenix. Afraid to fight me as Fashion Girl?" The Phoenix said, "I'm not afraid to fight you period. I still don't why you're doing this but you and all of you are in terrible danger." Satanra replied, "What danger are you talking about?"

The Phoenix said, "That swill you and the others have been guzzling is nothing more than a pharmacy in a bottle. There are dangerous drugs in it. And look at what it's done to you. You used to fight for what's right. You built this complex with good intentions. Look at you now. You're ugly, you're fatter than an elephant. And for what? Doing someone else's bidding? But most of all, you've had a grudge against me since I turned eighteen. If Grandma Daphne were still alive, she would be ashamed of you. And you should be ashamed."

Satanra replied, "When you were born I told you that you would one day take my place. I was foolish to give up being a model and being Fashion Girl. To see you and Harry grow up, I did it so I could be there for you both. When you hit puberty and in high school, every boy wanted to score with you. I was like that too. But you took it to another level. I missed the power and prestige Fashion Girl gave me."

"As Madame D, I wanted to fight crime my own way by subduing bad people. Many times I was asked by both the Crypt Keepers and the Hell's Hotties to join them. And when you wanted to speak with your father in the cemetery, a man I loathed and despised. I decided to join them. As your mother, I gave you everything and more."

"My mansion, my money and even my heroine name. And how did you repay me? By defying me in the worst way possible. So if it's a fight you want, a fight is what you're going to get you little bitch. I enjoyed seeing you getting your ass kicked by Miss Muertos' minions. You will have to fight everyone in this camp including me. And who's going to help you?"

Just then, the Archangels appeared as Solara said, "We're here too Slutanra!" Serpentina's group also appeared and she said, "We're here as well blood sister!" And the Style Chicks, Cosmo Chicks and the Phat Kats appeared too as Saks said, "Count us in too." Cover Girl got out of the strip club to join in and stood by the Phoenix's side.

The Phoenix said, "I think we've evened the odds just a little bit. Satanra it's you I'm after so be prepared to fight me one on one." Up to this point, Satanra was seen looking beautiful but then she showed the image of what she looked like at that point.

She replied, "Look at me daughter, look at how evil I've become. I married the Skull King and we all became this way. But when we look at each other, us girls are drop-dead gorgeous and the men are beefcake supreme. Our babies will be harvested so let's settle this now. My master Satan will be pleased with our efforts."

The Phoenix said, "After we are done with all of you, your master won't be pleased. Style Chicks, Archangels, everyone, ATTACK!" The fight begun as Satanra's gang got the worst of it as the women were taken down easily because of the babies they were carrying. Those who had the special daggers, cut the women's bellies open and the fetuses came pouring out. The Crypt Keepers also took a beating as the former Skulls and Vipers had the upper hand. The Skull King fought his former gang with ferocious might, but he was simply no match for them.

But it was Satanra and the Phoenix who fought the hardest. Satanra didn't let up on her attacks as she bit, punched and clawed the Phoenix. She returned the onslaught with an attack of her own. Her punches sent Satanra to the ground. As she punched, she said, "This is for your unborn grandchild!" As she continued the punching barrage. Then she said, "This is for ruining my wedding night!" The Phoenix sent Satanra flying with a roundhouse style kick.

And finally she said, "And now mother, this is for me!" The Phoenix began to glow with fire, accumulating it and shot at Satanra and was badly burned. However, her wounds, bruises and the burnt flesh was returned to normal. Satanra laughing maniacally replied, "Look around darling daughter, your fellow Style Sluts are losing. Their numbers are dwindling. Now I will finish you off!"

Satanra grabbed the Phoenix by the throat and began to choke her. Struggling, the Phoenix couldn't say anything as Satanra continued, "Now my daughter, prepare to die!" With the last bit of strength she had, the Phoenix took out Fashion Girl's improved sword and made a slashing "X" across Satanra's stomach. Her hundreds of fetuses were spilling out in full force.

Satanra screamed, "MY BABIES! MY PRECIOUS BABIES! THEY'RE ALL DEAD!" She let the Phoenix go and she was about to perform the ultimate strike. She said, "NOW MOTHER, PREPARE TO JOIN MY FATHER IN HELL WHERE YOU BELONG!" The Phoenix took her sword and stabbed Satanra right in the heart. The silver covered sword pierced Satanra to the point she landed on the ground gasping for breath.

The Phoenix continued, "Mom I'm sorry I did this to you but you had to be stopped. I hope you can forgive me." Satanra was dying and replied, "I'll never forgive you Daphne. I will never forgive you. You cost me everything." A moment later, Satanra was pronounced deceased. The Phoenix began to cry as her group gathered around her and her mother.

Serpentina said, "Daphne, you had to do this. She was no good anymore. She became a pawn in Satan's sickening goal. Don't feel bad. You won." The Phoenix replied, "I can't believe it, I killed my own mother. Why mom? Why did you become so evil?" Serpentina said, "Don't fault yourself, if you hadn't done this someone else would have."

The Phoenix asked, "What about the others? Are you all okay?" Cottonmouth answered, "We're okay honey. We did sustain some injuries but nothing serious. As for them, we did the same thing you did to your mother. We slashed their bellies to lose their fetuses and struck them all in the heart. As for the men, they all fled. It's over Daphne, it's over."

The Phoenix hugged Cottonmouth and said, "Is it really over Cottonmouth? Is it? Those men may have fled but they're still alive. All they have to do is find more willing women to poison their minds and bodies with wolf's blood." Serpentina replied, "Not if we can help it Daphne, we found where they stashed the wolf's blood and broke every single bottle. They won't impregnate women like that ever again."

The Phoenix said angrily, "Don't you get it Aunt Cindy!? Don't you all get it!? Satan will provide them with more potion! He will get those men to seduce innocent women and turn them into baby making machines! This madness will never end unless we find those men who escaped and execute them! My mother joined willingly, some of those women didn't! And they all paid the ultimate price! IT'S NOT OVER WITH! NOT BY A LONGSHOT!"

Minutes later, the police arrived by the dozens to assessed what had happened. They questioned everyone involved and they realized that based on what did happen that any killing was considered justified homicide. No charges will be filed. After the coroner's office took the victims away including Satanra, everyone left the scene and returned to their vehicles. Cottonmouth wanted the Phoenix to ride with him, but she decided to fly away and find a place to reflect on what had happened.

She flew to Makeout Mountain outside the Colognia city limits. She sat down on a rock and began to cry again. She began to envision how her mother was before she turned evil. How beautiful she was, how kind, generous, helpful and all the great things she did for her community and the world. Now she's faced with an even bigger problem. Her brother was there as a Phat Kat so he understood the situation. However, there were two young siblings that were on her mind. Charlotte and Dean Jr..

How can she explain to them why their mother died and what can she say to her grandmother, both of her grandfathers, her uncles, and other family members. She became confident that the reactions won't be good. She needs to find a way to let them know as gently as possible.

As for the Aurora Gardens complex, the Phoenix realized that the complex should never be used again for any purpose. Not to welcome travelers, passersby, and yes the criminal element. It needed to be destroyed. And what about the Style Chicks and Archangels reputations? Will they get a reputation of being killers? Even if it was justified? This was one problem that might haunt the Style Chicks and Archangels for years to come.

The Phoenix's mother did cost three people their lives when she was Fashion Girl and all three deaths were justified. After pondering everything, the other Archangels joined her. They all hugged the Phoenix to comfort her. Solara said, "Daphne what you did tonight had to be done. It simply couldn't be helped."

The Phoenix replied still shedding tears, "Was it right Sarah? What right did we have to kill otherwise innocent people? I know we won't be charged with any crime or go to jail, but this will forever be in my mind." Nighthawk said, "Daphne, whether you want to believe it or not, we saved the world tonight from the worst fate imaginable. Don't feel guilty."

The Phoenix replied, "Isabella, do you realize that this is only a temporary victory? No one can buck the almighty Satan. Next time it could be us that will do his bidding. Do you all want to become baby making machines one day? I suffered a miscarriage at the command of my mother. Sarah is pregnant right now. Again I ask, do you want to be the next Satanra? Slutan or Miss Muertos? I sure don't and neither will you. We have to remain as diligent as possible."

Seagirl said, "You're right Daphne. You're absolutely right. Even if I am at sea, I'm not safe." The Phoenix replied, "You see, Indira has got the idea. And you should too." Nothing more was said as the others joined the Phoenix in silence. And from that moment on, the Style Chicks, Archangels, Cosmo Chicks and Phat Kats have officially entered the next chapter of the legacy of Fashion Girl.

EPILOGUE

One month passed as everything returned to normal. The Phoenix's idea to have Aurora Gardens destroyed was agreeable with the citizens of Monterrey County. Fashion Girl oversaw the proceedings but she emptied the Den of Sin by taking her mother's dominatrix outfits and equipment. She felt it would come in handy as a femme fatale.

Fashion Girl ordered that Aurora Gardens be burned to the ground and never to have anything else on the property. As it burned, she did have a small sense of satisfaction that the complex met the same fate as her mother and Hell's Hotties. The buildings topside did burn down, but the casino, strip club and the Den of Sin didn't. The elevators that went down to those places also were destroyed. The eerie music that was heard in the Den of Sin could now be heard above ground. Whatever that was playing or where it came from was never revealed.

The dean at UCLA allowed Fashion Girl a chance to catch up in her schoolwork. She took advantage of this chance fully. She officially became a member of the Alpha Beta Omega sorority. She also was assigned to keep her sorority sisters in line so they wouldn't do things like get drunk or have wild parties.

In Colognia, Fashion Girl made Amber Watley a permanent member of the Style Chicks as a token of gratitude for her service especially while she was recovering in the hospital. Fashion Girl gave Amber a new

Style Chick name. She decided to call her Estee Lauder when she learned that Amber used the perfume and other products. As a Style Chick, Amber's costume was similar to that of when a woman dresses up as a sexy nurse at Halloween.

Although she wasn't in attendance for the ceremony, She-Ra learned of the new addition of the Style Chicks being a nurse, she gave Amber a special gift. She-Ra gave a small portion of her healing power in the form of a bracelet so Amber can do the same thing of heal by touch.

Saks, Bloomie and Nine West continued to be Fashion Girl's personal assistants and be used as a first line of defense. Nike was growing up fast but was still a puppy. He loved Fashion Girl too much to harbor any resentment. Dogs have that feeling of how their owner are good or bad.

Fashion Girl and Cottonmouth's marriage continued and their love grew even stronger. When she got the green light, she and Cottonmouth tried once again to raise a family. After several tries, Fashion Girl was pregnant again. And this time, until she started showing, she would greatly limit her Style Chick duties. Tiffany's pregnancy continued without any difficulties.

The former Victoria decided to reopen Victoria's Café in Colognia along the beach. The others did their jobs they way they were meant to do. No member of Fashion Girl's family maternal or paternal were upset by the Phoenix's actions that killed her mother. Fashion Girl's mother was buried in an unmarked grave so no one would know about her. All people will know is she was the former Fashion Girl and the legacy she left behind.

And finally, what kind of legacy will Fashion Girl 3.0 leave behind when it's her turn to pass the torch? She's just getting started but she hopes for a great legacy of service, community, and justice. The kind of justice the former two Fashion Girls performed. She knows it will be a rough road ahead. But if she doesn't encounter what she did at Aurora Gardens, her legacy will be a bright one and if she has a daughter, Fashion Girl 4.0 will hope to continue the tradition.

I hope you enjoyed my first full novel and the coming of age of Fashion Girl 3.0. Hopefully, I will be able to continue to chronicle the new Fashion Girl and her friends as she will continue the tradition of fighting crime with style. Until we meet again, take care and stay safe. And as Fashion Girl would say, "Stay Stylish".

THE END

Printed in the United States
by Baker & Taylor Publisher Services